NOT A HERO

Sons of the Survivalist: 1

CHERISE SINCLAIR

VanScoy Publishing Group

Not a Hero
Copyright © 2019 by Cherise Sinclair
ISBN: 978-1-947219-13-7
Published by VanScoy Publishing Group
Cover Art: I'm No Angel Designs
Edited by Red Quill Editing, LLC

ACKNOWLEDGMENTS

I had so much lovely help with this book that I'm not sure where to start.

Bianca Sommerland and Monette Michaels—where would I be without you guys to keep me on the plot path? Love you!

The reason y'all can read this book without tripping over typos and bloopers are due to the fantastic Red Quill's editors and my wonderful beta readers, Marian Shulman, Lisa White, and—despite just getting out of the hospital—Barb Jack.

Big hugs go to my Alaska beta readers, Jennifer Foster and Kathleen Cole, who provided so many wonderful details about living in Alaska and also kept me from making idiotic Outsider errors.

PROLOGUE

Don't wait for someone to hand over a red cape and call you a hero. Jump the fuck in. - First Sergeant Michael "Mako" Tyne

Heading out to play baseball with Kana and Miguel, two other foster children, ten-year-old Gabriel MacNair heard whimpering. The sound came from the master bedroom.

Pausing, he reached for the knob and stopped. *No, dummy.* Although he'd only been in this foster home for two weeks, after a year in the system, he knew better than to go into a foster parent's room...and that went double for this man.

Phillip had big hands and a mean temper.

Inside the room, Phillip cursed, then growled at someone, "Shut your trap, you ugly little shit."

"Don't touch me! Get off!"

That was *Derek's* voice.

Gabe sucked in a breath. All three foster boys in this house were almost Gabe's age and as streetwise as he was. He liked them. Derek didn't talk much at all, and he had a mean-looking scar on his face, but when Gabe'd first arrived, the boy had scooted over and shared his bench. He was okay.

But...if Gabe opened the door, Phillip would probably hit him. Hard.

There was a slapping sound and something ripped. Derek screamed in fury.

Fear thick in his throat, Gabe tried to turn the knob. *Locked.* He swallowed. *Okay, okay,* he could do this. He'd always helped Gramps in the locksmith shop. Gramps said Gabe could pick a lock before he could walk.

Grief slid over him. *Why'd you have to go and die, Gramps?*

Taking the jackknife from his sock, he silently slid the blade past the lock's strike plate, edging the spring latch from the jamb. When it gave, he tucked his knife away and shoved the door open.

"Hey, Phillip, can I—" The weak excuse died on his lips as he stared in shock.

Phillip had Derek shoved face-first on the bed. The man's fat dick bobbed out of his unzipped jeans. Seeing Gabe, he turned red with rage. "Get the fuck out of here!"

Terrified, Gabe took a step back.

Shirt half-ripped off, Derek was kicking, struggling.

2

Can't leave. Heart pounding so hard it hurt, Gabe yelled, lowered his head, and charged. His skull hit Phillip right in the gut and knocked him against the wall. "Run, Derek!"

Wheezing, Phillip shoved off the wall and backhanded Gabe to the floor. "Pissant brat."

Gabe slammed into the floor and tumbled against the dresser. Head spinning, he tried to stand. And fell.

Derek scrambled up onto the bed and launched himself at the man.

Ear-splitting shrieks came from the doorway as the other two boys tore in from outside—and attacked.

Kana, a big kid with long black hair dove at Phillip, hitting him at the same time as Derek. Phillip tossed them back.

Miguel, the short Mexican, swung his bat. The wood hit Phillip's dick—and the scream was terrifying.

Phillip dropped to his knees, holding his junk.

Panting, Gabe made it to his feet. *Man, they were all so screwed.*

Miguel looked like he'd puke, and Kana backed away.

When Derek staggered, Gabe slung an arm around him to hold him up.

"Jesus, what kind of clusterfuck is this?" A huge man stood in the doorway, filling the frame completely. All muscle. Short, dark brown hair going gray. Eyes sharper than Gabe's knife narrowed on Phillip who was holding his naked dick. The stranger's jaw tightened as he looked at the bed, then Gabe and the others. "Who was the pervert after?"

Derek edged closer to Gabe, but bravely raised his chin. "Me."

"Goddamn city isn't safe even for rugrats." He studied them. "Which one of you attacked the asshole?"

Holding his aching jaw, Gabe forced out the answer. "Me."

"Me." "Me." "Yo." Four kids; four answers.

Gabe braced himself to be hauled away. The others were doing the same.

Instead, the guy's mouth curved into an approving smile. "You boys got guts. And already made yourselves into a team."

Phillip leaned toward the bedstand, fumbling for the phone. "You hit me with a god-damned *bat*. They'll lock you little bastards up forever."

Lock us up? Fear chilled Gabe's skin. His knees wobbled.

The stranger's gaze went icy. He took two steps, slammed his huge fist into Phillip's jaw, and knocked the jerk out cold.

Turning, the big man put his hands on his hips and looked them over.

Shakily, Gabe braced his legs and stared up. Why'd he do that? What did he want?

With relief, Gabe felt Kana's shoulder rub his on the left. Miguel moved to stand on Derek's other side.

The man nodded, like he was pleased or something.

"Name's Mako. I've been next door, visiting an old buddy. He said this here is a foster home?"

That was a safe enough question. Gabe nodded.

Mako glanced at Phillip. "Is the pervert your father or uncle?"

"Uh-uh."

Mako frowned. "How about the rest of you? He a relative?"

The three shook their heads.

"Guess that's good. Do any of you got family around here?"

"No," Miguel muttered while Derek and Gabe shook their heads.

Kana snorted. "If we did, we wouldn't be here."

"Yeah, guess not." The man's face tightened. "When the asshole wakes up, sounds like you're going to be in trouble. True?"

Gabe blinked back tears because it was true. No one believed what kids said—not if a grownup said different. If Phillip told the social worker that the foster kids ganged up on him or tried to steal something—jeez, he could say anything—then they'd get dumped into a group home.

Gabe'd heard awful stories about those places. *Got to leave before Phillip wakes up.* He eyed the door and then realized Mako's gaze had followed his.

"You'll run." The man's eyes narrowed.

No one answered.

"The streets are no place for kids," he muttered. "An' if

shit hits the fan, y'all will be like ducklings in a lake of hungry bass."

Miguel made a worried sound. He was the youngest and really nice.

Saying stuff to scare kids wasn't right.

Gabe tried to stand taller. "You shouldn't try to scare us." When the ice-cold gaze came to rest on him, he almost fled right then. Instead, he forced out the words. "We don't have any choice, mister."

"It's Mako, kid, or Sarge works." The man ran his fingers through his hair and scowled. "This's fucked up."

He stared at them a minute, then sighed. "My home is a long way from here, and that's where I'm headed now. If you come with me, I'll raise you till you can stand on your own two feet."

Silence.

The other three looked at Gabe, waiting for him to decide, as they had since the first week he'd arrived. As if he knew what he was doing, which was totally a crock.

But if they trusted him, he'd better be careful. Couldn't let them get hurt, and this guy was awful big. When Gramps was dying, Gabe had scavenged on the streets to get money for food and medicine. He'd seen bad stuff happen.

He studied Mako. Clean. Good sturdy clothes. Scary tough. Probably kinda mean. But his gaze was straight; his body was straight. No sign of drugs or alcohol.

And he'd called Phillip a *pervert* like he hated perverts.

"You'll take care of us?" Gabe asked carefully. "Feed us an'...and send us to school?"

The man snorted. "Got no school in the wilderness, but you'll learn, boy. And you'll eat a far sight better than here. You'll learn to hunt your own meat. Live off the land. And you'll be safe when the world goes to hell."

Was the world supposed to go to hell? That sounded kinda crazy.

Gabe glanced at Phillip, still not moving. Crazy was better than a...a pervert. Or being locked up in a group home. Getting a long way from here would be smart.

"I'll go with you." Gabe met the other kids' looks and spoke for them all. "We'll go with you."

"Good enough. Let's get out of here." The man turned, and his voice drifted down the hallway. "Start thinking of new names for yourselves."

Mako hadn't been joking about a long way away. The sarge took them to *Alaska*.

Within a month, the other three had found their new names.

A bull moose charged Kana, making him dodge around trees *forever*, before Mako'd gotten a shot at it. The kid dropped onto the ground, panting and laughing—cuz Kana could laugh at anything. He stared at the monster-sized moose and slapped his chest. "I'm gonna eat him and get as big as him. I'm gonna be a bigga-badda *bull*."

Bull had found his name.

When Miguel had trapped a rabbit using just stuff from the forest, Mako said he had the makings of a hunter. Miguel had stared at the trap he'd built. "Cazador. *Me llamo Cazador*."

Miguel still hadn't picked up much English, but the sarge knew Spanish. "You want to be called Cazador?"

Miguel nodded.

Mako crossed his arms over his chest. "Means *hunter*. Yeah, that's a good handle, kid. You're Cazador."

The first time Derek saw a hawk launch from a branch and snatch up a mouse in its sharp talons, he knew what he wanted to be called. In all the years since, Hawk had never lost his fascination with the predatory birds.

Only Gabe had refused to choose a new name because Gramps had said Mama chose his name especially for him. For who she thought he'd be. *Gabriel* was a guardian angel, the messenger of God. She'd said she knew her son would someday be a protector. A *hero*.

He wouldn't give up his name...or her dream for him.

Trying not to tremble like a coward, that's what he'd told the sarge.

Mako had been quiet for a long time and then said, "Can't argue with a mother's hopes. God knows this fucking world needs more heroes."

CHAPTER ONE

Gabriel had tried being a hero. Served as a Navy SEAL, a police officer, and as a mercenary. *Yeah, no.* He'd hung up his cape for good.

People didn't want heroes.

And he was done risking his neck for anyone ever again.

Nope, he'd stay far, far from the job of hero and away from people, as well. *Damn straight.*

Stiffly, he rose from where he'd been kneeling on the porch. The ladder-back chair he'd made with hand tools was finished. Limping slightly, he carried it inside and set it beside the kitchen table. Not bad, but it'd taken him forever. He grinned ruefully. If he tried to make a living by building furniture, he'd starve.

Shaking his head, he headed back outside. Long winter, small cabin. He needed to be outside.

Spring had finally arrived on the Kenai Peninsula in

Alaska. A couple of weeks before, the river near Mako's old cabin had been an impressive flood of water with massive chunks of ice. Now, the water level was returning to normal, and the snow was disappearing.

Back on the porch, he stretched. His left shoulder and hip only throbbed resentfully, far improved from the stabbing pains he'd suffered when he arrived last fall. Back then, he'd moved like a gunshot cripple—because he was—now, his limp only appeared when he was an idiot and overexerted himself. Like ever since the snow began to melt.

He should go into Seward sometime. He hadn't been there since he arrived last fall. He probably had mail piled up in the post office box.

The mail could sit and rot. After the disastrous ambush of his mercenary team, which could have been prevented if the company hadn't lied to him, he'd quit and come here, to where he'd grown up.

The total isolation of Sarge's old cabin was what he'd needed—to get away from people. He shook his head. How so-called humans could do such unspeakable things to each other, he would never understand. As a cop, he'd seen crimes committed for money, sex, and drugs. In the Navy SEALs and as a mercenary, he'd seen people fight over power, territory, religion, and race. The atrocities he'd seen...

The ambush of his merc team last fall had been the breaking point. His jaw tightened to the level of pain before he breathed out. *Stop, dumbass.* The past was the past.

There weren't any people out here. The cabin was off the grid. No electricity, no running water. Rather rundown, despite the work he'd put into it over the winter. When Mako'd brought him and the other boys here—over twenty years ago—the log cabin had been one room with a loft. That summer, they'd doubled the size and started the first of their lessons. Construction techniques, obedience, respect, survival, and first aid.

Seven years ago, Gabe and his three brothers had talked the sarge into leaving this area and moving near Rescue where he had an old war buddy. Together, they bought a huge, isolated chunk of land and built five cabins, despite the fact that only Mako had lived there permanently.

Jesus, Gabe'd visited as often as he could wrangle time off—they all had—but he hadn't been there when Mako really needed him. When he'd died last fall.

God. The swamping guilt and grief hollowed a place around his heart. October. It'd been a dark, ugly month. First, the ambush down in South America. His men shouting, screaming, falling, dying. He hadn't known them long, but they'd been his, and he'd failed them. He should never have trusted the intel provided...or the company.

After surgery to repair the damage from the bullets, he'd been flown back to the States to finish his recovery. He'd wakened after the long flight, smelling the astringent odors of a hospital, hearing people in a hallway. Feeling the searing pain in his shoulder and hip.

When he'd opened his eyes, Caz and Bull were there. They'd looked devastated.

And they'd told him about Mako's death.

Gabe swallowed against the thickness in his throat. Why did he still feel as if he'd lost a part of himself? The sarge had died in a car accident months ago.

Car accident, my ass. He'd killed himself. Said so plainly in the note he'd left.

- - - -

If you're reading this, I'm dead. Soon now, I figure on taking a quick right off a high cliff—although it's a waste of a good vehicle. Got a diagnosis a while back. Cancer. No surprise after that crap they sprayed on us in 'Nam. The docs say they can't do shit, and I always said I'd check out when life lost its flavor—that time is now.

The nightmares are getting worse again, too. The PTSD— Jesus, who the fuck thought of such a stupid name—got better when I got you four. Raising you all gave me a mission. Staved it off— mostly. I'm sorry for the times it got the better of me and I scared you.

- - - -

. . .

Gabe shook his head. Yeah, Mako had scared the crap out of them off and on. The sarge'd been a Vietnam vet, and some triggers made him crazy. The sound of a chopper, the unexpected smell of diesel. Fireworks with staccato, sharp noises sent him diving for cover, or worse, running into the forest. Days later, he'd return haggard and silent.

But if he didn't run and was fighting off a flashback, his temper would erupt.

Drill sergeants had cruel tongues.

Being clueless kids, they hadn't understood, not at first, but Cazador, the smartest with people, had eventually figured out the sarge had PTSD from a war that had occurred before they were even born. Slowly, they'd discovered how to avoid the triggers...and what to do when shit happened anyway.

Gabe rubbed his face and the rough beard he hadn't bothered to trim. He had his own nightmares of war and death now and a hell of a lot of respect for how well Mako had managed.

The sarge would be the first to understand why Gabe had holed up in the cabin...and would be the first to kick his ass out of it.

But Gabe hadn't found any reason to leave.

Leaning against a porch post, he inhaled. The crisp green scent of spring smelled like anticipation. It was...annoying.

With his free hand, he massaged his throbbing shoulder.

It didn't hurt too much, considering the amount of work he'd done this week. The injuries were pretty much healed.

His mind, though? Not so much. Like Grayson, the sarge's psychologist friend, had warned, the isolation had made it worse.

The land was thawing under the spring sun; he wasn't sure he ever would.

But he'd found some peace, too, out here in Mako's old cabin. Seemed like he could feel the sarge here now and then. Mako'd loved this place where dense spruce, birch, and cottonwood forest surrounded the cabin on three sides. A slope filled with alders led to the river where the sun sparkled off the last remaining ice along the riverbank. A few chunks still bobbed in the swift-running, turquoise water.

As he watched the water, the birds went silent. He heard the approaching noise of one—no, two—four-wheelers coming down the nearly impassible dirt road to the cabin.

Stepping inside, he pulled his old Mossberg shotgun off the rack and returned to the porch.

Just inside the clearing, two men dismounted from their ATVs and approached the cabin. One bear-sized man. One shorter, more slender guy who moved with the deadly grace of a lynx.

Jesus. Fuck.

Shoving back his hood, Caz eyed the shotgun. *"Buenos días, 'mano.* Are you shooting visitors now?"

Bull snorted. "He always did take after the sarge."

Gabe's brothers sauntered up to the porch.

With a grunt of irritation, Gabe went inside to put the shotgun back in the rack as the two pulled off their boots and coats in the entry. "What the hell do you two want?"

"Wanted to make sure you were alive." Bull walked into the main cabin.

"I'm alive." Gabe motioned toward the door in a not-so-subtle hint.

They didn't leave.

"Nice try. Won't work." Bull pulled him into a one-armed hug.

Gabe froze. It'd been a long winter without people. But okay, okay, he loved his brothers. With a sigh, he hugged back. "Hey, bro."

"I've missed you, *viejo*." His other brother grabbed a hug too. A medic first, then a nurse practitioner, Caz had the biggest heart of them all and the hottest temper. "It's been too long."

Yeah, from fall until... "What month is it anyway?"

Caz shook his head. "May. Happy Cinco de Mayo in two days."

May? It *had* been awhile. He snorted. "I'm surprised Zachary Grayson didn't show up. Last fall, he said that if I didn't leave after break-up, he'd come and dig me out."

Bull grinned. "He called me last week, actually, to ask if you were out. His wife just gave birth, so he couldn't leave right away but said you'll be getting a visit in a few weeks, if you're still holed up here."

"Damned psychologist." Yet it felt...good...in a way, to know that Grayson had worried about him even with a new baby in the house.

Wait. New baby? He counted backward on his fingers. "Jesus, she must've been pregnant last fall." Back when Grayson's stalker had almost shot her. The thought shook him to the core, and he pulled in a harsh breath.

At ease, MacNair. Baby was born. Everyone was good. He looked at Bull. "So you're here to answer his questions on how I am?"

"Nope. We want to talk to you about a problem we're having." Bull walked over to the kitchen area.

The two extra people made the cabin feel much smaller. "I don't do problems. Not anymore."

Still, guilt trickled through his glacier-cold numbness, because problems were what he did. Or used to do. He was used to taking the lead...in foster homes, with his brothers, in the military and law enforcement, with the merc company. He pulled people together and fixed what was broken.

Trouble was...*he* was what was broken now.

"Then listen and tell us what you think we should do." Bull poured himself a cup of coffee, then ran his palm over the new kitchen chair. "Nice work."

"Yeah, thanks."

Coffee mug in hand, Bull dropped down onto the old brown couch and put his feet up on the ottoman.

Gabe scowled. *Dammit.* Once settled in, his brother couldn't be moved. Not that Gabe would care to try, because Bull's childhood wish to be a big man had come to pass in spades. Thankfully, he didn't have the irritable personality of a male moose. He didn't have to. He'd simply flatten whatever annoyed him.

With a resigned sigh, Gabe got his own coffee and took a seat.

Caz filled a cup and glanced at the open shelves in the kitchen corner. "You're low on food."

"End of winter. Of course I am."

Choosing his favorite armchair, Cazador opened his backpack, took out a package, and tossed it in Gabe's lap. "Eat those while we talk."

Gabe looked down. Oreo cookies. Double-stuffed. His favorite junk food. Caz understood people—and he never forgot anything.

Gabe's mouth started to water. He'd run out of sugar and sweets well over a month ago.

He had to clear his throat. "Thanks." The first bite was a symphony of taste and texture, like having sex after a long drought. "Good bribe."

Which meant he'd have to listen to what his brothers had to say. Maybe they weren't related by birth or even adoption, since Mako'd never bothered with the paperwork, but they were brothers, nonetheless. Their ties had grown strong from facing off against Phillip, growing up together, shared experiences, deaths, spilled blood and terror, and from practical jokes and late-night whispers.

The sarge had originally said they were a team. Later, he just called them brothers.

Gabe picked up another cookie and shot Bull a look. "What's this so-called problem?"

"You should have gone into town to pick up your mail."

"Too much work."

"Too barn sour, more like."

Gabe scowled. He wasn't a horse unwilling to leave the stable, dammit.

After a glance at the coffee in his cup, Bull frowned, took a careful sip...and grimaced.

"Coffee not to your liking?" Gabe's lips twitched up. He'd made the pot hours ago.

Bull was a fussy bastard about food and drink. After leaving the SEAL Teams, he'd opened a brewery in Anchorage, then a restaurant that'd grown so popular he'd launched another on the peninsula.

Gabe motioned with his cup. "Drink it. It'll put hair on your chest."

"I'm Polynesian. We don't do that hair-on-the-chest bullshit."

The trickle of amusement was unexpected and brought back memories. They used to tease Bull about his smooth skin...back when Gabe, Caz, and Hawk had counted each newly sprouted hair on their skinny chests. Gabe raised an eyebrow. "Just out of curiosity, did you happen to notice your skull is also bare as a baby's butt?"

"No, *really?*" Bull ran his hand over his shaved scalp and looked appalled.

Caz laughed and glanced at Gabe. "Shocked me, too."

"He accused me of having a midlife crisis." Obviously unconcerned, Bull grinned and stroked his trim goatee.

Gabe noticed the black beard had speckles of gray. Gray hair—already. In the hospital, Gabe had noticed a few streaks in his own hair. Then again, he'd hit the thirty mark a couple years past.

But thirty wasn't that old. "Midlife, my ass. So what's this about my mail?"

"Here, old man." Smirking, Caz passed over a few letters along with a manila envelope. "We stopped by the PO box on the way here."

After glancing through the junk mail, Gabe opened the big envelope and withdrew a sheaf of papers. The signature on the first page gave him a jolt. "From Mako?"

"His lawyer had orders to mail these last month," Bull said. "It's about Rescue."

Mako'd chosen the tiny town because he had an old Vietnam War buddy there. Although having a friend nearby had helped his PTSD, the sarge'd never stopped bitching about living close to people. He'd been a survivalist to the bone, a prepper before the word was ever coined.

Gabe swallowed his grief and read the short hand-written letter.

. . .

My boys,

The greatest pride I have in my life is you four, and if I did nothing else worthwhile in my life, getting you out of LA and into Alaska was worth everything.

Gabe blinked as his eyes burned.

I learned the hard way that, after leaving the military, a man can get lost. That he needs to either fight for something or build something. My inheritance to you is this—a new mission. Welcome to Rescue. Guess what, men. You now own half of the town.

Death has been part of your lives. Time to create something instead. Bring this town back to life.

That's an order.

What the hell? They owned part of Rescue?

Unsettled, Gabe read the letter again.

Located a couple of hours from Anchorage, the mountain town had started life as a roadhouse and general store for the 1890s gold rush miners. Rescue grew again when the McNally Ski Resort opened mid-twentieth century. But, a decade ago, the resort closed, leaving Rescue to die.

"How exactly did the sarge figure we could revive the town?" Gabe looked up.

"Read the lawyer's letter." Caz motioned to the packet. "It seems a consortium dumped a ton of money into upgrading the old resort. The place re-opened this spring."

Bull nodded. "There's a fancy hotel, ski lifts, hot springs. Proposed golf course. Summer recreational shit."

In the papers, Gabe found a map of Rescue. When visiting Mako, he'd rarely gone into the town itself. The town was a branch off the big Sterling Highway that went to Homer—and the road through town continued up to the mountain resort.

There was no other way to reach McNally.

"Interesting. There'll be a ton of tourists, including skiers, looking for cheap lodging." But, if he remembered right, the town didn't have much more than a few businesses. Hardware. Post office. Mako's old war buddy, Dante, owned the grocery.

"Resort employees, too," Bull commented.

An influx of tourists into an unprepared town? "It's going to be a mess. Damn first sergeant and his missions."

Gabe leafed through the rest of the papers. A note from the lawyer. Copies of titles to land and buildings all over town. In addition to their homes, they now owned a restaurant, gardening center, hotel, and quite a few stores. All had closed down some time in the past.

Mako's expectations were clear.

Gabe's balls shrank at the thought of disappointing the

sarge. They'd learned early on that giving less than 110 percent of effort earned a scathing dressing-down. Even Navy SEALs' Hell Week had been easy compared to his first year with the retired Green Beret.

He glowered at the letter. "I miss that crazy bastard, but Jesus, nobody can manipulate a person like an old drill sergeant."

"I bet he's laughing his ass off right about now." Caz grinned. "He probably figured it was suitable revenge for the way we coerced him into moving to town."

"Of course he did." Bull's deep laughter was like a foghorn.

"I can't believe he took the money we sent him and bought property," Gabe muttered. They'd all sent a portion of every paycheck to Mako. "It was to help support him, not…this."

"It's not like he ever spent money on anything—except maybe military surplus, bomb shelters, and MREs." Bull glanced over. "Speaking of military, we haven't heard from Hawk since last December. The company says he's out of the country."

Private military companies weren't particularly good at reassuring families. And this company had turned into a shit operation. "Hawk will check in when he returns to the States. He'll get the packet then."

"Guess that's all we can hope for," Bull said. "So, about the town. Caz and I have been in Rescue a month now. I'm remodeling the old roadhouse there."

"What about your restaurants in Anchorage and Homer?"

Bull put his hands behind his head. "That's why God created managers."

Yeah, that was Bull, the most easy-going guy on the planet. Gabe glanced at Caz. "And you?"

"They had a health clinic there, once upon a time. I'm going to re-open it."

"Sounds like you have it covered. Why are you here?" Gabe leaned back in his chair. The pleasure of seeing his brothers was fading. He needed to be alone, isolated, surrounded by forest.

Trees didn't talk. Trees didn't need him.

Caz studied him over the rim of his coffee cup. "We wanted you to know about Mako's request."

Bull snorted. "Request, my ass. Those are orders."

"And, as it happens, we're having problems in town," Caz said.

Gabe stiffened. "And that applies to me...how?"

"The remodeling of the roadhouse is being sabotaged." Bull scowled. "Equipment and materials have been stolen. Two days ago, someone busted all the new windows."

Caz nodded. "Same with the health clinic."

Concern sparked inside Gabe as quickly as he stamped it out. "What did the police do?"

"Rescue doesn't have a police force." Caz shrugged. "The state troopers are the only law enforcement available, but they're not exactly on site. Or very interested. Since

Rescue is still incorporated, we're supposed to have our own police."

Hell. "Is anyone else having trouble or just you two?"

Bull ran his fingers over his goatee. "I haven't talked much with the locals. Been too busy. And my construction crew is from Soldotna since Rescue doesn't have a general contractor."

Caz shook his head. "I don't know either. I'm buried in paperwork. And trying to get moved."

"You figure someone is singling out the sarge's kids?" Gabe asked. Fuck knew Mako wouldn't have been polite if he took a dislike to someone.

"Doubtful," Caz said. "Aside from Dante and a couple of others, no one in town even met Mako and no one besides them knows us."

Gabe considered. Old sleepy town. Resort opens. Tourists. Bull and Caz opening businesses. "Could be that someone isn't pleased with the changes happening. Maybe a back-to-the-land type." Right now, Gabe was feeling more sympathy than not toward someone who wanted to avoid a bunch of noisy tourists. "You might..."

Gabe's voice trailed off as he saw his brothers' expectant looks. Yeah, they'd sucked him in. The assholes.

"We need someone to enforce the law in Rescue. We need you, *viejo*," Caz said softly.

Old man. One of Gabe's nicknames. Because he was all of a year older than Bull and Hawk and two years older than

24

Caz. Because they'd heard the sarge affectionately refer to his company commander as the old man.

Because Gabe had always led, and his brothers had always followed.

He tried to thicken the ice around his soul and felt it thin instead, like river ice before break-up.

Dammit, he wasn't a fucking hero. He didn't give a shit about the Rescue residents. He didn't want to protect them. People weren't worth his life—or his death.

But his brothers were worth...anything he had to give.

Hell.

He wasn't about to give in without a fight. "I'll think about it."

CHAPTER TWO

The first week in May at the University of Illinois-Chicago was an intense time as students and faculty revved up for final exams the following week. End of the school year and commencement parties had started, as well.

Thursday evening, Audrey Hamilton glanced back at the university in her rear-view mirror. Her fellow university librarians were heading off to a faculty party.

As always, she'd made excuses not to attend.

She scowled at herself in the mirror. *You are one timid, vacillating, spineless coward. An invertebrate in human form.*

The truth hurt.

She loved the reference part of her job. She enjoyed helping students and faculty locate the materials needed to complete their work or studies.

The liaison responsibilities? Having to schmooze and

build relationships? Totally not in her skill set and way outside her nerdy comfort level.

And tonight, rather than facing her fears and attending the staff party, she'd fled. With a sigh, she settled down to a rainy drive through rush hour traffic.

In her apartment complex's parking lot, she started to turn into her designated slot and almost rear-ended a beat-up yellow car parked there. The high-pitched squeak she gave probably woke every cat in the neighborhood.

She glared at the trespassing vehicle. *Seriously? That's my parking space.* Growling, she backed up and quickly discovered that building C's visitor slots were filled...as were building D's and E's.

Finally, she found parking at building F. *F* for *eff-it-all*—a word infinitely satisfying to mutter under her breath.

Before getting out of the car, she pulled her cell out of her purse. No calls from Quentin.

Eff-it-all, eff-it-all, eff-it-all. She punched in his number. Again.

No answer. Again.

Worry festered in her stomach. Where was her client? He'd promised to call her, and yes, as an author, he was absent-minded when writing, but today, he'd gone to interview some people. Possibly scary people.

There was nothing she could do now. Slinging her purse over her shoulder, she picked up her groceries. With a heavy recyclable bag on each arm, she paused in the drizzling rain and eyed the distance to her building. Her laptop would have to remain in the trunk. Laptops and rain—not a good combination.

She was drenched before she'd gone past the first building. Spring in Chicago was so...nice. Really. She loved the rain. Loved it more when she didn't have to walk in it.

As she approached her building, she was panting like a steam engine. Sheesh, maybe she should visit the complex's gym now and then.

Or not.

She huffed a laugh. She was a lazy nerd and proud of it. Which was why winter was the best season. She could curl up on her big cushy couch with a mug of hot chocolate and read.

At the front, the security door on her building was propped open. Driving rock music and raucous laughter poured like a waterfall of noise from an apartment upstairs. Someone was having a party. No wonder the parking lot was full.

There were days she wished she lived in a cave.

She headed down the hall to her ground floor apartment. Should she call the manager to complain about the noise or the cars? *No.* Just because she was a boring rule-follower didn't mean she'd ruin some college kid's weekend by having his car towed.

Maybe this was a good incentive to stop living nose-to-nose with others and buy a house. She was twenty-seven, after all. However, she'd always lived in apartments, and the thought of buying a house all by herself was somewhat nerve-wracking.

Her mouth twisted. She and Craig had planned to buy a house. She'd envisioned a cute fixer-upper that would fit in her budget since she was excellent at looking up how to repair things. However, Craig had wanted an eye-catching, client-impressing house—and that's what he and his new girlfriend had bought.

It turned out that Craig had also wanted an eye-catching, client-impressing woman.

Audrey shook her head. How had she missed the signs their relationship was doomed? His interests didn't mesh with hers. In fact, after the initial excitement, she'd usually been relieved when he *hadn't* come over and she could have an evening alone. The way he'd criticized her clothing, her makeup, her social skills.

Eventually, she'd have understood that their personalities were incompatible.

It sure did burn that he'd been the one to dump her.

Inhaling slowly, she let herself into her apartment. As she carried her groceries into the kitchen, she tried not to remember their last time together. Two months ago, he'd told her they were done.

Her biggest mistake was asking him why he was breaking up with her.

"Because I need someone at my side who likes people, who is

sociable. Someone who can impress my clients and my boss rather than trying to avoid even meeting them."

The words had shriveled her soul.

Truly, introverts shouldn't try to have relationships. Nerds should be content with being alone. These days, aside from casual university friendships, her relationships were online, and she was perfectly happy to have them that way.

The jagged ache in her chest didn't count.

Maybe she should get a cat.

After putting her groceries away, she checked her phone again. No calls. Still no answer when she rang Quentin. Could he still be interviewing people at the pharmaceutical research facility? No, it'd been too long. He knew how worried she was. He wouldn't have left her hanging like this.

He'd gotten in trouble.

She scowled. He'd been positive his credentials would gain him access to the scientists and managers there and that his well-known name would keep him safe. What if he'd been wrong?

Her fingers felt like stiff icicles as she booted up her desktop computer in her office alcove.

Quentin wrote conspiracy thrillers and occasionally ran across criminal information he'd share with the law. The FBI agent he usually talked with was here in Chicago and had a name like a restaurant chain. *Denny...no, Dennison.*

Although Audrey's specialty was biology, since becoming

a freelance internet researcher, she'd become very eclectic. And she was damn good at digging out information. It didn't take long to locate the FBI Special Agent and only a few minutes longer to find his cell phone number.

She punched the number into her cell.

"I don't recognize this number. You have ten seconds to prove you're someone I want to talk with." The man's voice had a harsh New York accent.

"Quentin's missing."

A pause. His laugh was a bitter bark of sound. "That works."

Over the phone, giggles and a high voice called, "Daddy, come and play. We got Candyland."

"I'll be a minute, kids. Ask your mommy to start the game with you."

The disappointed whines disappeared as a door shut. His voice came back on the line. "Who is this? Why do you think he's missing? Start at the beginning."

"I'm Audrey Hamilton. I do internet research." Moonlighting from her university job had seemed like fun last year. Her clients had the oddest requests—from articles on resilience in foster children, to apple production numbers in Wisconsin, to how to disappear in the computer age, to horseback travel times in the nineteenth century.

But blundering into an actual crime? Perhaps she should rethink her career choice.

"Quentin hired me to collect data about recent viral

epidemics and vaccines." Her hand clenched around her cell phone. "I found... First, do you remember the influenza last year? Because of the high mortality, the CDC recommended everyone get a vaccine booster that'd been developed by a small pharmaceutical research company. Xeno Labs."

"I remember." He snorted. "I got the booster."

"Perfect. Quentin requested I find him articles about creating mutations in the influenza virus. Several scientists wrote about their research in developing vaccine boosters for unexpected mutations."

"Ms. Hamilton, there are tons of articles about the flu, aren't there?"

She could almost see him deciding to cut the conversation short.

"Of course. The point is I discovered the top three researchers were hired by Xeno Labs two years ago. At the same time."

Silence. "Were they now?" he muttered. "Quentin suspected something?"

"He's pretty sure Xeno engineered a viral mutation, one that would necessitate a booster. Their booster. The profit must have been enormous." The bastards.

"That's a serious accusation." Dennison exhaled noisily. "But Dane's instincts are rarely wrong. Did you say he's missing?"

"Quentin went to visit Xeno labs this afternoon. Now I can't reach him."

The sound of a keyboard being tapped came over the line. "Xeno Labs—north of Chicago."

"Yes, that's where he was going."

"I'm sending someone there and someone to his home. What else can you tell me?"

"Uh, not much. I merely looked up articles for Quentin."

"I see. If you have my phone, I assume you also have my email?"

"Yes."

"Email me with the names of the people he planned to talk with. Attach the pertinent articles and anything else you think relevant. Can you do that?"

Quentin hadn't been willing to point fingers at the lab, not without more information. But now... His scruples could go hang. "I'm emailing you the names now. I'll send the files in a second email after I get them together."

"Perfect."

She'd never met Quentin. Her business was conducted over internet and phone, but he lived somewhere in Chicago. If she—

"Miss Hamilton, I know you're worried, but I want you to stay put. I'll call you once I know what's going on."

Darn it, she wanted to go and check out that lab herself, to look for him at his house. "All right."

After getting the emails sent off to Dennison, she waited with her cell phone beside her. No one called.

Finally, she gave up and worked on information for a

health food store client. Stats on the correlation between pesticides and early dementia for their blog.

Hours passed as she worked. Despite the loud music from upstairs, her small apartment felt adrift from the world and far too lonely. Now she really did wish Craig were here. Or a cat.

Or anyone.

———

A sound roused Audrey, and she blinked awake. Pushing her hair back, she sat up in bed. Her camisole and silky boxers were twisted around, and she wiggled them into place.

Had her phone rung? Maybe Quentin or the FBI agent called?

No...that wasn't what she'd heard.

A sound came from the living room.

Did she have mice? Startled, she reached past the crystal vase of silk flowers on her nightstand to turn on the lamp.

Footsteps sounded.

Her eyes widened. There was someone in her—

The bedroom door was flung open, and a man charged across the room. He landed on her, knocking the wind out of her. His palm covered her mouth.

Screaming against his muffling hand, she fought with everything in her, hitting at his head, trying to scratch his face. The covers over her legs destroyed any chance to kick. His arms were leather covered, defeating her fingernails.

Silently, he rolled her over in bed, all his weight on her. He shoved her face against the mattress until she couldn't breathe. Panic ripped through her.

"You gonna be quiet?" He brutally wrenched her arms up behind her back until her shoulders felt dislocated.

Frantically, she nodded.

Gripping her by the hair, he yanked her over and up.

All she could do was gasp for *air*. But her mouth was free. *Scream, fool.*

Before she could, the man hit her so hard the left side of her jaw exploded in pain. She fell back. Hot tears streamed down her cheeks.

"I got a knife, cunt. You make a noise, and I'll slice you up." He was dressed all in black. Like a prizefighter, his face was battered. Scarred and swarthy with a big nose and black eyes. His black hair was buzz cut. His raspy voice held an accent—one she recognized from her college days watching foreign films. Greek.

He yanked her up to a sitting position and made a quick movement. Suddenly, warm liquid trickled across her left biceps, followed by searing pain. He'd *cut* her. She choked back her cry.

"Yeah. Better." He held the knife up. "Pretty, huh?"

Frozen with fear, she could only stare as blood—her blood—dripped off the blade.

A nasal voice from the doorway said, "Nobody's here."

"Good. Search the place." The man in front of her smiled. "Who'd you tell about your research, cunt?"

"Research?"

His fist impacted her ribs, and she felt a crack. As pain engulfed her, she hunched over her left side, sobbing for breath. Oh God, it *hurt*.

He repeated louder, "Who'd you tell about Xeno Labs? Besides Quentin Dane."

Only a whimper came out.

Leaning forward, he whispered, "The author is dead, *poutana*. He gave me your name. Your address. And then he died, screaming. Do you want to die like that?"

Grief mixed with her terror. *Oh Quentin.* "N-no, please."

"Who did you tell?"

If the man realized the FBI knew about the labs, would he leave?

"I—" Yet, if she gave him Dennison's name, he might go there. The agent had small children. They'd been playing Candyland. No, she couldn't. "Quentin. I only t-talked to Quentin."

A crash and hammering noises came from the other room, then the other man appeared. "I trashed her desktop computer." He had a thick New York accent. "Did she talk with anyone else?"

"She says no. I think she's lying." Gripping her hair, the Greek tossed her on the floor.

Her hip hit first, the pain muted by the carpet. She caught herself on her elbow and instinctually kicked his leg with all her might. Her bare foot glanced off his shin.

"Cunt." He stomped his boot down on her left thigh.

As pain blasted through her leg, she tried to scream. His hand covered her face, covered her mouth and nose. No air. She panicked, flailing at him.

When black filled her vision, he laughed and let her go.

As he rose, he casually kicked her in the belly. Her whole body jerked at the impact. Curling into a ball, she gasped for air—and cried. Her arm burned, her leg and hip throbbed, every shuddering wheeze stabbed into her ribs and stomach. *Oh, God, help me.*

"What? Yeah, at her place." The New Yorker was talking on the phone. Vision blurring with tears, she tried to focus. If she was going to die here, she wanted to see who'd kill her.

He was shorter than the Greek and burly with muscles. Blond buzz cut. Nose thickened—had been broken. Front tooth half-broken off.

The New Yorker shoved his phone into his pocket with a scowl. "Hey, Spyros, the Xeno boss says a cop showed up at the lab."

Audrey tried to even her voice. "You'd better run. The police and FBI will be here soon."

The Greek hissed a laugh. "Nah. I got men in both places. I'd know. Why do you think I'm still free?"

He had his own people in the police and FBI.

And his name was Spyros. A tremor shook her. He didn't care that she'd heard his name—because she'd never identify him. She was going to die.

"Why're the cops looking for Quentin Dane at the lab?" the New Yorker asked. "The Xeno dude was pissed."

"Dane said he didn't call them. He wasn't lying—not at the end." The certainty in the Greek's voice was terrifying. "I bet this cunt sent the cops after him." He looked down at her with black eyes. "What else did she tell them?"

The air was so thick with her fear she felt as if she was drowning in it.

"Dunno, but we been here too long already." The New Yorker slapped the doorframe. "Time to go."

"Yeah, I know." The Greek reached down and gripped her upper arms, his thumb digging cruelly into the knife wound on her biceps.

Hurts, hurts, hurts. Her stomach heaved as she tried to choke back her sobs.

"Bring the car around," Spyros said. "Park at the side exit. I'll clean up our package."

"Fuck, you're bringing her?"

"I want to take my time. It'll get bloody."

"Your call." The apartment door opened and clicked shut.

Spyros lifted her and set her on the bed, then fondled her breast through the camisole.

No! When she shoved at his arm, he carelessly backhanded her.

Her head whipped back, the skin beside her mouth tearing from his ring. Her head spun from the new horrible pain.

"Where's your phone, *poutana?*"

Her phone. It would show the call to Dennison. She stared at him, too terrified to speak.

He set a big hand around her throat and squeezed. "Where?"

Red streaks shot through her vision as she struggled for air. Her fingers scrabbled uselessly against him. Lifting her by her neck, he stood her up. Her feet touched the carpet; her legs took her weight...

Yanking her knee up as fast as she could, she smashed his balls so violently she could feel cells bursting.

He choked, wheezed, and struck out, punching her in the cheek, before his legs buckled. He hit the floor, wavering on his knees.

Half-blinded, she fumbled for the nightstand lamp. Her fingers brushed cold glass. She grabbed the crystal vase and, with a terrified howl, swung with all her strength.

The heavy glass struck his head—and shattered.

"Aaaah!"

Terrified at the tortured yell, she scrambled to the other side of the bed and stood. Looked.

He was on his side, hands pressed to his face. Shards of glass covered the carpet and pincushioned his cheek. Blood poured from between his fingers. Gut-wrenching moans filled the room.

Backing up, she thumped into the wall.

His head turned, and she gasped.

A huge glass shard had penetrated his right eye.

Bile rose into her throat. She couldn't move.

"I'll kill you...kill you, kill you, cunt." At the guttural cursing, fresh terror gripped her.

Run, oh God, run. She banged into the dresser and grabbed her phone, purse, and keys. *Don't use the door.* The other man would be coming back.

Opening the bedroom window, she shoved out the screen. Crying at the pain, she crawled through.

The back of the building was dark, the only illumination from the windows above.

Arms wrapped around herself, she staggered toward building D. Each footstep sent pain stabbing into her ribs. Keeping to the blackest shadows behind the buildings, she splashed through puddles. Icy rain plastered her skimpy clothes and hair to her skin.

Stopping at the corner of building E, she heard a car and froze. A black van drove past.

Her heart hammered so loudly it drowned out the sound of the rain, of anything. The New Yorker would find Spyros. Would come after her.

"Move, Audrey. Move."

The night blurred around her as she lurched forward. Building F.

There was her car. Hot tears spilled over.

The engine started. *Oh thank God.* Grabbing a stocking cap from the glove compartment, she pulled it on, bunching her hair under it. She put on her driving glasses.

Taking painful shallow breaths, she drove slowly out of the parking lot.

No black van. No cars at all.

Blocks away, she pulled into an all-night grocery parking lot, stopped, and tried to pick up her phone. Her hands trembled so hard that it took three tries to get her fingertip in the fingerprint reader.

As the screen lit, she paused. What should she do? Her fingers hovered over the display of numbers. Over 911.

But Spyros had a person—or more—in the police department. And FBI. The sinking feeling of despair made her eyes burn. She couldn't turn to law enforcement.

Nonetheless, she needed to warn Quentin's Fed.

Dennison didn't answer.

Eff-it-all. In a quavering voice, she left him a voicemail—about Quentin's death, her attack, informants in the cops and FBI.

She got through it...and then cried, and oh God, crying hurt. Her face burned as tears ran over the cuts and gashes. Each sob hurt her ribs and her stomach, and she couldn't *stop.*

A lifetime later, the weeping slowed. Shudders shook her as she wiped off her face. Bloody streaks stained the camisole.

Now what? What could she do for herself?

She was alone. So alone.

The memory of Spyros's threats made her tremble. Once he healed, he'd come after her. He'd kill her.

She had nowhere to hide. No one to call.

But that wasn't new. Her chin rose. She'd manage running on her own. Her first client had been a mystery writer who'd had her look up the various ways a fugitive might hide in this modern world.

Research would save her.

CHAPTER THREE

At the railing of the MV *Ketchikan,* Audrey watched the rocky British Columbia coastline flow past. She tilted her face to the chill wind off the water, hearing the cries of the gulls. Beneath her feet, the deck rolled slightly.

Her first day on the ferry had been spent staring at the horizon and trying to calm her stomach. Her ribs were cracked—or broken. Throwing up would really hurt.

Today, her queasiness had disappeared.

And look at me go. She'd never traveled before, but in the last seven days, she'd crossed most of the continent. Wasn't it odd how fear could spur a girl to doing new things?

The morning after her attack, she'd pulled on the spare snow clothes and boots she kept in the trunk, cleaned up in a gas station bathroom, and then gone shopping. She'd figured she had a short window of time before Spyros started to hunt for her. After all, he'd need to get his eye treated.

The thought made her stomach turn over.

A department store visit gave her an assortment of wigs and makeup, hats, scarves, and cheap clothes, vanity glasses, sunglasses, and jewelry.

After covering what she could with makeup, she'd visited an internet shop, using Bitcoin and the Dark Web to purchase two different sets of fake ID, then arranged delivery to Denver and Seattle. The IDs probably wouldn't pass a close inspection, but they'd be good enough.

She hoped.

Then she'd visited her bank to cash out almost all of her savings. When the teller voiced concern, Audrey'd said, "My boyfriend is abusive, and I have to get away. Please hurry." It'd worked. The sympathetic female teller sped through the withdrawal process.

She'd considered flying to the opposite side of the country, but airport security was too tight. Her credit card and ID would be scrutinized; she'd be on camera. It'd be too easy for Spyros's bribed FBI agents to trace her.

So, after leaving her car in long-term storage, she bused to South Side Chicago and used her credit card to buy a nondescript, used car. If her pursuers could access her credit card usage, this would make it look as if she was headed south. Hopefully.

She drove west.

Even now, she winced at the memory of those long painful days of driving. Twice, in scary slum areas, she abandoned her current vehicle, leaving it running with keys in the ignition. Each time, before buying another car, she altered her hair and skin color. Various glasses and hats covered her eyes and ears. Lipstick changed the shape of her mouth. Facial recognition systems were scarily accurate.

After picking up her ID in Seattle, she bused to Bellingham, Washington and boarded the ferry to Alaska.

As one of the boat crew passed with a nod, she smiled. Men had been friendly to this persona. She was wearing a dark red, short-and-perky wig, hooker-heavy makeup, and a padded bra that made her a couple of sizes larger.

She'd used the men's interest to get them to talk about Alaska's small towns. Because she needed somewhere to disappear. She wanted a town small enough to have no traffic cameras. It'd be even better if it lacked any law enforcement yet was big enough to have a way for her to earn a living, no matter how pitiful. She also needed to be close enough to Anchorage to have a way to fly out.

Homer was too big and too far from the city. Girdwood, Cooper Landing, and Moose Pass were all about the right size.

Or there was Rescue, a town not too far from Cooper Landing. It had a small lake on one side and the Kenai River on the other. The boat crew wasn't impressed with the place. Said it was rather dead.

Rescue had possibilities.

Anticipation rose within her. In a few more days, when the ferry docked in Whittier, she'd break out her final ID and change her appearance. After that, she'd take the train to Anchorage to buy a used car.

And then find the town where she wanted to live.

CHAPTER FOUR

M *en, we are surrounded by the enemy. That means we have the greatest opportunity ever presented to an army. We can attack in any direction we choose.* - General Tony McAuliffe

Rescue had two whole blocks of businesses, and most of them were empty. Gabe slowed his Jeep as he drove down Main Street. Like an old derelict living on the streets, the town looked gaunt and faded. Older than its age. Paint was chipping off the wooden storefronts; the sidewalk in front of the stores was cracked, and most of the streetlights were busted.

He didn't see any massive wave of tourists wandering the streets. Only a few cars were diagonally parked in front of businesses. Then again, the middle of May was a bit early for fishing season.

If there was a tourist season here.

There were no stop signs. No *Welcome to Rescue* signs. If the townspeople wanted this place to be welcoming, they needed to up their game.

He drove to Grebe Avenue, made a left, and left again down the gravel alley.

Caz said the municipal building housed the town offices and records rooms, the police station, and the medical clinic. All the departments shared the reception area. As he parked in the huge parking lot at the rear, he spotted a tattered windsock. Apparently, the lot also served as a helicopter-landing pad.

Three back doors led to the different sections of the building. Rather clever, actually, to house tax-funded services together. Many Alaskan towns were census-designated areas, not incorporated, and the services came from the borough. Rescue, though, had been large enough at one time to have incorporated and gotten a home rule charter.

As Gabe got out of the Jeep, movement caught his eye. He froze, adrenaline flooding his system.

Seeing the furry black rump disappearing into a clump of bushes, Gabe relaxed. The black bear had probably been scoping out the garbage cans.

And Gabe's heart rate was still elevated. He shook his head. The minute he hit town, he started looking for insurgents behind every building.

Because a village was where he and his mercenary squad had been ambushed.

The hypervigilance from being in town would diminish with time and familiarity. Although it sucked at the moment.

He breathed out, forcing his shoulders, his chest, and his gut to stand down, then walked to the police station's back door. In his pocket were the station's keys he'd found on the kitchen table after Caz and Bull had left.

It'd taken him two weeks to leave his refuge. Bull was right about him being barn sour.

Damn brothers. Gabe scowled and entered the building. He was a fool, stepping back into a war zone...because that's what being a law enforcement officer meant.

At least he'd just be a lowly officer and not responsible for anyone but himself...and the town. The entire damn town.

The tiny police station was empty. Somewhat dusty.

One long room obviously served as the bullpen with scattered desks for the officers. He'd have to pick a desk and settle in.

The front had a window to Main Street. The left side of the room had a door that opened into the building's main reception area.

He kept exploring. On the right wall was the door to the staff area with a few lockers, a shower, and toilet area. Another room functioned as the lockup for evidence and contained the gun vault—open and empty.

The final door near the front opened to the police chief's office. Gabe studied the dust and the desk piled with junk mail and notices. Didn't look as if anyone was filling that position.

To his surprise, he spotted a paper with his name on top of one pile.

- - - -

Gabe.

The town council appointed you Chief of Police. Here's your badge, stars, and the contract. Welcome to Rescue.

Caz

- - - -

Chief of Police? What the hell?

Gabe closed his eyes. Talk about being railroaded. *Welcome to Rescue, dumbass. You're now the person in charge of enforcing the law.*

Growling, he glanced through the paperwork—all in order. Of course it was.

Was he going to let himself get pushed into this shit? He considered the papers, the badge, the stars. Considered saying no. But did it matter what title he carried—officer or chief? In a one-horse town, there wasn't much difference.

With a sigh, he signed the contract. All right, he'd play. For now. He'd find whoever was sabotaging his brothers' construction, beat the shit out of him...no, wrong. *Arrest* the bastard. After that, he'd help Rescue hire on an officer or two.

Then, he could return to Mako's old cabin with a clear conscience.

After tossing the badge up in the air a few times, feeling it grow heavier each time, he pinned it onto his jacket. He attached the stars to his jacket collar tabs.

He'd need to give the State Troopers' dispatch a heads-up that he was in Rescue. Later.

What kind of idiotic council did Rescue have anyway to appoint a police chief sight unseen?

They might well change their minds once they met him. Gabe snorted. At one time, he'd been friendlier. Not like Caz, who could charm the hair off a poodle, but more approachable than Hawk, who'd rather be skinned than dole out an entire sentence.

Gabe frowned. As a kid, he'd actually liked people. As a Navy SEAL too. Then his years in law enforcement had sent his idealism into a nosedive. Too much corruption in the force. Too much hatred from the public he was pledged to protect. Eventually, he realized he was risking his life for the same people who'd break the law a second later. He'd hated how he'd grown cold and calloused.

After a goatfuck of a drug raid, when Gabe'd been shot and his partner killed, Hawk had talked him into joining a mercenary outfit. Gabe'd figured, why not? The LA citizens sure hadn't appreciated their police. He might as well get paid the big bucks if he was going to risk his life.

But merc work turned out to be ugly. Even worse, after the private military company was sold to investors, the jobs had become questionable. He'd lost the feeling of doing anything worthwhile with his life.

With the inexorable movement of a glacier, ice had finished burying his emotions. Aside from the gap he'd left for his brothers.

He shook his head and caught the bright glint of the badge on his chest. Back in the force again. "You are a dumb son of a bitch, MacNair."

Fuck, he needed some coffee.

As Gabe walked into the squad room, the door from the receptionist area opened.

The person who entered was male, 5'10". Short, dark blond hair, light blue eyes, muscular, wearing a khaki shirt, jeans, and tan jacket. And a police badge.

The man frowned, then grinned. "Hey, you must be Gabriel MacNair." His eyes narrowed at the stars on Gabe's jacket. "*Chief* MacNair."

Gabe nodded. "So it seems."

Crossing the room, the man held his hand out. "I'm Earl Baumer. Your one and only patrol officer. Welcome to Rescue." He had a pleasant tenor voice with a strong southern accent.

"Thanks."

Baumer tried to dominate the handshake.

Not that he could. Mildly irritated, Gabe asked, "When did you get hired?"

"About two weeks ago after the town council approved the budget to reopen the station." Baumer shrugged.

"I heard it'd been closed for a decade. Why open it again?"

"Eh, with McNally's Resort open, we've got tourists who get upset if there isn't an officer right there to hold them up. Most of the town council jumped on the *increase tourism* bandwagon."

Most, not all? *Interesting.*

Gabe eyed Baumer. The patrol officer was friendly enough, but was he competent? "Where did you work before?"

"I put in close to ten years in Thibodaux. It's in Louisiana." Baumer headed for the coffee pot on a table against the wall.

Ten years should have netted Baumer the rank of sergeant, if not higher. Gabe'd been a lieutenant when he quit the force after eight years. Then again, maybe Baumer didn't like the god-awful paperwork.

That'd be a shame since Gabe was already wondering—after he cleaned up Caz and Bull's problems—if he could dump the chief job on Baumer and head back to the cabin. "Louisiana to Alaska. Quite the change."

"Yeah, sure was." Coffeemaker primed, Baumer flipped the switch. "It's why I wasn't working when this position opened. We moved to Alaska over a year ago, but my wife and I wanted to make sure we liked the winters before I committed to a job."

Not a foolish notion. Although Alaska summers were glorious, the cold, gray winters drove a lot of people south.

Gabe eyed the coffee drizzling into the pot. Pale brown. Might as well be piss. Mako'd taught his boys that coffee should be strong enough to use as an offensive weapon.

"I need to scope out the town before anything else." And get some decent coffee. "Let's meet here at one o'clock. We'll discuss scheduling, and you can brief me on the town's problems."

"Sounds like a plan." Baumer gave him a laid-back smile before turning to pour himself a cup of coffee.

Gabe went out the front, walked down the sidewalk, and studied the town. Scattered among the closed stores were a few open businesses. The grocery. A hardware store.

A buzzing from the right caught Gabe's attention. A floatplane soared upward from the lake, a graceful silver silhouette in the fathomless blue sky. The far end of the lake had a non-manned airport. One gravel strip and a couple of floatplane docks. Probably all in poor shape.

Hawk lived to fly. Maybe he'd return and take on the upgrading.

Gabe's mouth tightened. For two years, he and Hawk had been on the same mercenary squad. Then, a month before the ambush, Hawk'd requested reassignment to another squad. When Gabe asked him why, he'd walked away.

The asshole. Gabe shook his head. If he'd done something his brother didn't like, would it have killed the bastard to tell him?

Despite Gabe's anger, he thanked God that Hawk hadn't been with the squad that day. Hadn't been ambushed. Hadn't died like the others.

Gabe hadn't seen his brother since the reassignment. The terse, rude bastard. His absence left behind a hollow ache.

To hell with memories. *I need coffee.*

He crossed the street to an old-fashioned coffee shop. The bell over the door clanged softly as it closed behind him.

Aged wooden pews, probably from a church, formed booths along the front windows and right side. A few tables and chairs dotted the center. Customers sat in the booths, enjoying coffee and desserts. To the left, a glass-fronted pastry display ended in a short counter with stools.

Behind the counter was a small woman, lean as a whippet, with short brunette hair. She smiled. "I haven't seen you in years, but you're Mako's Gabriel. It's good to see you again. Can I get you a cup of coffee?"

After a minute, Gabe recalled her name from the time a couple of years before when he'd visited Rescue with Mako. "Sarah. Yes, coffee would be good." Odd how difficult it was to be around people after months of isolation. "Drip and black, please."

She prepared a cup and handed it over, then spotted his

badge. Her smile widened. "I'm so pleased you're here. Caz warned us that you weren't too enthusiastic about returning to civilization."

Damn Caz. "I've found that honest people are scarcer than rattlesnakes in Alaska, but it's not a—"

"We don't have rattlesnakes in Alaska."

"Exactly."

Not taking offense, she laughed. "I hope our Rescue citizens will change your mind. I know Mako wanted you here. He knew how much we need you."

Did he? Mako'd sure been more involved with the town than he'd told them. Since when had the survivalist loner concerned himself with anything other than an impending apocalypse? "Bull mentioned there are anti-tourism sentiments?"

"Oh, yes. We have..." Her voice trailed off as a clean-shaven, spare-framed male entered. Probably late forties. Average height. Light brown hair.

Armed.

Gabe tensed, then relaxed again. The man was a civilian, not an insurgent. Jesus, he'd forgotten that open carry of firearms was allowed in Alaska.

Sarah's voice cooled. "Good morning, Reverend Parrish. What can I get you?"

"I'll have a latte." The man had a Texas drawl.

"Coming right up." Sarah turned a warm smile on Gabe. "I look forward to talking with you more at a later time. Welcome to Rescue, Chief."

Chief. Gabe froze for a second. Chief of Police. God help him. "Thanks."

When Gabe nodded at Parrish, the man tore his gaze away from the badge on Gabe's jacket. Mouth flattening, he nodded back.

Something told Gabe they weren't going to be bosom buddies.

In no hurry, Gabe strolled the business section of Main Street—two blocks—reached the end, and headed back on the other side.

It'd take a while to get his footing here. Get to know the place. When visiting Mako, he'd only come into town to pick up groceries.

But police work was police work, no matter the size of the town.

He was a retired SEAL, had been a police lieutenant in Los Angeles, and even led a merc squad. He could deal with paperwork. Didn't mean he looked forward to managing an entire station's budget.

He glanced at the store he was passing, saw it was Dante's Market, and entered. The owner was a Vietnam vet and the reason why the sarge had chosen Rescue as a place to live.

Not spotting Dante, Gabe glanced around. Sometime in the last year or so, the owner had walled off the right-most third of the building. Probably as the population diminished, so did the need for a large grocery store. With an influx of tourists, resort staff, and more residents, Dante might be able to open that section back up.

Only one person was in the store, a white adult female, who was perusing the cookie section. She had stunning hair. The thick, wavy tangle was every shade of gold and reached halfway down her back. About five-five, she wore jeans and a flannel shirt bulky enough to disguise any curves.

Before he could speak, she picked up a box of cookies and tucked it into her purse.

Well, fuck. Disillusionment washed through him. Even here, people were no good. Odd, he hadn't realized how much he'd hoped for Rescue to be different until that desire was crushed.

He cleared his throat.

She spun, saw him, gasped, and began backing away down the aisle. Hand on her throat, she looked so terrified, he almost had a moment of pity.

Almost.

Staring at the man, Audrey retreated as fast as she could... and he came toward her. *Oh God.*

He blocked the narrow aisle completely. Her heart began to pound painfully inside her rib cage. She glanced over her shoulder at the back door, but the locked door would take time to get open.

She turned to face the man. He was frighteningly big. Over six feet tall, with short brown hair. The beard shadow was darker than his outdoorsman's tan. Harsh lines bracketed his unsmiling mouth, and he looked...threatening.

Could the hitman or his people have traced her?

A glance didn't reveal Spyros; the man was alone. Besides, she hadn't left a trail. People disappeared all the time into remote Alaskan towns.

No, she was safe here. Surely she was. "Wh-what do you want?"

He crossed his arms over his chest—a very broad chest. "It's simple. Hand me everything you stole, and then we'll go down to the station and have a chat."

Have a chat? She wasn't going anywhere with him. The rest of his sentence registered. *Station... Oh my God, he was the police.*

She stared at the badge on his black fleece-lined jacket.

Wait. What did he mean "stole?"

"I didn't steal anything." Fear blossomed anew. Even if her photo ID looked real enough to her, it wouldn't hold up to a police background check. She took a step back.

His eyebrows lifted slightly. "I saw you. Bring your purse up to the counter."

Outrage swept through her, vying with anxiety. "I'm not stealing. Dante said I could take whatever I wanted to eat."

"Mmmhmm." Disbelief was obvious in the man's deep voice. "Let's ask him."

Audrey crossed her arms over her chest, imitating the man. "He's not here."

When his gaze pinned her in place, she saw his eyes

weren't black—they were midnight blue and brimmed with skepticism. "He wouldn't leave his store unattended."

"He asked me to mind the register."

"And steal the goods?"

"Listen, Sheriff—"

"There are no sheriffs in Alaska. Call me Chief."

"Chief." Oh, she was so screwed. He wasn't merely a small town cop, but the Chief of Police. She swallowed. Where was Dante? Shouldn't he be back by now? "Chief what?"

"MacNair. And you are?"

"Juliette Wilson." She'd done her homework. Wilson was almost as common as Jones, Johnson, and Smith. Juliette was a popular name, too.

"Wilson, huh?" His mouth flattened in a cynical way.

The door opened. As Dante moseyed into the store, relief filled her.

Only a few inches taller than she was, the wiry grocery store owner had receding white hair and a thick white mustache and beard.

He saw her, and his bushy brows pulled together. Turning to Gabe, he snapped, "Yo, buddy, leave my girl alone."

When the chief turned toward him with a scowl, Dante blinked. His face lit. "It's Gabe, isn't it? I'll be. You're really here?"

The chief didn't even notice Dante's delight. "Ms. Wilson here was stuffing her purse with groceries and says you left her to mind the place." The cop's low baritone held enough sarcasm to fill a lake.

"Heh, working in LA done made you cynical, boy." Dante might've left Oklahoma behind a long while back, but the southern twang in his voice remained.

"She told the truth?"

"Yep, she sho'nuff did." Dante stepped behind the counter and set down a travel cup and white paper sack from the coffee shop. "She's working now and then in exchange for one of my rental cabins and some groceries. Room and board, you might say. Keeps me from having to close up every time I want to leave the store."

Audrey's muscles began to unknot.

"I see." The chief glanced at her, and his sharp gaze lingered on the yellowing bruises on her face. His suspicions didn't appear much abated, but he said, politely enough, "I'm sorry to have bothered you, Ms. Wilson."

"Quite all right. I can appreciate how guilty I must have appeared." If she'd been a criminal, she'd be running from him as fast as possible.

To her relief, he nodded and joined Dante at the front.

After the two men shook hands, Dante glanced over. "Julie, how about you unpack those boxes of cereal?"

Yes, she totally needed something to keep busy. "I would be delighted."

"You shopping or walkin' your beat?" Dante asked the chief.

"There's no food in my cabin, but I'll shop later." The

chief shrugged. "I wanted to see what I had to deal with here."

"A lot, boy. A lot. Get yerself settled in, and then we'll talk." Dante's smile widened. "You might check on your brother across the street. There was a shit-ton of swearing coming from over there."

Pretending not to listen, Audrey blinked. The man had a brother. There were two of them in this town. *What an awful thought.*

"No surprise. He hates paperwork." The chief's lips didn't move, but the sunlines beside his eyes crinkled.

Oh. Dear God, the man would be lethal if he ever really smiled. She realized she was staring.

He noticed. His eyes narrowed, and his expression hardened. Even though Dante's explanation should have placated the cop, he obviously didn't trust her at all.

A chill ran up her spine because she knew she must have looked guilty as hell.

As Gabe left the grocery store, he eyed the buildings on Main Street. A shiver crawled up his spine. Too many places for a sniper to hide.

After a second, he headed back across the street. *Get over it, MacNair.* The antsy feeling wasn't new, after all. Every combat vet went through something similar.

And his discomfort at being in town? All too familiar during his childhood. Each spring break-up, Mako'd take them to the nearest town where Gabe and his brothers would bunch together like terrified sheep. People would be talking, cars whizzing by... Of course, being resilient kids, they were fine within half an hour and driving the sarge crazy.

He wasn't a kid any longer, but he'd get over his nerves soon enough.

And it'd been pleasant to see Dante. The vet had taken the young woman under his wing. Room and board in exchange for working a few hours? *Riiiight.* The old guy was good people.

It'd been nice to see a pretty woman too. Although she obviously hadn't felt the same about him.

Was she avoiding him because he was in law enforcement?

Or because he had a dick?

Her face was thin with hollows in her cheeks. Her fair skin looked slack as if she'd lost weight recently. Despite her liberal use of makeup, faded bruise shadows over her left jaw and cheek showed. Even more damning, she had faint shadows of bruises on her neck. A healing cut by her mouth made him think of what happened when an abuser wore a ring.

The damage to her face and neck indicated that whatever—or whoever—had occurred, it had been brutal. He growled under his breath. Be nice to meet the asshole who'd hit her.

She'd sure been terrified when accused of shoplifting.

He felt a touch of shame. He hadn't believed for even a moment that she might be telling the truth.

In his experience, everyone lied.

But she hadn't been—at least about shoplifting. Thank fuck, he didn't have to haul her in. Yeah, it was sexist, but arresting a woman bothered him. *Protect the women and children* had been one of Gramps's dictates. Mako, also, had lived by that code.

Gabe scowled. Even if Ms. Wilson was innocent of stealing from the store, his "guilty" sensor had gone off. The woman was hiding something.

When she'd first seen Gabe, her big eyes had filled with fear. That had hurt. But the fear hadn't left when she'd realized he was a police officer. If anything, her worry had escalated.

Very astute of you, Ms. Wilson.

He didn't like secrets. Might be he'd take an interest in finding out what she was hiding.

And, appealing or not, that's all he wanted from her—her secrets. Women were...

His mouth thinned, remembering when he'd quit the LAPD. To derail an organized crime investigation, the subjects had bribed a woman to set up the detectives. Gabe had been shot. His partner had died. When interviewed, the woman had shrugged and laughed. *"Who gives a damn if a pig or two dies?"*

He lost his taste for *serve and protect* that day.

Enough. Shaking his head, he forced away the rancid memories. *That was then; this is now.*

He walked through the glass-fronted double door and into the two-story municipal building. The wide entry held a receptionist desk guarding the door to the police station on the left, the stairs to the second-floor city hall offices and the health clinic on the right. A handful of folding chairs served as a waiting area. The off-white walls were freshly painted, but the hardwood floor still needed a good sanding and some coats of varnish.

The receptionist desk wasn't staffed. Something else to worry about.

Turning to the right, he walked into Caz's health clinic.

Mako'd been damned proud when Caz had joined the Army Special Forces—the sarge's old branch—and even more so when Caz became a medic. After his discharge, Caz finished his Master's with a Family Nurse Practitioner license and set up practice in Anchorage. Every so often, he'd disappear for months to do volunteer work in third-world countries.

With his FNP license, he could run a health clinic without a doctor in residence. And Rescue needed a clinic here. Even if the drive to Soldotna or Seward wasn't long, a snowstorm or avalanche could render the Sterling and Seward Highways impassible for a couple of days.

Inside the clinic, a dented metal desk blocked the door to the various exam rooms and offices.

Hearing the thunk of something hitting the wall

followed by another two thunks, Gabe paused. The thuds were accompanied by cursing that started with *chinga*-something and ending with *cabrón*.

When irritated, Caz pulled out his throwing knives. Sounded like someone was in a pissy mood.

Gabe walked down the hallway.

In an office at the end, Caz sat behind a desk. His short black hair was uncombed, his dark brown eyes bloodshot, and he hadn't shaved in a couple of days.

Gabe cleared his throat.

Caz slowly turned his head. "'Bout time you got your ass moving."

Since his brother held a knife, and the three in the bulletin board were still quivering, Gabe took the path of wisdom and stayed silent.

As Caz's scowl lightened, he leaned back. "It's good to have you here, *viejo*."

Uh-huh. Gabe glanced at the piles on the desk. "Looks like you've got more paperwork than you have patients."

"The clinic's not open, so yes. But the paperwork is filed and approved, and I'm getting some equipment from Community Health Services. Basic supplies are already ordered."

"Progress."

"*Sí*. Slow, but sure." Caz rose and stretched with a groan. "I *hate* filling out forms."

The police station would need a budget, staffing, requisitions... "I hear you."

"I'll be able to open soon, but it'll be just me at first." Caz pulled his knives from the bulletin board.

Gabe grimaced. "The police station has a total of two—patrol and chief."

"One end of the pendulum arc. We start with too few businesses and not enough money and, with luck, swing to too many tourists and not enough services. Back and forth."

"With no one happy."

"Beginnings are like that." Caz massaged his shoulder—the one he'd busted the year Mako'd taught them rock climbing. "I could sure use a beer. Did you talk to Bull? The bar's grand opening is tomorrow night even though the restaurant half isn't quite ready."

A bar. That was a civilized notion he could get behind. "Good."

"Be warned, *mi hermano*, he hopes we'll wait tables if he gets too far behind."

"It's good to have dreams, no matter how unrealistic."

Caz grinned.

There. The explosively tempered Hispanic had been defused. *My work here is done.*

"Since you'll be at the bar..." Caz rummaged in a drawer, pulled out a small box, and tossed it to Gabe. "Welcome back to civilization."

"Condoms? You're getting more like Mako every day." The sarge had usually concluded his *safe sex* lectures by tossing them boxes of condoms. Gabe felt a smile tug at his lips as he opened the box and stuck the three packets in his wallet.

"Thanks, bro." Not that he had any intention of using them, but arguing anything health-related with his medic brother was an exercise in futility. "I better get going. I need to work out schedules with Officer Baumer."

"We'll talk tonight, the three of us. Mako's freezer still has some salmon, and we can light up the grill at the Hermitage."

Gabe snorted. After they'd built the semi-circle of five cabins on the far side of Lynx Lake, Bull named the compound the Hermitage. "*What? It's the dwelling of a hermit, isn't it?*"

Mako hadn't been amused.

"Getting together for supper sounds good. I still have to get my cabin opened up and stocked." Tomorrow, he'd attend Bull's grand re-opening...if he could stand being around that many people all at once.

He paused. A bar. Bull needed staff. Dante's blonde helper was getting only room and board. No cash. She could probably use a real job.

When Caz's lips turned up, Gabe eyed him. "What are you smirking at?"

"You haven't lost that *I've got a plan* expression you had as a kid."

"It's not my fault you all were stupid enough to follow me."

"Good times. Remember when you decided we should help that cub get back to its mama?"

The mama had been a brown bear—and all those grizzly movies were spot on about the dangers of a pissed-off mother. Gabe'd almost gotten them all killed. "No wonder the sarge's hair turned white."

Caz laughed. "So, what's the plan?"

"Might have a barmaid for Bull." But he still didn't trust her.

He'd just have to keep an eye on her.

CHAPTER FIVE

After the police chief left, Audrey continued restocking the shelves. Her anxiety hadn't lessened, though. She dropped a can. Picked it up. Her hand was shaking so hard she dropped it again.

Eff-it-all.

That police chief had studied her as if she was an ax murderer or something. Sheesh, he was scary.

"You all right, girl?" At the dairy aisle, Dante looked up from unpacking milk cartons.

"Just clumsy, but I'm fine." What a lie. Everything inside her wanted to flee back to her rental house.

Wasn't it funny how quickly the tiny log cabin on the lake had become her refuge...despite a few hair-raising night noises from outside. One sounded like a high-pitched timer going off, peep, peep, peep, for long periods at a time. Another went up in pitch like a saw being sharpened.

Or...far worse...she'd heard something rustling in the brush down by the lake. And, like a courageous soul, she'd actually pulled the covers over her head.

Welcome to Alaska, city girl.

Maybe if Spyros came after her, some huge carnivorous animal would chow down on him before he reached her cabin.

Speaking of primitive Alaska, her tiny cabin didn't have internet service or phone coverage. She sure hadn't realized how addicted she was to an online connection...not until the day she arrived and found she had none.

Now, every morning, she visited the coffee shop to use the free internet there and check her emails.

Not that her emails had good news.

She scowled as she stacked cans of beef stew. Spyros still hadn't been caught. Special Agent Dennison thought the hitman had holed up somewhere to heal. The day after her attack, an ophthalmologist's body had been found in his clinic's bloodied surgery room. Had the eye surgeon been forced to operate on Spyros's eye?

Feeling guilty about the doctor's death was foolish, but... if she hadn't hurt Spyros, the doctor would still be alive. God, the last thing she'd ever wanted was for someone to die because of her.

But here, a continent away, she didn't pose a risk to anyone—not buried in a small town no one had ever heard of. There were no traffic cameras, no reporters. She'd abandoned the wigs and disguises...aside from makeup to cover the remnants of bruises. It'd been nice to look in a mirror and see herself again—blonde hair, gray eyes, a few freckles.

The store door opened and a bearded man in overalls and flannel shirt walked in accompanied by the stench of an unwashed body.

Ew. She gave him a polite nod and took her place behind the counter to ring up his purchases. Because that was her job now.

How long was she going to have to hide out in Alaska? Her life was in Chicago. Her library job, her cozy apartment, her friends. Okay, maybe she had possessed more work acquaintances than friends, but still...

Surely, she wouldn't have to scurry around like a terrified mouse forever.

At least she'd figured out how to use software to hide her IP address so she could keep in touch with Dennison by email. He'd told her they'd found Quentin's body. The author had been tortured before being killed.

Tortured. Her hands fisted with her fury. Her fear.

Dennison wrote that, despite frustrating obstacles, the pharmaceutical research company would be prosecuted.

However, he hadn't found Spyros's informants in the FBI. And when a task force started investigations, her involvement with Quentin had surfaced—and her picture had appeared in the Chicago papers.

I want to go home. Depression settled like a heavy weight around her shoulders.

Footsteps crossed the store from the back, and she shook herself. *Smile.*

Scowling, the bearded man thumped a six-pack of beer on the counter. "Gimme a pack of cigarettes. Those." He pointed to the brand.

She took the pack and rang everything up. Before she could tell him the total, he tossed her a wad of bills, his mouth still turned down. Someone had really woken on the wrong side of the bed today.

Silently, she made change. He headed out, passing Chief MacNair at the door. When the chief got an identical glare, Audrey felt better. The man's animosity wasn't confined to her.

Her relief disappeared as the cop headed straight for her.

Why did he have to be so big and mean looking? God, he was almost as scary as her attackers had been. No, no, he wasn't. What was she thinking?

Wiping damp palms on her jeans, she forced a smile. "Chief, can I help you?"

"No." He didn't smile back. "Do you want a job?"

Hope rose like a helium-filled balloon. A job. Only... She eyed him. Men who offered to hire a woman without knowing her skills might be looking for...intimate services. Even nerds like her occasionally got propositioned.

No, she was being overly cautious. Despite being intimidating, he didn't seem like a horny jerk. Or a needy one. He wasn't exactly gorgeous, but his rough masculinity probably drew women like bees to clover. It was doubtful he'd ever had to pay for sex. "Doing what?"

"Serving drinks in a bar. Or maybe working as a waitress in the restaurant section."

"Uhhhh..." A place filled with people? She usually dealt with one person at a time at the library—or over the internet for freelancing. She'd take the client's request, do the work, and hand back information or books. "I don't..."

She paused. Maybe serving bar customers wasn't all that different. Take an order and hand back the requested drinks. She pulled in a breath. "I'm interested, but..."

How honest should she be?

"But what?"

Behind the cop's back, Dante smiled encouragement.

"I've never waited on tables before."

The police chief studied her, then shrugged. "It'll be up to the owner." He motioned to the door.

"Right now?" Her voice came out a squeak, and she flushed. But seriously? No time to prep? Look up what waitresses did? Put on the right clothes?

"Good a time as any. The roadhouse opens tomorrow."

Oh. She should get over there ASAP if she wanted the job. She hesitated and looked at Dante.

"You go on, girl. Get a cash-paying job. Even if you do, you can still work here for room 'n' board."

He was such a nice man. When he'd offered the cabin, he told her she looked like his daughter who'd gone on ahead. The grief in his eyes had broken Audrey's heart.

She smiled at him. "Thank you, Dante. That sounds perfect."

"It's not far," the chief said. "We'll walk."

Silently, he walked beside her, taking a right, then a left down Sweetgale Street.

She gave him a sidelong look. Why couldn't the guy have a potbelly and double chin or something? No, his stomach was flat, his shoulders broad, and his jaw was hard.

Mean-looking hard. Even a faint limp didn't diminish the menace he radiated.

He caught her looking at him. "Relax. The jail is the other direction."

"There's a relief," she muttered, and his low chuckle made her stumble. He did have a sense of humor. Who knew? "Where is this place?"

"There." He pointed. The building sat at the intersection of Sweetgale and Dall—the road that led to the resort. A long outside deck overlooked the oval-shaped lake.

"That's a great location."

He eyed the place, as if he hadn't noticed before, and nodded. Not exactly the type to talk a girl's ear off, was he?

A huge wooden sign hung from the aged log building. The name: *Bull's Moose Roadhouse* arched over the silhouette of an antlered moose. "I thought the term was *bull moose*."

"It is. The owner's name is Bull."

The man's parents had named their child Bull. How wrong was that?

The chief pulled open the door, and she walked inside.

The massive logs making up the walls had been stained a satiny dark gold.

Wagon wheel chandeliers hung from solid beams, high overhead. A frame of stretched animal hides divided the bar section from the restaurant. In the bar, distressed wood tables and wooden chairs took up the middle of the sawdust-covered wood floor. A small raised stage on the right had an open area for dancing. The décor included antlers hung on the walls, but thankfully, there were no animal heads or bodies.

Was there a decorating category called *Alaska rustic*?

"We're not open," a loud bass voice yelled from the back. "Come back tomorrow."

"Got possible wait staff for you." The police chief guided her forward with a hand on her low back.

When he stepped away, she felt the loss of the almost-comforting touch.

"Gabe? 'Bout time you got here!" The owner strode out of the back.

Good God. No wonder he was called Bull.

This man was taller than the big police chief by another two or three inches and simply huge. With a shaved head, a graying black goatee, and black eyes, he was frightening in a whole different way from the cop. Meeting the chief was like unexpectedly coming face-to-face with a wolf—a danger she'd never had to worry about in Chicago. Bull was a city bus that'd flatten a person without the passengers even feeling the bump.

Bull gave the chief a rough one-armed guy-hug, complete with a wallop on the back. "What took you so long, old man?"

Look at that. Chief MacNair actually almost smiled. But...had Bull called him old? She frowned. The cop looked a few years older than she was, probably in his thirties, but still, nowhere near forty.

"Did you say you had help for me?" Bull asked.

"Yeah." The chief nodded toward her. "Juliette Wilson."

Bull's eyes narrowed as he looked at her face.

Eff-it-all. In the bright light, her bruises probably showed through the makeup.

The black gaze swept over her again. "From Outside, I'd guess."

Seriously? She glanced at the door and said politely, "Yes, we came in from outside."

The chief's expression was unreadable. "He means you probably came from the Lower 48—the rest of the States."

"Oh." She hesitated. Unfortunately, she couldn't possibly pass as a long-term resident. "Right. Yes."

"Figured." Bull frowned at Chief MacNair. "Teach her to survive so I don't lose her to a moose the first week."

Great. Her potential boss was already laughing at her. "I'm not that naïve. Even *I* know that moose aren't carnivorous."

Chief MacNair almost smiled again. "No, they're just half a ton of irritable."

Eeeks.

Bull waved at the bar in the back. "I finally got the taps and soda dispensers hooked up. Want something to drink while we talk?"

"A root beer would be good," she said.

As Bull strolled toward the bar, Gabe motioned to a table and pulled out a chair for her. For a frontier sort of guy, he had nice manners.

He was still scary as all get out.

Rather than joining her at the table, he put his foot on a chair and leaned his forearms on his thigh, looking down at her. "You going to be all right with Bull?"

She stared up at him. He was being...kind. That was so unexpected. "I'll be fine. Thank you for giving me the opportunity to interview."

His eyes narrowed like Bull's had, and she wondered what she'd said wrong this time. "Is there a problem?"

"You sound like you should look for a college professor job instead."

Oh, damn. She didn't want to sound like a nerd. Pulling her shoulders back, she lifted her chin. "I'm trying to impress him."

"Mmmhmm," he agreed politely, and his mouth twitched. Then his dark brows drew together. "A warning. Alaska bars can be rough."

Suppressing a cringe, she straightened her shoulders instead. *Sound confident, woman. Grow a spine.* She needed this job. "Don't worry about me. I can manage."

Still frowning, he glanced at Bull, who'd walked up with two drinks. "You'll keep an eye out for her?"

"Count on it."

Gabe gave her a nod. "Good luck, cheechako."

What the heck was a cheechako? Her fingers twitched toward her phone, only it wasn't a smart phone, just a cheap prepaid. Google wasn't available to help her out.

As the chief abandoned her to her fate, Bull sat down across from her. "Where have you waited tables before? Have you worked in a bar or restaurant?"

"Um, no." She managed a smile and prepared to give it her best. "But I learn quite fast." Especially if she had time to get online first.

"No experience, huh. You're over twenty-one, yeah?"

When she nodded, he eyed her. "I've got a couple of under-twenty-ones who can't serve alcohol, but they can work in the restaurant. What I need right now is bar staff."

She laced her fingers under the table. "Give me a try."

He rubbed his mouth, then sighed. "Okay then. Gabe's rarely wrong about people. Let's see how you do." He held out his hand. "Welcome to the Bull's Moose, Juliette."

Rather than getting up and doing a hip wagging, victory dance—something she'd never do in public—she smiled and shook his hand.

Audrey left the tavern, her feet barely touching the gravel parking lot.

But, wow, what a short interview. To obtain her reference and liaison librarian position, she'd had to submit her resume, have a preliminary dialogue by phone, then spend an entire day interviewing at the university as well as give a presentation.

This interview... She hadn't even had time to finish her soda.

Despite the abbreviated nature of the meeting, she'd snagged herself a job. Best of all, Bull agreed to pay her in cash during the probationary period, which meant her fake ID wouldn't be tested.

Once on the sidewalk, she hesitated. She could retrace her steps and go back downtown. However, she could see the lake behind Bull's Moose Roadhouse. Her cabin was on the lake. If she followed the lakeside trail through the tiny unkempt city park, she should arrive home.

It was a lovely sunny day and would be a pretty walk. Assuming she didn't run into any irritable moose. Had Chief MacNair been joking about that? She'd gotten the impression he was serious, although amused at *her*.

Maybe Dante would tell her the truth. Or when she was online in the coffee shop, she could investigate potentially dangerous Alaskan animals.

As she strolled down the gravel path, she smiled at the sight of a floatplane taking off from the lake. It rose effortlessly into the sky. So cool. Dante said if she'd arrived here earlier in the spring, the planes would have landed on the snow using skis rather than floats. Alaska certainly was different.

And the lake was a lot bigger than she'd realized.

By the time she arrived at her cabin, she was exhausted, and her legs ached. It was embarrassing to realize how out of shape she was. Honestly, in Chicago, she'd never hiked anywhere. That's why God created the taxi.

She turned off the lakeside path onto the narrow dirt trail that led to the four rental cabins. Dante had been extremely generous to her. He said he'd built the cabins years ago when the town was bigger, and these days, the only time all the cabins were rented was during fishing season.

Her place resembled a furnished studio apartment—one big room with a living area in the front half. The kitchen and dining table in the back left, and a bedroom behind a curtain in the right corner. The tiny bathroom had an equally tiny shower.

Nothing fancy. But the cabin held a woodstove for heat, a table and two chairs, a couch and armchair, and a bed and dresser. The kitchen had a small fridge and stove, pots, silverware, and dishes. Everything necessary to survive... even if her laundry had to be taken to the downtown laundromat.

And she was still picking up new skills.

The first day, Dante had shown her how to build a fire in the woodstove. She'd started all the rest since then. It was embarrassing how much pride the accomplishment gave her.

Smiling, she walked through the cabin, out the back door, and climbed onto the top of the picnic table. She'd always considered herself a practical person. Living in a rustic cabin with no internet, no washing machine or dishwasher or even air-conditioning was...hmm...an adventure?

And when she sat out here and looked at the sunlit lake and the magnificent mountain range behind it, the need for modern amenities faded into the background.

This was where she wanted to be.

Although... A quiver of worry ran through her. How did a person go about being a waitress?

When she'd been served in restaurants, the job hadn't appeared too complicated.

Tomorrow morning, she'd have to buy some coffee, pull out her laptop, and find out if there were tricks to waiting on tables in a bar.

CHAPTER SIX

The next night, Gabe pulled his Jeep into the Bull's Moose Roadhouse parking lot with a rising sense of anticipation.

Bull had hired the newcomer. That was good.

Nonetheless...Gabe was a tad worried, since: (a) He'd recommended her from instinct, not actual knowledge of her character, and (b) She might not be prepared for a bar like this.

At least his brother had managed to find another server —a youngster who'd just turned twenty-one. The young man was hoping for a job at McNally's Ski Resort, so he might not be around long. Ms. Wilson wouldn't be stuck waiting the tables alone.

And Gabe would be there tonight to make sure he hadn't led his brother wrong.

After beeping the Jeep's locks, Gabe headed for the bar.

A "Grand Opening" banner hung between two trees to inform the world that Bull's was now in business. At least the bar portion was.

Inside, at a table near the door, two men in their sixties were people-watching. Gabe gave one a double take. "I know you. Tucker."

"Yeah?" Tucker eyed Gabe. His smile was almost hidden in his bushy gray beard. "Yeah, you're Mako's kid."

Kid? After two decades of fighting in one battle or another, he felt ancient. "Good to see you."

A subsistence homesteader, Tucker lived in an off-grid cabin in the bush. When he busted his leg a couple of years ago, the sarge had drafted Gabe to truck in food and water a few times. It'd made for an interesting vacation.

Tucker waved his hand between Gabe and the other man. "MacNair. Guzman. Guzman owns the land next to mine."

From Guzman's faded clothes and weather-beaten appearance, Gabe would guess he was another back-to-the-lander. He nodded politely, then asked Tucker, "How's the leg?"

"Healed up all right. Mostly. Gotta say I can now tell when the weather's about to change." The man's smile faded. "A shame it didn't warn me the town was going to change into a tourist trap."

Yeah, well, Gabe knew how the old guy felt, especially about an influx of people. "Could be some good come from the change. Did you know Dante had planned to close the grocery if the population kept decreasing?

Guzman's jaw dropped, showing a batch of silver fillings. "We'd have to drive to Soldotna to get food?"

"Yep." Gabe remembered Tucker's ancient pickup and doubted it'd gotten any younger.

"Well, hellfire, I'll put up with the damned tourists if that's what it takes to keep the grocery open." Tucker shrugged. "Not like they're gonna bother me at my place."

Gabe almost grinned. Tucker's place was well hidden and down a nearly impassible dirt road. "No, I doubt you'll see any tourists unless you come to town. When you do, you can enjoy having a bar again."

Both men smiled at that. Even people who embraced subsistence living needed to buy the items impossible to make by hand. And Alaskans did like their alcohol. A bit too much, any law enforcement officer would say.

Gabe frowned. "The trick will be to keep our way of life —mostly—and still reap the benefits."

Walking that tightrope would be a bitch. The off-the-gridders didn't want any increase in the town's size. Other residents saw the money and resources tourism could produce. Rescue needed to find a middle ground.

Taking his leave, Gabe found himself an empty table. He was off duty and more than ready for a beer. The other officer was on duty this evening.

After the meeting with Baumer yesterday, Gabe called

their schedules in to the dispatch office and arranged for state troopers to cover their off hours. Someday, if the town's coffers filled, he'd hire seasonal patrol officers for the tourist months.

After pulling off his jacket, he settled in to watch Bull work.

His brother was laughing and exchanging jokes with the bar crowd. Lots of women were there, of course, all trying to gain his attention. The sarge used to say Bull attracted women like a cat in heat drew toms.

Bull served an older lady a frothy drink, and with one intimidating glance, silenced an obnoxious sourdough who was disparaging visitors from the Lower 48. Yeah, Bull was in his element when surrounded by people.

Gabe shook his head. Guess he'd gotten bitter over the years. Too many people were cruel...or just plain idiots. Unfortunately, as a law enforcement officer, he wasn't allowed to silence stupidity with a fist.

Now there was an idea. "Excuse me, sir, you were speeding. Step out of the car, please." One busted nose later...

Think of the paperwork he could avoid.

Leaning back in his chair, Gabe gauged the room. A good mixture, looked like. There were locals in old Carhartt jeans, Xtratuf boots, and flannel shirts over tees. The ones wearing designer jeans and fancy tops were tourists. The summer tourist season had begun.

Most of the tables were full. Very nice.

"Can I get you something to drink?"

The sweet, clear soprano was so utterly female his dick

shot to attention. With a rueful grunt, he shifted to a more comfortable position and smiled at Bull's new barmaid. No, not politically correct. The *server*.

Her shining golden hair was pulled back in a low ponytail. She was dressed in jeans, sneakers, and a green T-shirt with the script: "*There are two kinds of people: 1) Those who can extrapolate from incomplete data.*"

It took him a second, and then a snort of laughter escaped him.

Seeing where he was looking, she grinned in delight that he'd gotten the joke.

"Good evening, Ms. Wilson."

"In this place, using miz is ridiculous. How about Julie?" Her friendly smile could melt ice cubes.

"All right, then. How are you holding up, Julie? You look a bit tired."

Hands occupied with a tray of empties, she puffed at a wayward strand of hair in her eyes. "This is insane, isn't it? Thank God, Bull found another waiter. Where did all these people come from?"

"I'd guess there are some transient fishermen from the fish camps and lodges. Some tourists from the resort or wherever. The rest are locals, both from inside town and outside."

"Outside of town?" She frowned. "Dante said there was electricity only in town and along the highway. But when I drove down the road, I didn't see very many houses—not enough to fill the bar."

"You can't spot the cabins that are off the highway. And they're dry cabins. No electricity, no water, no plumbing—and variations thereof."

"No plumbing?" Her nose wrinkled. "They have to use an outdoor facility like an outhouse?"

Damn, she was cute.

"I'm afraid so." He smothered a smile. All last winter, he'd bared his ass in an unheated honeypot. A man's dangling testicles in minus-twenty-degree weather gave new meaning to *freezing your balls off*. "Outhouses are a necessity if you don't like civilization."

"People are perplexing, aren't they?" She shook her head. "Can I get you anything?"

"I'll have a stout—Off-the-Road."

She beamed at him. "You didn't even have to ask for the list. I'll be right back."

And she was. After delivering the beer and pocketing his money, she checked the next table before heading to the bar. Why did she only deliver one table's worth of drinks at a time?

Gabe studied her closer.

She was guarding her torso, tucking her elbows down whenever someone might bump into her. He'd had his ribs busted a couple of times, compliments of a bad freefall landing and later, an ugly fight in the Iraq sandbox. He'd guarded his ribs against being thumped for a good month after each injury.

Yeah, when she'd picked up all that bruising, her ribs

must have been broken or cracked. No wonder she carried light loads on her drink tray.

Who had hit her? Was the bastard in Rescue?

Anger simmering, Gabe drank half his beer, realized it, and shoved the glass to the middle of the table.

He shouldn't jump to conclusions about Julie's injuries. Maybe she'd been in a car accident.

But...she feared the law. That, right there, was a concern. Was she running from a man? Or because she might be arrested?

Running a finger through the dampness on the table, he watched as she tended her section, growing more comfortable minute by minute.

Her smile came easier. She was chatting with even the rougher customers without looking worried...although she flinched whenever shouting broke out. He nodded in respect for both her courage and determination. Despite being shy and a bit overwhelmed, she was doing a damn fine job.

Audrey's aching feet felt pancake flat, and every time she lifted a heavy tray, a knife stabbed into her ribs. Nevertheless, her spirits were soaring. She *rocked* this job.

She'd been worried, especially since the waitressing tips on various websites had emphasized, "be sociable." But the basics were do-able: *Smile. Be interested and upbeat. Ignore rude comments. Keep tables tidy by incorporating cleanup as part of serving.*

Remembering drinks and people wasn't difficult.

The instruction about making eye contact? That was more challenging, but she was improving. And people seemed to like her.

She'd never dreamed she'd make a good bar server.

Smiling, she stepped up to a table of four men near the room's center. "Hi, guys. What can I get you tonight?"

"I can think of a few things." The man reached around her to squeeze her bottom. Hard.

Gasping in shock, she barely kept from bashing him over the head with her tray. Instead, she stepped out of reach. "No touching."

Over the evening, she'd received a few pats on the ass—which was annoying—but this guy had actually groped her.

"What's the matter, girlie? Not used to a man's hands on you?" The scarecrow-thin, black-bearded man in his forties wasn't the one who'd grabbed her.

"No touching, please." She managed a light, firm tone. "What can I get you men to drink?"

The scarecrow-looking man leaned back and looked her up and down as if she were a commodity he was purchasing. In fact, all four men had the same appalling attitude.

She took another step back and made her voice louder. "Did you want to order or not?"

Scarecrow-man raked his gaze over her again, leaving

her feeling as if she needed a bath. "Four beers—the cheapest on tap."

As she sped away, the sick feeling in the pit of her stomach eroded her enjoyment of the evening. How could people act like that? And what was she supposed to do?

She'd managed well up until now, even if she moved slower than the other server. Somehow, Felix managed to flirt with other cute guys while carrying a ton of drinks, all without spilling a drop. She was in awe.

Of course, he didn't have cracked ribs.

She gave her orders to Bull.

"Thank you, Julie." He grinned at her before continuing his conversation with three customers. At least, he didn't seem to be worried about her being slow.

In fact, everyone was wonderfully welcoming. Okay, a couple guys had been overly friendly—why were some men so obnoxious?—but overall, the night had gone well. Till now.

Maybe Scarecrowman and his friends would leave soon.

After Bull set the four glasses of beer on her tray, she wound her way across the crowded room. At one table, Sarah from the coffee shop and Dante greeted her. At the next table, the gray-haired, bearded hippie, who owned the gas station, lifted his bottle in a salutation. His tie-dyed shirt was a work of art. She caught a whiff of marijuana as she passed.

The bar was a heady potpourri of scents. The fishermen sported a pungent combination of sweat and fish. A couple of Alaska Natives and several backwoods-looking men smelled of wood smoke. Tourists wore cologne and perfume in jarring mixes.

At Scarecrowman's table, Audrey chose the opposite side and stepped between the two beefy blond men across from the groper.

As she set the glasses down, the bearded blond to her left shoved his hand between her legs and dug his fingers in.

She squeaked, jerked away...and the last glass on her tray landed in his lap.

"Shit!" He jumped to his feet. His jeans were soaked. "You fucking bitch."

"I'm sor—"

There was a loud crack of flesh meeting flesh. He'd *slapped* her.

As pain blazed across her cheek, the impact threw her sideways. Unable to catch herself, she fell against the table's edge, hitting her cracked ribs. *Oh God.* A short scream escaped. Her legs buckled. Her knees hit the floor, and she hunched, trying to breathe despite the agony.

Angry shouts and thudding boots sounded over her sobbing gasps.

As the pain started to recede, she heard a woman ask, "Are you going after that guy?"

"I'll find him later, if Officer Baumer doesn't nail him first." That was the chief's deep, masculine voice. Slow and even and calm. "Julie, where are you hurt?"

Julie. That was her name now. He was talking to *her*.

Before she could answer, warm fingers under her chin lifted her head. "Look at me, Goldilocks."

The command couldn't be ignored. Her eyes were so filled with tears he was only a blur.

He was down on his haunches in front of her. His dark brows were pulled into a frown, his hard jaw tight.

An unfamiliar feeling seeped into her. *Safe.* She was safe.

She tried to smile. "I'm fine."

"Bullshit. I've collected fists to the face. I never called it fine."

"Can you take her home, Gabe?" Bull walked up behind the chief.

"*No.*" Still holding her ribs, she shook her head frantically, increasing the ache in her cheek. She needed the job. "I have customers... I need to—"

"If anyone complains about the lack of service, I'll give them a few truths about how women should be treated." Bull's voice silenced the bar.

"Am I fired?" she whispered.

"Not a chance." Bending over, he patted her shoulder with a huge hand. "I'm damned sorry this happened. I'll try to make sure it never happens again, but there are no guarantees. I'll understand if you want to quit."

She gave a sigh of relief. The work wasn't that bad; she just needed to dodge better. "I'll be back tomorrow night."

"You're too brave for your own good." Gabe scooped her up and cradled her against a rock-hard chest.

How had he managed to rise with her in his arms?

"Bull, call in a report to Baumer, would you? He's on duty tonight."

"Will do."

"Here, MacNair. Got your stuff." Someone laid his black jacket and her own coat over her.

"Thanks, Tucker." With her still in his arms, Gabe strolled out of the bar.

It was past nine o'clock. Expecting full dark, she blinked at the soft twilight.

The parking lot was full. On the adjacent road, a car went past, heading for the resort. Gabe stopped beside an unfamiliar Jeep. He intended to drive her home?

"I'm fine. I don't need a ride."

"I need to see how much damage you took." He set her on her feet and gave her a look. "Unless you want me to check you in the bar?"

"No." Her answer came before she thought.

"Then, I'm taking you home," he reiterated.

Even as she frowned at him, relief swept her. She wouldn't be alone. Not yet. "Yes, sir."

Her answer made a corner of his mouth curve up.

After putting her in the passenger seat—and fastening her seatbelt for her—he drove down Sweetgale Street and turned left onto the gravel road leading to the lake.

Each bounce over the rough road stabbed into her aching ribs. She wrapped her arms around her waist.

He slowed even further. "Which of Dante's cabins are you in?"

"Number three."

When the vehicle stopped, she fumbled at the seat belt.

By the time she had it unfastened, Gabe had opened the passenger door. He reached for her as if he'd carry her again.

She pushed his hands away. "I'm fully capable of ambulation."

"Feeling better, are you?" After picking up her coat, he gripped her arm as she slid out onto the muddy dirt path. "I noticed a bear headed for the lake. Let's get you inside."

"A bear? Here?" No way. Wild animals didn't come close to houses...did they?

He motioned toward the last cabin in the line. And there was a *bear*. Big and black and way too close. "Oh God."

Following the big animal were two balls of fluff. Cubs.

Even a city girl knew mother bears were dangerous. She'd seen the movies.

Backing up while watching the bear, she bumped into Gabe. "Sorry."

He took her arm again and guided her to her cabin. At the door, she fumbled for her keys...and dropped them.

Gabe caught the key ring in midair—and didn't she just feel like a clumsy idiot?

Without saying anything, he opened the door and hung her coat on the hook. When he flicked the switch beside the door, the lamp on the end table came on, bathing the room in a golden glow. After removing his boots, he went down on one knee and pulled off her muddy shoes.

"Um, thanks."

As she moved toward the couch, he stopped her. "I want a look at your face in decent light. Be a good girl and go into the bathroom."

"But..." Her protest died at the set of his jaw. Maybe it was a police thing. Perhaps a cop needed to ascertain the extent of injuries to determine the correct charges.

After turning on the bright lights over the sink, she gingerly lowered herself onto the closed toilet seat. Why did her *ribs* hurt when she sat? That seemed anatomically impossible.

At least the stabbing pains had disappeared.

Thumping sounds came from the kitchen. The chief appeared with a dishtowel wrapped around a baggie of broken-up ice.

After giving her the improvised ice pack, he set his hand under her chin and tilted her head so he could get a look at her face. With gentle, but merciless fingers, he pressed on her sore cheek, making her eyes water again.

"He got you good, but I don't feel any loose bone fragments." He lifted her hand to press the ice pack to her face. "Keep that there."

"Um. Thank you."

"Now let me see those ribs."

Her eyes widened. "I'm not—"

"Did you get an x-ray when it happened?"

Pinned by his dark blue gaze, she couldn't lie. "No."

"I'll take a look. If you're still this sore a couple weeks after being injured, then—"

"How did you know how long it's been?"

"Bruises change colors as they heal. It's not difficult to judge how long ago an injury occurred." He squatted in front of her, his gaze unwavering. "Lift your shirt up for me, Julie."

With a sigh, she complied.

"Take a deep breath."

As she pulled in air, his gaze flickered from her ribs to her face. "Pain?"

"Uh-uh."

"Any trouble breathing? Do you get short of air?"

She shook her head. "It hurts if I cough, but my breathing is fine."

His hands were warm and sure as he touched the bruise on her left side. "Tell me if this hurts." He pressed on her rib cage, over the bruise, then on each side as he watched her face.

The low throbbing didn't increase. Or maybe she was just too distracted by how close he was. She swallowed. "It's tender, but nothing horrible."

"Has the pain decreased over the last few days—or gotten worse."

"It's less." Until she'd been knocked into the table.

"Good enough. There isn't an x-ray machine in the clinic, but Soldotna has one."

"No."

He snorted. "How did I guess that was what you'd say? I'd guess at a cracked rib or two, but as long as the pain improves, you're probably all right. It's your risk to take."

"I'm good with that." A medical clinic would photograph her ID.

"All right. Ice will help your ribs, too. Use it."

"How do you know so much about broken ribs? From law enforcement?"

"Actually, I learned basic first aid as a kid, picked up more in the military." For a second, his eyes looked haunted. Shaking his head, he gave her a faint smile. "Finish cleaning up. I'll wait in your"—his brows quirked—"living room."

Her only room.

She dearly wanted to get out of her beer-soaked clothes. "All right."

After stripping and wiping down, she glanced at the door. *Well, stupid, you should have gotten your clothes from the dresser out there first.* No way was she re-dressing in the filthy garments.

Her nightclothes—a loose shirt and sweatpants—hung on a hook beside the shower. After being attacked in bed and being touched by Spyros, she couldn't stand wearing anything sexy or silky at night. The shirt and sweats were far...safer.

The attire would be adequate to wear to talk with the police chief.

After pulling on the sweatpants, she frowned. Her bra

was soaked with beer. *Oh well.* The big police chief wasn't interested in her *that* way. And the shirt was loose. He probably wouldn't notice she had no underwear on.

In the living area, he was patiently leaning against a wall.

She settled herself on the long couch. "Now what?"

He took the armchair next to her. "Tell me what happened with those men tonight."

Oh, no. Was she in trouble? "I-I didn't mean to start a fight."

"Julie." His face softened. "You did nothing wrong. I didn't see what occurred, but I'd guess one touched you in a private spot, and that's considered sexual assault. All you did was accidentally spill a drink on him. Unfortunately."

"Unfortunately?"

"As a law officer, I frown on retaliation"—his mouth quirked. "However, it's not unheard of for a waitress to knock an obnoxious customer right off his chair."

"Oh. Wow." She really should have gotten out more.

"Next time you think there'll be a problem, tell Bull. He enjoys throwing assholes out. If he's in a good mood, he might even open the door first."

Good. Grief. It was appalling that she liked the visual of that blond jerk being thrown into the door. "So, I'm not in trouble with the law. And Bull won't fire me?"

"*Fire* you?"

Why did he have to be so good-looking when he smiled?

"Didn't you hear his announcement as we were leaving?"

"Um, no."

"He shouted that any bastard who touches his staff will be tossed out and never allowed inside again."

A warm feeling tugged at her. Someone had stuck up for her. Two someones, actually. "I hope his edict won't affect his business. Although people seemed happy to have a bar in town."

"It should quiet down some after tonight. Alaskans like opening nights—of anything. We don't get much excitement."

"Uh-huh. Just bears and bar fights, huh?"

When he grinned, looking so...so male, competent, and fun, her heart did a slow somersault in her chest. He'd saved her, sent the jerks fleeing, brought her home, and made sure she was all right.

How did a girl deal with being cared for like this?

Politely. *Try politely, Audrey.* "Well, thank you, Chief. For the help. And the ride. And the ice. And...uh...carrying me like Rhe—" Like Rhett with Scarlett? Good God, had she almost said that? She felt her cheeks heat with her chagrin.

He chuckled, low and deep. Laughter looked good on him, even if she was the cause.

She slumped against the couch cushions. "This is why I prefer to be a loner. I'm not adept with people."

"A loner, hmm?"

"Yes." However, she didn't want to be alone now. Not when her center felt hollow and quaking. Being hurt again... "Usually."

She ran a trembling hand through her hair, and his gaze followed the movement. "Uh...would you care for a drink?"

In that way he had, he studied her. His intent focus resembled how she examined data to puzzle out anomalies.

"Bears and bar fights," he said softly. "Quite the adjustment for a little cheechako. You're still shaken, aren't you?"

Without waiting for her answer, he strolled over to the kitchen area. He found the "Welcome-to-Rescue" bottle of wine Dante had gifted her with when she moved in and glasses in the cupboard.

After pouring them each a glass, he set the bottle on the end table and settled on the couch.

She blinked, not having expected him to sit beside her. Then again, no intelligent person would prefer the lumpy armchair where a spring was trying to push through the seat cushion.

But the police chief was close enough that his body heated her side.

She picked up her glass and took a hearty gulp. "What's that word you keep calling me—*chee-chah-ko*?"

Glass in hand, he leaned back, stretching his legs out. Even sock-clad, his feet were masculine and strong. And sexy. That was just wrong. "Cheechako is what we call a newcomer to Alaska."

"Oh." That wasn't so bad. At least it didn't mean *clumsy blonde* or *chronic liar*.

"Is that a New York accent you have?"

"No, Chic—" She stopped, bit her tongue, and sighed. Way to get tricked into volunteering her city. "Chicago."

"A real city girl, then." He tucked a strand of hair behind her ear. "Alaska must be terrifying at times."

Most of the time, thank you very much. "I manage." She stared at him. He'd known she was scared and stayed, and now he was actually...conversing. The chief of police had a protective nature, didn't he?

"Good to know. Be aware, the lake draws a fair amount of wildlife."

"Like bears?" Her voice tried to squeak.

"Yeah. Hibernation's ended, so they're hungry and cranky. Be watchful and give them space."

"I intend to give them lots of space." Bears. Beside her cabin. As uneasiness crept down her spine, she edged closer to him. "You can't possibly know how alien this place seems."

"Actually, I do know." When she shivered, he put his arm around her shoulders.

She stiffened. Her entire side was pressed against his very hard, very large male body. Oh God, he had muscles all over. She swallowed and pretended she was comfortable. "How can you know? Dante said your father settled out here over thirty years ago. Mako...was that his name?"

"My father, hmm?" His arm was heavy, and his fingers traced circles on her upper arm.

Even though the coals in the woodstove barely glowed, the room seemed excessively toasty.

"I guess there's no need to protect him from the law any longer." His eyes filled with sorrow, and the lines beside his mouth deepened.

Dante had mentioned Mako died last fall. "I'm sorry, Gabe."

"Yeah, me, too." He shook his head as if to cast off the grief. "Mako rescued me and three other boys from a Los Angeles foster home and brought us here. Stole us, essentially. I was ten."

Stole them? *Whoa.* She stared at him. "Wait, you were from LA and came to Rescue? Talk about culture shock."

He huffed a laugh. "Rescue would've been easy. Back then, Mako lived way outside of Seward in an isolated dry cabin."

"Dry cabin. No plumbing or power. With *children*? Was he crazy?"

CHAPTER SEVEN

Gabe looked down at her, seeing her eyes flash with outrage. She had a tender heart, didn't she?

Staying until she'd calmed wasn't the chore he'd thought it would be. Julie was quietly intelligent and sweet. A pleasure to be with.

"Was Mako crazy? Oh yeah. He was a paranoid survivalist, figuring the end of the world or a war was imminent."

"Oh my God." Turning to face him, she set a hand on his shoulder, and was close enough, one full breast pressed against his side. Her pink lips were slightly open...and looked soft. "Were you boys all right? Did he hurt you?"

How long had it been since he'd enjoyed a woman—let alone one who worried about him? The combination of sweet and sexy was irresistible.

Before he'd thought things through, Gabe set down his glass, picked her up, and settled her on his lap.

Oh, hell, this was a mistake. Her thread-worn T-shirt and sweatpants let him feel every inch of her lush curves.

The position put her head slightly higher than his. Her eyes were wide and confused as she looked down at him. She might not be a virgin, but he doubted she was very experienced with men.

"What are you—" She motioned to her position. "Why did you do that?"

Fuck, he liked honest women. And honest questions.

"This is more comfortable than looking down at you. Now you get to look down at me." But his idiotic testosterone was making him stupid. She'd been manhandled and hurt. "Yeah, I like having you on my lap, but I'm not going to put any moves on you, Julie."

This was as far as he'd go—now and probably ever. Although damn, she was appealing. Such fair, fair skin. Her big gray eyes were the color of the morning fog.

And she had worried over what happened to young boys two decades past.

"Ooookay." Her voice was uncertain, but she didn't move. "Did Mako... Was he good to you?"

"He was." As much as he could manage. In hindsight, Gabe realized how at a loss the first sergeant had been. "The sarge'd been career military and had managed hundreds of new recruits. Even so, taking on four boys terrified him worse than any battle."

The worry in Juliette's face eased.

Gabe watched the red coals in the woodstove. "He had

CHERISE SINCLAIR

no experience of how to parent—or be gentle—but he was fair. Honest. Careful. He taught us everything he knew and raised us to stand on our own two feet. I owe him everything."

When he looked up, Julie's eyes were wet, offering Mako the tears Gabe hadn't been able to shed.

Her lips trembled slightly as she smiled. "I'm glad you had him, then."

"Yeah." He reached up, his hand behind her head to pull her down to him—and caught himself. *No, dumbass, no sex. Not going to happen.*

She bit her lip, and her fingers curved over his shoulder. A flush turned her cheeks a delicate pink.

His cock hardened.

Ah, hell. There was only so much temptation a man could take, and giving in wouldn't be right.

"I'd better be going." He gripped her hips, planning to set her down on the couch.

"No." Audrey blinked, not believing she'd protested, but she had. She meant it. He was going to leave—and she didn't want him to.

Of course, sex wasn't especially tempting since she couldn't get off with a man without taking a hand herself. And she was usually too embarrassed to do so.

But Gabe's presence made her feel incredibly safe. She didn't want to be alone. Not tonight. Nightmares were

106

already edging out of the shadowy corners. She could hear the unfamiliar sounds outside the cabin, the ones that always sent her to check door and windows repeatedly.

If she made love with Gabe—okay, use the blunt terminology—*fucked Gabe,* maybe he'd spend the night. And even hold her.

Was having sex with someone in exchange for affection afterward a variation on prostitution?

She stroked her palm across his chest, disconcerted at the feel of his bunching muscles. "Why don't you...stay?"

When he shook his head, humiliation hit her like a blow. He didn't want her. She'd misread his interest completely— another confirmation of what Craig had said about her social ineptness.

And yet, heat lurked in Gabe's eyes, and the color in his darkly tan face had heightened. Beneath her hip, she felt his thick erection. That was interest, right?

"I don't think that would be wise, Julie."

At the compelling huskiness in his resonant voice, arousal swept over her, leaving her skin overly sensitive in its wake. Even the brush of her own hair against her cheek felt tantalizing.

She'd gripped his wrists to keep him from setting her away and off his lap. He was strong enough to move her anyway. If he wanted to.

Her veiled invitation for sex hadn't worked. What did women do when they wanted to entice a man?

In movies, women often made the first pass. How? Oh,

yes. Gripping the hem of her shirt, she pulled it over her head, leaving herself naked from the waist up.

For a second she felt incredibly, powerfully sexy.

The moment died.

She wasn't sexy; she was stupid. Oh God, he was going to laugh at her and—

"Hell, woman." His jaw went taut, and his hands closed around her waist—not to move her. Instead, his warm, callused palms skimmed up and down her newly bared skin.

A thrill of awareness heated her blood. What had she unleashed?

Cupping the back of her head, he drew her down. His lips were firm as he nibbled on her mouth.

Shocked, she didn't move.

With a low sound, he nipped her lower lip, and when she gasped, he took possession. His technique held nothing gentle about it. His kiss was as direct and commanding as he was himself—and she was swept into responding.

Even as he kissed her, he captured a breast. She startled —and he deepened the kiss, his tongue invading in a seductive, fierce demand.

As heat swept over her skin, her head swam. Low in her belly, everything was melting.

His palm on her breast was hard, rough, and the abrasion over her delicate skin sent tingles coursing through her.

When she moaned, he stilled, then gripped her shoulders and moved her slightly back.

At his frown, she couldn't resist running a finger over his dark brows. They were so straight with only the tiniest hint of a curve, as if to say, *no pretense, no games.* The line between them grew, and he tugged on her hair, making her blink. "Did you hear anything I just said?"

Had he spoken? "Uh. No."

"Fuck," he said under his breath, before cupping her face gently. His eyes were the blue of the lake at twilight. "Julie, although I'd love to be balls-deep inside you, I don't want anything more."

"I don't understand."

"I don't do relationships." No smile showed in his eyes. "Don't jump in thinking this is more than a night. Anything between us will be physical only."

"Oh, I see." Her relief at his qualification was edged with illogical disappointment. "That's fine, really. I don't want you."

His quizzical look made her giggle. "No, I do want you —right now—but I certainly don't want a relationship or ties or anything."

The mesmerizing fan of lines beside his eyes appeared. "Guess I've been told."

"Just this once. Okay?"

"Okay." He put an arm behind her back, one behind her knees and rose with her in his arms.

"Wait—"

"Goldilocks, I'm not going to fuck you on this poor excuse for a couch." He crossed the room, stepped around the curtain hiding the bedroom corner, laid her on the bed, and followed her down. His fingers tangled in her hair as he took her mouth again, kissing her mindless.

After a while, he moved to lie beside her. When she made a protesting sound, he ran a finger over her lip. "I'm too heavy for you." He leaned over and kissed her again.

Her heart gave a warning squeeze...because, despite his blunt speech and forbidding face, he was more protective than any man she'd ever met. Through the curtain, the lamp in the living room cast a dim glow that sharpened the roughness of his rugged face and darkened the beard shadow along his jaw. She ran her palm along his cheek, feeling the scrape of the stubble.

He smiled ruefully. "Will it bother you?"

On the contrary, she was wondering how it would feel in...places. Like between her thighs. Not that he'd do that, but... Her face heated as she realized he was watching her. "Um. No?"

His eyes lit with laughter in a way she hadn't seen before. "Let's check. See if it's a problem." He lowered his head and kissed the curve between her neck and shoulder. His velvety lips contrasted with the deliberate scrape of his chin that followed.

Oh, my God. A disconcerting pleasure sent goosebumps over her skin.

Without pausing, he moved down. His hand closed over one breast, plumping it, as his thumb circled the nipple. "Such a pretty pink. Like a Sitka rose."

He licked around one nipple, then the other, switching back and forth, before his fingers teased each to a jutting peak.

Hunger pulsed in her bloodstream. Her breasts swelled, and her pussy ached for the same touch. No one had simply...played...with her before, but he looked as if he was enjoying himself. Her protest died.

He rubbed his cheek lightly over one sensitive nipple, making her gasp at the unexpected rasp, so different from his velvety tongue. When his lips closed over the nub, his mouth was hot and wet. Soothing—yet...not. When he sucked, the rush of exquisite pleasure made her back arch, pushing her breasts upward for more.

His laugh was a rolling rumble. "You don't seem to mind beard stubble." He switched back and forth between her breasts until they were tight and swollen and acutely sensitive to the lightest touch.

"You *are* fun, Goldilocks," he murmured.

Damn, she was beautiful. Somewhat unsure, but delightfully honest. And as responsive as a dream.

Sitting up next to her, he pulled off his shirt and took hold of the waistband of her sweatpants to strip them off.

A low sound broke from her. Dismay filled her face.

Uh-oh. "Easy, Julie." He dropped his hand and lay back beside her, propping himself up on an elbow. Cupping her face, he set his thumb under her chin and tipped her head up so he could meet her tear-filled eyes. "What's the matter, sweetheart? Shall we stop now?"

"What happened to you?" Her voice shook.

"Me?" He frowned. "What do you mean?"

With a trembling finger, she traced over last year's gunshot marks on his shoulder, then the older ones on his arms, shoulders, and torso. Scars from shrapnel, knives, a dog bite, gunshot, barbed wire. She found the ugly spot on his ribs from a jagged alder stump he'd landed on during a fight with Bull.

"These are... *Look* at all this. What *happened* to you?" The appalled, distressed edge in her voice was oddly heart-warming.

And fuck, he loved her straightforwardness—far better than the women who pretended not to notice. "Some happened in combat when I was in the military. I collected a few more in the police force"—he gave her a bitter smile —"which is another kind of a war."

"Oh, Gabe." She shook her head, her eyes damp. "I would have quit after the first time I got hurt."

Somehow, he doubted that. After all, she planned to return to the roadhouse tomorrow. The girl had guts.

And her sympathy worried the crap out of him. Because he liked it.

He should leave.

All the same, when she pulled him down to kiss him, he didn't resist. Hell, he let her—and then took back control, enjoying the way her breathing sped back up when he caressed her breasts. Perfectly plump breasts.

"Gabe." She stopped him so she could whisper, "I...uh... haven't done this in a long time."

"Been awhile for me, too." Since before he was shot, in fact. He circled one rosy tip with his finger. "Let's see if I can remember what the next step of the process is."

Her tiny laugh made him grin.

His painfully erect cock knew what *it* wanted next. But no man with a functioning brain would ever take his dick's advice.

Moving slowly enough that he wouldn't jar her ribs, Gabe slipped his fingers under her waistband and stripped her sweatpants off.

Oh yeah. Her pale skin glowed in the dim light, and he could see the golden hair covering her pussy. Her calves were sweetly curved. Moving her left leg out, he settled between her thighs and bent down.

She put her hands over his target.

Seriously? He looked at her and lifted an eyebrow.

"I-I don't shave. Guys don't like that."

Fuck, she was cute. "Some do, some don't." Trying not to laugh, he moved the roadblocks from his path, set her arms at her sides, and gave her the intimidating stare a cop quickly mastered. "Stay right like that, or I'll find my handcuffs."

Her mouth dropped open, but her arms stayed at her sides...and she flushed a rosy pink.

The thought of her in his handcuffs was damn tempting. He squeezed her wrists in approval. "Very good."

Obstacles removed, he settled between her legs and opened her folds. The things a woman found to worry about. As if a man couldn't move something out of his way, whether it be criminals or delicate hands...or labia.

At the top of her pussy, her clit was a gleaming, wet, pink pearl, already swollen and begging for his mouth.

Perfect. "I'm going to do this hard and fast, little cheechako, since it's been awhile for both of us. Later, we'll go for slow."

When he licked over her pussy, the burst of glorious sensation nearly sent Audrey off the bed. "Oh, God."

His unexpected masculine laugh melted every bone in her body—even as his teasing tightened her muscles. His tongue started an intimate dance with her clit, leaving her breathless. Then he drew his cheek over her inner thigh, rasping his beard shadow over her tender skin.

Her leg jerked, and he leaned his weight against it and slowly drew his abrasive chin up her thigh, toward her pussy.

Her muscles tensed. And when he reached the top, he licked over her and sucked the sensitive nub back into his mouth.

The noisy moan she gave startled her.

By the time he repeated the pattern on the other side, her clit was tight and throbbing with need.

When he lifted his head, she couldn't suppress a protest. *More.*

After studying her a long moment, he smiled. Continuing to watch her intently, he slowly pressed a finger inside her.

Her pussy was already throbbing, and the merciless penetration shocked her senses with pleasure. She couldn't think, couldn't move. Every cell in her body focused on the feel of his finger as he pulled back and pressed in.

"You're tight, but you can take me." He added another finger.

As he pushed his fingers in, she felt her body stretch slightly. A tremor ran through her.

Bending his head, he closed his mouth around her clit. As his tongue flicked over the nub and he sucked lightly, his fingers increased speed, thrusting faster.

She never came unless she used her own hand, but this time...

Her pussy tightened around the intrusion, her hips tilted, and the pressure inside grew with each touch, each thrust, each slide of his tongue over her clit. He was going to make her come. Did she want this? "I don't..."

He didn't relent, didn't slow.

Sensation piled on sensation, so unstoppable, building higher.

And everything inside her *erupted.*

"Oooooh." The irresistible pleasure seared through her veins in an overwhelming lava flow, one raging wave after another.

As she gasped for air, he pinned her hips down, licking over her, sending new rushing thrills thrumming in her system.

Slowly, the spasms eased. The roaring in her ears decreased.

"That was fucking gorgeous." Rising up, he pressed a firm kiss to her lips.

She could taste herself.

"I..." What could she say? Was *thank you* appropriate?

Sitting back, he took a condom from his wallet, opened his jeans, and sheathed himself.

She had a moment to think, *he's awfully big*, before his cock was at her entrance.

Gradually, he worked his way partly in, big enough she felt the burn as her core stretched to accommodate him.

Her pussy kept contracting around him in fresh bursts of pleasure.

Carefully, he lowered himself on top of her, bracing a hand beside her shoulder to keep most of his weight off her sore ribs.

Pausing, he evaluated her expression. His smile flickered, and he rubbed his cheek over hers. "Hang on, Goldie."

Even as he spoke, he pressed in, the relentless advance stretching her impossibly full. The feeling of being...taken...

rocked her to the core. Possession. No choices, no worries, no decisions.

And then he was in. So very hot and thick.

Oh God. She panted as new ripples of pleasure shot through her.

"You feel amazing." Ever so slowly, he pulled back and pressed in again. "Put your arms around my neck, Julie."

She obeyed and ran her palms over his back. The skin over his shoulders was satin stretched over rock-hard boulders of muscles. A patch of bumpy scarred tissue was palpable proof he was a warrior.

He pulled back, thrust in. Each slow slide of his shaft sent heat lancing across her senses.

His eyes were slightly narrowed, his gaze on her face.

With each controlled thrust, his pelvis rubbed over her exquisitely sensitive clit, setting up a pulsing cadence in her center. Helplessly, she tightened around him.

"That's right," he murmured…and increased the pace.

Her body wound tighter and tighter, the pressure building. *Oh, oh, oh.* The surge of her impending climax was so strong, so terrifying that she whimpered.

She heard him whisper, "Hang on to me, sweetness," and as she gripped his broad shoulders, it hit.

She was *coming*—coming so hard that every single cell in her body joined in the fireworks of pleasure.

As her hips lifted, he ground against her clit in a stab of brutal pleasure. A wailing cry broke from her.

Then, with a low growl, he pressed in, so very huge and deep inside her, and she could feel the jerking of his shaft.

As his muscles relaxed to putty, Gabe moved far enough to lie at Julie's side. The sweetness of release simmered through his body. Yeah, it'd been a long time.

Propping his head on his hand, he smiled at the pink flush that ran from her breasts to her face.

Her eyes were closed, and her breathing was still fast, her lips reddened from his kisses. Damn, she was touchable, and he couldn't resist stroking her silky skin. Under his palm, her breasts still felt tight and swollen, although her nipples were softening.

As was his dick. With an unspoken curse, he eased off the bed.

After he used her bathroom to clean up, he frowned at himself in the mirror. Should he leave now?

He should. There were a lot fewer misunderstandings if a man left after sex.

But...no. She'd had a rough evening earlier, and—relationship limits or not—he wouldn't chance making her feel worse by pulling a *slam-bam, thank-you-ma'am*. So he stripped completely.

When he came out of the bathroom, she'd already crawled under the covers. Seeing him, she gave him a hesitant smile and lifted the sheet. Yeah, she was a sweetie.

He tossed his jeans over the footboard and joined her,

carefully easing her against his side, so her head could rest on his shoulder. The way she snuggled closer and gave a contented sigh made him smile.

Hours later, he realized he'd fallen asleep.

And that his hand was cupped around a sweetly plump breast. Hell of a way to wake up.

Well, he had said that "later" they could go for slow. Seems like he'd made a promise he should keep.

And he still had two more condoms in his wallet.

Reaching around, he slid a finger in her wetness and over her clit. Just a touch at first. Ever so gradually, he roused her, increasing the pressure and the strokes, and she was so responsive that she was already coming before she fully woke.

"G-Gabe?" Her back arched, and her hips bucked under his arm.

"Mmm, that was nice." He rubbed his cheek in her hair, inhaling the light lemony fragrance of her shampoo...and the scents of female and sex. When he moved his hand up to cup a breast, he could feel her heart hammering with her release.

Since playing with her had him harder than a rock, he rolled her over, set her on elbows and knees, sheathed himself, and slid into her from behind.

Fuck. Her slick pussy closed around him like a hot fist, and his grip on her hips tightened. Pausing to regain control, he curved an arm around her and put his fingers back on her clit.

CHERISE SINCLAIR

When he started rubbing the bundle of nerves, she moaned. Her hips wiggled irrepressibly, making him grin, and damned if his control wasn't shot, just like that.

So much for slow.

He raised her hips for greater penetration and took her with mercilessly driving thrusts. A second before he lost it, he slowed long enough to tease her clit again, pushing her into another orgasm.

And as her cunt clamped down on him in rhythmic pulses, he came in violent juts.

Feeling her post-orgasmic shudders was incredibly satisfying all by itself. Damn, she was fun.

This time when he came back from the bathroom after disposing of the condom, he chuckled. She wasn't hiding under the covers this time. No, she lay in a limp, sated sprawl.

Simply gorgeous.

As he walked up to the bed, he frowned. During sex last night, he'd been focused on her curves, her breasts, her pussy.

Now his head was clear enough to see...damage.

A faint bruise showed on her thigh—the outline clearly a boot mark. Someone had stomped on her leg.

Her right arm, draped over her chest, showed tiny dots of yellow—the remnants of a punishing grip.

Above that was a thin pink scar. He knew too well what a knife wound looked like.

Kinky sex?

Doubtful, despite the fact he had a feeling she'd enjoy submitting to a lover. But she said she hadn't had sex recently. An untruth? People *did* lie all the time—cynicism was a side effect of a law enforcement career—but he doubted she'd lied about this. Unless her last lover was pencil-sized, she hadn't been taken for quite a while.

Someone had beat her up. His jaw tightened to the point of pain. Hitting any woman was screwed-up, but to hurt someone this sweet was...

He had no words.

Sitting on the edge of the mattress, he traced the mark on her thigh and studied her torso. On her ribs, a red line from the edge of the table last night crossed older yellow-brown bruising. Another shadow on her softly rounded belly might have come from a punch or kick to the gut. "Jesus, the bastard really did a number on you."

When he looked up, she was watching him, worry in her eyes. Her muscles had tensed.

"Tell me the asshole was arrested."

"I... I don't want to talk about it." She looked away.

Gabe scowled at another spot on her hip and then caught her chin, forcing her to look at him. "Tell me he's behind bars, Julie."

"He's behind bars." Her voice came out a snap. Her eyes said she'd lied right to his face.

Pulling in a breath through his nose, Gabe released her. Anger roiled uncomfortably in his gut along with disappointment. And he was a dumbass. They'd just had sex, yes.

She'd welcomed him inside her body, yes. That didn't mean she trusted him.

Hell, he didn't trust *her*.

But, God, he hated liars. His shoulder ached as if to remind him what happened to gullible idiots. He tried to fight the unwarranted feeling of betrayal and gave up. No need to continue being an idiot.

He rose. "I should get going."

"Oh. Right. Of course."

After dressing, he turned to look at her.

She sat on the bed, staring out into the black night. The covers were wrapped around her in a way that indicated she'd cocooned herself against him.

The visible barrier made his chest hurt. What the fuck had happened to his defenses?

He moved closer. Maybe they could talk. Work through...whatever this was. "Julie."

She didn't respond.

He lifted his voice. "Juliette."

She jerked and turned.

Realization dawned. "That's not your name, is it?"

Her face told him the answer.

Yeah, okay, he was done. "Have a good day...whatever your name is."

CHAPTER EIGHT

When his alarm went off, Gabe silenced the damn thing with a curse and squinted against the bright morning light. His bedroom on the second floor overlooked the living room—and he hadn't closed the wooden pocket doors that gave the loft some privacy. Sunlight streamed through the huge downstairs windows right into his room.

Hell. After stretching, he walked out of the bedroom. Naked, but it wasn't as if anyone could see him. Mako'd insisted on buying enough acres to make the Hermitage as isolated as possible while still being close to town. It'd cost some bucks to get electricity to this side of the lake, but even the sarge had admitted he enjoyed the convenience.

Leaning on the railing, Gabe looked out over the downstairs and then outside.

The lake was buried in a dark gray mist...the color of Julie's eyes.

His mouth twisted. *Welcome to a crappy new morning.* Even if his shoulder felt better, his conscience now had an ache that massage wouldn't relieve.

Sure, Ms. Juliette Wilson had lied about her name and probably other things. Liars pissed him off to the nth degree, especially when it came to the female gender. Guess he could thank his ex-wife for that.

Even so, he could have handled last night better.

He scowled at the urge to retreat to the wilderness. Away from people who'd do anything they wanted without a care for whom they hurt in the process.

And now *he'd* hurt someone—he'd seen her face as he left—and even if she was a liar, he still felt like shit. For all he knew, the city girl had a damn good reason for being in Alaska and lying her head off.

Hell, people were always moving to Alaska and changing their names, hiding their pasts. Starting over. He, Bull, Caz, and Hawk had done the very same thing.

Yeah, he'd overreacted.

With a sigh, he walked into the master bath's big tiled shower that he'd installed with his first merc paycheck.

As the nearly scalding water beat against his back, knotted muscles began to relax. Civilization did have some rewards, after all. Damned if he hadn't missed inside plumbing and hot water last winter.

As he scrubbed, he caught faint whiffs of a light spicy scent. Julie's—or whatever her name was.

Dammit.

A shave and clean clothes later, he headed downstairs to the kitchen and brewed up a cup of strong black coffee. Cup in hand, he walked out onto the lakeside deck and leaned on the railing.

The temperature was a few degrees above freezing—not bad at all. It was almost 7 a.m., a couple of hours after sunrise. In the lake shallows, a moose breakfasted on early aquatic greens. With slow grace, two trumpeter swans glided past the dock, stirring the mist, before landing on the water. They probably had a nest nearby.

It was spring, after all.

He gave a dour snort. *Bah, humbug.*

And yet...

He'd fought insurgents in the desert, policed in the polluted stench of overcrowded Los Angeles, and spent the last couple of years in and out of South America's steamy jungles.

Spring in Alaska had to be the most beautiful time and place on the planet.

Sipping coffee, he stood and watched the mist dissipate as the world came to life.

To his right, he could see the semicircle of the other cabins, similar in design. His was the leftmost arm, then his brothers' three houses, and finally Mako's empty cabin at the other end of the U. The enclosed two acres contained a chicken yard, garden, patio, and gazebo.

The other night, when he, Bull, and Caz had grilled

outside, he'd kept waiting for Mako's gruff comments. His death had left such a big hole behind.

"Dammit," Gabe said under his breath. "I miss you, Sarge."

In the chicken yard, the rooster spotted Gabe and crowed a challenge. Caz had bought the flock from a prepper who was moving back to Missouri. Alaska winters, not for the faint-hearted.

Over the last couple of days, Gabe had worked on repairing the coop to keep out weasels. This afternoon, his day off, he'd start on the garden. There was something calming about planting, he had to admit. Baumer volunteered to work the late Friday through Sunday shifts, so Gabe had weekdays, and the state troopers would cover the rest.

Until things were under control, Gabe'd be putting in a lot more than full-time.

A few minutes later, Gabe backed the Jeep out of the garage and punched the remote to close the garage door, then grinned. Mako's idea of high tech had been a coffee maker, and the paranoid old survivalist would've preferred the cabins wall-to-wall with only tiny, sniper-sized windows. It'd almost turned into a war. Gabe had been damned if he'd give up that gorgeous view of the lake and mountains. To keep the peace, they'd put closable shutters on the huge windows, electric fencing between the cabins to make the compound bear and moose proof, and used a solar and battery-operated pump on the well.

When the power went off a few years ago, they'd been warm, dry, and fed...thanks to Mako's foresight.

Gabe grinned. That's when they'd discovered that Mako had dug out the root cellars beneath each cabin, creating one long tunnel tying each house together. *In case of war.* As Gabe drove down the tiny gravel road, he shook his head fondly. The sarge'd been one paranoid bastard.

At the intersection of Lake Road and Swan Avenue, he slowed as he passed Dante's rentals.

The lights were on in Julie's place.

Dammit. When he'd driven Julie home last night, he'd figured on getting her keys so he could fetch her car from the bar. So much for good intentions.

After opening the police station and making coffee, he checked the log. Officer Baumer had taken witness reports from the people in the bar, but hadn't located the asshole who'd slapped Julie. It seemed the man had left town.

Gabe growled.

Nothing particularly interesting in the log.

One moose killed by a truck. Baumer had called the Alaska Moose Federation to deliver it to the next name on the list. Someone would have plenty of meat this year.

A drunk had joined a bunch of toms serenading a female cat in heat. Apparently, the nearest neighbor had been unimpressed with the music. Maybe there should be an infraction called drunk and discordant as well as drunk and disorderly.

Baumer had written that a few unhappy customers

created a ruckus when Bull closed the bar at 2 a.m. By Alaska law, the place could remain open until 5 a.m. *Fat chance.* Gabe grinned. His brother liked sleep too much to stay open into the morning hours.

Staccato loud noises brought Gabe to his feet, heart pounding. Gripping his pistol butt, he scanned the room. Wait, no, it wasn't gunfire.

Someone was pounding on the back door. "Gabe, you in here?"

Stand down. Gabe exhaled, long and slow, and went to open the door.

"Hey, boy." Dante strolled in followed by two teenage boys carrying a long crate. The man pointed to the center of the bullpen. "Put it on the floor there and fetch the rest."

After the kids brought in several more crates, Dante passed them some money and shooed them out. He told Gabe, "I was here when the station closed down and took charge of the contents. I figured you might want these back."

Gabe leaned against a desk and eyed the boxes. They were the right size for... "The armory?"

"Yep."

As they pulled off the lids, a variety of weaponry and ammunition was revealed. Handguns, rifles, shotguns.

Dante pointed to two 12-gauge shotguns and two AR-15 rifles. "Those were department issue. The officers used their own personal handguns—they won't be here. All the rest is shit the department confiscated over the years."

"Good enough. This'll help my budget." The ammunition would be around a decade old. Might be all right depending on where it was stored, but he'd order new and test out the old. The beanbag rounds for the shotgun would come in useful for wildlife. "Thanks, Dante. Any other surprises up your sleeve?"

"One big one, yeah." Dante settled into a chair next to the coffee pot. "Something me an' Sarah arranged. The council appointed us to set up and oversee the police force." The old guy grinned. "Be grateful; you almost had Parrish watching over your shoulder. But since he voted against reopening the station, he wasn't given direct oversight."

"Parrish... Reverend Parrish?"

Dante poured himself a cup of coffee. "Yep."

"I saw him in the coffee shop the other day. Interesting to see an armed clergyman."

Dante had a distinctive *heh-heh-heh* raspy laugh. "That "clergyman" is the founder of the Patriot Zealots."

What the...? "Do you mean someone like David Koresh? Religious antigovernment paramilitary?"

"Yep."

"Oh wonderful." Gabe rubbed the back of his neck.

"See, aren't you glad Parrish isn't in charge of the station?"

"You have my undying gratitude." Fanatics. Rescue had armed fanatics, including one on the town council. Gabe shook his head. "So what's this big surprise you and Sarah set up?"

"Should arrive today. Sarah has friends on the Anchorage PD—and they helped us lease a police vehicle. SUV. All wheel drive to deal with our shit roads. Nothing fancy, mostly standard equipment with a few things Sarah's cop friends recommended."

Gabe started to smile. Things were looking up. "Unmarked or—"

"Nope. Black and white. Lights and sirens, cage in the back. Fun stuff." Dante grinned.

"I'll be damned. That really is good news. Thank you." He and Baumer's shifts only overlapped on Fridays so one car was adequate. "We really needed an official vehicle."

"A man needs the tools to do the job. Let's get your weaponry locked up." Dante pushed to his feet with a groan. "By the way, I heard the new craft store got spray-painted."

"Well, hell." After he and Dante got the weapons stored in the gun vault, he walked the Okie out.

Not fifteen minutes later, the new patrol car was delivered.

And damn, the Ford Police Interceptor was well stocked.

He had to grin because it felt like...like break-up when Mako'd bring them all to town to get supplies. So damned exciting.

In addition to normal vehicle supplies, the cargo area drawer had police equipment like body armor, evidence kits and bags, yellow tarp, and police tape. There was no ambulance in town, so he wasn't surprised to see first responder supplies like a car-opening kit, fire extinguisher, first aid kit, emergency blankets, latex gloves, and portable defibrillator. Being as this was Alaska, bad weather gear was essential, and the car was equipped with chemical hand warmers, heavy flashlight, emergency food and water. There were also supplies for highway accidents—tape measure, HAZMAT suit, bolt cutters, traffic cones, flares and vest, breathalyzer, and shovel.

Nice job, Dante and Sarah. They'd done well by him.

Gabe added extra ammo and a paperwork box, stored the AR-15 and shotgun in the interior rack, and climbed in.

Jesus, it even had that new car smell—along with the underlying smell of gun oil. It took him a second to wipe off the big grin and put an appropriate serious police chief expression on his face as he pulled out and drove out of town.

He drove the back roads for a while before returning onto Main Street.

And there was the graffiti.

Garish red lettering "GO HOME" was painted on a pale yellow storefront.

Anger simmered in his gut.

Mako had bought this building last year, and Bull had just leased it to a couple of sisters from Juneau. They planned to open an art gallery and craft store, specializing in Alaskan-created goods.

They sure didn't deserve this kind of shit.

Gabe snapped the SUV into a diagonal parking space and headed for the store.

Obviously seeing him coming, a stout, brown-haired woman bustled out. A quilt decorated with bears, moose, and bald eagles was bundled in her arms. She studied his uniform shirt for a moment. "Oh, excellent. You must be the new police chief."

He held out his hand. "I'm Gabe MacNair. Mrs. Johannsen, isn't it?"

"Ms. or even better, Glenda." She motioned to the spray-painting. "Do you see what someone did?"

"I see." His jaw clenched. So much for the hope that a local police presence would discourage vandalism.

On the contrary. This felt like the asshole was thumbing his nose at the cops.

And the business.

The two new owners were in their fifties, both divorced, both hard-working businesswomen—and artists, as well. In Juneau, one had owned an art gallery, the other a craft store. What kind of asshole picked on women like this?

The red paint was garish, the sentiments clear. "Someone either isn't happy about increasing tourist traffic and-or hates seeing the town change at all.

She gave a sniff of displeasure. "Too late now. He should've kept the ski resort from opening if he felt that strongly."

"Too late to put the cork back in that bottle. I'll see if

Bull can free up a construction worker to repaint your storefront."

"That would be wonderful."

And he'd recommend that Mako's trust cover the expense. Not that he'd mention that to Glenda. He and Caz wanted Bull to remain as the front man for the trust. It helped that very few people had ever met Mako or knew about his kids.

Although Glenda's scowl had disappeared, a line appeared between her eyes. "Do you think the vandalism will keep happening?"

Optimism gone, he eyed the graffiti. "So it seems. However, I plan to install some security cameras." Gabe motioned toward the streetlight outside Dante's store. "We'll cover high-target areas, including your store. No one will be monitoring real-time, but we should be able to identify the culprit."

"That's very reassuring. Thank you, Gabe."

After a disconcerted moment, he headed back to the patrol car. No civilian in a city would call him by his first name. But he rather liked Glenda's informality.

A shame he was so unfamiliar with small towns. Growing up, they hadn't been part of town life. Mako'd taken them into Seward only a few times a year for groceries, the post office, or home schooling checkups.

As he started to unlock the patrol car, a shout drew his attention.

Turning, he huffed a laugh.

A moose was sauntering down Grebe Avenue. After crossing Main, it stopped to nibble on a young budding tree.

Only in Alaska...

Outside the coffee shop, three tourists bounced up and down with excitement. "A moose! Right in town!"

A couple of old-timers heading into the grocery paused, probably in hopes of a bloody human-versus-moose battle.

Attracted by the commotion, more people exited the coffee shop—followed by Baumer.

The officer noticed Gabe and loped across the street, detouring widely around the moose. He skidded to a stop and stared at the patrol car. "Lookee there. Is that ours?"

"It is. Whoever's on duty gets the vehicle, otherwise it'll be in the parking lot in case one of us gets called in. Your keys are on your desk."

After opening the cargo door, Gabe grabbed the shotgun and loaded it with beanbag ammo.

Baumer's eyes narrowed. "You look like you know what you're doing."

Jesus, the officer acted like Gabe'd never seen a moose before, let alone dealt with one. Then again, Baumer might not know more than Gabe had served in the LAPD as a lieutenant.

"Oh-oh," Baumer muttered.

Gabe turned to see two young men and a woman headed straight for the moose. "Oh, hell."

"Tourists." Baumer snorted. "They're dumber than rocks."

"They're from Outside. Probably think moose are as skittish as deer." Gabe raised his voice. "You three. Get back to the sidewalk, or I'll arrest you for jaywalking."

"That's a threat?" Baumer asked in disbelief.

"It is in the city."

"Guess you'd know, wouldn't you?" The comment fell... just...short of being insulting.

The three tourists dutifully trotted back to the sidewalk and turned, phones out and recording. The wide eyes and expressions of wonder made him remember his first moose sighting.

Twenty-some years ago at Mako's old cabin. He and Hawk had dashed straight toward the animal before realizing how big the damn thing was. And that it didn't like them at all. They'd run even faster the other direction. Thank God, it'd only chased them a short distance.

The sarge had laughed his ass off.

Would probably be laughing now.

Pushing the grief aside, Gabe turned his attention to work.

If the moose kept moving down Grebe Avenue, it'd reach the lake. That would be good. If it stopped here in town, well, wildlife on Main Street was an invitation to disaster.

"You going to shoot him, Officer?" one person yelled.

Gaze on the loudmouth, the animal halted in the center

of the street. Its ears went back. The hair on its spine rose. Moose were exceedingly territorial about their space.

Pointing at the spectators, Gabe shouted, "You people move back half a block. Now, now, *now*."

"Good idea." Baumer turned to the two observers on the left side of the street and yelled the same instructions.

As people retreated, the moose's ears came up.

Better.

Baumer motioned to the shotgun. "You'd better let me handle this."

Not bothering to answer, Gabe strolled into the street until directly behind the beast. "Go, you idiot," he muttered at the moose. "Visit the lake."

Instead, the damn thing headed straight toward the noisy tourists.

Shit. Before it got too close to them, Gabe fired the shotgun. The beanbag nailed it in the right ass, and he shot again. Another hit.

Startled, the moose jolted forward, turning leftward to escape the stinging "insects." Once it started moving, the animal continued down Grebe Avenue.

"Have a nice day at the lake, Bullwinkle." As Gabe returned to the SUV, he chuckled. Damned if the spectators weren't cheering as if he'd made a touchdown.

Still beside the car, Baumer studied him. "Nice job, Chief."

"This time." Gabe stowed the shotgun. "Let's hope this isn't a regular route for him."

"Might be. I've seen him here before." Baumer turned to look down the street. "Idiots. You should've let him kick a couple of them."

Gabe gave him a look. "That's not the job."

"No, guess not." The officer's grin reappeared. "You know, I kinda wanted the chief job, but not if it means sucking up to Outsiders."

"Unfortunately, it means sucking up to everyone."

Baumer barked a laugh. "Never thought of it that way, but guess so."

Maybe the officer's attitude explained his slow promotions in the past. Closing the cargo door, Gabe pointed at the graffiti defacing the craft store. "Last night, did you notice anyone downtown?"

"No. That must've happened after I went off shift."

"Probably so." A shame Gabe didn't have enough staff for round-the-clock coverage of town. The cameras would help. "By the way, I plan to get—"

Baumer interrupted, "What are you doing on duty today? I thought Saturday was my day on, your day off."

"I'm putting in extra hours until things are caught up."

"Hard on your wife and kids."

"Divorced, no kids." Three brothers. No father. The sorrow was still a hollow ache around his heart. "And you?"

"I got a wife and a couple of little boys. Still in diapers." As Baumer leaned against the SUV, settling in like a true southerner for a spate of gossip, Gabe felt...crowded. Enough already. He checked his watch. Two o'clock. "You're on in an hour. After you start, take some time to familiarize yourself with the SUV and then keep an eye on downtown and the tourists."

Baumer blinked and straightened. "Will do."

As they parted, Gabe headed for the coffee shop. He fucking needed some coffee.

Inside, a few locals were at the counter, getting refills after the *show*. The hippie gas station owner looked up from choosing a pastry to give Gabe a nod.

And there was Julie. Her golden hair brightened the dimly lit back corner where she sat. Her laptop was on the table, and, after a glance at him, she focused on her work. The tension in her shoulders said she didn't want to talk with him.

Just as well. This wasn't the place to deliver an apology. He wasn't sure how to phrase the sentiment anyway. *Sorry your lies pissed me off.*

With an exasperated grunt, he moved to the counter.

"Good afternoon, Chief." Behind the huge coffee-making apparatus, Sarah held up a to-go cup. "Drip again?"

"Thanks. My last cup was a lifetime ago."

"Some days are like that." After passing him his coffee, she rested her hands on the counter and straightened—a private preparing to give report to the sergeant.

"Yes?" He eyed her as he took a sip.

"The man who slapped Julie last night. His name is Keaton. He's a member of that cult—the PZs."

"The who?"

"Patriot Zealots." Her mouth twisted with repugnance. "Captain Nabera, Parrish's second-in-command was also at the table. The older black-haired man. I didn't recognize the other two, but the population out at the PZ farm changes constantly."

"Keaton. Got it, thank you."

When she turned to a new customer, Gabe grabbed a pastry and left enough money to cover the bill. Setting his coffee on a table, he leaned against a wall and ate while watching people come and go.

Seeing his badge, most smiled and nodded. Two of the women said, "Welcome to Rescue." One man in his thirties didn't trouble to hide his glare. Another frowned.

So, some were in favor of a police presence, others weren't.

Julie never looked up.

Dammit.

Gabe had just finished his coffee and pastry when the good Reverend Parrish walked in. How convenient was that?

This time, Gabe gave him a closer study. Mid-forties. About 6-2, two hundred pounds, and in good shape. Short brown hair, blue eyes. Still wearing a pistol.

A young man and two women followed him like chicks after a hen.

Seeing Gabe, the reverend motioned the three to the counter—and headed for Gabe. "Chief MacNair. I'm Reverend Parrish.

Gabe took the offered hand. "It's good to meet you. Actually, I wanted to speak with you about—"

"About Keaton. I heard about the unfortunate incident last night." A flash of amusement was quickly masked.

"That incident was assault." Gabe kept his voice mild.

"Of course, and I was appalled. We don't condone violence. That is why Mr. Keaton's membership was revoked, and he was expelled from the fellowship and the grounds. I so informed Officer Baumer last night."

Son of a bitch. Although the crime would be considered a misdemeanor, it was still assault. "Where did he go?"

"In fear of being arrested, I believe he planned to return to the Lower 48. He was from Kentucky." Despite a slight smirk, Parrish appeared to be telling the truth.

In fact, he probably was. He'd undoubtedly tossed Keaton out to keep Gabe from getting onto the militia's grounds. Rounding up a judge to get a warrant for Keaton's arrest at this point was probably futile.

That's why Baumer's log stated the man had left town.

"I appreciate the information." Gabe kept his voice level, not letting his frustration leak out. "Please let your... members...know that violent behavior isn't acceptable and will get them in trouble."

"I'll do that." The reverend tilted his head. His gaze on Gabe stopped barely short of being a challenge. After a long moment, he turned and rejoined the others.

As Gabe watched, the man spoke to the three,

switching on his magnetism, as someone would turn on a light.

His "flock" hung on every word.

Rubbing his neck, Gabe watched with a sinking feeling in his gut. The good reverend was a charismatic fanatic with firearms.

Great, just great.

CHAPTER NINE

Audrey sighed in relief when Gabe finally left the coffee shop.

Earlier, when customers had poured out of the shop to see the moose, she'd gone to the door to watch, and seen Gabe take charge, ordering people around with that military command voice of his. Then he'd strolled into the street, just like those old cowboy movies where the sheriff stalked out to face a gunslinger.

She grinned. He'd faced down a moose.

Actually, it wasn't all that funny. The animal had been massive. As tall as Gabe. With antlers. That was no Bambi.

Gabe had been as cool as if he'd been out for a nice walk.

Just...wow.

Then, the chief had entered the coffee shop, and she'd felt herself turn red.

Rather than working, she'd sneaked peeks of him as her memory relived last night. The way he'd held her in place. The low resonant sound of his voice when he called her Goldilocks. How hard she'd come.

He'd been understanding and patient—and adamant about caring for her. Sheesh, she couldn't even pretend he'd taken advantage of her since having sex had been her idea.

It had been wondrous. Amazing.

And a total disaster.

Why did the man have to be so perceptive? After sex, any other guy would've been half-asleep, not noticing how she didn't answer right away to her fake name.

Why was he so unbendable? It wasn't as if she'd killed someone; she was just using a name that wasn't hers.

Of course, she *was* getting paid in barter and cash, so she was kind of escaping taxes. But, *please*, the IRS was well equipped to come after her if they wanted to. She sighed. And Bull said there was a limit on how long he'd pay her in cash.

She didn't need to look up to know that the chief had left. The man exuded power that could be felt all the way across the room. The badge might give him legal standing, but the intimidating authority? Oh, he'd have it without the badge.

Why did she find that so sexy?

She closed her eyes. *My girl, who are you and what have you done with super-nerd Audrey?*

Unfortunately, a brainy bookworm was who she was—an

introvert to the nth degree— possessing a total inability to handle relationships with lovers, friends, and family. Even her mother hadn't loved her.

Oh honestly, she was whining like a baby. *Stop. Now.*

It was good that Gabe had walked out before she got in too deep. Because if she did—and God, it would be easy to fall for a man like him—then when he tired of her nerdiness and pulled away, it would really hurt.

She grimaced. It already hurt.

Unable to concentrate, she checked her emails and cringed inside.

Special Agent Dennison had written.

Her fingers almost crossed as she punched the keys to open the email.

—

Audrey,

The investigation of the pharmaceutical research company and their created virus is going well. I believe all those involved will end up destitute and behind bars.

Spyros hasn't been apprehended. Rumors are flying that one of his targets injured him badly—and escaped. He's going to want revenge and to repair his damaged reputation. As you feared, until he's imprisoned, you will be in danger.

—

. . .

Audrey's stomach clenched. She'd learned Spyros had escaped law enforcement agencies, including Interpol, for well over a decade. What if they never caught him?

Her fingers shook as she scrolled the page.

—

I understand your hesitance to reveal your whereabouts. If you change your mind, I'll do my best to see that you stay safe.

—

Safe. Now there was a feeling she hadn't felt since leaving Chicago. Not until last night when wrapped in Gabe's arms. She shook her head. *Not going there.*

She wasn't going anywhere, it seemed. Until and unless Spyros was caught, she needed to stay put and stay quiet. Here in Alaska.

Maybe for a long, long time.

As she fought back tears, the laptop's screensaver came on. Fractal patterns appeared, grew, and dissolved, chaos in action. The story of her life these days.

Eff-it-all.

She pulled in a breath. All right then. It was time to get the contents of her Chicago apartment packed up and stored. Maybe Dennison could help with that.

And then?

She couldn't keep taking Dante's charity, and face it,

charity was what it was. The waitress job brought in cash, but would it last after tourist season was over?

The freelance online research could bring in enough to survive on, but she'd have to use the internet for hours every day. There was no way she could justify sitting here, taking up a table all day.

After packing away her laptop and papers, she pulled on her denim jacket and waited for a lull at the counter.

"Sarah?"

The woman turned away from refilling the pastry display. "More coffee?"

"Uh, no, I don't need more to drink—and that's why I wanted to talk with you." Darn it, why was it so easy to answer research questions and so difficult to talk with people any other time? "I know you have free internet, and I need the internet. But I can't drink coffee all day long. Is there a way I could simply pay for the use?"

Sarah let out a pleased laugh. "And here Gabe said honest people were rarer than rattlesnakes in Alaska."

Audrey stiffened. She was one of those people who'd lied to him. "Um..."

"I'd be delighted to work something out rather than you wasting perfectly good coffee."

Apparently, Sarah had noticed how many of Audrey's half-full cups were abandoned.

Audrey winced. "You make wonderful coffee. I just can't drink more than a couple of cups a day."

"Let me talk with Uriah and get back to you with some figures."

"Perfect."

"I take it you're going to stay in Rescue for a while?" Sarah leaned on the counter, ready to chat.

"Um. Yes. Rescue is a quite attractive location. The populace is pleasant. Congenial." And she sounded like an idiot—a well-read idiot. Audrey took an awkward step back. Small talk was so out of her comfort zone. "I should go" —*bang my head on the pavement*—"pick up my car. Let me know about the internet."

"Of course." Sarah's cheeks dimpled, but her voice was even.

Audrey fled.

Outside, a biting cold wind slapped her face. Incoming gray clouds to the west confirmed the forecast for rain later in the day. From her jacket pocket, she grabbed her green stocking hat and pulled it on as she headed toward Bull's Moose.

Paying for internet would be a hit to her cash, but she could afford a month. After that, with luck, the freelance research jobs would have picked up. Since she had to start over with a fake name, it was taking time to get a good reputation again. But if Spyros had people in the FBI, she couldn't risk them tracing her real name through a PayPal, credit card, or bank account.

This staying hidden was sure tricky.

Even trickier was trying to socialize.

When Sarah switched from business to chatting, Audrey had...run like a coward. *I can't do that anymore.* Unlike in Chicago, Rescue residents liked to stand around and talk. She couldn't afford to stick out as a newcomer.

Somehow, someway, she'd have to learn to be comfortable with people. She could do it. She *would*.

So...she smiled at the next two people she saw. Turning off Main, she strolled down the gravel street of Sweetgale. To her left was an older home and two newer ranch-style houses.

One front yard held an old red wagon like the one her grandparents gave her one summer. She'd given her doll frequent wagon rides...until Mother cut her playtime in favor of studying.

Audrey shook her head. Children shouldn't be forced into being intellectual stars. In college, she'd realized how unfit she was for living in the real world. How gray her childhood had been. Other children's mothers had played with them, spent time with them. Not had extra homework from her mother on top of what the private school required. Not had nannies who read physics texts to her rather than bedtime stories.

She shook her head, wrapping her arms around herself. Sometimes, she'd just wanted a hug so badly.

When she changed her college major to biology rather than physics, the final break had occurred.

Her mother had been furious. Audrey was to have been her achievement, a shining example of superior genetics and training. *"But you must take after your sperm donor. Weak, emotional. Stupid. Fine. I wash my hands of you, Audrey. Get out and don't return."*

Audrey huffed a laugh. Why did those words still hurt so much? Why had she stood there, wanting to beg her mother to love her?

She shook her head, remembering the neighbors gossiping about Mother, saying, *"That woman has no love in her soul."* Maybe it wasn't Audrey who was lacking.

Most days, she believed that. *I won't be an emotionless machine. I won't.*

Biting her lip, she frowned. Because she'd been on that path, hadn't she?

Well, she could change. Pulling her shoulders back, she lifted her chin and determinedly smiled at the world around her. Pure white peaks, dark green forests. The glint of the stunningly turquoise lake. So real and immediate. Not a painting or photo in a museum.

She could smell the wetlands by the lake and hear the *thunking* noise of someone chopping firewood.

And from a backyard came an English-accented woman's voice: "Plague you, knee, you bolting-hutch of beastliness. You..."

Audrey hadn't heard such cursing since attending her last Shakespearean play, and she stopped in amazed admiration.

"Support me, you villainous, foul deformity of nature." The Elizabethan swearing ended with a muffled groan.

That didn't sound good. Audrey hurried around the side of the house.

Inside a fenced garden, an older woman with chin-length white hair was on her hands and knees, struggling to stand.

"Wait. Let me help," Audrey hurried through the gate. "Are you hurt?"

Blue-gray eyes sparkled with annoyance. "Don't ever get old, child. It's the pits."

Audrey choked on a laugh.

"I could use help getting up, yes." The slender woman smiled.

"All right." Bracing her sore ribs with an arm, Audrey bent to give the lady her hand.

"Uh-uh, Goldilocks." A firm grip closed on her shoulder.

Releasing the lady, Audrey spun. Her eyes widened. "*You*."

"'Fraid so." Gabe's mouth twitched. He put an arm around her waist and purposefully moved her back before speaking to the older woman. "Ms. Wilson has cracked ribs and shouldn't lift anything. Let me help."

Audrey wanted to argue, but her voice didn't work, silenced by his touch, by his commanding baritone, even by his scent. The fact that he was right made it all worse.

"Chief MacNair, I believe?" The lady smiled, as self-possessed and dignified as if she were at high tea. "I would appreciate your assistance. I'm Lillian Gainsborough. Do please call me Lillian."

"Good to meet you, ma'am." Gabe bent, gently scooped the woman off the ground, and straightened. "How badly are you hurt?"

He strode out of the garden toward the long back porch, and Audrey followed.

"I didn't fall, and I'm not hurt," Lillian said. "I knelt to see if the soil was warm enough to begin planting, but my knee refused to cooperate when I tried to rise."

"Ah." Gabe climbed the two steps of the back porch and settled Lillian on a chair. "Considering the distance between houses here, you might consider getting a medical alert system. In the house or your garden, you can push the button and get help.

"Honestly, what's next—a walker?" Lillian said under her breath. "Of course, you're right, Chief. I'll get one."

Leaning forward, she massaged her right leg. "I planned to schedule a knee replacement surgery after ice-up...so I could enjoy my summer without being laid up. I was quite excited that the ground was ready to plant." She gave them a rueful smile.

"We always waited to plant until Memorial Day." Gabe leaned against a porch railing. "But you're right; it's been a warm spring."

Audrey shook her head. Was there anything the man didn't know?

The movement caught Lillian's eye. "This chair is empty, dear. Please do sit."

After Audrey settled into the adjacent chair, she noticed

most of the wrought-iron tables and chairs held trays of seedlings.

Although Lillian's back was straight and her voice was level, sadness showed in her eyes as she looked at the tiny plants. "It appears I won't be putting in a garden this year."

Audrey couldn't stand it. "Um. I don't have any experience, but if you want to direct me, I could help you out."

Gabe smiled at her, then folded his arms over his broad chest. "Planting is fine, Goldie, but no digging. Not with those ribs."

She opened her mouth to argue, caught his unyielding expression, and turned to Lillian. "I'd like to help you plant."

The woman's blue eyes lit. "Accepted. I'll find someone else to use a shovel."

"I've got a few minutes now, long enough to turn over the soil enough that you can get those seedlings in," Gabe said.

"That would be wonderful, Chief." Lillian smiled. "A couple of locals, Knox and Chevy, do handyman work. They'll be happy to do the rest."

Gabe pointed at a small shed at the side of the backyard. "Tool shed?"

"That's it."

As Gabe headed to the shed, Audrey could relax without his overwhelming presence. Without his every movement reminding her of what they'd done together.

"You have no experience in horticulture?" Lillian asked.

"When I was younger, I wanted a garden, but we lived in an apartment." She frowned. "Actually, I've always lived in apartments. Now, I actually get to play in the dirt. I'm thrilled you'll let me help."

"We will both have fun." Lillian lifted a perfectly groomed eyebrow. "I have an offer for you. When my husband was alive, we utilized all of the space. Now, without him, I only need half. If you would do the planting, weeding, and harvesting for the entire garden, you are welcome to use the left half as your own. I'll provide seeds and plants, tools, and directions."

Really? Happiness danced through Audrey's bloodstream. Her own garden space along with an experienced teacher to help her with it? Her fingers twitched with the need to start. She should read a few books, see what—

"I've been presumptuous," Lillian said. "I didn't ask if you'd be here long enough to enjoy the harvest."

The words were like a blast of cold water.

"I'll definitely be here through harvest. Probably for a long time after that. I won't leave you in the lurch," Audrey said slowly, feeling off-center. She recognized the hollow feeling in her stomach as homesickness. But there was also a flutter of anticipation.

She wanted this experience, even if the thought of visiting someone every day was a bit daunting.

What a perfect way to fulfill her goal to learn to socialize. "I would love to exchange labor for learning."

"Excellent." Lillian gave a nod of approval. "I believe we'll do quite well together."

In the garden, Gabe motioned with the pitchfork. "Are you planting in this row first?"

"That is the plan," Lillian called. She smiled at Audrey. "That's where our short salad greens will go."

Audrey eyed Gabe, wondering how he knew a certain row would be planted first. And she couldn't pull her gaze away as he rolled up his sleeves and started turning the soil. The way his steely muscles bunched under the uniform shirt dried her mouth.

"He's done that a time or two, hasn't he?" Lillian noted. "Mako was an excellent teacher."

Audrey caught the sadness in Lillian's tone. "You knew his father?"

Lillian smiled. "He and my husband were friends, and after my husband passed, the sergeant and I grew to be close."

Audrey saw the slight curve of Lillian's mouth and understood exactly what she meant by "*close*." "But you hadn't met Gabe before?"

"No. When his boys visited, they stayed home with Mako. And Mako, well, he preferred to deal with people in small numbers." Sadness filled the woman's face. "I'm sure that was why he chose to exit the world the way he did. Being in a hospital would have... He wouldn't have done well."

Exit the world? Did she mean the man had killed

himself? The thought was like getting hit in the chest. "But Mako had Gabe...and his other sons."

"And he loved them dearly. He knew they'd come running to help out, but Mako wasn't a man to tolerate weakness in himself." Lillian shook her head. "Such a narrow vision is its own kind of failing."

"His poor sons."

"Yes." Lillian's brow creased. "I must say, Mako led me to believe Gabriel was a friendlier sort. This chief is quite reserved. I do wonder how difficult Mako's death was for him."

"I think...very difficult." Audrey had heard the sorrow in his voice when he'd talked about Mako. Gabe's body had so many terrifying scars. Would the suicide of his father-substitute add scars on his soul, as well? No wonder his face was etched with hard lines.

As Audrey watched, Gabe reached the end of the row.

After stowing the pitchfork, he returned, and his gait held a slight limp. "Ready for planting, ladies."

"Thank you, Gabriel."

He smiled at Lillian and rolled down his sleeves over pumped-up forearms.

During the night, as she'd kissed her way down his body, her lips had brushed over those powerful muscles. As she looked at them in the daylight, heat ran through her. The air seemed to turn thick and sultry.

When her gaze lifted, he was watching her, his expression unreadable.

She wanted him to hold her again. And...she wanted to run away.

Audrey averted her gaze. Because she was a smart woman, she'd choose option B.

And stay far, far away.

CHAPTER TEN

A couple of days later, the patrol car was starting to feel...almost homelike, Gabe thought as he drove down Sweetgale. He slowed.

With Julie beside her, Lillian stood on her porch, arms waving angrily.

Now, that looked like trouble. Gabe parked the car and jumped out. "Is there a problem here?"

Lillian didn't even look at him. "You vile, scum-filled dunghill of metal."

Gabe blinked. Whatever she'd just said, it was an insult; however, she seemed to be addressing the door. He gave Julie a puzzled look.

Julie's hands covered her mouth. Her eyes were crinkled with laughter.

He did have to say that laughter looked damn fine on her. "What's going on?"

"She locked herself out."

"Thou art unfit for any place but hell." Lillian kicked the door and turned. "Why hello, Chief MacNair. How are you this day?"

Here was an actress who'd spent too much time performing Elizabethan plays. "Good. I'm good. You're locked out, I hear?"

The look she gave her door was scathing. "Vile, treacherous creation. If I had an axe..." Lillian turned to Gabe. "Can you break a window for me, please, Chief?"

That seemed a bit extreme. But, wait... The town had no locksmith. "No need for violence. How about I unlock the door for you instead?"

Lillian tilted her head regally. "That would be most convenient. Why do you have a key to my door, I wonder?"

"No key, ma'am. Hold on a minute." Trying not to laugh, Gabe returned to the patrol car. As he opened the cargo door, he noticed the dust caked on the vehicle. Most of the roads in Alaska were gravel—or dirt—and he'd been driving everywhere, getting a feel for the town.

For *his* town. For someone who'd come just to clean the place up for his brothers, the sense of possession was fucking disconcerting but very real. If he were a dog, he'd've been lifting his leg and marking his territory.

After a quick rummage in his personal pack, he pulled out his old locksmith tools.

As he knelt in front of the door and opened the kit,

Lillian's eyebrows rose. "Did you indulge in burglary as a child?"

Actually, after Gramps died, he had. "I'll take the fifth on that, thanks."

When Julie made a smothered sound of laughter, Gabe grinned and set to work.

A couple of minutes later, the rumble of a bad muffler made him glance over his shoulder. A battered red pickup pulled up to the curb, and two men in their late twenties climbed out of the truck.

With bushy red hair and a drooping mustache, the lanky driver stared at Gabe's black & white. "Chevy, that ain't no state trooper rig."

"Says *Rescue Police*. Since when do we have cop cars in town?" Chevy scowled. The short man was so bulky with muscles his neck almost disappeared into his shoulders.

"Gabriel, meet Knox and Chevy. They're doing the garden work that Julie and I can't manage. Men, this is our new Chief of Police, Chief MacNair." Lillian motioned toward Gabe.

Gabe turned far enough to nod at the two. "Afternoon."

No answer. Just irritated stares.

Oh well. As the lock released, Gabe pushed the door open and rose.

Julie smiled. "Where did you learn to pick locks? I wouldn't have thought they'd teach that in a police academy."

Depending on the specialty, they did. However, he'd

already known how. "No, my grandfather was a locksmith in LA. As a kid, I'd go with him on calls."

"City boy, born and bred," Chevy said to Knox. His voice was lowered...not far enough. "What's a damn LA cop doing here?"

Gabe blinked and almost laughed. Apparently, Chevy had heard Gabe was a cop in Los Angeles. Now, he knew Gabe'd been a boy in LA. Two and two added up to a wrong conclusion because Gabe'd spent all the intervening years in Alaska. Same mistake Baumer had made. He considered telling them the truth.

Nah.

"We don't need some city pig poking into our business." Chevy's aggressive attitude made Gabe think of the sarge's maxim that a short man could be as proddy as a moose in rut.

Probably not a saying to share right now. And giving Chevy a lesson in manners... Well, Mako hadn't approved of violence in front of women. Although Lillian probably wouldn't bat an eye, Gabe had a feeling Julie had seen far too much violence already.

Ignoring the two men, Gabe stowed his lock kit away.

"Chief, do you know when the health clinic is due to open?" Lillian asked.

Pulling gardening tools from the pickup, Knox turned his head to catch Gabe's answer.

"A couple of weeks. The building needs to hire a receptionist. The clinic didn't want to open without one."

"Makin' all sorts of changes, aren't you," Knox butted in.

"Actually," Gabe kept his voice polite, "a shared receptionist isn't a change. It's the way things worked prior to the closing of the services. Before your time." As the ginger's face turned dark red, Gabe knew the last part hadn't been the most diplomatic.

Jesus, sometimes he missed being a merc where he could shoot first and talk later.

"He's correct, Knox," Lillian said. "I do believe I'll enjoy having a medical facility available closer than Soldotna."

"Yeah, well, we don't need all those asshole Outsiders cluttering up our streets," Knox snapped.

Gabe shrugged. "Not everyone in town is into subsistence living. Some of them want a good school for their kids and—" He stopped. Why waste time on bozos who weren't about to listen?

"What should we work on first, ma'am?" Chevy asked, shouldering a hoe.

"Come with me, and I'll show you." Lillian motioned to the side gate, pausing to say, "Thank you so much for unlocking the door, Gabriel."

"My pleasure, ma'am." He'd always enjoyed the challenge of opening locks.

After giving Gabe dirty looks, Chevy and Knox followed Lillian toward the backyard.

"They were awfully grumpy," Julie said with a frown. "And for no reason."

Gabe shrugged. "Some people see the police uniform

and nothing else." He'd dealt with the same problem in Los Angeles...and had hoped a small town would be different. *Guess not.*

Turning, he tried to throw off the gloomy thoughts. He probably wouldn't stay long enough to change anyone's mind anyway. "Just the way it is."

"It shouldn't be." She eyed him, dug in her purse, and walked over.

"Here, Chief." As she tucked something in his shirt pocket, she was close enough he could smell her spicy lemon-and-orange fragrance.

"Is that a bribe, Goldilocks?"

"No." She had the cutest snorty laugh. "Of course not."

"Well, all right then." Unable to resist, he ran his hands up and down her arms.

She startled, all big eyed as she looked up at him. Took a step back. "Um, right. Enjoy."

He let her go and watched her flee—and flight, it was. *Bad Chief—shouldn't have touched.* But, Jesus, how he wanted to touch.

He settled for checking his shirt pocket. Damned if she hadn't given him an oversized Snickers bar. His favorite, in fact.

His mood lifted as he grinned.

CHAPTER ELEVEN

Cities were fucking annoying. Especially when having to be in one for *hours.*

On Tuesday, back in the station, Gabe dropped down at his desk and let out a long sigh. Like a shorted-out circuit board, his nerves were still misfiring. From being in Anchorage. From the drive there and back.

Tourists had clogged Seward Highway, turning it into bumper-to-bumper traffic. He'd been stuck at twenty-five miles per hour because an RV driver refused to pull over and let the faster traffic by. Despite the law that stated he had to. *Asshole.*

A man's irritated voice came from the bullpen. "Anybody in here? Doesn't anyone staff this damn place?"

Yep, he and Caz definitely needed that receptionist. Gabe rose, hauling in a breath to smooth his frazzled nerves. *Don't break the unhappy citizen, MacNair.*

He walked out of his office into the squad room to find a middle-aged man in a golf shirt and Dockers. "I'm Chief MacNair. How can I help you?"

"You can take care of this." The man waved a ticket in the air before shoving it into Gabe's hands.

Gabe took a look. "A state trooper wrote you a speeding ticket."

"And I wasn't speeding." The man crossed his arms over his chest. "You morons have bad radar. For pity's sake, he could have just opened his eyes and seen that I—"

Gabe noted the location on the ticket. Twenty miles away. "I'm sorry, sir, but the Rescue Police Department doesn't have any authority beyond the city boundary. You need to—"

"I don't care what authority you have; I just care that this ticket be killed. Do you know what this will do to my insurance?"

Patience, MacNair. Part of police work was public relations. "You're going to have to discuss the problem with the Alaska State Troopers. I can't assist you with a ticket they wrote."

"Jesus, it's pass the buck time, is it?" The man's chest puffed up. "Listen, mister, I pay taxes, and that means you work for me."

Riiiight. Gabe tried, he really did. Made the proper sympathetic noises, tried to tell the good citizen what to do, that he was in the wrong place. Didn't even ask if those so-called paid taxes were in Alaska.

The rant continued and escalated to making threats to the blue shirt who'd written the ticket. At the fifteen-minute point, Gabe was done.

"Sir, the trooper was simply following the law. If you don't like the law, you and your fellow voters can change it." Gabe realized his voice had lowered to a growl. "Once the law says that asshole speeders who endanger the public can go unticketed, your law enforcement agencies will be pleased to comply."

Gabe walked around him and stopped next to the station door. "Until then, I'm afraid I have work to do. Have a nice day."

When the man's face darkened, Gabe opened the door.

The good citizen walked through.

Shaking his head, Gabe closed the door.

What an asshole.

No, he shouldn't be thinking like that, even if it was the appropriate term.

Closing up shop, Gabe headed out.

At home, hearing noise from outside, he walked onto the back deck. Bull was working in the garden, humming to himself. Caz stood at the grill.

Gabe's brothers were home. As peace wrapped around him and his muscles unknotted one by one, he leaned against the deck railing.

Caz had a fire going in the patio grill. They'd all had a hand in making up the big patio area that sat in the semi-circle of their houses. Hawk'd designed and done the brickwork for the pad. Gabe'd built the thick, solid table, benches, and chairs. Caz and Bull had constructed the stone grill and fire pit.

Stepping back from the blazing fire, Caz noticed Gabe. "Once this dies down, I'm making bacon-moose burgers. You in?"

Gabe hesitated. "Ah..." He'd hate to take his mood out on his brothers.

Caz headed back to his house, calling over his shoulder, "Two burgers coming up."

With a half-grin, Gabe shook his head.

Yeah, he could have stayed inside. But no, he'd headed right out here where they all tended to spend their time.

Because...he wanted to be with his brothers.

Slowly, he drew in a breath. The air was rich with the scent of the lake, the smell of fresh spring plants and newly turned soil.

Over the years, Mako's old cabin had become a safe place, one the world couldn't touch. The haven where he'd found a new family and a home in nature.

Yet, after the sarge moved here and they'd built their houses, the Hermitage had become just as special. Like homing pigeons, they'd all return to be with Mako and to renew their brotherhood ties.

That's what he'd needed today. His brothers. And the peace of home.

In the semicircle of cabins, chickens clucked content-edly in their yard. The lake water lapped quietly along the shore and the dock. Humming quietly, Bull worked his way down the garden rows.

Smiling, Gabe cast off the day's annoyances and started carrying boxes from the Jeep out onto the deck.

By the time he'd gotten the first camera assembled, Bull had finished in the garden. He and Caz walked up the steps.

"Looks like a bunch of tech." Bull dropped into a chair at the table.

"Security cameras." Gabe smiled slightly. "We're going to install them around town, including at your bar. Tonight after sundown."

"We are, are we?" Bull picked one up and nodded. "Good plan."

"Someone is in for a surprise." Caz grinned. "I like it."

"Like that's a shock. You're as sneaky as Hawk," Bull said.

Gabe chuckled. Bull and sneaky didn't belong in the same sentence.

After the devices had been put together and rigged up to communicate with Gabe's phone and computer, they chowed down on burgers and chips, along with Bull's baked beans. Gabe contributed the Oreos and ice cream he'd bought in Anchorage.

The sun set late these days, around eleven at night. To kill time until dark, Bull pulled out some beer—ones from his brewery.

Two beers later, Caz disappeared into his cabin and returned with a hand drum and harmonica.

"Oh, yeah. Let me get my guitar." As Bull went to fetch his acoustic guitar, Caz turned an expectant look on Gabe.

Brother pressure was peer pressure on steroids. Gabe grinned. Yeah, he'd missed them.

All last winter, his guitar had sounded...lonely...without the familiar accompaniment of the men who'd always been there.

With a token grunt of annoyance, he went to get his guitar.

Returned and settled into his chair, Gabe started tuning. "Been a long time since we played together."

With no electricity to Mako's old cabin, the entertainment choices growing up were what they could do themselves. The sergeant had started the boys off on boot camp cadences. But, being a history buff, Mako'd also known songs enjoyed by the earliest British sailors to ones sung by soldiers in World War II.

Hawk, who loved the old west, had demanded country-western music. Gabe liked folk rock. Caz had a fondness for harmony, and Bull liked it all, including jazz.

Music could lighten the longest, darkest night.

Mako'd insisted he taught the boys to sing in sheer self-defense. With four kids in a small cabin, if they weren't singing, they were fighting. Sometimes they managed both —like singing Queen's "We Will Rock You" while having a knockdown bloody brawl. Mako'd been laughing so hard that they'd gotten to fight far longer than normal. Right up until Gabe caught Bull with a roundhouse and knocked him into the river.

Gabe smiled. Good times.

After playing a quick intro riff on the harmonica, Caz sang the first verse of one of Mako's favorites—the "Battle Hymn of the Republic," and Bull was right there with him. Gabe strummed along and tried to clear the thickness from his throat. Eventually, he joined in, plugging the gap between Caz's tenor and Bull's bass with his baritone.

Hawk hated the sound of his own raspy voice and never joined the singing. Mako'd figured his vocal cords were damaged from screaming and hadn't pushed. Even now, Hawk had nightmares from before he'd entered foster care. So, he'd learned the fiddle. When Hawk couldn't sleep, his music would drift over the lake like a mournful fog.

After a couple of songs, Caz asked Bull, "Did you find any more help for your place?"

"Yep, I'm on schedule to open the restaurant section this weekend. I hired another bartender. Julie and Felix will cover the bar. Got a couple of younger college kids for the restaurant. Two cooks from my Anchorage restaurant want to work here to see if they like small town living."

"That's not enough people to staff the roadhouse," Gabe said.

"I know. For right now, I'll only be open Wednesdays through Saturdays. That gives some flexibility with my personnel until I can find more staff."

"What will you serve?" Gabe asked. On Sunday, they'd

visited the ski resort restaurant to check out Bull's competition. The food was damn good there.

"I'll leave the fancy chef-created meals to McNally's, and offer the same menu as my other restaurants—food that goes well with beer. Mid-range priced, hearty fare—burgers, steaks, and comfort foods. Somewhere to enjoy a leisurely meal with a lake view. I should get locals who want to just get out and tourists who don't want to pony up for a five-star restaurant."

"Good," Gabe said. "That's my kind of place."

Caz nodded his approval. "You'll draw guests from the resort—and their staff, probably."

"That's the hope."

"Well, the clinic should be open soon, although—like you—I need more help." Caz glanced at Gabe. "How about a receptionist? Where are we at?"

"Hired." Gabe smiled. "When I stopped to visit Lillian, she sent me to Regina Schroeder. Mid-forties, husband works on the Slope, so he's gone every two weeks."

"She probably gets bored and lonely." Caz nodded. "Any experience?"

"Years ago, she was a receptionist in a dental office in Nebraska. Raised a couple kids here. They're in the Lower 48 and working now." Gabe paused. "She's honest, blunter than tactful, practical. Seems unflappable."

"Not a bad mix. I'll take a calm person over a tactful one." Caz tilted his head. "She'll work Monday through Friday, nine-to-five?"

"That's it. The police department won't open until eleven when I come in."

Bull lifted his eyebrows.

"I'm targeting the hours of the highest number of tourists—and they don't get up early. I'll work eleven to eight on weekdays. Baumer will be on three to three on Friday and Saturday, then eleven to eight on Sunday." Gabe shrugged. "We'll readjust as needed. If we have too much demand, I'll look at hiring seasonal help."

Caz passed over the bag of chips. "What kind of calls are you getting?"

"Shoplifting in the grocery, drunk passed out in the street, fighting on a homestead out in the bush, a domestic call in town"—and damn he hated domestics—"a brown bear near the elementary school, someone tried to break into a post office box, two burglaries. Pretty quiet."

"Shit." Bull stared. "That's quiet?"

"Yeah." Looking back, he'd enjoyed some of the calls. He liked an occasional adrenaline rush. Liked helping out. Liked keeping people safe.

Dammit, he was getting attached to this damn town.

He sucked back some beer. "Anybody heard from Hawk?"

Both his brothers shook their heads. Caz added, "I called the offices. They won't give out any information. They won't even take a message, which is taking operational security too far."

"Yeah. They're over the top." Previously, the admin had

passed on messages and a family would be notified of an operative's death. With the change in owners had come increased security to the point of a total informational blackout.

"Would anyone there know if he's all right?" Caz asked.

"I don't know people there any longer." Gabe shook his head. "Only me and another member of my squad survived —and he quit when I did. The admin sure won't talk with me—not after what I called them."

"Hawk texted at Christmas," Caz said. "Just that he was all right and would be out of touch for a while."

"He didn't answer when we texted back," Bull added.

"Probably a burner phone." Hawk'd probably stomped the phone after sending his text. "Give him longer."

Gabe strummed his guitar in the introduction to a Spanish song Caz'd made them learn on his last visit home —"Despacito."

When Caz took the lead singing, setting the beat with his drum, Gabe dropped to backup, with Bull joining in on the refrain and fancy guitar fingering.

As they finished, Caz started laughing.

"What?" Bull asked.

"Ah, I was with a woman in Colombia and singing this to her. She...ah...didn't like some of the lyrics." Caz grinned.

Gabe spoke Spanish, too. The song was pretty explicit.

Bull laughed. "Knowing you, she forgave all."

Caz only smiled and said nothing else.

The sarge hadn't been an officer—he worked for a living

—yet he'd been a gentleman to the core. A man protected women, which included silence about intimate matters. Mako had taught them all his morals...and walloped them when they didn't learn fast enough.

Caz openly enjoyed women, many women, but each woman was treated with respect and honesty—and never discussed afterward.

Setting his drum to one side, Caz asked, "So, *viejo*, how is your patrol officer? Baumer, right?"

"Earl Baumer. He's experienced. Polite enough. I want to actually see how he does when he doesn't know I'm around." Gabe tasted the lingering bitterness left from when he'd worked in LA and observed an officer taking a bribe.

If and when Gabe headed back to the wilderness, Baumer would be first in line for the chief position.

Eyes narrowed, Gabe gazed at the mountains. Baumer looked all right on paper. Had experience. Had a good ol' boy disposition that fit well with Alaskans. So why did he evoke an uneasy feeling in Gabe's gut?

Strumming softly, he saw a large rectangular light appear across the lake. Dante's cabins were over there. In fact, that was Julie's cabin. He could make out her silhouette in the doorway as she came outside, and damned if his body didn't tighten in acknowledgement. In desire.

As the door closed and her figure disappeared in the dusk, he missed a chord. In fact, he couldn't even remember what tune they'd been playing.

In the gathering twilight, Bull's grin flashed white. "Guess the naughty lyrics drew her out, hmm?"

Caz snorted. "The other side of the lake is too far away to hear more than faint music."

Good thing, Gabe thought, considering how innocent she was. Although she'd been yielding in his arms. Giving. Responsive.

He wanted to hear her voice again. Hear her laugh. Take her mouth and pull her against him and...

When he looked away from her cabin, his brothers were watching him.

"Pretty little thing, isn't she?" Bull said. "I like her."

Gabe shot him a look that made his brother's big laugh bust out.

"Got it." Bull lifted his arms, palms forward, in a "hands-off" gesture, the way the brothers acknowledged a claimed woman.

Grinning, Caz duplicated the movement despite the fact that Gabe hadn't said anything.

Dammit. With the experience of years of diverting them, Gabe started singing a song they couldn't resist. "O, America!"

And...he had to say, it was nice to be home.

Across the lake, Audrey perched on her picnic table. The walls of the cabin had seemed to be closing in on her, so she'd come out to enjoy the quiet evening.

It was so different here. In Chicago, the city hummed with noise all night. Was never really dark.

In Alaska, sunset came so late the sky never turned completely black. Even so, the stars were still huge and brilliant and so close it felt as if she could reach up and touch.

There was no hum of traffic or people or horns or sirens. The stillness wrapped around her until she could hear each lap of the lake water against the shore. There were singing insects in the shore grasses. The more distant hooting of an owl.

She blinked as another sound whispered across the lake.

Music? That was music. Almost too soft to hear, but beautiful. Men's voices in harmony. Someone had found a pleasant radio station.

Then the music stopped, and she'd heard Bull's big booming laugh.

Wait... The music started again, playing a few seconds and broke off. That wasn't a radio station, but real people. Her boss and some friends. Singing together. Playing real instruments. Guitars and a drum.

Wow. The only people she'd ever heard creating music were people in church or teenagers wanting to start a band.

These guys were just...having fun.

A deep laugh made her nerves jump to attention. That was Gabe.

He was over there, too. Sitting and talking. Occasionally singing with the other two. Just having fun.

She bit her lip against the ache of loneliness, the longing to be over there with people.

No, more than that. To be with Gabe, to be the one making him laugh. To see him smile and have the sound of his low voice washing over her. Maybe to take his hand and...

She rolled her eyes.

You're a fool, Audrey.

CHAPTER TWELVE

One more tie with Chicago had been broken. The movers had emptied Audrey's apartment.

After reading Dennison's email, she'd returned to the cabin and just...sat at the table. A morass of depression sucked at her spirits, and she tried to back away.

It was just an apartment.

It was my *apartment.*

Decorated the way she wanted.

No, don't think that way.

She'd planned to move someday, anyway.

Eventually.

She blew out a breath. It felt as if she had shifting sand under her feet. No home.

Because although she was living here in the cabin, it wasn't hers. The place was a charity loan, plain and simple. Somehow, she needed to make enough to pay Dante rent.

Speaking of making money, she needed to get moving. Her job at the roadhouse started in a few minutes. A Thursday night should be busy. She'd get tips.

As she gathered her keys and coat, she gave herself her orders for the evening. Tonight, she would be outgoing and sociable. She *would*.

While working on the garden this morning, Lillian had given Audrey advice about fitting into a small town. Don't try to be chatty—*like that would ever happen*—but participate in conversations. Express interest. Ask questions. Get involved in the groups and events going on in town.

Audrey sighed. Lillian insisted that dealing with people was as much a skill as playing the piano or hitting a baseball. If an activity didn't come naturally, of course it needed practice. Being sociable might feel as awkward as learning a new sport.

No kidding. *Practice, practice, practice.* She grabbed her keys. *And try not to be late for work.*

Moving quickly, Audrey stepped out of her cabin, locked the door, and—

"Oh *shit*."

A shaggy monstrosity stood beside her car. Munching on a bush.

Whoa, that was a *moose*.

Talk about huge. Its butt and humped shoulders were feet higher than her car roof.

And it had antlers. Not huge ones. Covered with fuzzy velvet. And still frighteningly deadly looking.

She backed up, bumped into her door, squeaked. As it looked over, she hastily unlocked the cabin and dove inside.

When she peeked out again, the beast hadn't even moved. It was eating.

And it kept eating.

"No, no, no. Don't you realize I have to get to work?" She stuck her head out. "Go away."

No reaction.

She raised her voice. "Go away!"

Ears flicked. It looked up, showing a flap waving below its chin.

Still eating.

It reminded her of the perpetually hungry university students. Stepping out on the porch, she yelled at it. "Go away, you stupid thing. Shoo!"

Its ears went back.

Oh, good, she was getting somewhere. It'd heard her. Now it would move.

Head down, it stared at her, licking its lips.

Eff-it-all, this was ridiculous. It was just a big deer, right? Stepping out onto the two-step landing, she jumped up and down, waving her arms, and yelling, "Get out of here."

The hair on its back went up, and it charged. Right at her!

She jumped back inside so fast, she tripped and landed on her butt. Frantically, she kicked the door shut. "Oh God, oh God, oh God."

The moose hit the doorframe so hard the entire cabin shook, and she heard a cracking sound.

She screamed then clapped her hands over her mouth. Don't make it *angrier*. Her heart pounded like crazy. What if it knocked the door in?

Get away from the door! She scrambled to her feet and moved to the center of the room, dancing on tiptoes so she could run.

Run *where*?

Nothing hit the door again. Was it still there? Had it left?

She rushed over to the small window that faced the road.

Gripping the windowsill, she stared. Her hands shook as she watched the moose move away from her cabin.

Her knees buckled, and she dropped to the floor. Cold sweat dampened her shoulders, and she was panting like a bellows.

Oh God, that had been *horrible*.

Belatedly, she remembered Gabe had said something about half-a-ton of irritable. *No kidding*.

And people came here to see the wildlife?

They were *insane*.

She watched as the animal reached the next cabin. *Keep going, please*.

Conscious of the minutes passing, she waited and waited. Then, after easing out the front door, she paused. It was near the last cabin in the line.

She darted to her car and jumped in.

Even as she turned the key, the moose swung its big head to look, then took a step toward her.

Oh, God, it would totally win an encounter with her tiny car. She turned the key and stomped on the gas. As her car spat gravel behind her, she glanced in the rearview mirror.

Not accepting the challenge, the moose had resumed its stroll down toward the lake.

Her fingers were still trembling. She pulled in a breath and glared at it in the rear view mirror. "You big bastard." Her voice came out hoarse.

A few minutes later, she walked into Bull's, saw how packed it was, and almost cried in relief. She'd never realized how wonderful a crowd of people could be.

Both Bull and the new bartender were behind the bar. An old Gordon Lightfoot song was playing. The slow ballad smoothed her jangled nerves, and she pulled her shoulders back. Okay, she could do this.

After locking up her purse and donning an apron, she swung by the bar to let her boss know she'd arrived.

Mixing drinks, Bull bantered with a half-dozen people. Not wanting to interrupt, she stood at the cocktail waitress section and leaned in so he could see her.

After a glance at the clock behind him, his brows drew together, and he didn't look easy-going at all.

Her voice came out higher than normal. "I'm sorry I'm late. I... There was a moose."

A big man seated at the bar turned to look at her. *Gabe.* As she met his intent gaze, her pulse performed a weird skipping beat for several disconcerting seconds.

"Are you okay, Julie?" he asked in his smoky voice.

"Of course she is, darling." The brunette beside him patted his hand. "Outsiders frighten easily. The moose was probably a mile away."

Audrey stiffened. "He was right beside my car and wouldn't move. When I yelled and waved my arms, he *charged* me."

Now everyone was staring at her.

"Damn, Julie." Bull had turned to look at her.

"You deliberately annoyed a moose?" The woman was stunning with huge doe eyes, wavy brown hair, full lips, and a flawless tan. Tight jeans and a clinging royal blue top showcased her slim figure.

When she cuddled up to Gabe, Audrey wanted to slap her.

Gabe's gaze ran over Audrey. "Are you all right, Goldilocks?"

I could have died. Her heart was still racing. "Fine. Just fine."

"I'm surprised the moose didn't stomp her." The woman sounded regretful it hadn't. "Considering how dangerous our wildlife is, Outsiders should be evaluated for common sense before being allowed into Alaska. Of course, we might lose ninety percent of the tourist trade that way."

Everyone around the bar laughed.

Audrey turned away. The woman had implied Audrey was an ignorant idiot.

Right now, Audrey felt like an idiot—as well as clumsy and ugly.

"Oh, my. You're all red." The woman gave Audrey a sugary smile. "Don't be that way. I was just joking with you."

"Brooke." Gabe growled in obvious disapproval.

Brooke tossed back her long hair in a flirtatiously feminine move. "Don't worry. *Julie.* The moose is undoubtedly gone by now."

Aaand there was no good response to that—not one that wouldn't be horribly rude. Cocktail waitresses weren't supposed to be rude. So she channeled Lillian's English upper-crust manners.

"Thank you so much for your concern, Brooke. It's quite heartwarming." The smile Audrey offered was equally saccharine.

Brooke's blink of surprise was satisfying, but the woman hadn't released Gabe's arm.

She heard Bull say something, heard Gabe say her name, but she picked up her tray and turned away.

Gabe could have the woman.

Not my problem, not my concern. Trying with all her might not to care, Audrey headed off to take orders.

At least the surge of anger had wiped out the quaking feeling in the pit of her stomach.

An hour later, she felt the tired ache in her leg muscles as she waited for Bull to fill her orders. Still out of shape, but she was doing better than her first nights here. Walking to the grocery store and coffee shop was making a difference.

Her lips quirked at the thought. Honestly, moving to Alaska was an awfully extreme way to get some exercise. She could have just joined a gym.

Well, except for having a hitman after her.

"You all right, champ?" Bull asked, studying her.

"I'm fine, thank you." She smiled at him. "I won't be yelling at any more big animals, trust me."

"Good to hear."

The tray of drinks went to a table of three women—massage therapists—who worked at McNally's Ski Resort. Audrey held up the first one. "Here's a Long Island Iced Tea."

"That's mine," the sturdy redhead said unnecessarily. Her gaze went past Audrey, and she nudged the blonde on her left. "Isn't that Brooke at the table by the door?"

The blonde turned and nodded. "That's her. I see she's already found herself a hottie."

The redhead snorted. "Of course she has."

Taking the last drink, the third woman asked, "I've seen her around, I think. Who is she?"

"Resort public relations." The first woman shook her head. "She pretty much ignores us. For her, it's all about the men."

Audrey picked up the empties, swiped over a damp area,

and headed for the next table. Her mood soured as she realized the "hottie" beside Brooke was Gabe.

Even worse, they were in her section.

After tending to two other tables, she ran out of reasons to stall.

Sitting with Gabe and Brooke was a dark-haired Hispanic-looking man. He smiled at Audrey as she walked up.

"Are you folks ready for another round?" Audrey asked.

Brooke gave her a cool smile. "Lovely, a waitress at last. I'd like a mojito."

"All right." Audrey nodded toward the Hispanic man. "And you, sir?"

"It's Caz, and you're Julie, I hear." The calm Spanish-accented voice was like warm velvet. "I've heard so much about you. It's good to finally meet you."

She froze, feeling her heart stutter in her chest. People were talking about her? Would that draw attention? Get back to Spyros?

When Gabe's eyes narrowed speculatively, she forced herself to pull in slow breaths. *No panicking.* Tilting her head toward Caz, she said, "It's good to meet you, too. Can I get you a drink?"

"I think Bull's Moose Brewery has a seasonal spring beer. I'd like that, please." He grinned at Gabe. "And bring Bull's Off-the-Road stout for the *viejo* here."

Viejo meant old man in Spanish. "He's not old."

Gabe's low chuckle sent happy chills up her spine. Oh, he really should laugh more.

Brooke leaned into Gabe and her suggestive whisper was far too audible. "You aren't old at all...and you can prove it to me later."

Audrey moved swiftly back to the bar because if Gabe kissed that obnoxious woman, she didn't want to see it.

And she didn't want that knot of unhappiness in her stomach. The one that grew every time Brooke touched him.

Gabe considered cuffing Brooke to her chair. Not for fun and games, but simply to get her the fuck off of him.

When he'd arrived at the bar, he'd been surprised to see her. It'd been years since he'd dated her in Anchorage, and he'd no idea she had a job at the resort.

She hadn't changed any. Still flirted with anything with a dick.

He'd discovered early in their relationship that she had all the fidelity of a cat in heat and had planned to break up with her even before she'd latched onto Bull. Then, still dating Bull, she'd tried for Caz.

Just as well that Mako had a talk with them when they'd first discovered women. The sarge had explained the mess that could arise if a woman was allowed to come between teammates. So, in their teens, they'd come up with their own rules.

If not for their bro code, Brooke could have caused serious problems. She was the kind of a person who thrived on causing havoc. And in putting down other women.

Now, he was regretting being friendly to her when he'd come in tonight. She was a beautiful woman, but Gabe had never been into playing games. Not then, not now.

With a flirtatious bat of her eyelashes, she pressed against him.

"Brooke," he warned.

She leaned into him even more, shoving her breast against his arm.

"If you rub on me one more time, I'm going to assume you're itching. Bull probably has flea spray."

She jerked back. Her face went red, then cold. "That was rude."

"So is rubbing your tits on someone." He lifted a hand to Caz—the poor bastard could deal with the fallout—and walked away.

In the middle of the room, he saw Julie picking up their drinks from the bar.

She'd been damn shaken when she came in tonight. Scared. And he was wondering what else scared her. She was lying about her name, her past, probably about everything. Was he judging her too harshly for those lies?

Turning, he headed for her and picked his beer off her tray. "Thanks."

"Oh, of course." She glanced at the table and blinked.

Following her gaze, Gabe saw Brooke was flirting with

Caz now. Good enough. Caz was more than equal to extracting himself and would undoubtedly do it with charm.

Gabe turned his attention back to Julie. "Brooke was right."

Julie's back went straight...and Gabe remembered all the other insulting statements Brooke had made. Hell, at the rate he was going, he'd soon have every female in the road-house aiming for his balls. "About the wildlife, I mean. You need lessons."

"I'll do some reading about—"

"I work tomorrow, you work Saturday. Let's make it Sunday morning. I'll pick you up in the morning at nine. Wear shoes you can walk in." He tucked a strand of hair behind her ear, enjoying the sweet curve of her cheek. "In the meantime, park closer to your door and avoid that moose. Call the station if you need help."

He left before she could argue...because as smart as she was, she'd undoubtedly win.

CHAPTER THIRTEEN

God grant me the serenity to accept the things I cannot shoot, the courage to shoot the things I can, and the wisdom to hide their bodies.

~ Unknown

Well, that didn't take long. The next afternoon at the station, Gabe leaned back and watched a video play out on his computer. Words appeared on a building.

"OUTSIDER GO HOME"

He, Bull, and Caz had positioned one of the security cameras outside an old Victorian-style house that a married couple had purchased for a B&B. Built by a millionaire in the 70s, the house was a broken-down beauty with ornate trim, towers and turrets, wrap-around porch, and a bay window.

On the camera, a short man with no neck was wielding a can of spray paint. Finishing the "OUTSIDER GO HOME" lettering, he exchanged fist bumps with his comrade in crime—a tall man with a distinctive drooping mustache.

Knox and Chevy, the handymen he'd met at Lillian's house.

Gabe scrubbed his hands over his face. Man, this was going to be a mess.

From the lobby, Regina's voice came through the open station door. "Earl, you're right on time."

"Hey, Regina. I heard you're our new receptionist. That's great if you're ready to get bored. The police station doesn't get much action."

She laughed. "I'll stay busy enough, since I'm covering the municipal offices and the health clinic, as well."

"Whoa." After a second, Baumer added, "That's pretty smart."

"I thought so. Before you ask, the chief is in his office."

"Thanks."

A second later, Baumer strolled through the open office door. Gabe gave him a sweeping glance. Clean uniform shirt, jeans, and boots. Duty belt on. Good.

"Afternoon, boss. How's the week gone?"

"Not too well, but it might get better." Gabe turned the monitor so the officer could see it.

"What the freaking eff? Hey, that's a camera feed. Was someone filming them?"

"Me. I put up security cameras."

"Yeah?" Baumer's face clouded over. "Just when were you planning to tell me we had cameras, *boss*?"

The anger seemed excessive, considering Baumer hadn't been on duty all week. Still, if positions were reversed, Gabe might've resented being left out of the loop. "I was planning to tell you at our first Friday meeting...which started a minute ago."

Baumer stood still for a moment, then sighed. "Yeah, sorry. I'm not good with surprises."

"You might have chosen the wrong career." Moving on, Gabe tapped the screen. "What do you know about these two men?" Considering the size of the town, Baumer would know most of the inhabitants after living here a year.

"Chevy and Knox? They share a few acres off the grid. Each has a cabin. Winters, the guys work up in Prudhoe Bay to bring in cash. Chevy has a wife and a couple of youngsters. Knox's woman left him a few months ago."

"Any idea where we'll find them today?"

Baumer glanced at the window looking out onto Main Street. "Actually, I saw them going into Dante's a few minutes ago."

"They probably wanted to see the reaction to their vandalism."

Baumer shrugged. "All they'll see is a pissed-off owner. No one else cares. Even a judge would only slap their hands."

"For the paint, true. They also busted the windows."

And the Victorian had a lot of windows. "I figure that'll cost over five hundred dollars to fix and elevates this to Class C criminal mischief."

"That's...that's a felony."

"Yep." Gabe motioned to the screen. "Notice they're not wearing gloves."

"Shit." Baumer frowned. "You got them on tape already. You don't need their fingerprints."

"Not for this crime, no. However, our perps never pick up after themselves, so I've got the spray paint used on other vandalized sites. And the ax used to destroy construction supplies at Bull's bar. Everything has been fingerprinted and logged in as evidence."

Gabe half-grinned. It'd been awhile since he'd processed a crime scene. The LAPD was big enough that fingerprinting was usually done by techs. Here, in Rescue, he and Baumer would do everything.

He rather liked the idea. "I'm afraid these two are in for a world of hurt. Bull's pissed-off."

"No gloves. The dumbasses," Baumer muttered.

"Yep. Let's go get them."

Outside, Gabe headed for the grocery store, followed by the officer.

The two vandals stepped out of Dante's, each carrying a grocery bag. Chatting amiably, Julie and Bull walked out after them.

"Chevy is yours," Gabe told Baumer before raising his voice, "Knox, I'd like to speak with you, please."

Both men froze. When Baumer pulled out his cuffs, the idiots attacked.

Gabe blocked a swing by Chevy and kicked him toward Baumer. The officer was sure slow as molasses at stepping into the fight.

"Fucking cop." Knox threw his groceries at Gabe.

Gabe dodged the hail of cans and raised his arm in expectation of a follow-up punch.

Nothing.

Instead, he saw Knox stagger sideways. Recovering quickly, the man attacked.

After blocking Knox's haymaker, Gabe jabbed his fist into the man's breadbasket, folding him over.

Damn, that felt good.

As Knox straightened, Gabe delivered a sweet uppercut.

Knox staggered back.

Advancing, Gabe kicked the idiot's feet out from under him, followed him down, and snapped on the cuffs.

Baumer had finally jumped in and was struggling with Chevy, so Gabe walked over and delivered a sharp kick to the back of the vandal's knee. The man dropped.

Baumer pulled out his cuffs.

"You're getting slow, *viejo*." Caz was crossing the street from the clinic. "The sarge would have you doing drills all day to speed you up."

Gabe gave him a grin. "Yeah, I was slow. You're right."

"That was *slow*?" someone said in a hoarse voice.

Turning, Gabe saw Baumer and the two vandals were staring at him.

Gabe frowned. In Iraq, after he'd killed a knife-wielding insurgent, his team had worn similar expressions. Because he'd taken a gut-wound and hadn't noticed.

He looked down at himself. No blood. No knives. "What's with the stares?"

Caz laughed. "Those two have been calling you a pussy city-cop Outsider."

"Well, that's just rude." Gabe yanked Knox to his feet. "It is true that I was a city cop, though."

The rest, not so much. But he rarely spoke about his past. Terrified the law would return them to foster care, Mako's boys learned to stay silent about where they lived. That wariness became entrenched. Being a SEAL—not gonna share. And he sure wasn't about to discuss working as a merc.

"Hey, Chief." Leaning against the grocery store wall, Bull had a grip on Julie's upper arm.

At the sight of her wide eyes, a pang of guilt shot through Gabe. While he'd been enjoying himself, she'd been terrified at the violence. Not surprising considering her recent past.

He should have tried harder to avoid the fight.

Then he blinked. Damned if she wasn't holding a bottle of apple cider by the neck. Like a weapon. And Bull's grip on her was one of restraint, not support. The realization she'd wanted to help him warmed his heart. "You were going to whack Knox for me?"

Bull snorted. "She *did* whack Knox for you. I'm surprised the bottle didn't break."

Ah, that was why Knox had staggered.

"He...he could have killed you. Are you crazy?" She sputtered for a second. "You were smiling. When you hit him, you *smiled*."

"Yeah, well, there's no law that says law enforcement can't derive a smidgeon of pleasure from a good fight."

She sputtered some more. Fuck, she was cute. "Thank you, Goldilocks. I appreciate the help."

Eyes on Gabe, Knox wore a perplexed expression.

Gabe couldn't help laughing. "What? Pussy city-cops can't have fun on the streets?"

"Sure doesn't act like a city boy," Chevy grumbled.

Gabe glanced at Bull. "As long as you're here, do you have the damage totals for me?"

"Yep." Bull pulled a paper from his pocket and handed it over. "All itemized and everything."

"Thanks." Gabe turned the paper so Chevy and Knox could see the sum at the bottom. "This is the dollar amount of damage done to the roadhouse during the remodeling."

Although Knox just shrugged, Chevy went whiter than the snow on the Chugach Mountains.

"The other businesses are digging up the figures for me, as well," Gabe said.

"Hey, Chief. Are you transporting them for AST lockup

or am I?" Baumer had Chevy by one arm.

"First, let's take our guests into the bullpen for a chat."

Audrey stared after Gabe and the other officer as they led the two handcuffed men across the street to the police station. The chief was limping slightly.

In front of the building, the new receptionist crossed her arms over her chest. Her voice carried clearly. "As a mother, I can only say, your mamas would be ashamed of you."

The two men flinched.

In the coffee shop doorway, Sarah gave a snorty laugh. "Here I thought it was the tourists that would provide the entertainment today."

As Sarah returned to her counter, Audrey shook her head. "I'm not sure I consider that entertainment." No matter what the big police chief thought.

"Oh, it was." Bull chuckled.

She frowned at his hand on her arm. "You can let go of me now."

"Sorry, champ. I couldn't let you charge into that fight; you might've gotten hurt," he rumbled.

Anger simmered as she looked at the huge man beside her. "*Gabe* might have gotten hurt. You didn't even help."

"If he'd been up against a half dozen, I'd have stepped in. But just a couple of rednecks against the old man? No contest."

"Old man. Why do you call him that?" Caz called him *viejo*. Old man. "He's not old."

"He's older than me. That's all that counts." Bull's grin was white against his light brown skin and dark goatee. "It's also a nickname for a commanding officer. When he refused to choose a call sign, we had to give him one."

"Because he bosses you around?" Gabe did, she'd noticed. Wherever the chief was, he'd probably end up the one in charge.

"Because when he leads, people follow." Bull's gaze was on the municipal building, and his mouth turned up into a satisfied smile. "Even when he doesn't want them to."

Oh.

Bull glanced at the bottle Audrey was holding. "Hang on to that. I'll tell Dante to put it on my tab."

"But—"

"Keep it as a souvenir of the day you returned to the fight."

As he disappeared back into Dante's, she looked down at the bottle, weighing the heft of it. In spite of Spyros and her fear, she'd acted.

To save Gabe.

Feeling powerful, she tucked the bottle under her arm. Tonight, she'd pour herself a glass of cider...because she deserved it.

Two subdued vandals sat side-by-side in the main room of the station. Seeing the camera footage and being finger-printed had silenced Knox and Chevy's bluster.

As if distancing himself, Baumer sat at his desk across the room.

Leaning a hip against the center table, Gabe crossed his arms over his chest. "What with the evidence we have, a prosecutor would go for a third-degree criminal mischief charge. That's a felony offense."

His words fell into the silent room, and as the two shrank, Gabe...paused.

He'd been damn pissed at their deliberate destruction of what people were trying to build. Barbarians versus civilization.

Only...these two had chosen a dying town and to live in the bush, obviously to escape civilization. Now, an influx of people was ruining their primitive sanctuary. They wanted their world to stay the same. The men were scared and cornered and, like animals, had fought back.

Unfortunately, no one could prevent change, no matter how much he spray-painted and destroyed.

"All right, here's how I see it. I can give you over to be prosecuted. You'd probably end up in prison, a tax drain on our law-abiding populace. Or you can visit each business you screwed with, tell the owners what you did, and work off the damage...within a month's time. In addition, I want your word you'll stop this shit."

When Baumer started to speak, Gabe shot him a warning look. The officer settled back in his chair.

Knox stared at Gabe. "You'd let us go? After fighting with you?"

"That fight was the best five minutes I've had since I started this job. Yeah, I'm taking a chance here, but neither of you would do well in prison." It would feel too much like he'd be locking up the sarge. Mako's PTSD would've gone through the roof if he'd been put behind bars.

Under Knox's long mustache, a muscle twitched.

Chevy opened and closed his hands repeatedly. He had kids. A wife.

No matter their hatred for Gabe, the new businesses, and the tourists, neither man wanted to go to jail.

"I'm serious about you paying for the damages." Gabe shook his head. "My oath is to the citizens here—to protect them. If they don't feel they've been recompensed, we'll have a problem."

Knox's gaze met his. He was openly furious at being caught, furious at being trapped, furious at being indebted to Gabe, let alone the businesses that were destroying his world. "I'll do my part."

Chevy looked like a badger with its paw caught in a trap. "Same."

Their voices, their body language, their eyes held no lies. Good enough.

"I'll hold you to that." Gabe pulled out his handcuff key. "Let me get those off so you can get started."

CHAPTER FOURTEEN

On Sunday morning, Audrey scowled at the loud staccato rap on her door. Gabe had said 9 a.m., and he was annoyingly on time.

And if she complained, he'd probably tell her the sun had risen hours ago. It had. *This crazy state.* Last night, the sun had still been up at 11 p.m., and who could go to bed before sunset?

But tired or not, she couldn't sleep late this morning. Just not possible. Because Gabe was gorgeous and terrifying, and just seeing him, let alone hearing him, made her go weak in the knees.

And because she'd been to bed with him. That so wasn't who she was. She wasn't a woman who did one-night-stands with police chiefs. That would be someone like Brooke.

Audrey was a nerd—a brilliant one, true, but...a nerd. Socially inept, somewhat clumsy...sheesh, look how well her moose encounter had gone. That was who she was. Being with Gabe today would undoubtedly leave her feeling as stomped as if she'd tried to pet that moose.

However, if he wanted to teach her about Alaska, she should take advantage of it.

Putting her shoulders back, she pulled open the door. Bright morning light streamed into the cabin, blinding her. Then something blocked the light—a body. Squinting, still half-blinded, she realized she was staring at Gabe.

His faded red flannel shirt was open enough she saw the edge of his collarbones above the thick muscles of his chest. The base of his corded neck had a tantalizing hollow.

Oh, wow. Swallowing hard, she stepped back and looked up.

Well, hmm. He'd demanded this appointment, but he wasn't bursting with enthusiasm, was he? His carved face held no expression. His dark blue eyes were unreadable.

She glanced past him. No moose. Didn't that figure?

Noticing her frowning at the cars, he shook his head. "I checked. We are moose-free at the moment."

"Okay."

His gaze took her in. He nodded approval of her lightweight boots, one of the first things she'd purchased in Alaska.

Her jeans got a frown.

"What's wrong with my jeans?"

"You've lost weight. More weight."

Men. A girl just couldn't win. She'd thought her hips

looked better. "I'm not sick—I'm just not used to such an active job."

"Ah." His keen gaze lifted to stab her in the eyes. "What did you do before?"

"I did a lot of sitting." She smiled. He already knew she was lying about her name. Why give him more ammunition?

A crease appeared in his lean cheek. "You're a frus-trating wench." His scrutiny resumed. "The T-shirt and hoodie work. Do you have a waterproof jacket?"

"Waterproof?" She frowned at the blue sky.

"Weather on the Peninsula changes quickly. Stuff a jacket in your daypack."

"My what?"

He nudged her inside. "I've seen you carrying a small pack. Get that."

But she'd put her wallet and keys in her jeans so she wouldn't have to carry anything. *Aaand* she could see from his face that arguing wasn't the right response. "Right."

She'd bought the lightweight backpack to carry her laptop when she walked to town. After emptying it, she stuffed her waterproof jacket inside.

Returning from his Jeep, Gabe gave her a plastic grocery bag with several items inside. "Add that in. From now on, you wear your daypack anytime you go hiking."

She added the plastic bag to the backpack. "What's in there?"

"Bunch of stuff. Bug juice—repellent. A bottle of water

and a filter. Couple of granola bars. Sunscreen. Matches and greasy cotton balls. A multi-tool." He thought for a second. "First aid kit. Space blanket, hand warmers, socks. Compass, flashlight, and whistle."

She stared at him. "Do you have this stuff sitting around?"

"It's extras I had lying around. I figured you wouldn't have much, and you need these to stay safe."

Stay safe. She dropped her gaze, and her eyes prickled with tears. He was such a protector.

"Come, Goldilocks. Let's get going." He took her hand and pulled her to her feet. When he looked down at her, his gaze softened for a second.

And her insides melted.

Later that day, Audrey lay on a riverbank beside Gabe. As the sun soaked into her shoulders, her calves ached and burned. Hiking up and down trails was far different from walking around in a bar.

And, boy, Gabe had walked her. And talked.

In fact, her brain felt overstuffed with information. Moose precautions. Scaring off black bears as opposed to protecting vulnerable body parts from brown bears that didn't scare. And she'd seen a brown bear that would be called a *grizzly* if it'd lived inland. Talk about scary.

He pointed out the nasty cow parsnip plant that'd burn

a person who blundered into it. And countered that with amazing views of the Kenai Mountains. The river was lovely, too—an impossible blue-green color.

She could now recognize alder. "*Good for smoking salmon.*" And spruce trees—and the spruce grouse. A ptarmigan had burst out, almost from under her feet, and she'd landed on her butt.

Then a woodpecker loudly hammering a tree above her had startled her into a squeak that made Gabe laugh.

She'd never realized woodpeckers were so big.

Speaking of big, nothing compared to the size of the bald eagle that'd landed on the riverbank to tear apart a fish. Its head would be level with her waist.

Beside her, Gabe sat with his back against a tree, playing with a strand of her hair. Why did she like that so much?

"Now that you've lived here awhile, are you enjoying Alaska?" he asked.

How in the world could she answer that? "It's not what I expected," she said finally. "It's—"

A rustling sound from behind them made her stiffen. "*Bear.*" She grabbed Gabe's hand, ready to run.

"Not a bear, a bull," he said. "Listen. The *thud-thud* indicates a two-legged animal. A human."

Seriously? Her hearing didn't work like that. "Then—"

"It's Bull," he said. "Not many people are as heavy, and he has a slight hitch in his stride."

She stared at him. She could barely hear the footsteps, and he could tell who it was?

Bull stepped out of the thick forest on the path that led to the road. Despite the chill, he only wore a T-shirt covered by a flannel shirt. Like Gabe, he had a daypack. "Hey, you two."

With a breath of relief, Audrey settled cross-legged on the blanket. "How'd you know we were here?"

"Gabe left word where he planned to take you, and I saw the Jeep beside the road."

"Oh."

"Always leave word where you'll be hiking." Gabe's smile flickered. "You know, so someone can rescue you...or retrieve the body."

Men had such a warped sense of humor. "That's not funny."

"Just the truth." Bull smiled at her. "But rescues aside, sometimes you get good stuff when people know where you are. You know, like bribes."

"Yeah?" Gabe raised an eyebrow.

"Yeah." Her boss set down his pack, pulled out a bottle of beer, and passed it to Gabe before winking at Audrey. "Want one?"

How could she resist? "A beer would be lovely, thank you."

He handed over a bottle, took one for himself, and leaned against a tree. "By the way, Chief, your two graffiti artists showed up at the roadhouse and are working their asses off. You're not their favorite person right now— neither am I—but they *are* trying. Reminds me of when

Mako made us rebuild the meat cache after we'd misjudged felling that tree."

With a smile at Audrey, he added, "When we were cutting down a dead spruce, the trunk caught on another tree—something we should have predicted. The spruce came down and smashed the platform where we stored meat in the winter."

"Those were good days." Gabe chuckled.

Wait a minute here. Audrey gave Bull, then Gabe, a long stare. "You said, '*Mako made us*'. Does that mean you two grew up together?"

"I guess I never told you, did I?" Gabe patted her knee. "Yes, Bull's my brother. Caz too. The scrawny Hispanic you met at the roadhouse the other night."

He meant the devastatingly gorgeous, leanly muscled Hispanic? Then again, Caz and Bull called Gabe *old man*. Brothers were weird. "Does anyone in town know you men are siblings?"

"Only a few." Bull flashed his signature grin. "The sarge only had a couple of friends in Rescue—and when we visited him, we weren't into being sociable. I was building a business in Anchorage, and Caz was in grad school and being a nurse practitioner. Gabe was in LA, then South America. And Hawk—hell, like always, he was off getting shot at."

"I see." She took a long gulp of beer. Dante and Lillian knew about the guys being brothers, and maybe Sarah, too, since the coffee shop owner seemed to know everything about everyone.

But sheesh, these guys took private to a whole new level.

Gabe took a drink of beer and then waggled the bottle. "Why don't you tell me what the bribe is for?"

"I'm supposed to remind you about the town council meeting this evening. As chief of police, you're expected to be there."

"It's good to have expectations," Gabe said mildly.

"Listen, old man..."

Why did Bull sound so worried? "He'll be there," Audrey told Bull.

Gabe lifted an eyebrow. "Will I?"

"Well, yes, of course. It's your job, your duty, and I know you take that seriously, even when it makes you unhappy."

Bull's grin was wide. "You have a good read on him, woman. Looks like I'll see you both tonight."

"Me?" Her mouth dropped open. "I don't need to—"

"If I have to go, so do you." Gabe gave her a really mean look.

Uh-oh. She'd really over-reached her bounds. "Oh my, it's getting late, and I should get cleaned up. If you're leaving now, Bull, how about I catch a ride with you?"

As she started to rise, Gabe gripped her hand and drew her back to the blanket. "I don't think we're finished here, Goldilocks."

"But..."

Gabe waved his brother along. "See you later, Bull."

Bull's booming laugh sounded before he disappeared into the forest.

Audrey frowned at Gabe. "I thought you said we were finished hiking."

"We are. There might be a couple of other things to finish up." He ran a finger over her lower lip.

Tingles spread from his light touch in a wave over her skin.

"Other things." Her voice came out husky.

"I could be wrong." He bent. His mouth brushed against hers. Tantalizing. Tempting.

Oh, the way he kissed... Needing more, she leaned into him. Gripping his shirt, she resisted when he started to straighten.

He huffed a laugh. "Or not."

"Yep." His mouth settled on hers again, firmer, claiming a response.

Her mouth opened under his. And as everything inside her melted, he pressed her back onto the blanket. His weight came down on her, his hand behind her head.

Unable to help herself, she put her arms around his shoulders. His lips turned upward against hers as he smiled.

"You planned this, didn't you?" she whispered.

"This, no. I did want to talk with you." Fingers tangling in her hair, he tugged her head sideways and nibbled a place under her ear. "But this is good, too."

Goosebumps coursed over her skin.

"I really should torture you some," he murmured, "for pushing me into that damned council meeting."

"But you're good with people. At least they don't scare you."

He lifted his head, his eyes the blue of the twilight sky. "People scare you?"

"A little." She bit her lip. "A lot. I prefer to find my friends in books. The characters there don't expect me to say anything."

"So it's not really people, it's conversing?"

She nodded. "I'm not a...sociable...person."

His teeth closed on the muscle at the top of her shoulder, leaving a heady sting. Her breasts felt fuller, tighter.

"You seem sociable enough to me." He nipped her jaw. "Hell, you work in a bar."

"That's different. When I'm working, I know what to say. There isn't any time for inane chitchat."

His head lifted as he considered. "That makes sense."

She sighed. "I promised myself I'd try to be more of a...a joiner. Lillian says it takes practice."

Gabe propped himself on his elbow beside her and idly played with a strand of her hair. "Practice will help. After spending winter in an isolated cabin, coming to town was difficult. Too many people." A corner of his mouth turned up. "But it got easier. I don't growl quite as much now."

She laughed because she'd heard him snarl a time or two. "I knew you'd been out of touch for a while. But...all by yourself?" Both Bull and Dante had acted as if they hadn't been sure he'd come to Rescue. "Why an isolated cabin?"

The creases beside his eyes deepened with his smile. "Did you realize that when you're curious, you're not shy at all?"

"Uh, maybe." No, she hadn't, actually. "Asking me a question won't let you escape an answer."

"Stubborn, too," he muttered. The laughter faded from his eyes to be replaced by...grief? "It's an ugly story, Goldilocks."

His hand had closed around her hair. Laying her hand on top of his, she waited.

His gaze lifted, focusing on the flowing river. "I ran a crew of security contractors for a private military company. When Hawk and I joined, it was a decent place to work, but the ownership changed, and the missions changed. On my last job, we provided security for a CEO inspecting his factories in a third world country."

Audrey frowned. Factories in third world countries weren't always good places.

"At the fourth factory, we were ambushed. By the factory workers and the villagers, too." His mouth tightened. "I lost three men in the first few seconds. The last two of us were shot up, but we got the CEO out alive— along with a villager. I needed to know who'd ordered the killing."

"Did the CEO have a rival or something?"

"No." His grip tightened on her hair. "As we were driving

away, I asked the villager why they'd attacked us. Turns out the CEO had a habit of helping himself to any pretty woman working in the factories, especially the young ones. The month before, he'd raped the headman's twin daughters."

Oh, God. Gabe was a protector down to his bones. "What did you do?"

"The CEO was babbling scared, and he admitted it." Gabe's eyes held a darkness she hadn't seen before. "We turned around, dumped him and the villager outside the factory, and we drove away."

After a pause, he said quietly, "The factory burned down that night; his body was found inside."

Her skin felt cold. Clammy. The world seemed an uglier place than a few minutes ago. And she knew how ugly life could get. Look at her own past. "Did your company say anything?"

"I quit. They hadn't told me that the CEO might require far more than standard protection because I'd have asked why. They knew about his...habit and knew none of us would've taken the job—not even the worst of my men."

His company had betrayed him. "The ambush. That's where some of your scars are from?"

"Hip and shoulder, yeah."

That's why he limped sometimes when he was tired. "Add Mako's death in, and you didn't want to be around people any longer." She closed her eyes, still feeling sick. "I don't blame you."

He was quiet, his gaze on the water. Eventually, he started to play with her hair again.

When she opened her eyes, she saw the shadows had lifted from his face.

"I feel like a wimp," she said. "I've always been nervous around people, but not for any particular reason. Not like yours."

"You're trying, Goldilocks. That counts." He gave her hair a light tug.

"I might venture out, but it doesn't take long before I want to run back to my cabin and away from everyone."

"Yeah, I know the feeling." He shook his head. "But you're right—people don't scare me, and I can get along with them if I want."

She sighed. "I wish I could."

His brows drew together. "I had men like you in my command. Some guys, like Bull, thrive on company. A few at the opposite end needed alone space, or they'd get weirded out."

Alone space. That was it exactly. "I guess that means I shouldn't try to be a joiner."

"Wrong." He nuzzled her cheek. "Solitary isn't healthy for herd animals. But in your case, you'll want to indulge in quiet time, too, or you'll feel like people are crawling inside your skin."

His advice made sense.

He bent down and kissed along her jaw before taking her mouth in a slow, gentle kiss. As he nibbled her lower lip, excitement heated her blood. She realized he'd abandoned her hair and was playing with the buttons on her shirt.

She grabbed his wrist.

He studied her, his gaze watchful. Controlled. "We can stop at this point if you want."

She didn't want to stop—and he knew it. Her whole body hummed with desire. But she didn't release her hold. They were *outside*, for heaven's sake. "What in the world are you thinking?"

He pulled free only to cup her chin, forcing her to meet his intent gaze. "I was thinking I'd like to strip you bare— right here—and take you, hard and fast and very, very thoroughly."

Oh, the thought of him touching her, being inside her, made her heart kick up and stomp the insides of her ribcage. "B-b-but, here? Now?"

"Ah, having sex is fine, but being outside is what's throwing you?"

She nodded.

He undid one button. Another.

"No one can see us, sweetheart." He moved his hand down between her opened buttons and ran his knuckles over the tops of her breasts. "This is a yes or no question. Yes to continue or no to stop."

The word slipped out. "Yes."

She was rewarded with a devastating kiss. Slow and sensual, tongue and lips, nibbling and sucking. Then he kissed down her throat, between her breasts. Without a pause, he undid the front catch of her bra so he could fondle her breasts.

Oh, the feeling of his callused hand on her breast was amazing. Lust pooled low in her belly.

Slowly, his gaze on her face, he rolled her nipples between his fingers, pressing until the sensation was all she felt, the carnal pain sending her somewhere else.

His lips grazed over her stomach, then he was unzipping her jeans and pulling everything down to her calves.

She felt a second of worry. "What if something comes— a bear or..."

"We'll hear it. And I won't take your pants all the way off, Julie. I just want them out of my way."

"Is that possible?"

"Yep." Holding her gaze with his, he unbuckled his belt and unbuttoned his fly. His cock was fully erect, a bead of liquid at the head. He pulled a condom from his wallet and sheathed himself.

"Over you go." He turned her over and positioned her on hands and knees.

Hungry shivers sprang to life as her shirt and bra gaped open, leaving her breasts dangling. On the blanket, her knees sank into the spongy ground.

And he was behind her, his knees straddling her calves, his erection pressing against her pussy.

"Already wet and ready for me." Satisfaction was in his masculine rumble. His fingers ran over her, spreading the moisture, and pushing between her legs to tease her clit. He thrust, slowly, firmly, not stopping until he was completely inside her.

Her pulse went erratic. Her nipples contracted into tiny, tight, aching buds.

"Damn, you feel good." But he didn't move.

Why didn't he move? Fine, she'd move. She wiggled slightly, then rocked forward.

He started to slide out until, with a low chuckle, he gripped her hips and held her in place. "Hold still, Goldie."

"But..."

Pressing in again, he leaned over her, one hand closing on her breast, the other moving between her legs—and finding her clit.

"Oooh."

His laugh was a low rumble in her ear. "Let's take care of you first, sweetheart."

Slowly, he moved his slickened finger up one side and down the other, rubbing firmly, never too long in one place.

His shaft was thick within her, and unmoving as he played her, teased her. He pinched a nipple gently—and did the same to her clit until electricity sizzled between the two sensitive sites.

Involuntarily, her hips wiggled, trying to get him to thrust, but his cock remained unmoving, even as she throbbed around him.

His finger never stopped, circling, tapping, rubbing, teasing. Driving her right to the edge of climax. The pressure inside grew, desire an insistent pulse between her legs. Her hands clenched on the blanket.

"Gaaabe..."

He squeezed her breast, making her gasp—and clench down around him.

Finally, he moved. Sliding out, pressing in once gently. Then he set up a driving rhythm, one that jolted her hips. Every thrust rubbed her clit against the fingers still between her legs, and each time, he rubbed the side firmly before his cock withdrew.

Need gripped her with demanding claws, tightening all her muscles, and each ruthless slide inside her became unbearable and *wonderful*. Each light touch, each deep penetration increased her urgency, until she was trembling and poised on the brink of coming.

With a low laugh, he thrust harder and moved his finger to the very top of her clit.

Pleasure flooded her senses, wave after dizzying wave pouring through her body, fueled by the unrelenting pounding of his shaft.

His hands closed on her hips, and he pulled her back to penetrate her more fully. His low rumbling groan sounded as he came.

Her breathing was still fast, her heart pounding as she tried to recover.

His thickly muscled chest was warm against her back, and she could feel the thump of his heart. He rubbed his cheek against her hair. "See, no bears. They probably heard your screams and ran."

She froze. "I...screamed?" She hadn't. No, she'd have... "You're teasing me."

His masculine chuckle sent tingles along her skin. "Mmmhmm. I'll have to work on you some before I get a good scream out of you."

Work on her? More than he had? When her pussy clenched around him, he laughed, and slowly pulled out.

As she rolled onto her side, too drained to move, he dealt with the condom and buttoned his jeans.

And, to her delight, he lay down and pulled her on top of him. Her jeans were still around her knees, but somehow it didn't matter. Not when his arms were around her. She rubbed her cheek against his shirt and rested her head against his shoulder.

"Mmm." He stroked her hair. "I hadn't planned for our hike to end this way, but I can't say that I'm unhappy about it."

Unhappiness was the farthest thing from her mind.

However, she did remember they'd both said one time only. That one night and no more.

She didn't care. The sweet contentment of being held, of hearing the slow thump of his heart under her cheek, of inhaling his clean scent washed away any second thoughts.

His hand stopped moving, and she felt his head tilt.

"Time's up, I guess." Gently, he rolled her off, rose to his feet, and pulled her up, too. "Better dress, sweetheart. Someone is on the path."

"What?" Eff-it-all.

Laughing, Gabe dropped to one knee so he could tug up and zip her jeans.

Hastily, she fastened her bra and buttoned her shirt. She could hear people on the path now.

By the time the two men emerged from the forest, she was decently clothed. And felt as if her flushed face probably broadcast, *"We just had sex."*

"Folks." The first man was the hippie who owned the gas station. He had long hair, a patchy short beard, tie-dyed T-shirt, and a peace emblem on a necklace.

"I take it you closed down the mini-mart to come fishing?" Gabe asked.

"Hell, yeah. There's nothing better than dropping a line on a sunny day."

The other man was probably about the same age, but looked...rougher. Definitely not a hippie sort of guy.

"Julie, I don't know if you've officially met these two, although you've probably served them beer. That's Tucker." He pointed to the rough-looking man.

Then the hippie. "And Zappa."

Only one name apiece. Was this an Alaskan custom or something Gabe did?

"It's nice to meet you both." Julie stopped and then mentally kicked herself. *Add to the conversation, girl.* "Will you be fishing for salmon?"

"No, miss," Tucker said. "The salmon runs won't start for another month. This is just a plain-ol'-trout day."

Trout? She liked trout. She watched as Zappa started putting together his gear. That looked...complicated. How did a person go about learning to fish?

When she looked up, she realized the men had gone silent—and Gabe and Tucker were watching her.

"Got an interest in fishing, miss?" Tucker asked.

"I... Yes?" She pushed her hair back, feeling twigs and grass. "Dante said he'd show me how if I got a license. But he's been busy."

Gabe's eyebrows lifted. "You have a license?"

"In my wallet."

Zappa looked up with a gap-toothed grin. "Nothing more fun than teaching a new fisher-person. Got your tackle with you, Chief?"

Gabe also knew how to fish? "Do you know how to do everything in the whole world?" Belatedly, she realized her tone was totally vexed-sounding.

He only laughed and tucked an arm around her. "If I say yes, are you going to hit me?"

"With my luck, you'd arrest me," she muttered, and the two fishermen laughed.

"Damn straight." Gabe ran his fingers through her hair, picking out a couple of twigs. "But I do have my fishing tackle, and you can have a fishing lesson right now, if you'd like."

"Really?" Delight rose like froth on the waves. "You'd really show me how?"

Gabe's piercing blue eyes softened. "Sure."

"Hands-on," Zappa said. "That's the best way. Get your shit, Chief."

An hour later, Audrey caught her first fish.

On the way back to Julie's house, Gabe couldn't stop watching the little cheechako. Yeah, she was a tad uncertain with people. He'd seen moments when she'd start to retreat and then push herself into talking again. She had courage.

And she'd learned everything they taught with frightening speed, never needing to be shown anything mechanical twice. Fuck, she was smart. However, her physical skills weren't up to par with her mental ones. It'd be awhile before she got good at casting.

Hadn't dimmed her enthusiasm, though.

She wasn't a jump-up-and-cheer sort of person. No, she was far quieter, but her eyes would light, her face would pinken, and she'd focus in like a laser sight. He'd had SEALs under his command like her. Smart, brave, determined.

Yeah, he liked her and for more than her curvy body and sweet lips and generous response. For more than her pretty gasps when she got off.

He still couldn't believe he'd told her about the ambush.

She'd listened. He'd expected her to be horrified at what

he'd done, but she hadn't run. Had simply nodded, her expression showing the same unhappiness he'd felt.

She'd been...a friend.

Seemed like she could use one in return.

He glanced at her and couldn't keep from asking, "Are you ever going to tell me what brought you here? And let me help?"

The way she stiffened up gave him his answer before she opened her mouth.

"I'm sorry, but it's none of your business."

He pulled the Jeep to a stop in front of her cabin and turned to face her. "I've been inside you, Goldilocks. Can't get much closer."

She turned red, first with embarrassment, then he saw her eyes spark with anger. "I thought you were a no-more-than-one-night guy. No relationships or ties, remember?"

His frustration died as her anger lit. As she hopped out of his Jeep, he started to grin. "Seems like you said the same thing. Just once, right? Does twice mean we have a relationship?"

"*No!*" She slammed the Jeep door shut so hard the vehicle rocked.

CHAPTER FIFTEEN

Following the crowd is a fine strategy if you're a sheep. Are you a sheep, boy? - First Sergeant Michael "Mako" Tyne"

A domestic feline call made him late to the town meeting. In the municipal building, Gabe strode past the reception desk, turned into the large meeting room, and stared.

The place was packed. The number of vehicles on the street should have warned him, but who ever heard of citizens actually attending a town meeting?

In the front of the long rectangular room, the six commissioners and the mayor sat behind a long table, each with a nameplate in front. Gabe eyed the names and titles.

Dante, Sarah, and her husband, Uriah, were town council members. So was the Patriot Zealot leader, Reverend Parrish. Two were unfamiliar. Joe Kolbeck was a stocky bearded man who looked like an off-the-grid sort. The other, Eugene Jones, was a tall, lean, fifty-year-old male in casual business attire.

Julie's friend, Lillian, was the mayor. *Interesting.*

As Gabe entered, Sarah was speaking into the mic about the council's goals. That they hoped to balance the rural quality of life, protect the natural environment, and support the area economy. With the resort opening, the town needed to prepare for increasing numbers of tourists and to decide how to direct the growth.

She was an optimistic one, wasn't she? Cynically, Gabe studied the audience.

The left rear corner was filled with men, some barely in their twenties to seniors in their sixties. Country clothing predominated—work shirts, jeans, and boots.

Where were their women?

Most of the preppers and off-the-gridders were scattered through the left side. The right half of the room held the business and town folk and many families.

As Gabe moved to stand along the right wall, he spotted Julie in the back row beside Regina.

If it came to watching her or the speaker, he knew which he'd choose...so he stopped where he could watch her profile. He hadn't seen anything so pretty in a long, long while.

Her hair was damp from a shower and forming springy waves as it dried. Freckles sprinkled her nose and sunburned cheeks.

He also noticed that whenever someone shouted, she flinched.

Dammit, he wanted to help. When would she realize that?

Seated with Tucker on the anti-business side, Guzman rose and pointed to the council table. "Did you see all the new businesses? You're turning this place into some damn tourist trap."

"Now, Guzman," Uriah said, then stopped as if unsure what to say.

Near the front of the room, Bull rose and faced the back-to-the-lander. "What businesses make this place a tourist trap? Is my bar a problem? I noticed you've been enjoying the beer."

The crowd laughed—and Guzman had a rueful grin.

Bull continued, "Have you noticed the new art gallery also has a crafts section for people who like to make things? I don't know about you, but I get bored in the winter. You can even pick up an embroidery hoop and pattern to keep your wife from murdering you before winter solstice."

People exchanged looks. Anything to relieve the long, dark winters was welcome.

"If you're skilled with your hands, you might find a way to bring in a few extra bucks. The store only sells Alaska made crafts and artwork."

A hum of interest ran through the room.

Bull folded his arms across his chest. "The hotel at McNally's Resort is pricy and not every skier can afford to stay there. We're going to have bed and breakfast places. One place at the end of town will open in two weeks. More people in town means there will be enough customers to support a pizza place. Happens I love pizza, so I'm happy someone wants to start that business."

Interested comments ran through the room. Bull wasn't the only person who liked pizza.

Bull smiled. "A woman wants to open a video rental next to Dante's, and I'm good with that because I don't like those empty buildings. They look creepy as all get out."

Before Bull could go on, the rising noise cut him short.

Alaskans had no problem expressing their opinions...loudly.

The councilor wearing business attire tried to talk above the crowd. "We're not planning drastic changes, and we want to keep a small-town atmosphere. No box stores or franchises will be given a license."

That got a roar of approval from both sides, and Gabe almost grinned. Rescue residents could be a pain in the ass, but they got involved. That was impressive.

"Yes, increased tourism means we need a police presence," Uriah said, "but also means money for our elementary school. People, these are our children, and even homeschooling takes money."

Gabe remembered the correspondence school's tests and materials. He doubted the process had gotten less expensive to the town and borough.

A few rows back from Bull, Caz rose. "The projected

increase in population means the health clinic received enough grant money to reopen."

That won a few cheers.

At the council table, Reverend Parrish frowned. His gaze shifted from Caz to the mass of men in the back left.

Gabe followed his gaze and recognized some of the men in that corner. The man who'd followed Parrish into the coffee shop. An older man who'd been at the table with the asshole who'd slapped Julie.

The men of the Patriot Zealots had shown up in force.

When Parrish gave an infinitesimal nod, one of the PZs rose with a belligerent scowl on his face. "What's with hiring a bunch of cops, anyway? We don't got any crime here."

Sarah didn't...quite...laugh.

Every morning, Gabe would drink coffee and get her rundown of the local gossip. In return, he gave her a verbal police report.

Sarah knew exactly what law enforcement did in this town. "Chief MacNair, would you give us a synopsis of your first week?"

The sarge had taught his boys to be prepared, whether for a fight or a march...or to answer awkward questions.

Nonchalantly, Gabe pulled out the list he'd made and started reading. First, the station's on-duty hours. The numbers and types of calls he and Baumer had handled—several domestics and assaults, and one attempted sexual assault on a minor, which had pissed him the hell off. They'd covered wildlife problems when the state wildlife troopers couldn't respond in time—bears and moose to a pack of sled dogs that'd gotten loose.

He elaborated about the various burglaries. Mentioning vandalism even without using their names netted him glares from Knox and Chevy. He went on with traffic violations, motor vehicle accidents, and dealing with medical emergencies until an air ambulance helicopter could arrive.

"Several intoxicated residents were assisted home after a visit to the bar." Gabe's frown at Bull made people laugh.

"We're here to help, people. Even if it makes us late for a town meeting." He showed the long vivid scratches on the back of his hand and said in a wry voice, "Even if the job is rescuing a kitten from a tree."

Along with the laughter came a wave of applause.

In truth, returning the kitten to the little girl had topped off a very enjoyable day.

This being sociable wasn't all that bad, Audrey thought. And sitting in the back row meant no one was looking at her.

She'd sure been surprised when she'd realized Gabe was leaning against the wall...really near where she sat.

And didn't that give her a frizzle of excitement?

No, don't go there. She couldn't afford to get involved with him, no matter how nice he'd been in teaching her about being in Alaska. Although...nice...isn't what she'd have called him when he'd started unbuttoning her shirt. Devastatingly dangerous would be a better description.

How did he make her feel like that, beautiful and sexy? And as if her bones had melted. As if she had no willpower of her own. Yet she knew he'd honor any concern she had. He'd also be able to discern if she was truthful with him—and herself—about what she wanted.

It was both scary and heady to be with someone who read her so easily.

Which also meant a person with a fake ID shouldn't get too close to him. To a cop. She shouldn't try to have a relationship, not even a friendship, really.

But, oh, it'd been fun to be with him. To learn about Alaska. To simply watch him.

He was amazing in the forest. When he'd checked ahead on the trail, he would silently disappear into the green, and she couldn't hear him move. Herself, she sounded like a buffalo tromping around.

He noticed and identified the tiniest tracks. Her nose wrinkled. He even knew what animal had left poop on the trail. Bear poop was disgustingly enormous.

After they'd...when Tucker and Zappa had arrived, she'd realized Gabe would never be one of those guys who shouted at football games or got stupid and drunk. Even relaxed and fishing with other men, he'd looked deadly. That dark and dangerous intensity never diminished.

She frowned. Wasn't it odd that, after Spyros, she could find reassurance in how lethal Gabe was?

Because he'd protect a woman. She smiled. And kittens.

She listened as two citizens requested new streetlights, repairs to the Main Street pavement and sidewalks, and beautification of the downtown. Their requests sounded reasonable, especially fixing the potholes in the street.

She'd noticed most Alaskan small towns had no paved streets at all. Off the main highways, Seward and Sterling, graveled streets were the norm. Rescue should be proud it had something better.

Most of the council members seemed open to the requests, but two were vehemently against spending money. She eyed the nameplates. Reverend Parrish and Joe Kolbeck.

As the argument continued, Sarah's color rose along with her temper.

Dante put his hand on her arm and said mildly, "I figure us business owners can work together on making the town pretty. However"—his chin rose—"unsafe streets, sidewalks, and lighting might well get us sued, especially from lawsuit-happy Outsiders."

That got an unhappy buzz.

"Outsiders aren't the only unhappy ones," an older woman stated. "I almost broke my neck when I tripped on the crack in front of the post office."

"Yeah, that's a bad one," another person chimed in.

"That sounds like a good compromise. We'll fix the pavement and sidewalks. We can even spring for the money to fix the streetlights, too." Uriah grinned. "There are all of eight lights total. For now, the businesses will beautify the place on their own."

That vote carried.

Other issues were brought up, increasingly petty, and the meeting grew more rancorous. As the voices rose, Audrey shrank in her chair, wishing she were home. But people would notice if she stood up to leave.

Someone touched her arm, and she jumped.

Gabe was down on his haunches beside her. "You look like you need to get out of here," he murmured.

"But—" She flushed and glanced at all the people in the room.

"They're busy bickering. Come on." He rose, pulled her to her feet, and with a firm grip on her arm, guided her out of the room.

To her surprise, he didn't release her once they were outside the building.

"Thank you, but I can get to my car myself. It's still light out." A glance at his unsmiling face told her that protesting was useless.

An ache grew inside. She missed the easy camaraderie of earlier. Before he'd asked her about her past. *Eff-it-all*, why did he continue to dig for information?

But he was a law enforcement person through and through. Cops probably resented mysteries in the same way she resented a search query that returned incorrect answers. With a silent sigh, she simply walked beside him to her car.

Releasing her arm, he opened the car door. "Drive

safely."

"I will." She looked up. "Are you going back in?"

"Yep. Attendance is part of the job as *someone* pointed out earlier today."

"True enough." She gave him a half-smile. "At least the issue of police funding is done. You rocked that report."

The lines in his face eased. "Good to hear.

"Thank you for pulling me out."

"Julie." He stood close enough she could feel the heat from his body. Another inch closer, and her breasts would rub on his chest. Her skin felt too tight, as if she'd gotten into clothes a size too small.

Everything inside her wanted those arms around her.

He wanted to know her past. She couldn't tell him. "No. No more."

When she edged away, he studied her face for a second and nodded. "All right." He took his own step back.

Eff-it-all. She slid into the car...and he closed the door.

Letting out a forlorn sigh, she glanced in the rear view mirror. Yes, duty done, he was striding toward the municipal building.

Every woman knew chocolate ice cream would fill her with endorphins and make the world better. Being with Gabe was even better than chocolate ice cream.

She couldn't.

And from the expression on his face, he wouldn't try to tempt her further. The knowledge closed her throat and filled her eyes with tears.

CHAPTER SIXTEEN

At five on Tuesday afternoon, Gabe crossed the street toward Dante's Market. He was out of milk and cheese. Be nice to have a dairy cow or goat, but no. Mako had tried livestock in the past, but it was damn difficult to cougar-proof a cattle-sized pasture.

As he walked into the store, he spotted Dante at the end of one aisle. Since the grocery would close within the next few minutes, Julie had already left.

Biding his time, Gabe had avoided the bar, grocery, and coffee shop for the last two days. Julie liked him. Wanted him. She'd pulled away only because he was too inquisitive for her comfort level.

He chuckled. Considering how curious *she* was, she should have more sympathy. He picked up a block of cheddar and a quart of milk. Well, he'd give her another day or so to relax before approaching her again.

Frustrating woman. If she'd only bring herself to trust him, he could help with whatever frightened her.

Of course, if she were a serial killer and fleeing the law, they might have a problem. But—he smiled—he knew her now. Julie liked rules and order too much to be a crook. And she was far too tenderhearted to hurt people.

It was odd to miss someone he didn't really know—but he did. Hell, just a glimpse of her could bring him to a full stop. Maybe because he remembered all too well how her curvy body felt beneath him, how soft her lips were, the velvet of her nipples against his tongue, the way her cunt closed around his dick.

The tiny sounds she made when she came.

Gabe grunted his exasperation because now he had a boner. *Dumbass.*

He'd sure never figured on entangling himself with a woman when he'd arrived in Rescue. After his divorce during his SEAL days, he'd had a couple of longer relationships. Like the one that'd taken him to Los Angeles. But no woman had truly upset his equilibrium.

But now... Damned if he could get Julie out of his mind.

At the counter, he waited for Dante to make his way to the front.

"How's it going, Chief?" Dante stepped up to the register and rang up the purchases.

Gabe handed over some money. "Good enough. Been quiet. And you?"

"Fine. Maybe I can liven up your life." Dante grinned. "Lillian wants you and Caz to come for supper tonight."

A meal he didn't have to cook? "Sure. When?"

"Now, boy. Now." Dante motioned Gabe out of the store, flipped off the lights, and turned the sign on the door to CLOSED.

Gabe grinned as he got into his Jeep. Small town living. Everyone knew he had nothing planned.

He glanced at the grocery sack. Good thing the late May temperature had been cold today; the food would keep for a few hours. A few minutes later, he parked behind Dante's car. Caz's SUV pulled in behind.

"I see Dante found you, *viejo*." Caz slapped Gabe's shoulder and followed Dante up to Lillian's house.

With an easy informality, Dante opened the front door, yelled, "We're here, woman," and walked in.

The grocery store owner and the Englishwoman?

Gabe exchanged a glance with Caz.

Caz's eyes lit...of course. Despite the way Caz went through women, he'd always had a fondness for romance—at least when it came to others.

And hey, best of luck to Dante. He was Mako's generation and far more sociable than the sarge had been. Gabe rubbed his hand over his jaw. A man like that needed friends. A lover.

Now Gabe, he wasn't as withdrawn as Mako had been. He liked having a few friends. His brothers. A woman, now and then.

At one time, he wouldn't have wanted more from a woman, but...now, there was Julie.

Lillian's home suited the Brit well. Her high-ceilinged living room was filled with antiques, Oriental carpets, tall plants, and stained glass windows.

Dante walked through the room, through a dining area, and into a bright kitchen.

To the right, Lillian was putting a pan of biscuits in the oven.

Biscuits. Gabe's mouth started to water.

Turning, Lillian smiled a welcome. "Dante, my love." A quick kiss confirmed Gabe's suppositions of their relationship. Stepping past Dante, she took his and Caz's hands. "Welcome, you two."

"Thank you for the invitation," Caz said smoothly. "Whatever you're cooking, it smells wonderful."

"Julie had a successful time fishing, so we're comparing our favorite trout recipes." As Lillian spoke, Julie came in the back door with a platter of grilled trout.

Apparently, his avoidance policy had a new expiration date. Gabe couldn't hide his smile. "Julie." *Or whatever your name is.*

Surprised delight flashed in her eyes before wariness appeared. "Gabe."

As she greeted Dante and Caz more easily, he studied her. The bruise shadows had finally disappeared. She moved more easily. Her silky skin had a light tan, and her cheeks had filled out enough that she no longer looked like she belonged in a Dickens novel.

She got sexier every time he saw her. *Dammit.* He searched for the manners that he'd acquired from Gramps —sure hadn't been from Mako. "I see you've turned into a good fisherman."

Her expression brightened. "I'm getting better. Lillian gave me her old gear. Tucker and Zappa invited me along yesterday for more instructions."

Pretty pitiful to feel envious of her time.

"What bait did you use?" Caz asked.

As she turned to him, Gabe asked Lillian, "What can we do to help?"

"With the cooking?" She moved the trout to a white china platter.

"Yep. I was raised in a *no work, no eat* regime."

Lillian laughed. "Yes, that does sound like the sarge."

"You knew Mako?"

"Over the years, we grew to be good friends." She smiled. "The winters here are long and cold. It's pleasant to have a way to keep warm."

"Huh." Gabe'd thought Mako had remained a hermit, despite the move to Rescue. It seemed the sarge'd had friends...and friends with benefits, as well.

Gabe frowned. He'd told Julie people weren't meant to live in solitude. Why had he assumed Mako was an exception?

He'd been wrong, hadn't he? Mako had made himself

part of this town—not as visible as Dante—but considering the type of properties the sarge purchased, he'd known a hell of a lot about the place. And had cared about it.

As Caz went to check the fish still on the grill, and the two women dished up food, Gabe stepped closer to Dante. "Mako discussed Rescue with you and Lillian, didn't he? How to get the town growing again?"

"Yeah, the three of us and sometimes Uriah and Sarah talked about what we wanted for the town."

"And the businesses Mako bought?"

Dante moved his shoulders. "Eh, that was his thing. He bought up the old hotel just to help the owner who was moving Outside for some fancy cancer treatment. Then he went kinda crazy."

That was Mako. The sarge gave everything his all. And yet... "He bought a lot of businesses."

"Living all those years in that old cabin, he piled up the savings—and said the money was just gathering dust. He wanted to leave you boys something more than piles of green paper." Dante looked away for a moment. "He wanted the town to have someone trustworthy guarding its future."

"And he wanted to see his boys building something." Lillian's eyes were soft. "He worried that you'd seen too much death. Especially, you, Gabe. And Hawk."

As grief shook him, Gabe looked away. *Dammit, Sarge.* "We better get the table set. Where are the plates?"

Lillian pointed to a high cupboard, and he caught the gleam of tears in her eyes.

Julie turned away to wipe her eyes, too. Tenderhearted sweetie.

The mood lightened as everyone worked to get the table set, and Caz carried in the last of the grilled fish.

It was a fine meal.

And the fish was damned good. Gabe grinned at the arguments over which recipe was best. To his mind, both versions were excellent. He jotted down the recipes for his brother. Bull loved collecting new dishes.

"Did you catch more trout than Tucker?" Dante asked Julie.

She laughed. "Hardly. But I had so much fun, it didn't matter who caught more. I never realized how satisfying it is to provide food for myself and others."

Gabe couldn't help smiling at her. "It is a good feeling."

"Usually." Caz gave him a wry look. "Except for the times you don't succeed."

Gabe laughed. "Some of us were less effective than others that year."

"What year?" Julie asked.

"Back when the sarge decided we didn't take our hunting and fishing seriously enough."

Dante leaned back in his chair. "Now, a man has to wonder what the ol' drill sergeant did when his boys gave his hunting lessons less than their best efforts."

Gabe glanced at his brother. "How many times did we go to bed without supper?"

"Too many," Caz said sadly.

An outraged red colored Julie's cheeks. "He didn't give you food unless you caught it?"

"We always got breakfast and lunch. Supper, though... Well, hunger can focus attention nicely." Gabe shrugged. "We did all right most of the time."

"The next year was worse. He doled out only two bullets or two arrows. And wouldn't let us share our kills." Caz scowled at Gabe. "You and Hawk ate good. Me and Bull, not so much. Not until we were allowed to set traps and snares."

"They took your food?" The appalled expression on Julie's face was truly cute. Tenderhearted and against injustice.

Yeah, he wanted this woman.

"No, no." Caz's mouth curved. "Pure skill levels. Gabe can hit anything he aims at, no matter the weapon. With a rifle, Hawk's even better."

"Oh," Julie said. "Of course."

Gabe shook his head. "I can't believe you accused me of stealing my baby brother's food. I thought you liked me. That we were friends."

"I'm...I'm sorry." Color rose into her cheeks, and her expression filled with remorse. "I didn't mean... Of course, we're friends."

Caz's laughter halted her apologies, and she turned.

The traitorous asshole pointed to Gabe. "Be warned, *chica*. That one can con a person with a perfectly straight face."

Her gray eyes narrowed before she speared him with a look. "You...are an evil person. I felt so *bad* for doubting you."

"As you should." He put his arm around her shoulders and leaned down to whisper, "Someday, I'll earn your trust, Goldilocks."

Her unhappy sigh lifted and lowered her shoulders.

Someday wasn't today, apparently. Nonetheless, Gabe left his arm where it was, enjoying the contact.

Amused, Caz quirked his eyebrows at Gabe before turning to Dante. "I explored the town building's second floor today. The municipal offices are over the police station, but the rooms on the other side are locked. The rooms that are over my clinic."

"Ah, those. The blue-doored room is the small conference room. When you want to use it for staff meetings, reserve it by writing your name and times on the calendar. Regina has the key." Dante leaned back in his chair. "Our library is behind the green door. It and the police station and health clinic all shut down at the same time."

Julie looked...appalled. "You had a library and let it close?"

Gabe chuckled. She really was the nerd she called herself.

"'Fraid so," Dante said.

Lillian smiled at Julie. "I'd forgotten about the library, and it was one of my favorite places. I used to read to the toddlers for children's hour."

"It slipped my mind, too." Dante scratched his bearded chin. "With the police and health offices open, the entire building has electricity and internet again. No reason not to open up the library."

"We could." Lillian rose and started gathering plates. "If we could get it staffed."

As Gabe, Caz, and Julie took over clearing the table, Dante filled the dishwasher, and Lillian put away the leftovers.

Julie cleared her throat. "I have a few hours I could work in the library."

"You know anything about libraries, missy?" Dante asked.

She drew herself up proudly. "Of course. I have a Masters in—" Her mouth snapped shut. When her eyes met his, her shoulders hunched.

Dante barked a laugh. "Too late, Julie. You have a Masters in..."

"Probably Library Science," Caz chimed in helpfully and caught a glare from gray eyes that made him grin.

"Julie," Gabe took her hand. "We all know you're running from something. But we won't share your information outside of this room."

Lillian, Dante, and Caz nodded agreement.

When the color eased back into Julie's face, Gabe wanted to pull her into his arms.

"Thank you," she whispered.

"Want to wrangle the library?" Dante asked. "It'd be

another part-time job for you. We can talk about giving you a budget to get the computers updated."

The joy that swept into her face was...stunning.

And heartbreaking.

For whatever reason, she'd left everything behind—including a career she loved.

Well, if she couldn't talk about whatever sent her here, then he'd simply do his best to help her build a new life here.

CHAPTER SEVENTEEN

Coffee in hand, Gabe walked through the open door of the library and looked for Julie.

She wasn't in sight, although the huge room was filled with activity. Tucker and Guzman were painting the walls a steel blue. Uriah from the coffee shop was hooking up the three computers.

Two women vacuumed the short steel-blue carpet. On a tall ladder, a man replaced florescent lights in the long ceiling fixtures. Women were dusting and vacuuming both the carpets and the old cobwebs in high corners.

"Welcome to the library, Gabriel." Off to the right, in the children's corner, Lillian painted the window trim an off-white color.

"The place looks good." After Dante and Lillian had talked Julie into taking on the library a week ago, they'd ramrodded the okay through the council. At first, Gabe had helped with setting up the place, but the weather had warmed up, and he'd been occupied with increased tourist traffic and crime.

"The room does look quite nice, doesn't it? We've had a surprising amount of assistance." The silver-haired, slender Brit motioned with her paintbrush at the people scattered through the big room. "I think we'll be ready for the opening on Friday."

"Good to hear. So, is Julie here?"

"Of course." Lillian smiled. "I'm very impressed with her. She hasn't neglected her gardening hours with me, Dante's grocery, or at the roadhouse. Every free moment is spent in here."

"Hard worker." Gabe wasn't surprised.

"She is. And honest, as well."

At Gabe's quizzical look, Lillian shook her head. "When the council tried to turn the library funds over to her, she refused. She says that since we can't check her references, it would be best if she makes out the orders for what she needs and has each order approved and paid at the time."

Gabe blinked. He hadn't thought about her handling large amounts of money.

Of course, the library would have operating funds. And Julie hadn't told anyone her history. Apparently, Gabe wasn't the only one who instinctively trusted her, despite her aversion to sharing.

Lillian lowered her voice. "I don't know what happened

to her in the past. I do hope that someday she'll let us help."

"She will." She'd get help whether she shared or not. "Where is she?"

"Somewhere back in the stacks. She's making a list for updating the books."

Knowing better than to wander through bookshelves with drinks, Gabe set her coffee on the front counter and went in search.

Audrey frowned at her list and scratched another note. Until she knew what the residents liked to read, she'd have to keep her book purchases to a minimum. The inter-library loan program would help.

She glanced at the electrician who was putting in more outlets. In today's world, everyone had devices to be charged.

The man gave her an interested look.

With a cool, but friendly smile, she moved past. The last thing she needed was to start anything with a man.

Well, with most men. Not when one man refused to get out of her head and out of her dreams.

Even worse, Gabe worked downstairs. Every time she came into the municipal building, she felt her pulse pick up. Knew she was listening for the sound of his voice.

He'd been the one to scrounge up a new printer for her. He'd fixed the broken tables in the research section.

She hadn't seen him for a couple days now. Wasn't it odd how much she missed him?

As if called, he appeared at the end of a row and walked silently toward her. Prowled toward her.

The high bookshelves cut off some of the overhead light, leaving the aisles in twilight, casting shadows on his stern face.

"There you are." Pleasure lit his eyes. "I brought coffee for you."

"Really? That would be perfect."

He didn't move, just smiled at her.

She glanced down at herself. Shirt was buttoned, jeans were zipped, nothing remarkable. "What?"

"You look...happy." With a finger, he tucked a strand of hair behind her ear, leaving awareness tingling over her skin. "I don't think I've seen you quite this content."

"I like libraries." She breathed in his distinctive woodsy scent, wanting to lean closer. "Mother thought fiction was frivolous, and if I wanted to read, there were textbooks and college preparatory manuals."

"Fiction is frivolous?" Gabe frowned. "Before high school, you were able to indulge, right?"

"No. But sometimes in English classes we studied classical literature." She sighed, remembering the joy of Dickens and...even better...the Bronte sisters.

Gabe looked around the library. "Ah. Libraries have fiction."

She grinned. He got it. "Exactly. If I had research to do,

I'd have to visit a library. Then I'd finish my homework quickly enough that I could curl up in a chair and read stories for the rest of the time."

There were entire worlds in which to escape.

She realized she was smiling when Gabe traced a finger over her upturned lips.

"A library is your happy place," he murmured.

"Yes. Always." And the reason she'd gone into library science—so she could share her love with others. "I take it you don't have the same fondness for book stacks?"

His laugh was a low rumble. "No, Goldilocks. I didn't see a library until college."

She stared at him. "But...where did you get your books?"

"Everything came through the mail. Of course, Mako had a wall of books in the cabin." He grinned. "His how-to-build and how-to-repair section was huge, and we learned early on to search out the proper way to perform a repair." He grinned. "Mako didn't care if we read fiction as long as the day's work was done."

"It doesn't seem right that your sergeant father was less restrictive than my mother."

"I'd have to agree." His eyes changed. Hardened. "Are your parents ... Mmm, do they know where you are? What's going on?"

He was trying to make sure she was all right without really asking, wasn't he? His concern filled her with light-ness. "There's only Mother. I was artificially conceived."

The unhappiness she'd felt as a child when realizing she'd never know her father had diminished to a mild ache.

She smiled slightly at Gabe's startled expression. "She didn't want to be bothered with a husband. Instead, she simply chose the smartest sperm donor in the manual or however it's done."

"I see. And does your mother know where you are?"

"No. We haven't spoken in years, since I refused to follow in her footsteps and major in physics. She's in Germany somewhere, I think."

Gabe frowned. "I'm sorry, but she sounds like a robot. The idea of you being deprived of fiction, something so essential to humans, bothers me."

"It wasn't—"

Putting two fingers under her chin, he tilted her head up and kissed her. Sheer shock silenced her.

He made a low masculine sound and then pinned her against the shelving. He curved his big hand behind her head, threading his fingers in her hair, holding her for a long, devastating kiss.

Every bone in her body turned to jelly. His other arm went around her waist, holding her up against him.

Her arms stole around his neck, and as she wiggled closer, her breasts crushed against his muscular chest. He hardened.

The sound of footsteps made him step back, and the electrician walked past.

Gabe smiled down into her eyes as he used his thumb to wipe the moisture from her lower lip.

"Gabe," she whispered. Longing rushed through her, a desire to break down and tell him everything. To destroy all the barriers between them. "I can't." *Can't share, can't be with you.*

"It's all right, Goldilocks." His midnight blue eyes conveyed infinite patience. He kissed her lightly again. "Don't forget you have coffee on the counter."

As he walked silently back toward the front, she leaned against the bookshelves.

Oh God, what was she going to do? The man had decided to hold off and wait for her to trust him.

And oh, she wanted to.

CHAPTER EIGHTEEN

On Friday, a week and a half after Lillian's dinner, the library opened its doors. Well, *door*. Upstairs in the municipal building.

Kneeling beside the shelves in the children's section, Audrey sighed in pleasure. It didn't matter if the library was merely a big room of book stacks and a tiny office behind the checkout desk.

The essentials were here.

The computer section—a table with three computers. The research section—a few tables with folding chairs. A children's area holding tiny tables for children with bigger chairs for mothers. Armchairs near the periodical racks for quiet reading.

Speaking of which, she needed to get the periodical subscriptions restarted.

Yes, the library was small. But it was hers.

She'd never felt so pleased or so possessive about any library she'd worked in before.

The entire town had helped her get it open—especially Gabe.

She shook her head. He was driving her crazy. Seriously crazy.

He'd run upstairs with coffee and her favorite cookies or pastries, then stay and simply talk. Like friends. About fishing and hiking, about some of the police work he'd done that day, although he never gave her names or specifics. They'd talk about whatever work she was doing for a client.

She knew he wanted her—and wasn't that simply amazing?—yet, he smothered his desire enough that she never felt pressured. He didn't ask her out or try to see her anywhere but in public.

The jerk. Now, she was past ready to knock him over the head and rip all his clothes off.

Ah, well. She was the one who'd said no to him more than once. It was up to her to change that to yes.

Why did the world have to be so complicated?

For now, though, it was opening day at the library.

Two people were already at the computers. Three were browsing the stacks.

Behind Audrey in the children's section, Sarah sat in an oversized armchair with her daughter on her lap, reading a book the girl had chosen.

Audrey grinned as she found the book she'd been looking for—*The Cat in the Hat*.

Still on her knees, she turned and handed over the book. "You might try this one. It's perfect for someone who can sound out short words."

"I had this when I was a child," Sarah said. Her eyes filled.

"Sarah?"

"I'm all right." The coffee shop owner wiped the tears away. "Just hormones. And happiness. You see, Rachel won't be an only child in a few more months."

Aww. "Congratulations. And congratulations to you, too, Rachel."

The little girl wiggled in delight. "I'm going to be a big sister. And we have to pick out names, boy and girl names, just the right ones. What's your name?"

"Audr—" God, what was she saying? "Uh, Julie. My name is Julie." Turning, she pushed to her feet—and realized that Gabe and the other law enforcement officer stood on the other side of the hip-high bookshelves.

From the narrowing of Chief MacNair's eyes, the two men had heard her slip-up.

Eff-it-all.

Her name started with *Audr*. Gabe smiled, enjoying the dismayed expression on "Julie's" face. Nice of her to give him a clue.

"Good day, gentlemen," she greeted politely...and fled toward the back.

Poor lost sweetheart. Now, what could the rest of her name be? He'd known a girl named Audra. Audre, maybe? Audria, Audris. No, probably just Audrey. It suited her quiet nature far more than the name Julie. *Audrey. Yeah.*

"Sounds as if she's using an assumed name." Baumer frowned after her.

"Maybe. She sure wouldn't be the first person in Alaska to leave her past behind. Or maybe she's a woman who likes to switch it up now and then. My ex went through a spate of spelling her name in different ways." Gabe half-grinned. "Got so I never knew what to use when I left her a note."

Baumer snickered. "Women. They can't—"

"What are you *doing?*" Filled with anger, Julie's voice echoed off the walls. "Stop!"

What the hell? Gabe stepped around Baumer and headed for the back in time to spot Knox heading toward the exit. "Hold up there, Knox."

The man realized he was caught and stopped. He spotted Julie, and his shoulders actually slumped.

"You." Her flushed face held an impressive fury. "What were you thinking? How could you do that to a book?" She sounded like a priest seeing someone spit on the altar.

"What'd he do?" Gabe interposed himself between Knox and the door.

"He was ripping pages out of books. I found two more that he destroyed. *Why?*" The last word was practically a wail.

Knox stared as if shocked by her anger and distress. He

shuffled his feet before throwing his shoulders back. "Don't want a liberry here. No need for it. It's a waste of my tax money to buy a bunch of useless stories."

"A library has more than just stories. The books help you decide where to go on vacation or how to start a business. You can come here to use the internet, read newspapers, and borrow movies and audiobooks. A library serves everyone in the community." The way her eyes lit with passion, Gabe knew this was her place. Her niche.

"It doesn't serve me." Knox's gaze caught on something behind Gabe, and he flinched. "Nobody asked me if I wanted a liberry."

Gabe turned to glance over his shoulder. A teen and an older man sat at the computers. Baumer stood behind the teen, looking at the display.

Breaking into Knox's rant, Gabe said quietly, "You gave me your word."

The words stopped Knox as thoroughly as if Gabe'd swung a 2x4. The man's face turned the red of his hair. "I did. I just...just got mad. Payin' out good money for some-thing I can't even—"

His abrupt stop left Gabe confused, but Julie's expres-sion filled with comprehension and, then, sympathy. She stepped closer to Knox, her voice low. "You can't read."

"I can, too." Knox glared...and deflated. "I can't. Can't even fake it anymore now my wife's gone."

Well, hell. Gabe frowned. Sending the man to prison

wouldn't solve anything. But Knox had broken his word and—"

"I'll pay for the books I ruined," Knox said.

"Yes," Julie said firmly. "And you'll meet with me here for two hours twice a week."

Knox gaped. "For how long?"

"Until you've learned to read."

When hope lit in Knox's eyes, Gabe knew the librarian had won.

———

A few minutes later, Gabe headed downstairs to the police station.

Baumer followed him. "That's a pretty woman. The librarian, I mean."

"She is." Beautiful. Brilliant. And, unloved as a child. Her mother hadn't let her read fiction. He still had problems with that. Maybe because novels had been essential to surviving the long Alaska winters in Mako's cabin.

Gabe nodded to Regina as they walked toward her receptionist desk.

"One call, Chief." The woman held out a post-it note. "All quiet."

"Good to hear. Thank you."

As they walked past and through the station door, Baumer persisted. "Do you and the pretty librarian have something going on? Seems like I've heard rumors..."

Jesus, was this the price of living in a small town?

At Gabe's irritated stare, Baumer held up his hands. "Just asking. I wouldn't want to arrest your girlfriend or anything."

"Why the fuck would you arrest Julie?"

"You know—fake name. No one knows where she came from. She never talks about her past or anything." Baumer shrugged. "I'm just a suspicious guy, and you gotta admit, women are devious."

"Sounds as if you've been burned a time or two."

"Shit, my first wife was a real feminazi and screwed around on me after the second month we were married. That burns, man, you know?"

All too familiar. Gabe poured himself a cup from the coffee he'd made that morning. Black as sin, but better than nothing. "I know. When I got deployed, my wife figured our vows went on leave." It'd hurt that while he'd been risking his life for the country—and being faithful despite temptation—she was screwing any soldier-boy she picked up at the bar. It'd been an ugly divorce.

Baumer nodded. "You get it."

Nonetheless, deciding a person couldn't be trusted because of his or her gender, race, religion, or what-the-fuck-ever was purely stupid. "Julie hasn't done anything illegal here, and she's from Chicago. Nothing suspicious about that. She's sure not the first person to come to Alaska for a fresh start and to leave the past behind."

"Maybe." Baumer's mouth twisted. "With the trouble

we're having here, seems like we need to be careful. For all we know, she's wanted for something—and has access to this building."

"Only during the hours the building is open and when Regina is here. Our budget doesn't extend to heating the place for the library alone."

"Oh. Yeah, okay. Guess that's different."

"But you're not convinced."

Baumer scrubbed his fingers through his hair. "She sets my instincts off, and I worry that you're not looking past a pair of breasts, boss."

Baumer was a cop; cops listened to their instincts. But Gabe hadn't been led around by his dick since he was in his teens. Hell, after a disaster or two, most guys figured out that the little head didn't have much for brains.

And he was done with this conversation. "Since your shift has started, let's have our meeting. I want to talk with you about my expectations for patrolling." Because the officer wasn't coming up to snuff.

Gabe led the way into his office and turned the conversation to problems going on in town and law enforcement talk.

CHAPTER NINETEEN

Around Monday noon, Gabe had abandoned the piled-up paperwork in the office to deal with a fight between an Alaska Native and an asshole over a fender-bender.

Then he'd gotten a call from the grocery store. Two teens had thought Dante's old eyes wouldn't notice one boy slipping a frozen pizza into the other's backpack.

An older woman called with a suspected intruder, which turned out to be a squirrel in the attic.

Minor problems but...yeah, he was having fun.

Back in town, he left the patrol car parked on the street and headed toward the municipal building.

"Chief Mac...MacNair?" A skinny boy with collar-length brown hair, well-worn jeans, and red T-shirt shifted from foot to foot. The kid couldn't be more than ten years old.

"What can I do for you, son?" Looking down at the child, Gabe had a sudden vision of how fragile he and his brothers must have seemed to Mako.

"Um, there's a dog. He...I can't get him out, but he needs help."

Gabe smothered a grin. The life of a small-town cop, right? "Show me."

Checking over his shoulder to ensure Gabe followed, the boy led him to the alley behind Dante's grocery. He dropped to his knees to peer under a parked car. "See? He won't come out. He's scared."

Gabe joined him. A half-grown pup, maybe four months. Fluffy enough to be part husky. Sunken flanks and poor condition. Half starved. The tiny whine and terrified half-wag indicated the dog wasn't feral.

With a hand on the boy's shoulder, Gabe pulled him away from the car. "What's your name?"

"Niko."

"Run into the grocery, grab some turkey lunch meat, and tell Dante to put it on the Chief's tab. Can you do that?"

"Yessir."

As the child whipped around the corner, Gabe got comfortable on his knees and started talking in a low voice. "Good thing for you, pup, that the gravel isn't wet or muddy. Looks like you found yourself a nice youngster... Behave and you might have a chance for a..." The puppy moved closer as he talked.

Before Gabe ran out of things to chat about, Niko was back. "What're you going to do?" The boy passed over the lunchmeat.

Teaching time. "Did the dog look well fed?"

"Uh. No. It's... He has a lot of fur, but he looks skinny. Shouldn't he be more round-like?"

"He should. No one's called the station with a missing dog report, so I'd guess someone abandoned him. He's been living hard and is probably back here to raid the garbage bins." Gabe didn't add that the pup was lucky not to have been a bigger predator's snack.

Niko glanced at the bins and nodded.

"Since we know he's hungry, we'll lure him out with some easy food." Opening the lunchmeat, Gabe ripped off a strip of turkey and tossed it under the car.

A second later, gravel scraped. There was a chewing sound.

Niko got down on his belly to peer under the car. "He took it!"

"Now, we work on getting him closer." The next piece of meat didn't get thrown as far.

With each offering, the puppy crept closer and finally out from under the car to get the meat next to Gabe's knee.

Gabe grabbed the little mite and held on through a frantic attempt to escape. When the dog settled, Gabe offered another piece of meat.

That was all it took.

Gabe gave the rest of the meat to Niko. "Your turn."

The kid's grin almost split his face.

"Will your parents let you keep him?"

To Gabe's relief, the boy stopped to think before answering. "Uh-huh. We lost our dog during the winter cuz he was really old. And Dad was talking about getting another."

Gabe eyed the pup who'd made itself at home in Niko's lap...where the food was. Despite its hunger, the dog took the turkey strips politely. It would probably grow up into a damn good dog.

He had a feeling Niko would grow up into a damn good man.

"Can you get the dog to your car, or do you want me to carry him?"

"Uhhhh." Niko bit his lip, looking awkward for the first time. "I can do it."

Gabe eyed him. Might be his folks weren't fans of the police? He shrugged. It wouldn't be the first time he'd run into this. "Okay then. Please keep a grip on him so we don't have to catch him again."

"I will. Thank you, Chief!"

Smiling, Gabe headed out of the alley, crossed the street, and entered the municipal building.

"Hey, Chief. No messages, no disasters," Regina reported with a smile.

"Good enough." Lifting a hand, Gabe strolled past and into the station.

In the bullpen, Baumer was seated at his desk.

"What're you doing in here on your day off?" Gabe asked. "Can't stand to be away from the action?" Shoplifters, drunks, road-kill, fender-benders...

Baumer grinned. "Not that. But I've got something you should see."

"Yeah?" Gabe walked over.

Baumer motioned.

Julie's photo filled half the computer display.

No, not Julie. *Audrey Hamilton. Reference and Liaison Librarian, University of Illinois.*

With a frown, Gabe skimmed the report.

A hitman named Spyros implicated in an author's murder. Assault on a woman who'd done research for the author.

That's where Julie's bruises had come from. A cold chill filled his gut. She was lucky to be alive. "Where'd you get this?"

"Yesterday, I queried the Chicago police to see if there'd been any incidents involving an "Audrey" in the month before she showed up here."

Anger rose. "Did you think you might have run that past me first?"

Baumer stiffened. "I didn't figure I needed permission to check into her background."

"She hasn't done anything to justify an investigation into her past."

"Someone needed to check on her, and you weren't doing it."

"Because I figured she had a reason to be scared and hiding."

Because he'd wanted her to trust him enough to tell him. Gabe scrolled down and found Spyros's rap sheet. Professional murderer. "Seems I was right."

Baumer flushed.

"You were out of line, Baumer." Gabe kept his voice even. "I realize it takes a while to learn the station policies and chief's boundaries." He left unsaid the warning: *Do not do it again.*

The way Baumer stiffened showed he'd gotten the message.

"Yeah, well, sorry." Baumer hit the keyboard, deleted the information, and pushed his chair back. "Guess I'll get back to enjoying my days off."

The door didn't...quite...slam behind the officer.

Late Monday afternoon, Audrey was at her usual spot in the back of the coffee shop. The scent of coffee mingled with the fragrance of freshly baked pastries. Her mouth watered.

Breakfast had been dry cereal and milk. Lunch a carton of yogurt.

Uriah had made chocolate chip cookies. Damn him.

Absolutely not, girl. The budget didn't allow for tasty goodies...and neither did her jeans. Although she'd stayed so busy here that the weight she'd lost hadn't returned.

One cookie wouldn't hurt anything.

Abandoning her analysis of the pedestrian patterns in New York that she was doing for a newsstand company client, she brought up her email. Anything to keep her mind off buttery cookies with chocolate and...

Oh, look, Dennison has written.

Hoping for good news, Audrey opened the email. And read the FBI agent's email.

Read it again.

Yesterday, the Rescue, AK PD queried the Chicago police department about you.

She stared at the email until the letters began to dance on the display. A sense of betrayal rolled through her in an ugly black wave. Slamming the laptop shut, she jumped to her feet.

Gabe knew she was running. Knew she was scared. And he didn't care. He wanted his questions answered and apparently would do anything to get answers.

Had Spyros's informants in the Chicago police department told him about the inquiry from Rescue?

Oh God. How soon would the hitman come after her?

A high whine filled her head—the beginning of panic. She shoved her laptop and papers into her backpack, pulled it on, and half-ran for the door.

Behind the counter, Sarah called, "Julie?"

Pushing open the door, Audrey ran full-tilt into Bull.

"Yo, champ." As she tried to dodge around him, his massive hand closed on her arm. "What's wrong?"

"What's wrong?" She broke into a bitter, ugly laugh. "Your brother Gabe is what's wrong. He...he..." Her mouth closed, and she turned.

The patrol car was parked in front of the station. He was there.

Pulling away from Bull, she ran across the street, past Regina at the reception desk, and into the station.

Gabe was in his office, filing papers in a cabinet. "Julie?"

"You insufferable bastard." She stalked over, wanting to make him hurt as much as she hurt. Because she'd liked him. Why had she liked him?

"What?"

"You've probably gotten me killed, you...you arrogant asshole. You *knew* I was hiding. You knew I'd been hurt, and you still went and made inquiries about me in Chicago."

He shook his head. "It wasn't me."

How stupid did he think she was? "Oh, it surely was. You heard me blurt out my name. You're the only one who knows I'm from Chicago." Frustration and anger grew so overwhelming that tears filled her eyes. "I t-trusted you."

No, no, she wouldn't cry. Not in front of this bastard. A sob broke from her, and she ran for the door.

He caught her arm, his grip as unyielding as his voice. "Uh-uh. This time we really *are* going to talk."

"No."

Gripping her shoulders, he turned her to face him.

"No, no, no." She shoved with one hand and used the other to pound his rock-hard chest. Blindly, stupidly, just wanting...wanting to make him feel.

"Julie, it wasn't me, sweetheart. I told Baumer you were from Chicago—I'm guilty of that. But he sent the inquiry without permission. I just found out what he'd done an hour ago and planned to talk to you about it today." His voice was calm. Direct.

And undeniably honest. He hadn't been the one who queried the Chicago police force about her.

Muscles turning to water, her arms dropped. Tears filled her eyes as the sense of betrayal drained away.

"Oh, hell, Julie. I'm sorry." He pulled off her backpack and firmly drew her into his arms.

Starting to cry, she tried to pull away.

"Shhh." He only pulled her closer, holding her as she sobbed. His palm moved up and down her back in slow, soothing strokes.

She'd been so scared and alone. And now, she felt safe.

Cared for.

His shirt smelled like laundry soap and wilderness, and she could hear his heart, a slow lub-dub...because she'd stopped crying.

He still held her, an enduring rock in an ocean of tears. Despite the way she'd yelled at him.

She flinched. "I'm—I'm so sorry. I need to go. Let me go, Gabe, I didn't mean to act like..." There was no word for her behavior.

"Like someone who felt betrayed?" She felt him rub his cheek against the top of her head before he let her pull back. Keeping a hand on her arm, he grabbed a couple of tissues from a box on his desk and snagged her backpack. "C'mon, let's get out of here."

As he walked her out, he paused at the reception desk. "Regina, I'm on the beeper for emergencies. Anything else, I'll deal with tomorrow."

"Yes, sir."

Audrey frowned. No, this wasn't right. "You shouldn't—"

"Goldilocks, you're not going to win this argument."

Ah, yes, that was obvious.

Silently, she let him guide her out the back door and into his Jeep. *His* vehicle? "I can drive myself."

"No. You can't." His jaw set.

When he drove past the turnoff to her cabin, she sat up.

"Gabe, where are we going?"

"My place. We're going to get this straightened out." He glanced at her, and a corner of his mouth tipped up. "Don't look so worried. I left the rubber mallets and handcuffs at the station."

She choked on a half-hysterical laugh.

Slowing, he turned onto a small, nearly invisible, dirt road. A few minutes later, the heavy forest opened into a cleared area. Four...no, five...two-story log cabins sat in a semi-circle with the open side facing the long expanse of lake. "I thought Bull lived here," she said blankly.

"He does. So do I—and Caz, too." Gabe pulled into the leftmost house's garage.

After they got out, he stopped at the inside door, toed off his boots, and waited until she removed her shoes. Then he led her up three steps and into a narrow hallway between two small bedrooms. Crossing under stairs that rose to the floor above, they emerged into a huge room that opened all the way to the vaulted ceiling. Immense front windows gave an incredible view of the lake.

"You have a beautiful place."

"Thank you." He waited as she looked around.

The rest of the house was beautiful, too. Off-white finished walls contrasted with the dark wood beams making up the ceiling. The window trim was finished logs.

On the left, the chocolate leather-and-suede sectional faced a massive stone fireplace with a black insert. She imagined cozy evenings in front of a crackling fire.

A wide flat-screen television hung over the fireplace mantel. Sturdy carved end tables and an equally hefty coffee table indicated a big man's home.

To her right, a brown granite-topped island separated the kitchen from the dining area under the front windows.

"Your house is lovely, Gabe." If the heavy brown furniture had been in a smaller room, it would have been oppressive. Instead, the colors balanced the spectacular views of the lake and mountains and gave a feeling of homey comfort.

"It's a good place." Gabe seated her on the sectional, fetched two sodas from the kitchen, and settled beside her.

Right beside her.

A fizzle of heat started low in her abdomen because she remembered what had happened the last time she shared a couch with the man.

He chuckled and tangled his fingers in her hair. "Talk, first. Then we'll see what happens."

God, how did he read the thoughts right from her head? Yet, she couldn't keep from tilting her head to press against the warmth of his big palm.

"You couldn't tell me about your past because..." he prompted.

"You must know why." She curled her fingers around his hand and held it against her chest, like a teddy bear. Needing the connection. "Fake name, fake papers. I figured that was probably illegal."

"The ID didn't come from witness protection?"

"No. I bought everything myself. No one knows—or they didn't—where I'm hiding."

His brows drew together. "Not even the FBI?"

"Spyros has informants in both the police and FBI on his payroll. I figured entrusting myself to them would get me killed. So I ran." The memory of that time sent a tremor of dismay through her...because she'd have to run again.

"You ran." Eyes narrowed, he looked out of the wide

windows for a moment. "How did you learn Baumer had asked the Chicago PD about you?"

"An FBI special agent. He's my only contact, and he keeps me updated about the investigation. He's been wonderful. He didn't like that I ran, didn't know where I went, but he understood my reason."

"Understood? Even though you didn't let him know where you were?" Gabe's eyebrows went up.

"I didn't want him put in a bad position if his higher-ups asked him where I was." She sighed. "That's why I didn't tell you, either."

Jesus. Gabe studied Julie.

As she stared down at their entwined fingers, her long eyelashes were a shade darker than her golden hair, making shadows on her pale cheeks. Her hand trembled in his.

She was scared—and with good reason.

In the time between Baumer's revelation and Julie's appearance in the office, Gabe had been busy. He'd called an old SEAL buddy who worked for Interpol. The agent said the quiet librarian had not only defended herself, but the fight had cost the hitman an eye. The few times Spyros had been spotted afterward, he'd worn an eye patch. Interpol was positive the assassin would seek revenge.

Gabe's jaw clenched. His buddy had also said Spyros's sources were reputed to be excellent. If Spyros had an informant in the Chicago PD, the hitman might already know Julie's location.

"I talked with a friend in Interpol," Gabe said. "He said they'll watch for Spyros entering Alaska, but he's gotten past them before."

"So I've heard." She still hadn't lifted her gaze, so he put a finger under her chin. The fear he'd seen in her eyes when they met had returned.

Fuck, he wanted to kill this Spyros.

And he wanted to assure Julie she was safe here in Rescue. But she wasn't a woman who'd appreciate lies.

He ran his knuckles down her cheek. "Whenever I see a movie hero promise a woman she'll be safe, it pisses me off. No one, no matter how skilled, can guarantee safety. But, Julie, I'll do everything I can to make sure you are."

"Instead, can you help me get out of here without anyone knowing where I went?"

He could.

"Are you sure that's what you want?" An ache grew inside him. She wouldn't have asked without weighing all her options. Yes, she'd be leaving, and he couldn't tell her it was a bad decision.

She nodded.

"Yes, I'll help, Julie."

Her lips curved slightly. "It's Audrey—as you know. I'd like it if you used it."

"Audrey." He bent his head and kissed her gently. The

CHERISE SINCLAIR

sigh she gave held the same sadness he felt. When her arms curled around his neck, he knew he wasn't the only one feeling as if life had screwed up something that might have been very good.

Well, he'd give her the traditional warrior's sendoff, even if it was the female who'd be going into battle.

Then, he'd declare open season on hitmen and do some hunting himself.

Rising, he scooped her into his arms, took her up the stairs, and laid her on his bed.

She sat up to look around.

He followed her gaze, trying to see his room with a woman's eyes. Smoothed to a glossy finish, the headboard, footboard, and nightstands were rough-hewn, heavy lumber. The exposed wood ceiling beams and walls were stained a light golden color. Beige shag rugs beside the bed greeted bare feet on cold mornings. The hand quilted spread was a colorful jumble of dark red, white, and cream.

He'd deliberately kept the room's colors lighter than downstairs. Getting out of bed was difficult enough during the black Alaskan winters; a cavelike room would make it worse.

Although waking up beside Audrey would brighten any man's day.

She looked good sitting right there.

"Goldilocks, I'd say you found a bed that fits you just right."

"I did." She patted the quilt, and her voice had turned

272

husky. Excited. "Are you planning what they call goodbye sex?"

Yeah, she was feeling what he was. "Only if you don't come back." She'd damned well better come back.

Her smile appeared even as tears filled her eyes.

Without saying more, he stripped her—T-shirt, bra, socks, jeans, and practical boy-cut briefs. *Nice.*

He straightened. "It's your turn to undress me, lazy one."

"Oh. Okay." As she slid off the bed and started on his clothing, her breasts wobbled in a compelling fashion.

While she removed his shirt, he played with her breasts, cupping, fondling, teasing, then teased her nipples to rigid peaks.

Her breathing changed. Deepened.

Pushing him back a step, she fumbled with his jeans buttons. Released, his erection sprang out, and she wrapped her hands around it.

All right—that would be a good diversion for them both. So he simply enjoyed the moment as she knelt in front of him.

She was adorably awkward, enough that he could tell she hadn't often given blowjobs. But her tongue was hot and wet, and she was careful with her teeth, something a man could appreciate. When she closed her mouth around him and started bobbing her head, heat swept through him, and his dick swelled with the urge to get off right then.

A wise man didn't let his cock rule the roost.

Gabe tangled his fingers in her hair, firmly slowing her, and letting himself savor the slow slide of her mouth, the flickers of her slick tongue, the sheer heat. Yeah, he loved how she threw herself into pleasing him.

Before he reached the point of no return, he gently pulled back, scooped her up, and laid her on his bed.

He hadn't closed the wooden pocket doors, and light streamed in from the lakeside windows. As he looked down at her, her cheeks flushed. She instinctively started to cover herself.

"Uh-uh, sweetheart." He caught her hands and curled her fingers around the thick vertical headboard pieces.

She blushed darker. Fuck, he liked that color in her cheeks. So, knowing it would fluster her, he said softly, "Open your legs for me."

Her protest died under his stern look. His cop look. In the academy, no one had mentioned all the potential uses.

He sat beside her, cupping a pretty breast to fondle as her legs slid apart...slowly. A snail would have moved faster, but he was in no hurry. Under his touch, her nipples were bunching tighter.

Bending, he kissed her, teasing her breasts as he did. Then he moved his palm down her stomach, enjoying the feel of the silken skin. A glance showed him that she'd stopped opening her legs way too soon. So he stroked over her mound, never lower, feeling the quivers as her need grew.

"Gabe..."

She put her arms around his shoulders as he kissed her.

"Hands up here, sweetheart." He put her hands back on the headboard, trying not to smile as she whimpered.

"You're a controlling, bossy...person," she muttered, obviously having thought better of the nastier word like bastard or asshole.

"Yes, I am." And wasn't it nice that she enjoyed that side of his nature. "Why? Did you want to be in charge?"

Her mouth dropped open. "Uh...no."

He hadn't thought so.

He dipped his fingers to graze the top of her swollen clit. "If you want more, your legs need to be wider apart."

Her low whine made him harder than a rock. Her legs spread.

"Very nice." Rising, he stripped off his jeans. From his nightstand drawer, he popped a mint lozenge in his mouth. Just for fun.

The quilt was cool under his knees as he settled between her legs and took a long appreciative look. "Damn, you're beautiful."

The surprise, then delight in her face hurt his heart. If she didn't disappear out of his life, he'd do his damndest to tell her often.

Because everything about her was lovely. Tiny freckles dotted the top of her breasts, shoulders, and arms. Her upper arms and shoulders had firmed up from carrying bar trays. Her high breasts had pink nipples that were peaked and rosy from his fondling. Her waist curved in then out to lush hips. He really liked the sweet roundness of her tummy.

The golden curls covering her pussy were damp with her arousal—and yeah, he wanted a taste before they got down to serious fucking.

She moved a hand from the headboard. "I want to touch you, too." Her gray eyes were stormy with the appeal.

Perhaps she wasn't comfortable with receiving and not giving? Yes, that would be like her. "All right. But hands and tongue only. No mouth."

Because he wanted this to last a lot longer than if that talented mouth started teasing his dick.

"Um...got it."

"Turn over onto your side."

When she was arranged on her right side, he lay down, facing her in a sixty-nine position, moving until his face was at her pussy, and her face was near his groin. He blew a puff of air and felt her shiver. Yeah, this would be fun...

When her warm fingers stroked down his shaft, he almost groaned. Fun and a pure test of his control.

So that he could use his hands, he positioned her left leg over him, knee pointing toward the ceiling, and her foot flat on the bed behind his head. Nice and open.

Resting his head on her soft inner thigh, he licked over her clit.

Her thigh muscles tensed, bouncing his head, and making him grin.

Her hot tongue ran over his erection, making it jump in turn, and she wiggled nearer. When her mouth closed around him, he almost laughed.

He might have known she wouldn't obey. Stubborn librarian. Well, it'd be his job to see she was panting too hard to suck cock.

Audrey rested her head on Gabe's left thigh and tried to keep her attention on fondling and licking over his velvet-skinned shaft.

But his fingers, his lips...

Oh my God, she kept losing track of what she wanted to do to him. As he teased her clit, his tongue was so very hot, and yet...each lick left a strange cold sensation behind. When he blew over the sensitive nub, his breath felt icy. The combination of warm and cold on her most intimate area was overwhelming.

A second later, he'd engulfed the area in the heat of his mouth.

Even as she moaned, he penetrated her with two fingers, pumping gently.

The incredible sensations drove every thought out of her mind.

Low in her belly, muscles tightened as her insides

clasped his fingers. Each long lick of his hot tongue increased the lust pulsing in her blood stream.

She tried to remember to stroke him, to suck him, and then his tongue would stroke over her with unerring precision.

She tried to pull her hips back so she could keep control and do her part, but he put an unyielding hand behind her butt, drawing her closer instead. His fingers plunged faster, deeper.

A moan broke from her as the ruthless hold sent shudders through her while the pressure grew.

His tongue circled her sensitive nub, even as he squeezed her buttocks and slid a finger down the crease.

The fireball of an orgasm burned from the inside out, shooting her higher and higher, and still, he didn't release her. His tongue kept moving lightly, ceaselessly wringing out the last flickers of pleasure.

A light kiss to her pussy made her spasm again before he sat up, pulling his rigid shaft from her limp fingers.

"I...I forgot. You didn't get—"

His eyes glinted with amusement. "That was the idea." After covering himself with a condom from the nightstand, he rolled her to her back and lowered himself on top of her.

She wrapped her arms around his broad shoulders. The feeling of his weight on her, pressing her into the mattress, fogged her brain and electrified her blood.

With a hand, he positioned the thick head of his shaft, and she held her breath at the sizzling thrill.

Then he thrust, surging inside so hard and fast they both gasped for air.

"Mmm. Right here is where I wanted to be." Seated deep inside her, he propped himself up on his elbows, moving his hands to bracket her face.

And he trapped her gaze as he started to move.

Oh, such a feeling, the heavy, thick shaft filled her completely. As her pussy throbbed around him, her eyes closed at the overwhelming sensation.

"Mmm, look at me, sweetheart," he whispered. "I want to see your eyes."

His eyes were a bottomless blue, burning into her. He took her with merciless, driving thrusts, possessing her, soul and body.

He slid a hand under her bottom to raise her hips for still greater penetration as his body turned rigid, the cords on his neck standing out as he came.

His body shuddered as he pulled in a long, slow breath.

Setting his forehead against hers, he huffed a laugh. His lips were gentle as he kissed her lightly. "I had planned to get you off again, but you're a bit too clever with those fingers of yours. You won't be getting a 69 very often."

No, she wouldn't. Never again.

An ache set up residence in her heart at the thought of losing him. Of never making love with him again. Never seeing him after tomorrow.

Nonetheless, she had no choice. To save her own life, she needed to get far away from here.

Even more important, she needed to be far away from Gabe. Because the thought of dying was far, far less terrifying than the thought of this man getting hurt or killed while protecting her from Spyros.

CHAPTER TWENTY

The next morning, Audrey got out of Gabe's Jeep, and he walked her to the coffee shop.

Although it was Tuesday and he had to work, he'd volunteered to drive her to Anchorage. She'd told him she'd wait until he got off work.

He thought the coffee shop was safe, since it was unlikely Spyros and his crew had already reached Rescue. Just in case, Gabe wanted her in a very public space. Spyros would want his revenge up close and personal.

Meantime, since she had a safe internet spot here, she'd order a new ID, figure out where to hide out in Anchorage, and where to get a new car.

Once in the city, she could hide until her ID came. After that, maybe she'd return to the Lower 48 or move to a village in the interior.

As Gabe held open the coffee shop door for her, she

looked up at his chiseled face, and blinked back tears. When had the deadly police chief become so dear to her?

And why did he have to be so amazing, in and out of bed?

Sex with him was...well, like all those romance books made it sound. But what had truly turned her to mush was when he'd pulled her into his big enclosed shower and washed her. Washed her hair.

How could such powerful hands be so gentle?

When she'd protested, he'd laughed and said, "Then you can wash me, Goldilocks, since you think you didn't get to play with my dick enough in bed."

Oh, what had followed had been amazing. Because when she'd washed his shaft, it lengthened. Thickened. After stepping out to grab a condom from the counter drawer, he bent her over the long tile bench and took her, fast and hard, using his fingers on her to ensure she came when he did.

Her legs had been so weak afterward he had to help her out of the shower.

And this wasn't what she should be thinking about right now. *Way to go, girl.* Now her lower half was tingling and needy, wanting to drag Gabe home for more.

Instead, she straightened her shoulders and stepped into the coffee shop.

He followed her in and ran a palm down her hair. "You sure you want to leave?" he asked softly.

She nodded. "It'll be safer." *For me and for everyone around me.*

But, God, it hurt.

As she stood there, he wrapped his arms around her in an all-encompassing hug. And her heart simply melted into a warm puddle.

They hadn't known each other that long, yet...she was totally in love with him.

She was leaving. *Leaving* him. The fog-filled morning air held a chill that matched the one in Gabe's gut.

After giving Uriah and Sarah a heads-up that Audrey might have someone bad looking for her, Gabe stalked through Rescue, nodding at the few people who greeted him. The rest scurried from his path. He was scaring the locals...and he didn't particularly care.

She was leaving.

He hadn't wanted to get involved with her—or anyone—but he sure had. Hell of a mistake.

Only he couldn't call the time he'd spent with her a mistake. More like a gift.

Still...she was leaving. His jaw clenched. He'd really like to hit something.

That wasn't like him at all.

"Chief's sure in a pissed-off mood," he heard a couple of women say. "Best stay out of his way."

That brought him up short. For fuck's sake, he was supposed to be the good guy here. With a sigh, he scrubbed his hands over his face. *Get a grip, MacNair. You have people to protect, and it shouldn't be from yourself.*

Pulling in a slow breath through his nose, he stowed his feelings away, a technique he'd mastered early in his SEAL career. Allowing emotions in battle got people killed. He'd think about Audrey when he wasn't on duty. Later.

As his balance settled, he nodded to the women. "Sorry, ladies. I don't think I got my full gallon of coffee."

They gave him smiles and "good mornings" and resumed their stroll down the sidewalk.

There. He gave himself two points for good community relations and continued.

He'd still rather beat the crap out of someone.

The day passed slowly. Knowing Audrey was in the coffee shop was a unique form of torture. She was safe there, far safer than if she was holed up in a lonely cabin or even trying to hide in Anchorage. But still...

He went in to check on Audrey every time he returned to town.

There'd been too damn many calls today.

Gabe parked the patrol car in front of the station, got out, and stretched. A concerned citizen had phoned in about abandoned sled dogs. *Jesus.* With dreams of big winnings or getting sponsorships, potential mushers would buy dogs, then discover it took work and money to develop competitive teams. And they'd kill or abandon the dogs.

Talk about asshole behavior.

Although Gabe had called a rescue organization to get the emaciated dogs, it'd be a while before his anger died.

Over the course of the day, the fog had dissipated, but the sky remained a leaden gray. Occasional rain smeared windshields and dampened clothing.

He'd be off duty soon. As he looked down the street, tourists still wandered the town, in and out of the few stores.

A sports equipment rental was looking at setting up on Main Street. If it did, the next step would be another restaurant since the fishermen and hikers would return their rented equipment around late afternoon and evening.

Gabe poked his head in the station to see if there was anything going on.

Regina was tidying her desk in preparation to leave. "Evening, Chief. Your messages are on your desk. Nothing needs your attention until tomorrow."

"How did I survive before you arrived?"

"Badly, Chief. Badly."

He smiled, enjoying how she'd settled into the job. Her manner and posture had changed in just this short time. It was as if she finally saw herself as she truly was—an intelligent, competent woman and a valuable member of the team.

"I'm going to make a quick foot patrol and call it a day." When he'd called, Audrey said she hadn't finished whatever preparations she'd been making.

"Yes, sir."

Gabe reversed course and headed down Main Street, detouring along the back alleys to check that the new business owners had heeded his orders about securing their garbage. There was nothing a black bear liked more than a free lunch.

So far, so good.

As he strolled down Sweetgale, he saw Lillian wasn't home. She was probably off at one of her numerous social things.

Reaching the end of the road, he stepped into the roadhouse. There were a good number of patrons...and no problems. *Perfect.*

Before leaving, he raised his hand to Bull and got a wide grin in return.

In the parking lot, a raised voice from the rear of the building caught his attention.

Gabe headed that way.

The lot held only a few cars. Several people stood around, watching something. Probably a wild animal. Tourists clustered like flies on carrion when spotting any wildlife.

But as he got closer, he realized the crowd was locals. And all male.

"Take it off, baby," one said loudly.

"Woohoo," another growled, "let's see those knockers."

"Hey, maybe this isn't a good idea." The skinny male's protest was drowned out by the rest.

Gabe drew closer.

Two women were in the center of the...mob. Both crying. One on her knees, the other trying to stand. *Damn.*

"What's going on here?" Gabe said in a loud voice.

"Shit, it's the *cop.*" Like cockroaches when a light was turned on, the entire group scattered and raced toward the front of the lot.

As pickups and cars screeched away, Gabe approached the two women and went down on one knee.

Both mid-twenties, terrified and clinging to each other. One's shirt was half-ripped off. The other had a swollen lip and a red handprint on her face.

When they cringed, he tapped the badge on his chest. "Police. How badly are you hurt?"

"Not...not really," one said.

Thank fuck. He was so angry, he had to work to keep his voice soft. "What happened?"

"We...we came out of the roadhouse to leave, but I saw..." The blonde was crying too hard to continue.

"Marcy saw a bear behind the building, so we followed. For a picture." The woman shoved her glasses up on her nose, looked around, and picked up her cell phone from the gravel. "That bunch of men... I guess they saw us, and they followed and just...just surrounded us."

Gabe managed to keep his face calm.

"We didn't do anything, weren't even talking to them. We tried to leave," the blonde said. "But they called us names and started ripping at our clothes. I tried to scream, and one slapped me." She held her swollen cheek with the stunned expression of someone who'd never been hit in her life.

That *his* town had taught her about violence made Gabe sick. He held out his hands and helped them to their feet. "Do you think you could identify any of them again?"

The blonde shook her head hastily.

The one with glasses actually hesitated. "No, no, I'm afraid not. And we leave tomorrow. We have to be back at work."

Jesus, what a way to end a vacation. Rescue sure wouldn't be the highlight of their holiday. "I understand. We have a medical clinic here. We can have the practitioner check you over and make sure you're not injured."

"The slap was the worst of it," said the one with the glasses. "At least as far as physical went." Her eyes teared. "I'm really glad you came along."

"Are you staying up at the resort hotel? How about I drive you up there?"

She shook her head. "No, I'm good." Her arm went around her friend. "Marcy's never been around this...kind of stuff. Unfortunately, I have."

Now that made a man feel like shit—that a woman was familiar enough with the general assholery of men that she'd experienced it more than once in her life. What the fuck was wrong with his gender?

At their car, he opened the door, helped them in, and gave the brunette a careful scrutiny. Yeah, she was recovered. Safe to drive.

She gave him a nod and headed out of town.

Out of his town.

Only it wasn't, was it? He didn't want to be part of a place where men acted like a dog pack, out after prey. Only one guy had even tried to protest.

Scowling, he headed back toward the downtown section. He hadn't met any of the men before, but he sure as hell would recognize most of them if he saw them again. If he did.

He glanced at the coffee shop and remembered Audrey was leaving.

Frustrated anger was a bitter taste in his mouth.

———

Audrey was in her comfy corner of the coffee shop. The low hum of the customers made a kind of background music. Business had picked up as people stopped in for the bargain-priced unsold pastries.

Oh, how she would miss this place—smelling the pastries and coffee, hearing Sarah and her husband mock-bicker, getting friendly greetings from the increasing number of people who knew her.

People seemed to like her, and how astonishing was that?

Unless Gabe got a call, he should be coming to get her soon. To take her to Anchorage. She'd better get her stuff put away.

She pulled up her email for a quick check to see if she had a delivery time for her new ID—and found, instead, an email from Dennison.

What disaster had ensued this time?

Biting her lip, she opened it.

Success!

Spyros was arrested today while boarding a flight to Alaska and is now safely behind bars. There will be no bail.

I'm pleased to say it should be safe for you to return to Chicago, Audrey.

Call me when you get into town. I'd like to meet you in person.

D.

A sound escaped her, then another squeak and another. As she jumped to her feet, her chair fell over.

They caught him. She wasn't going to die. No one was coming for her.

Oh, my God, she was *free*.

"Julie, are you all right?" Sarah hurried over, her hand

out. She halted, and her worried frown cleared. "Wait... Good news?"

"The best. The very best."

Realizing everyone was staring, Audrey flushed and raised her voice. "Sorry. I'm just...happy."

Grins appeared along with a few shakes of heads. They were probably thinking *idiotic Outsider*.

"Well, good." Sarah patted her shoulder and returned to behind the counter.

As Audrey resumed her seat, she saw again Dennison's sentence. *"I'm pleased to say it should be safe for you to return to Chicago, Audrey."* She could go *home*, where she knew how things worked. Where moose didn't attack her. Where she was a respected, valued member of the university.

Her fingers stroked over the keyboard as she stared at the swirling screen saver. Yes, she could return to work.

On her third day on the run, she'd called her boss to ask for a family crisis leave. Her superior had been understanding—after all, Audrey had never used her sick days—and said to take as long as needed.

Yes, she'd have a job.

Not an apartment, though.

That was gone, and her belongings were in storage. Not that she'd have wanted to go back to her old apartment. There'd been...blood in the bedroom. A shudder ran through her. The slightest noise would make her think someone was breaking in again.

No, it was good she'd have to find a new place. One with far better security.

Catching her eye, Uriah gestured to the bottled water, silently asking if she needed another. She shook her head.

She sighed. God, she'd miss coming here each day.

And she'd miss Gabe.

No, no, no, don't think about him. She shook her head and tried to shift her thoughts to ones that wouldn't make her cry.

Like how much she loved working with Lillian in the garden.

Lillian—oh, *no.* Audrey'd promised to take care of the garden until the harvest season. All the salad greens were planted, and the rapidly growing tomatoes in the sunroom would need to go in soon, and...

She couldn't leave now. She didn't *want* to leave now.

And what about the library? She had to finish deciding what to order.

Knox needed her. If she didn't keep teaching him, he'd never learn to read.

The children's hour programs had to be developed and scheduled, too.

Really, she needed to finish what she'd started. Leaving her tasks half-completed was...was *poor form*, as Lillian would say.

Besides, it'd be less stressful to return after Spyros had been behind bars for a couple of months.

August. She would stay until August.

"Problems, Goldilocks?" A warm palm cupped her chin and lifted, forcing her to look up into penetrating blue eyes.

Gabe.

If she stayed a couple of more months, what would he think? What if he didn't want her to? What if it turned awkward?

His brows drew together, and he took the chair beside her, his arm around her shoulders. "What's the matter, sweetheart?" His low resonant voice tugged at her.

"I...I'm going to stay until August. I need to stay."

"All right." His brows drew together, even as he wiped a tear off her cheek. "Do you need my permission?"

Oh, she did sound like an idiot. "No. I—"

"Chief, she was dancing around here a minute ago. Until you showed up." Sarah scowled at him. "Now, she's crying."

The criticism rolled off his broad back like rain off a newly waxed car. "Dancing? Did something happen?"

Her smile returned. "They caught Spyros. He's been arrested." She put her palms on his chest and bounced in her seat. "They caught him."

A crease appeared in his lean face as he smiled. "'Bout fucking time."

Leaning forward, he planted a kiss on her lips. Then his brows drew together. "Let me get this straight. You plan to return to Chicago, but not until August?"

Uncertainty made her hands clench. "Um...yes. I promised Lillian I'd stay until harvest, and I have to get Knox and the library settled. I have—"

"You have responsibilities." He turned to look out the window, toward the police station. She felt his chest rise and fall with a slow exhalation. "As do I, dammit."

"Gabe?"

"August, hmm?"

"I'll have things wrapped up by then." He'd mentioned his own responsibilities. She studied him. "Are you planning to leave, too?"

"Maybe. But like you, I can't right this minute, no matter what I want. I have to stay for tourist season at the minimum."

Gabe leaving. She couldn't imagine Rescue without its chief. It was as if he was the heart of the town. She frowned. "Doesn't a ski resort mean there's a winter tourist season, too?"

His jaw tightened. "Yes, but by then, the town can hire someone else for my position."

"Not Earl Baumer."

His eyes narrowed. "You don't like Baumer?"

"I...uh...don't know him. But I don't think he'd be as good as you are."

His stern face softened, and he rubbed his knuckles against her cheek. "I think you're a bit prejudiced on my behalf."

"Maybe." He was right in that she hadn't been to bed with Earl Baumer. Not that she would. But if she stayed, maybe...maybe she and Gabe... The words spilled out of her mouth. "Want to spend two months having a hot fling?"

She clapped her hands over her treacherous mouth.

"Fling?" The amusement in his gaze changed, darkened toward demanding. "Oh, yeah, little cheechako, that sounds good to me."

Oh my God, had he just agreed?

His mouth curved into a satisfied smile.

What had she done? Yes, she wanted nothing more than to be with him, but... Would she be able to leave him after falling more in love over the summer?"

"Chief." The call came from the door. "There's a fight in front of the bar."

Gabe gave a grumble of exasperation. "Coming."

Rising, he smiled down at her and repeated with a chuckle, "A fling."

"I..."

He stopped her with a kiss. "I'm damn glad you're safe from Spyros. I'll pick you up at your cabin tonight after I get off work. Because you'll spend the night at mine."

He strolled out of the coffee shop, leaving her staring after him.

He'd kissed her—right there in front of everyone. Like he was claiming her. Like a lover.

A lover. Oh, God, she couldn't have a lover. Even if she did love him—and she really shouldn't—. Talk about a stupid thing to do.

A chair scraped as Sarah sat down at the table. "You look like he slapped you instead of kissing you. Are you all right?"

Audrey swallowed as she met the woman's concerned gaze. "I—"

"We've been worried about you, but you looked like you were doing all right. Until today." Sarah took her hand and gave it a squeeze "Something's wrong. Let us help, Julie. Whatever you need, we can help."

God. Friendship. Without even realizing it, she had actually made a friend. The tears filling her eyes made her blink.

"No, no, don't cry. Just tell me what's wrong." Sarah's grip turned painful.

Audrey smiled and brushed the wetness from her eyes. "Not wrong—something went right. I have a story to tell you. First of all, my name isn't Julie. It's Audrey."

CHAPTER TWENTY-ONE

Leaving Audrey puttering around in his kitchen, Gabe stepped out onto his deck to check the grill.

The beauty of the early evening stopped him for a moment. The lake was peaceful, a shimmering reflection of the cloudless, blue sky. The trees and grass along the banks were brilliantly green. A pair of bald eagles performed a dance over the water.

The dry, clear days of late spring were the most beautiful time in Alaska.

Then, he laughed. He loved the appearance of termination dust—the first snowfall to whiten the mountains and signal the end of summer.

What about the unworldly quiet of a midwinter night? The glow of a full moon on a snow-covered forest? The intense cold that could steal a man's breath?

Or summer as the purple-pink swathes of fireweed

reigned over the meadows and roadsides. When the beginning salmon runs attracted the bears with their bumbling cubs.

Yeah, he liked all the seasons.

Especially at Mako's old cabin where wilderness surrounded him on all sides.

Yet...he was happy here.

The scent of the grill wafted to him. The alder wood had died down to the perfect embers for cooking.

Voice a low rumble, Bull strolled across the inner courtyard with Caz. Hoping for scraps, the chickens clucked as the men passed. Bull held the platter of salmon fillets he'd been marinating. Being a health nut, Caz had prepared a huge green salad.

His brothers. It'd been good to live here beside them rather than just visiting during vacations. Together, they'd fixed the woodshed, cleaned up the winter debris, and repaired snow damage. And they'd all silently grieved for Mako.

Working beside them had repaired the disconnect brought about by long absences.

He frowned. If he returned to Mako's cabin, would Bull and Caz see his leaving as a kind of betrayal?

At the sizzle of meat hitting the grill, Gabe headed inside to get the fixings for baked potatoes.

Audrey already had everything set out on a tray. She passed it to him.

"Perfect. Thank you. As soon as the salmon is done, we can get the potatoes out of the oven."

"Okay." She glanced out the window and rubbed her hands on her jeans. "Are you sure they're all right with me being here? I mean, at a family meal and everything."

He set the tray down on the counter and pulled her up against him. "Goldilocks, we're a bunch of guys. The addition of an intelligent, beautiful woman is always a plus."

The confused expression on her face made him frown. "Beautiful? I'm not...I mean, I'm okay, but not beautiful. No, that's not me."

He pulled her closer, his heart aching. She really did believe that.

It wasn't the first time he'd noticed this oddity in women. When younger, he'd thought maybe he attracted insecure females, but with more experience, he found most females doubted their attractiveness. During one late-night discussion, Caz had pointed out that society—and women's fashions—made each woman feel inadequate. Her figure was never the right size; she was either too curvy or too thin. Her hair was never thick enough or glossy enough. Her eyes weren't big enough. Her skin didn't glow enough. Her lips weren't red enough or full enough.

Honestly, if men were hammered with that kind of bullshit, they'd get out the pitchforks and rip apart the fashion industry.

He lifted Audrey's chin. "You are beautiful," he said

firmly. "You have the biggest, most beautiful eyes I've ever seen. They're the color of morning fog over the lake."

When he saw the hint of tears in her eyes, he panicked. And added, "Especially right after you've come."

The corners of her mouth tilted up.

Smiling, he stroked through her hair. "Your hair is silky and long...and perfect for holding you in place during sex."

She choked back a laugh.

He ran his thumb over the satin of her lower lip. "This soft mouth is simply perfect for sucking my dick."

When her eyes narrowed, he grinned. "Your breasts are the perfect size," *for my hands*, "and every time I see your ass, I get hard."

Pinning her against the counter, he pressed that very hard dick against her.

She began to laugh. "I think you've been sniffing the Viagra or something."

"I don't need Viagra; I have you." He nibbled his way down her neck. Yes, her breasts really were the perfect size for his hands.

She leaned into him, her fingers tangling in his hair. "Gabe, do we have time to..."

"Hey, bro," Bull yelled. "Bring us the taters."

"Hell." He pulled back and smiled down into her unfocused eyes. Her cheeks were flushed with arousal.

She blinked at him.

He grinned. "We'll finish this discussion later. For now, can you carry out the tray while I get the potatoes?"

"Right. Yes. Of course."

She picked up the tray and headed for the door, hitting the doorframe with her shoulder. He had to grin. She wanted him and still wasn't sure how to deal with it.

In fact, she'd surprised him completely by suggesting a fling. He'd never seen anything cuter than when she'd slapped her hands over her mouth, appalled at what she'd said.

Even if he'd wanted to say no, her reaction had sealed the deal.

Tossing the hot potatoes into a basket, he grabbed a couple of beers and headed out to the patio.

Nothing tasted as good as meat from the grill, whether salmon, moose, or cow. And Gabe was pleased to see Audrey ate as heartily as everyone else.

When they'd finished eating, he gathered the scraps and showed her how to give the chickens the treats.

Unable to resist her open delight over the task, Gabe pulled her into a long kiss. Was there anything sexier than the way she concentrated on each new "adventure," fully into each moment of time?

As they returned from the chicken yard, Bull and Caz had cleaned up the area and were heading across the lawn.

"Hey, you two," Bull called as he swatted at a mosquito. "The breeze is gone. Time to move to protected ground."

Grabbing their drinks, Gabe took Audrey's hand and followed his brothers into the screened pavilion on the grassy lake bank.

"So, *viejo*, how was your day?" Caz asked.

Earlier, Audrey had told his brothers everything about Spyros. Then Caz and Bull had run through the highlights of their Tuesday.

Now, it was Gabe's turn...because that was a Mako tradition. Growing up, each boy was required to give a summary of the day. The sarge had been devious that way. Hawk had been forced to use more than a couple of words. Caz had to speak in English.

Settling into a chair beside Audrey, Gabe told about the harassment of the two female tourists. "I didn't recognize the men involved."

He hadn't met everyone in town, but he'd keep an eye out for this group now.

Bull stroked his goatee. "How were they dressed?"

"Country, not city. Jeans, boots—"

"T-shirts or button-downs?"

Gabe replayed the scene in his head. "No tees." That was odd. The men had been under thirty—prime T-shirt wearing age. "None of them."

"They might be Patriot Zealots. Their illustrious leader, Reverend Parrish, doesn't approve of T-shirts. Too modern. The women's clothing is even more old-fashioned."

"I've seen their women in the grocery store, always accompanied by a man, of course." Audrey shook her head. "Blouses buttoned up to the neck. Ankle-length skirts. They look as if they stepped out of an episode of *Little House on the Prairie*."

Gabe eyed her. Had he ever seen her in a skirt? But...she probably only wore clothing she could run and escape in. The thought of how long she'd lived in fear was like a rough stone that grated against his heart. He reached over and took her hand.

"How do the PZs treat women?" Gabe asked. The man who'd slapped Audrey at the roadhouse was a PZ. Sounded as if the ones today were PZs. Were there going to be more sexual assaults from this crowd?

"I don't know about their own women, but from the few who visit my bar, they act as if single women are whores." Bull scowled. "I have Felix serve them, no matter where the bastards sit."

Obviously, Bull was watching them.

Gabe almost laughed. Poor bastards. No sane person wanted to piss off Bull. Gabe'd learned early on just how much pain his oversized fist could deliver.

"I'm glad you're keeping an eye on them." It meant Audrey would be safer. Gabe lifted her hand and kissed her fingers.

"You know, it's a relief to hear the assholes from this afternoon belong to that idiotic cult-militia." In fact, the ugly feeling he'd had since finding the men harassing the women had eased.

Bull and Caz looked puzzled.

"The PZs aren't really part of the town," Gabe explained. "When I thought the locals let shit like that happen, I was pissed off."

"I get it." Caz nodded. "Who wants to work to create something good if the residents aren't..."

"Aren't worth it?" Audrey asked.

"Yeah." Gabe rubbed his chest. Felt as if a wound had been ripped open.

"Who can say who's actually worthy, though?" Caz gave them a wry smile. "I doubt I deserved the help I received. Especially from Mako."

Gabe considered. The sarge had taken a chance on them —they'd all acted more like street rats than humans. "Good point."

"You're just like Mako, Gabe," Audrey said softly. "You gave Knox a chance, even though he says he acted like a jerk."

Gabe kissed the top of her head. Apparently, Knox was confiding in her during his reading lessons, wasn't he? Gabe might've let Knox off the hook, but it was Audrey who was steering the man onto a new path. A better one.

"We're going to have problems with that cult," Bull stated. "I don't know what Parrish is doing behind those fences, but he's sure down on attracting attention. It's why he doesn't want new business in the area."

"Too bad for him," Gabe said.

"Speaking of businesses, how's the leasing going?" Caz asked Bull.

Enjoying the way Audrey leaned her head against his shoulder, Gabe drank his beer.

Down the grassy slope, the lake lapped at their small

dock. Earlier, Caz had pulled two kayaks from storage and tied them on the left side. The space for Hawk's floatplane still stood empty, giving Gabe a pang.

Their gathering had a Hawk-sized hole in it.

When he returned his attention to the conversation, Bull and Caz were arguing about the empty building two doors down from Dante's. Bull had an offer from a guy who wanted to open a liquor store.

"I don't like him," Caz said. "Don't lease to him, *'mano*."

With a frown, Audrey tilted her head back to whisper, "How can Caz say no if the building belongs to Bull?"

Gabe kissed her fingers. "Mako left the buildings to all of us in one big bundle."

"He did?" Her brows drew together, then she giggled. "You're letting everyone in town believe Bull is the sole owner so he'll receive all the grief?"

She caught on quickly, didn't she? Gabe winked at her.

"It's because he's the best with finances." Caz grinned. "Really."

"You're so full of it," Bull said. "You're right, Jul—Audrey. They wanted me to deal with all the hassle."

Gabe chuckled. "Hell, yeah."

As the evening grew later, they gathered their instruments, and talking gave way to an interval of music.

It took a bit of coaxing, but Gabe got Audrey to sing with them. She had a beautiful clear soprano. Even better, once she relaxed, he could see the delight in her eyes.

And the pleasure in his brothers' expressions. They'd

occasionally brought home women—not often—but none had fit in the way Audrey did.

Caz did a quick drumroll to end the song and sat back. "I saw Knox and Chevy are repairing the B&B windows they broke."

"Yeah, they're working hard." Gabe snorted. "However, I'm back on their shit list since I warned them I'd be enforcing the dumping and hunting regs."

At Audrey's quizzical look, he added, "I'm hearing rumors the two aren't keen on following the rules, especially when it comes to hunting and fishing licenses."

She grinned. "Why am I not surprised?"

"At least the vandalism has stopped. Good job, bro," Bull said. "So, what's the next step to attract tourists to Rescue?"

Audrey opened her mouth, then closed it.

Still shy, was she? Tenderness lodged in Gabe's heart. "Do you have some ideas for us, Goldilocks?"

Caz and Bull set their instruments to one side.

"I...yes. Between working in the grocery and the road-house, I speak with a lot of tourists. They share what they'd like to see or feel is missing."

"Perfect. Let's hear it, champ," Bull said.

Shyness gone, she laid out what she'd heard, point by point. Logically. Concisely.

Gabe stared at her. After a second, he cleared his throat. "You are amazingly good at analyzing this business stuff."

She shrugged. "It's what I do for a living."

"All right then. The greatest demand seems to be for

more eating and lodging options." Bull rubbed his hands together. "People who want to open restaurants and B&Bs will be my first priority. I've had inquiries on the small hotel building, too. I'll sweeten a deal to get that moving."

"Audrey said Rescue needs recreational choices other than shopping. We could clean up the lakeside park," Caz said.

"That would be great." She frowned at the lake. "I noticed fishermen aren't always men, and often have their families with them. Maybe put in a playground?"

"Perfect," Gabe said. "That would benefit the tourists and the residents. Best of all worlds."

"How about advertising to attract people?" Bull asked.

Caz frowned. "Maybe hold off on spending until we have more infrastructure."

"Agreed," Gabe said.

"Social media is free, though. We could try to get the town's name out that way." Audrey pulled her phone from her pocket and held it up in front of her. "People take selfies all the time. We could give them a selfie site. Like the ones that have a statue of an animal to take a picture with."

"How does a person standing with a bear help us?" Caz asked.

"If the bear has a "Town of Rescue" sign at its feet, you have free advertising whenever pictures show up on Facebook and Instagram. As you beautify Main Street, keep an eye out toward creating interesting—and labeled—photo ops."

"Damn, you're good." Bull grinned. "I'll get myself a moose statue and put out a sign by the lake with the Bull's Moose Roadhouse logo."

"I don't suppose there are any historic buildings?" Audrey asked.

Caz shook his head. "The closest would have been Pearl's Roadhouse, but it burned down around World War II. Bull's was built on the original site."

Bull stroked his goatee. "I can devote a wall to the town's history, especially Pearl's."

"Good plan," Gabe said. "Let's see if the council and businesses will go for having a festival or two. We could use something to pull in Anchorage people between the fishing and ski seasons."

"Hold on, you guys. There's too much to remember." Audrey disappeared into the house and returned with a pen and paper. She quickly listed out their ideas.

Gabe stared. Some had already slipped his mind. "You've got an impressive memory, Goldilocks."

"Yes, I do." At her nonchalant response, he grinned. Calling her beautiful sent her into a tizzy. Remarking on her intelligence? Not a problem.

He leaned over her shoulder to look at the lengthening list, and when he put his arm behind her back, she relaxed against him.

And he smiled because, no matter how late the evening ended, she'd be in his bed afterward.

CHAPTER TWENTY-TWO

On Thursday, Audrey strolled through the sunny downtown, heading for Lillian's to do some weeding. As she walked, she jotted down notes on ways to make the downtown tourist friendly.

The empty spot on the municipal building would be a great place for a map of the businesses and maybe one of the interesting places outside of town.

She'd see what Lillian thought.

Lillian was so much fun to talk with. It was wonderful to realize she'd become a good friend. Even more, she acted almost like...a mother. Pushing Audrey, encouraging her, always on her side. When Audrey had told her about Spyros, Lillian had been furious. And terrified for Audrey.

Sarah had been the same.

I have friends.

And a lover. *Oh, God.* She pressed her hand over the quivers in her belly. Such a lover.

She'd grumbled about getting up this morning. Laughing, he'd given her a steaming cup of coffee and pulled her outside to see a pair of loons on the lake.

Why did sharing something so minor feel so special?

Smiling, Audrey popped into the grocery store to get a soda and check when Dante would want a break.

After getting his schedule, she stepped back out and stopped short. After the dimly lit store, the bright sun practically scorched her eyeballs. Remaining in the recessed doorway to let her eyes adjust, she opened her drink.

A voice came from someone around the corner on the sidewalk. "...soon be littering the streets with their garbage, plastic bottles, and soda cans." The man's voice was familiar.

A woman—no, two women—made sounds of distressed worry.

"Yeah, we're gonna be smothered with tourists, and, I hate to say it, but there'll be druggies and perverts with them. Crime'll go up." The man heaved a sigh. "I got a bad feeling our small town will never be the same. Our kids won't be safe here."

The man's Southern drawl was quite distinctive, and Audrey straightened in surprise. That was Officer Baumer. Heavens, did Gabe realize his officer was spreading such negative propaganda about tourism?

Surely, Officer Baumer knew how much the people here

needed the tourists and the money they brought in, and yet he was *scaremongering*.

When Audrey's hands clenched, she realized she was awfully angry for an outsider to the town. But she wasn't an Outsider, not any longer. She had jobs, friends, and people who'd helped her.

She'd do her darndest to help them in return.

Two women walked into the grocery's recessed doorway.

With a smile, Audrey moved out of their way and onto the sidewalk.

Officer Baumer was strolling away, his back to her. Yes, she'd identified him correctly.

Oh boy. Gabe wasn't going to be pleased. Her stomach tightened because *she'd* have to tell him the bad news.

After crossing the street, Audrey entered the municipal building.

Two people were seated outside the health clinic doors. Behind the reception desk, Regina pointed an elderly man toward the municipal office. "Go there, and George will help you with the licensing paperwork."

"Thank you." The man walked around the desk and headed to the back of the building.

Audrey lifted her hand. "Hi, Regina. Is the chief in? I need to talk with him a minute."

"He is. Go on in." The receptionist pressed a button on her desk, giving the chief an alert that someone was entering the station.

Inside, Audrey crossed the room Gabe called the bullpen and found him at his desk.

Even seated, he looked powerful. She wasn't sure why. Sure, he was tall and muscular. His strong jaw held the shadow of a dark beard—and his expression was often ruthless. The broad chest covered by the khaki uniform shirt, the badge, the heavy-duty belt with the weaponry—he had all the trappings.

But, even when laughing, even when in jeans and a ripped T-shirt, he had an air of authority. Of being someone to lean on.

The badge merely acknowledged what he was.

He rose as she entered, then came around the desk with a frown. "You're upset. What happened, sweetheart?"

It was troubling...and heartwarming...that he could read her so easily.

As he drew her to him, he smelled of the pine soap he used, freshly laundered fabric, and overwhelming masculinity.

Wrapping her arms around his waist, she leaned into him.

His steel-hard arms tightened, pulling her against his heavily muscled body. "Audrey?"

"Everyone else still stumbles over my name. Why don't you?"

He huffed a laugh. "You never seemed like a Julie, and I realized it wasn't your real name. Audrey sounds like you."

Cops. Of course, he'd never been comfortable calling her by a name he'd known was false.

"I don't think your name is what brought you into the station." Amusement was clear in his smooth baritone. He stroked a warm hand up and down her back.

She leaned her forehead against his chest. Would hearing about Earl hurt him? He never talked about the officer as if they were friends, but still... They worked together.

"Tell me, Goldilocks."

"I was in that recessed doorway at the grocery, and I overheard Officer Baumer talking to two women. He told them the influx of tourists would bring in more litter and criminals. Perverts and druggies. That the town would never be the same."

Under her fingers, Gabe's back muscles tensed. "Now, that's very interesting. I wonder how long he's been spreading surreptitious propaganda. And why?"

"Why is a good question. Creating a hostile environment in town will drive away visitors." Unable to think while in Gabe's arms, she walked to the window and back. "But the officer's job depends on having tourists. Without them, you two aren't needed."

"Yep. We're talking job suicide." Gabe leaned a hip on the desk, arms folded over his chest.

"What is more important to him than his career?" She stopped in the center of the room. "Is he one of those off-the-gridders?"

"You know, I'm not sure where he lives." Gabe sat behind the computer and brought up the officer's file. When he entered Earl's home address into the map app, his mouth went flat.

"What?" Audrey leaned in to look.

Gabe made a circle with his finger. "This area is the Patriot Zealot compound. He lives inside it."

"Oh...boy."

"Baumer being a PZ explains what he finds more important than his job." Gabe's expression hardened. "I've had concerns about him, but wrote them off."

That didn't seem like Gabe. "How come?"

His smile was rueful. "I figured he wanted the chief position and was ticked off when I got brought in. I thought he'd adjust to having someone over him."

Yes, unless the officer was a danger to the community, she could see Gabe giving Earl a chance to join the team. He'd done the same with Knox and Chevy. "Do you suppose Earl had been promised the chief position? I bet the PZs wanted him to be in charge of the police force."

"It's good they didn't get that choice." Gabe shut down the program. "Since Reverend Parrish was down on even reopening the station, he wasn't allowed input into the hiring."

Thank goodness. "What are you going to do now?"

"Watch and wait. I don't have grounds to let him go. Yet. Although his work as an officer is growing increasingly slipshod."

"Um...Chief?"

His mouth twitched. "Yes, Ms. Hamilton."

She almost grinned at the way he'd answered formality with formality. "I'm good at research and can collect different information than your standard law enforcement background check.

"Can you now?" he asked in a musing voice.

She flushed. "A while back, I did online searches for a PI, and he taught me some tricks."

"You're a wellspring of interesting skills." He ran his finger down her cheek. "I'd be interested in seeing what you come up with. I'll do the usual, you do your magic, and we'll compare notes."

He believed her, wanted her help, valued her skills. The sense of pride that washed through her was headier than any alcoholic drink. "Okay. I'll get that started right now."

"Maybe in a minute." He caught her around the waist and firm lips took hers, softened, and teased.

When he eventually released her, she had to cling to him to keep from falling. *Whew.* Heat swept in waves over her skin.

But...public place. *Behave.*

She gave him a severe look. "You shouldn't kiss people in your station. Bad chief." With an effort, she managed to walk in a straight line out the door.

And heard him chuckle behind her.

. . .

Standing at his window, Gabe watched Audrey cross the street. Her gorgeous hair swung back and forth, the sun turning it to a bright gold. Rather than the baggy clothes she'd worn when she first arrived, she now wore tight jeans that showcased a world-class ass.

So fucking pretty. He loved how she hadn't thought twice about offering her assistance. People might scare her, but her need to help won out every time.

He sure wasn't going to turn her down. The woman was brilliant.

Settling behind his desk, he frowned at the stacks of paperwork, then at the door. Anytime he wasn't in the station, his office was locked. Still, he'd thought a time or two that the piles weren't in the same order he'd left them.

Gabe scowled. He'd blown off the feeling, putting it down to being paranoid, to lingering PTSD.

Guess not.

As Mako had always said—just because a man was paranoid, didn't mean he had no enemies out to get him.

Was this anti-tourist whispering campaign new, or had Baumer been busy for a while?

He had a new thought. Had Baumer spurred Knox and Chevy to their destructive rampage?

The two had been caught because Gabe put up security cameras. Baumer had been ticked off he hadn't been informed prior to the cameras going in.

Leaning back in his chair, Gabe stared out the window.

Considering Rescue's politics and Parrish's animosity, Gabe needed to be careful about tossing Baumer out on his ass.

In the meantime, although the vandalism had stopped, female tourists, especially, were getting harassed. None of it was getting caught on camera. Because the instigators apparently knew exactly where the cameras were located.

Well, he could fix that.

CHAPTER TWENTY-THREE

A weather front had rolled through during the night and turned Tuesday into a cold, wet mess. Gabe had found it damn difficult to roll out of bed that morning, especially a bed with Audrey in it.

They'd been together every night for a week, since the day she'd told him she wanted to have a fling.

He shook his head. Weren't flings supposed to be all about the sex? Admittedly, he and Audrey were certainly having sex. They were also waking up together, making breakfast, and teasing each other about eating habits.

He'd visit the coffee shop and library to see her; she'd wander into the station with coffee and donuts—because *"isn't that what police eat?"*

He planted tomatoes with her in Lillian's garden, and she'd helped him weed the Hermitage garden. She'd taken over gathering eggs from the chicken coop.

Last Sunday on Father's Day, she'd talked him into fishing with her, Tucker, and Zappa. Later, after grilling their catches, he, Caz, and Bull had told her Mako stories that had her laughing, crying, and occasionally so spitting mad she'd have slapped the sarge if he'd been alive.

She'd not only joined them in singing, but also asked him to teach her guitar.

He'd never met anyone who dove into life with such enthusiasm. Having emerged from her Chicago cocoon and been reassured that introverts could win friends, there was no holding her back.

Next step, to get her to move from a fling into a real relationship...with him.

Gabe parked the patrol car by the grocery. He'd do a quick check of the businesses and stop in the coffee shop to collect a kiss from the prettiest woman in the state.

As he got out of the car, a spatter of frigid rain hit his face. No need for a cold shower when living in Alaska.

He glanced at the police station and turned away. The atmosphere there was nearly as chilly since, with no suitable reason to fire Baumer, the two-faced, lying bastard was still working.

Putting the frustration aside, Gabe entered the arts and crafts store.

"Good afternoon, Chief." Glenda's loom held some complicated weaving. "Did you come to check on your men?"

"My men?"

"Knox and Chevy." She motioned toward new shelving that ran up one wall. "After they bought the lumber, Knox sanded and stained it, and Chevy put the shelves up."

Gabe ran a finger over the wood. Nicely finished. "Looks good."

"It does, indeed. We feel the two have more than repaid the graffiti."

"I'm glad you—"

"Chief. Chief! Where's the Chief? And the Doc?" The woman's voice came from the street.

Hearing the desperation, Gabe ran outside.

A whipcord-lean, older woman stood between a pickup truck and his patrol car.

"What's wrong?" Gabe skidded to a stop beside her.

"Inside." She opened the pickup's passenger door.

Head slumped to one side, an unconscious Chevy lay with the seat reclined as far back as it could get. His shirt was in shreds. Blood covered his face and one shoulder.

Hell.

Gabe glanced around and pointed at a teenaged boy. "Run and get Caz from the health clinic. Tell him to bring the stretcher."

The kid darted across the street.

"Tell me what happened," Gabe said to the woman before leaning into the vehicle. Rope tied around Chevy's body was holding bloodstained gauze in place. Gabe took a quick look beneath and winced at the long parallel slashes. Caz'd have a job picking debris out of that mess.

Restoring the dressings, Gabe pressed down to help slow the bleeding. "Looks like he got crosswise of a bear."

"Must have. He staggered out of the forest, and sweet Jesus, I almost ran over the idiot. I pulled his jacket off, strapped a pressure dressing on him, and managed to get him into the pickup."

"All extremities moving?" Gabe asked. The head wound had stopped bleeding, but the surrounding swelling and bruising indicated the man had hit something solid.

"Yes. Chief, he said something about his boy. I yelled and yelled before leaving, but the boy never answered."

Oh...fuck. Gabe's jaw clenched. Leaning forward, he slapped Chevy lightly. "Wake up, man."

Chevy moaned. His eyes fluttered.

Caz joined Gabe. "What's going on?"

"Bear attack. Sounds like the guy's kid might be out there."

"With a pissed-off bear? *Dios.* Ask your questions. I'll transport him after."

"Chevy, wake *up.*"

Chevy's eyes opened and slowly focused. "MacNair. What the eff?" He moved, groaned, and looked down. "Oh God."

Reaching out, he tried to grab Gabe. "Niko. My son. Is he here?"

"No, he's not." Niko. That was the kid who'd found the pup under a car. *Hell.* Gabe took Chevy's hands. "Where did you see him last?"

"We got a mo—" Chevy's gaze caught on Gabe's badge for a long second. "Hell. Okay, I shot a moose. We were packing out the meat and walked between a sow and her cubs. A brown."

Shit. Pretty much what he'd figured. Brown bears could be aggressive, especially the mothers. "She attacked?"

"Yeah. I yelled at Niko to run and tried to get my weapon up, but..." He shrugged.

A bear's charge was fast. Unless Chevy had already been aiming his rifle that direction, he couldn't have done anything.

"Did you see Niko afterward?"

Fear was in the man's eyes. "Bear swatted me good, knocked me into a tree, and then I heard Niko yell. She took off after him. Jesus." A shudder ran through him. "After my *boy*."

Fuck, fuck, fuck. The kid couldn't be more than ten.

Chevy looked at Gabe. "I passed out. Don't know how long. When I came to, I tried to find Niko, only I kept falling."

"So, you walked out for help. Good decision, man." Gabe gave his pen and notepad to the woman who'd brought Chevy in. "Write down directions to where you found him as best you can. Then can you take me to the place?"

"Certainly." She took the pad and started writing.

Gabe gripped Chevy's uninjured shoulder in reassurance.

"I'll take a crew out to search. Anything else you can think of?"

"Uh-uh. Please find him."

"We will." Gabe remembered the boy's happy grin when the pup crawled into his lap. His gut tightened. *Please, let us find the kid alive.*

Caz bumped his shoulder against Gabe's. "My turn, *viejo.*"

As Gabe stepped back to let the medical shit begin, he saw townsfolk gathering around the pickup.

"Here you go, Chief." The woman handed over the pad of directions.

Gabe asked, "Do you want to come with me in the patrol car?"

"No, I want my vehicle. You can follow me."

"Good enough." Gabe glanced around at the crowd. "A pissed-off sow with cubs attacked Chevy. Chevy's son, Niko, is still out there. The kid's about ten years old. I need volunteers to search for him."

One person—only one—eased away and left.

Someone's voice rose. "Get Dante here. He'll be able to backtrack Chevy and the kid."

"Yeah, Dante's good at picking up a trail."

Dante's raspy laugh sounded off to the right. "From what I've heard, the Chief can leave me in the dust."

"No one follows a trail better than Gabe," Bull said.

Gabe saw the skeptical expressions. Looked like he shouldn't have been so close-mouthed about his past. No time to rectify that now, though. He motioned to Bull. "Organize volunteers. I want them wilderness-experienced and able to help with a carry-out."

Bull flicked his fingers in a salute and started barking orders to the people around him.

Caz would deal with medical. Bull had the search team. Next—support staff. It was hypothermia weather.

Gabe spotted Sarah and Audrey. "Can you set up a base station on the road? Blankets, warm drinks, and food for the searchers and hopefully the boy?"

"Absolutely," Sarah took the pad of directions from him and glanced at it before handing it back. "I know the area."

Beside her, Audrey hesitated as if unsure if she would be of use. A city girl would be used to calling 911 for shit like this. He gave her an encouraging nod.

Her chin lifted. "We'll get it done."

Yeah, she would.

"Good. We'll leave you a place to park." Spotting Regina, Gabe gave her the pad of directions. "This is where we're starting the search for those who aren't joining us right away. Also, get a wildlife trooper out here, please."

"Yes, sir."

Caz drafted men to help load Chevy onto the stretcher.

As they carried Chevy across the street, an older woman shook her head. "That idiot. Hunting out of season." She followed the stretcher.

"Chevy's aunt," Dante said.

"Ah." Looking around, Gabe was pleased by the number

of volunteers around Bull. If Gabe couldn't find the kid's tracks, the more eyes the better. "All right, people. We'll park where Chevy left the forest and backtrack him."

Nods showed their understanding.

"Gear up—cold weather and rain clothing, flashlights, survival packs. If you have bear spray or flares, bring them. Leave your firearms behind—we'll have too many people around to be shooting."

"No shit."

"Got it, Chief."

"Anyone who can't follow us out right now, get directions from Regina." He looked at Dante and Bull. He'd trust them to shoot and hit what they aimed at. "Bring your weapons."

He motioned to the pickup driver to get into her vehicle, then jumped into the patrol car.

Once they'd gathered supplies, Audrey rode shotgun as Sarah drove out of town and down increasingly narrow gravel roads.

"There." Audrey pointed to where cars and pickups lined the almost non-existent shoulder, turning the road into a one lane.

As they pulled up, the last of the searchers were disappearing into the forest.

How cool was it that two were women?

Although wishing she could search, too, Audrey knew she'd be more of a hindrance than a help. She'd keep learning, and next time a problem arose, she'd be with the searchers.

"I should learn to shoot, too," she muttered, getting a quizzical then understanding glance from Sarah.

Stay focused, Audrey. A line of orange cones caught her eye. "I bet that's the spot Gabe left for us."

Audrey slid out of the SUV and moved the cones so Sarah could park. As the cold, drizzling rain dampened her head and shoulders, she shuddered, thinking of the boy. Only ten years old. He'd seen his father attacked by a bear. He'd be terrified. And was lost.

At the back of the SUV, Sarah lifted up the rear hatch. "If you want to learn to shoot, ask the chief. Mako told us Gabe was ranked an expert marksman in the military."

"Oh, good idea." Gabe. She should have known. "I can't believe how quickly he got everything organized."

As he'd coolly handed out orders, people had jumped to obey. In fact, when he told Dante to fetch something, the old vet had absently saluted.

"The chief has a talent for being in charge." Sarah attached a tarp to the lifted rear hatch. "I think combat sergeants have an instinctual need to create order from chaos, and Gabe is a lot like Mako."

"I wish I'd known Mako." He'd certainly raised strong men. Audrey anchored two six-foot poles to hold up the other end of the canopy. "This is really clever. People can get under here and stay dry."

"It was Mako who gave us the idea." Sarah smiled. "He was a wealth of practical knowledge when we got here. Even after a couple of years in Alaska, we were still learning how to manage."

Audrey eyed her. "New York, right?"

"You can hear the accent, hmm?"

"New York to Rescue is quite a leap, isn't it?"

"Oh, *was* it. I blame my husband. He was determined our children would learn skills other than playing video games. It took us a while to find the right place, though. We tried Anchorage. Too many people for Uriah. A cabin without electricity? Not for me." She made a face. "There are certain skills I don't need—like doing laundry by hand."

What a horrible thought. "I'm with you there."

"So, we settled here in Rescue. It suits us both."

Audrey set up the oversized coffee and soup dispensers and then wrapped them with insulating blankets. Additional thermoses of hot water for tea or hot chocolate were lined up and insulated under more blankets. In case the search lasted too long, Sarah had a camp stove available to reheat the food and drink.

Blankets and heat packs were available in a box inside the vehicle.

"We're ready if we're needed." Sarah glanced toward the forest, her lips compressed. "Let's hope our work is in vain and they find Niko quickly."

Audrey said a silent prayer.

Ten minutes later, Tucker limped out of the forest, supported by a bearded man. The two headed straight for the SUV.

"Tucker, what happened?" Audrey hurried to open a camp chair so he could sit under the canopy.

"Stepped right into a be-damned hole in a clear-cut area. This ol' leg of mine doesn't bend like it used to." He slapped his thigh. "Twisted my ankle."

Sarah shook her head and gave the other man a cup of coffee.

"Thankee, Sarah."

Tucker looked up at his friend. "Appreciate the help, Guzman."

"No problem." Guzman chugged the coffee. "I'll get back to the search. You'll take care of him?"

Sarah nodded. "Leave him to us. Good luck."

As Guzman jogged back into the forest, Audrey handed Tucker a mug of coffee. "How is the search going?"

"Thanks, Audrey." He took a sip and sighed with pleasure. "I gotta say I was worried when Dante didn't lead us out. But the Okie was right. MacNair's damn good. He followed Chevy's trail slicker'n grease through a goose. After finding where the bear attacked, he picked up the kid's tracks. But we stalled out in the clear-cut."

A clear-cut meant loggers had taken all the trees down, making a treeless area filled with slash. "Why?"

"The clear-cut was where Chevy shot the moose." Shifting uncomfortably, Tucker rubbed his leg.

Audrey frowned. First aid manuals said sprains and such should be elevated. She pulled another chair close.

"Good plan." Understanding, Sarah lifted Tucker's injured leg so Audrey could push the chair under it.

"Wouldn't a clearing make tracking easier?"

"Thank you, ladies." Tucker glanced at Audrey. "Not easier. See there were moose tracks and lots of Chevy and Niko's tracks all over the place from them doing the butchering. Then you add in bear tracks, and you got a shitload of sign. The Chief was doing a wide circle to try to spot the boy's tracks outside the mess."

"The bear didn't attack the child?" Sarah asked.

"Nope. MacNair showed us where the sow's cubs caught up with her, and she lost interest in the chase."

Thank God.

Tucker scowled. "Chevy was probably so stoked about getting a moose, he wasn't paying attention to his surroundings. Stupid mistake. Now he's gashed up, will lose the meat, and get a hefty fine. I just hope we can find his boy."

"Yes." *Find the boy, Gabe. Please.*

As a gust of wind blew icy cold rain in his face, Gabe circled the clear-cut where Chevy had butchered the moose. He hoped to pick up the child's tracks and be able to narrow the search.

Everyone else was following the grid pattern he'd laid out.

No one had found anything. *Dammit.* Frustration gnawed at his nerves. Thank God, it was almost summer solstice, and they still had hours of daylight left. But a frightened boy could run far and fast. The kid was probably drenched and, with the temp in the low fifties, was headed for hypothermia.

What he wouldn't give for level terrain and open forest. But, noooo. Instead, the old slash from the cleanup of spruce bark beetle kill made for unstable footing—and his hip was aching like hell. Low blueberry and crowberry shrubs dotted the area, interspersed with reed grass and fescue. None of it was good for reading sign.

He shrugged his raingear closer and kept moving, gaze on what was under his feet.

There. A scrape, almost blotted out by the tracks of another searcher. Someone had missed the kid's footprints. Easy to do. Lightweight children didn't leave as much sign as an adult.

He looked out farther. That patch of crushed grass could've been from an animal, but no, there was the curve of a shoe. The semi-circle was too narrow to be from a man's footwear.

He spotted a handprint. Then a toe print. Wanting to ensure the sow lost sight of him, the boy had crawled through the low shrubs. Of course, the sow wouldn't have any trouble finding the kid's scent, but out of sight, out of mind never hurt. Smart kid.

Looked as if Niko had headed directly toward the closest edge of the forest, the place where shrubs gave way to spruce and hemlock.

"You got something?" Bull tossed him part of a granola bar.

"Yeah." Gabe pointed to the pattern from a hiking shoe.

"Good job."

Chewing the sweet oatmeal bar, Gabe followed the tracks for a few more feet. Yep, this was the way.

He raised his voice. "Over here. Fall in."

As he led the way, it felt good to have Bull at his back. The others followed in a fan pattern, watching for anything he might miss.

When they reached the forest, Gabe found muddy footprints and scraped bark on a trunk where the kid had scrambled up a tree.

Bull pointed out a deeper footprint where the boy had jumped down later. "He probably waited to be sure the sow was gone."

"There's no blood." Dante's comment made everyone smile.

"The sow never caught him. He's just scared and"— Gabe sighed as the footprints led right into the forest— "he's lost the way back."

Hell. Gabe glanced at the sky again. If they didn't find

Niko in another hour, he'd call in SAR dogs from Soldotna. He motioned to Guzman and Erica. "Mark the path, if you would, please."

They took out flagging.

A while later, Bull knelt and showed where a broken patch of grass was starting to spring back upright. "We're catching up to him."

"Yeah, we're close." Gabe nudged his brother. "You have a voice, bro. Use it."

"Niko. Niko!" Bull's roar could probably be heard in Rescue.

The searchers' startled laughter faded as they listened.

And got a response.

"Here. I'm he-re!" The boy's voice was faint—and broke on the second *here*. But the kid was alive. Able to shout.

Thank fuck. Gabe had to clear the thickness from his throat before yelling, "Stay put, Niko. We're coming. Stay where you are."

Stepping back, Gabe let the others surge forward. His crew had worked hard—and this was the best reward ever.

They found the child curled up in the hollow of a fallen tree. Wet, shaking with cold...and *alive*.

Relief weakened Gabe's knees. And the impact of a little body hitting him made him stagger.

"I knew you'd come, Chief. Knew you'd find me." The kid burrowed against him, skinny arms clinging like vines.

Gabe felt his heart turn to a slushy mess. "I think about

everyone in town is out here looking for you." And it was the truth.

Hell of a town.

Dante tossed him a blanket, and Gabe wrapped it around the kid before lifting him up. "Let's get you back to your family. Your pa's gonna have some interesting scars, but looks like he'll be all right."

Niko sagged and then buried his face against Gabe's neck and cried.

Gabe had to blink back his own fucking tears.

They'd walked about a mile before the kid's sobs turned to snuffles, and his head lifted.

Good enough. Smiling, Gabe ruffled his hair. "So, how's your new dog doing?"

"He's so smart!"

"Yeah, how do you know?" Bull took the exhausted boy, pretended to drop him, and made him giggle.

"We're not supposed to feed him people food, but he sneaks under the table when we're eating. And if I forget to give him a bite, he puts his paw on my foot."

Gabe grinned. "Yep, sounds pretty smart."

"And after he chewed up Dad's knife sheath—his favorite rawhide one—he hid in the back of my closet."

Walking in front of them, Guzman turned. "The pup's still alive after that?"

"Dad yelled," Niko admitted. "Then he laughed and said I owe him a new sheath, and he'll teach me how to make it."

Gabe blinked. Who'd have thought Chevy would be so patient?

When Guzman took his turn carrying the boy, Gabe joined Bull to play rear guard and ensure no one got lost. The entire group was in high spirits. Just about every damn person had slapped Gabe on the back with compliments on his tracking expertise.

Jesus.

In the clear-cut, Dante slowed to examine where Gabe had picked up Niko's tracks. "Can't believe you spotted this, Chief. Nice job."

Gabe shrugged. "I got lucky."

"Bullshit." Bull traced the faint outline of Nico's sneaker. "You were always better than any of us. Glad to see you haven't lost your skill, bro."

"Bro?" Erica, one of the two female searchers, looked back. "How do you two know each other, anyway? I thought the chief was new to Alaska."

Bull hesitated and lifted his eyebrows at Gabe. *Tell or not?*

Gabe rubbed his jaw. The sarge, being paranoid, had taught his boys not to share information about themselves with anyone.

But... Mako was dead. And they were part of this town.

Gabe nodded.

"We were raised as brothers," Bull said. "Off the grid down by Seward."

The half-dozen people within hearing all turned to stare.

"I'll be damned," one man muttered. "No wonder he tracks like that."

Gabe huffed a laugh. It'd felt good to put his skills to use. And to lead a team again. He glanced at the men and women. The townsfolk had dropped everything and pulled together to find the boy. Heartwarming.

Speaking of heartwarming... When they emerged onto the road, there was Audrey.

She ran over and threw her arms around him. "I knew you could find him."

When she went up on tiptoes to give him a lusty kiss, the men around him chuckled.

Gabe didn't give a damn. This right here, this open-hearted woman was exactly what he needed. He took himself another kiss before letting her go.

As Sarah took charge of the boy, Audrey bustled about, wrapping chilled searchers in blankets, giving them heat packs, and serving them hot drinks.

His mug of coffee came with a quick kiss and another hug, despite the fact he was soaking wet.

As she hurried to the next person, he stared after her. Because, one kiss...or one summer for that matter, wasn't enough.

He wanted more.

A lifetime sounded about right.

CHAPTER TWENTY-FOUR

At home, Audrey grinned at herself in the mirror as she got ready to head to the roadhouse for the evening. It'd been a great Thursday, so far.

Before leaving to shop in Anchorage, Dante had studied the grocery comparison pricing she'd prepared. It showed how he might cut his overhead with selective buying. Since the store ran close to the red, she'd hoped to give him a better profit margin.

After reading her notes, the tough old Okie had actually hugged her.

Once he'd returned, she spent the rest of the day in the library. With Knox's help, she'd unpacked—and gloated over—the new novels that'd come in.

Even better, Gabe had popped in to drop off sodas and steal a kiss.

She ran her finger over her mouth, still feeling the tingle.

Who would have thought such a deadly man could be so affectionate? He was polite—never grabbed her ass or fondled her in public—but whether they were alone or in public, he'd touch her. Put his arm around her. Even kiss her. He enjoyed being with her and didn't care who knew it.

God, she loved him.

No, no, no. Fling. We're having a fling, remember?

Firmly burying her wayward emotions, she studied herself in the ancient, rather hazy mirror.

Perfect.

Her lashes and eyebrows were a dark brown-black, her eyes sultry, her mouth lush. A touch of bronzer had emphasized her cheekbones.

And, look, Ma, I have cleavage.

Yesterday, when she was helping Lillian clean out her closet, the older woman had given Audrey grief about her shapeless, worn clothing. "*My dear girl, it's quite true Alaskans put little stock in a person's attire. However, it's a woman's prerogative to indulge in dressing up now and then. Just for herself.*"

Audrey had nodded her understanding.

"Good. Since I no longer wear low-cut clothing, you should take these and put them to good use." Lillian had presented her with several sexy tops.

Audrey grinned at the memory. Lillian was like the mother she never had.

Audrey checked the mirror again. Over the past weeks, she hadn't missed makeup, styling her hair, or wearing suits. But, Lillian was right. She was ready to go all female for one evening.

One of her escape guises had been an overly made-up redhead. After digging out those cosmetics earlier, she'd indulged.

Turning her head from side-to-side, she smiled. The makeup hadn't reached the *I'm-a-prostitute* heaviness, but she looked different. And good.

Who knew, maybe she'd get better tips.

Two hours later, Audrey knew her tips, especially from tourists, had gone up. Yay sexy clothing and makeup.

Having wall-to-wall customers didn't hurt. The roadhouse was celebrating summer solstice, the longest day of the year, and Bull had brought in live music.

Although she was running her aching feet off, she'd received so many appreciative looks that her ego was soaring. Wasn't it silly to invest so much into her appearance? And she really hoped Gabe would be in and see her all done up.

As Audrey stopped at a table to leave drinks, Irene patted her beehive hair. "I heard you helped out during the search the other day. Good girl."

The approving nod from the cantankerous postmistress made Audrey's day.

Irene's balding husband leaned forward. "Have you heard if Chevy is all right?"

"He came home from the Soldotna hospital last night." Between Gabe and Sarah, Audrey knew all the good gossip. "They had to pump him full of antibiotics since some of those gashes were down to the bone."

"Yeeouch," the man muttered.

"I know, right?" *Ew.* "But Niko is fine, and Chevy's wife told Sarah that people had dropped off food, so she could spend her time looking after Chevy—who is grateful to be alive and grumpy as all get out."

"That sounds like him." With a disapproving sniff, Irene looked at her husband. "Nonetheless, we'll go by his place this weekend and lend a hand."

"Yes, dear."

Audrey smiled. Yesterday, she'd heard the postmistress scold a teen for a poor packing job, and then Irene brought out tape and fixed the package for the boy. All bark and no bite.

A flash of pink drew Audrey's attention, and she waved at Felix who waited tables on the other side of the room. He gave her a big grin. Wearing a florescent pink shirt, he was openly flirting with a linebacker-sized tourist. *Go, Felix.*

She took drink orders from three fishermen, who were discussing the various Kenai River fishing charters. The salmon runs had started, and the riverbanks were crowded with fishermen.

Audrey grinned, remembering a blanket, a riverbank...

and Gabe. They'd been lucky not to be caught, really. No more riverbank sex during the busy salmon season, that was for sure.

But Gabe and Tucker had promised to instruct her in the intricacies of salmon fishing. She was looking forward to the fun.

At the bar, she gave Bull the new orders and started to pick up a newly filled tray. Then her feet seemed to freeze to the floor.

Leaning against the bar, Gabe stood next to Caz. On Gabe's other side, Brooke from the ski resort posed on a barstool. The woman's silky red shirt made her tanned skin glow and set off her brown hair.

Seeing all that vivacious beauty, Audrey felt dull and pallid.

"I love the idea of Rescue having a festival or two." Brooke's dark eyes flashed with her enthusiasm. "McNally's could co-host, and I'd be happy to set it up. Part of my job is finding ways to draw people to the area."

"I can see how more tourists would benefit the resort," Gabe agreed.

Brooke put her hand over his and leaned in. "Remember when we went to the jazz festival in Anchorage? Rescue could do something similar."

Picking up her tray of drinks, Audrey turned away. Deep in her chest, her heart ached. Why should seeing someone touch Gabe hurt so much? Audrey didn't own him, after all.

Brooke could help him with promoting Rescue. Like

Audrey's ex, Gabe probably wanted an eye-catching girl-friend who was skilled at working with people. Brooke not only had a history with Gabe, but also fit in here in Alaska.

And the woman wasn't leaving at the end of summer.

Remember, dummy? You're not staying here. Even though Gabe occasionally mentioned returning to his isolated cabin, she knew he'd stay. Neither the town nor his brothers would let him leave.

Brooke might weigh in, too. After all, the social director would be the perfect complement to the town's leader.

Audrey wanted to rip the woman's oh-so-perfect hair out.

Trying not to listen for Gabe's sexy low laughter, Audrey delivered her orders. The last three drinks went to Tucker, Guzman, and Knox, who'd settled at a table by the door.

She made her voice light and managed a smile. "How is your leg, Tucker?"

"It just needed a day of rest, and I was fine. Next time I tackle uneven ground, I'm taking a hiking stick."

"That sounds like a plan." As a roar of laughter came from the bar, she glanced over to see that Brooke was enter-taining everyone.

Audrey sighed. She'd never fit in the way Brooke did. Would always be the outsider as well as the Outsider.

Knox had followed her gaze, and his jaw turned rigid. "Don't let that bimbo bother you. You're worth a dozen of her."

Audrey blinked.

During their lessons, she'd gotten the impression he didn't like her much. "Um." Her voice came out rough. "Thank you."

He did like her. She was making friends. She gave them a bigger smile.

Having finally taken a bar stool, Gabe listened as Brooke waxed eloquent about putting on a three-day music festival. Her plans were too elaborate, especially since even a one-day would be a tough sell with some of the townspeople.

But she had good ideas, and the resort's participation would be beneficial.

He'd insist the festival be held in Rescue, though, not at McNally's ski area. If the town blocked off Sweetgale in front of the park, they could set up booths in the street. They'd have to figure out what would draw the city people, though.

Audrey would have ideas. Turning, Gabe spotted her as she headed toward the bar. He'd caught glimpses of her earlier, but she hadn't joined him, which seemed odd.

It'd taken a while to convince Miss Shyness, but she'd come to realize he valued her hugs. Her kisses. Now, she'd always greet him and grab a hug. But not tonight?

He frowned. Maybe she was avoiding someone? He glanced to his right and...

Shit.

In the crowded bar area, bodies were constantly jostling,

and he hadn't paid any attention to the way Brooke was jammed up against his side. If Audrey had pressed against him like that, he'd have damn well noticed—and gotten a hard-on—but he didn't view Brooke in that way. Because of their history, she wasn't even a friend—more like a business acquaintance.

Considering how Brooke behaved, Audrey might have gotten the wrong notion.

Even as he started to stand to move away from Brooke, someone growled, "MacNair."

Gabe turned.

Knox shoved through the three-deep crowd around the bar. His stance was belligerent, jaw shoved out. He looked Brooke up and down, and then glared at Gabe. "That pretty blonde waitress, Audrey...I got lots of friends who're interested. I take it she's free?"

"Fuck no." The words were out before Gabe even thought—but he'd spoken the truth.

Brooke leaned against him again. Yeah, he needed to deal with her. What was her problem?

"Good." Knox glanced at Brooke and scowled. "Our librarian looked a tad downhearted."

Oh, hell. The thought of hurting Audrey was a stab in the chest. He should have been more aware...of everything.

Before he could deal with Brooke, Audrey stepped out from behind Knox and thumped her tray of empties onto the bar to Gabe's left. "I'm not downhearted."

At Knox's disbelieving sound, she shook her head and gave him a wry *I'm-okay* smile.

"All right then." Knox nodded at her, shot Gabe another glare, and moved back into the crowd.

Next to the bar, Audrey watched Knox saunter away, realizing he *did* like her. Her smile faded as she saw that Brooke still clung to Gabe. That hurt like an ugly tearing around her heart.

And yet...

Gabe had said Audrey wasn't free. Emphatically said it. That discrepancy needed examination.

Biting her lip, she studied Gabe.

His gaze was on Audrey, his body turned toward her. His knees pointed away from Brooke. One arm was on the bar, the other holding his beer.

When Brooke gripped his arm, he turned to give her a disgusted look. "Stop it."

He wasn't...into...Brooke.

Brooke was the one doing all the flirting and touching. But what man would object to that? Brooke was gorgeous. Vivacious. Knew everyone.

I can't compete with her.

A loving relationship wasn't a sports competition. In the beginning, it was...a taste test, like deciding upon a flavor in the ice cream store. Cherry, vanilla, and hazelnut were good, but given a choice, she wanted chocolate.

Brooke might have been the right ice cream for a younger Gabe, but he wasn't interested in her now.

Unfortunately, the woman wasn't getting the message. As Audrey watched—probably *because* Audrey was watching—Brooke draped herself on Gabe again.

Oh, honestly. Audrey crossed her arms over her chest. "Brooke, you're giving the sisterhood a bad name. Hitting on someone's boyfriend, right in front of her? Seriously? That's just weird and...needy. Do you really mean to come across like that?"

Brooke gasped as if she'd been slapped, and she snatched her hands from Gabe's arm.

A mutter came from somewhere back in the very interested crowd. "She's always doing that. No man is safe."

Audrey's mouth was too dry. Her mother had taught her how ugly confrontations could get. But still... She glanced around and raised her voice slightly. "I'm sure Brooke doesn't understand that she's upsetting the sisterhood. For my part, I'll help by letting her know when she missteps again."

"Good plan."

"I like it."

A chorus of agreement came from nearby women along with suppressed laughter from the men.

Face a dusky red, Brooke sat back on her bar stool, leaving space between her and Gabe. Acting as if she didn't see Audrey, she picked up her drink. Probably no one had ever called her on her behavior before.

Audrey realized her own face was hot. Had she really just done that?

This probably wasn't what Lillian had in mind when she'd told Audrey to participate in conversations.

Smiling, Gabe pulled Audrey between his knees. "Thank you, sweetheart. I appreciate the help."

Behind him, Brooke looked shocked. "B-but, Gabe."

Gabe ran his hands up and down Audrey's arms, before turning to look at Brooke. "I'd already told you, but I'll repeat. We had ourselves some fun *years* ago, and it ended *years* ago. Done and over."

"But, I know you want me. You talked to me and—"

Audrey's anger was dying. Maybe the woman truly was that clueless. She stepped into her librarian-teaching mode. "Brooke."

Brooke looked over.

"Have you talked with guys and they immediately assume you want to go to bed? They'll get all pushy and try to manhandle you?"

Brooke rolled her eyes. "Oh, have I."

"Uh-huh. You're behaving the same way as those men, you know."

Such an indignant stare. "I am not."

"You thought Gabe wanted you merely because he was talking with you. Well, *I'm* talking to you. Does that mean I want to go to bed with you?"

Brooke almost gasped. "No!"

"Exactly. Just because a man talks with you, doesn't

mean he's interested in anything other than conversation. You need to learn the body language—the man-signals—that guys display if they want more than conversation. Because if you ignore those signals, you're just as bad as the male stalkers you hate so much."

The woman blinked, and then, surprisingly, sat back... and nodded.

All right, then. As Audrey tried to move away, Gabe pulled her closer, his knees closing on her hips. "I like you right here, little cheechako," he murmured.

Her exasperated huff made him laugh.

He curled his fingers around her waist and whispered, "Nice job with Brooke."

Maybe. Audrey might have been less aggressive if she'd realized how oblivious the woman was. "Thanks. Um, am I liable to run into a lot more ex-girlfriends?"

"Not here in Rescue. I only came here to visit Mako."

That was an interesting qualifier—*here in Rescue.* Was the rest of the world littered with Gabe's old girlfriends?

Catching her narrowed eyes, he raised his hands in pseudo-self-defense. "I'm not that bad, Goldie, not like Caz. One divorce in my early twenties—I believed in fidelity; she didn't. A few girlfriends since. No one at all in the last couple of years."

"Oh." He'd been married. Well, considering all that was Gabriel, she wasn't surprised in the least.

He certainly had been more forthright than she'd expected. "Thank you?"

He lifted an eyebrow and waited.

"You want quid pro quo?" Didn't that just figure?

"Well, yeah." His fingers were gentle as he tucked a lock of hair behind her ear. "I'll settle for marriages, the last important relationship, and why it didn't work."

This would sure be easier with alcohol. But fair was fair. She was the one who'd introduced the subject. "No marriages. Last relationship a few months ago." She drew an unhappy breath. "He wanted someone more outgoing. Someone more like Brooke."

"Really? What an idiot."

The sincerity in his tone warmed her. Then she winced. Had Brooke heard what she said? What Gabe had said?

She glanced over and was relieved to see the woman had left.

A man had taken the barstool. His appreciative stare made her flush.

With a menacing growl, Gabe leaned down and took her lips.

Oh, the way he kissed. Gently, firmly, teasing, taking.

When he finished, he ran his knuckles over her hot cheek. "That was another kind of man-signal, by the way."

"Mmm..." Her brain started to come out of the clouds. "What? What signal?"

"The one that tells other men I'll bust their faces if they touch what's mine."

CHAPTER TWENTY-FIVE

Watch your six, boys. Always watch your six. - First Sergeant Michael "Mako" Tyne"

Gabe finished the never-ending police paperwork and glanced at the clock. Outside, the sun was still up—of course—but it was well past time to leave. At least Baumer wasn't around. Since Audrey had heard the asshole scaremongering two weeks ago, the officer hadn't done anything out of line, at least nothing Gabe had caught on camera.

Hell, Baumer wasn't doing much of anything, in fact. He was a lazy bastard. He rarely did foot patrols, preferring to sit in comfort in the office or cruise the roads. During his shifts, he exerted only enough effort to keep from getting chewed out.

Made for an uncomfortable working environment. Politics or not, Gabe would give Baumer the boot before the man's probation period ended.

Rising, Gabe stretched.

The library was closed on Thursdays, so Audrey was already at home. Last night, they'd picked the first strawberries from the Hermitage garden, and she wanted to try making strawberry shortcake from scratch.

His mouth watered. They had fresh asparagus and snap peas. Caz had fished yesterday and caught a salmon. But... strawberry shortcake to top it all off?

Over the past week, the city girl had dived into catching and growing her own food. She was an excellent cook, insisting that cooking was a simple matter of finding a good recipe and proper adherence to the details.

He smiled. Her personality was a fascinating mixture of brilliance and logic and enthusiasm and compassion.

Since last week when he'd made clear that they were together, she'd relaxed into their fling. She was pretty much living in his house.

And he wanted to get home to her.

Regina had left a couple of hours before and locked the building's front door. Gabe latched the station's inner door and secured the gun-safe.

At the back, he opened the door and glanced outside. Two cars remained in the parking lot. No people.

Taking a step out the door, he heard an indrawn breath. A scrape.

Instinct took over. He dove forward...and the blow aimed at his head struck his shoulder.

He front-rolled to his feet, spun, and drew his Glock. A baseball bat hit his hand and knocked the weapon to the ground. Someone kicked it across the lot.

Knuckles burning, Gabe assessed the situation.

Five men. They must've been hidden against the side of the building. All wore ski masks. All carried weapons. One baseball bat, one club, brass knuckles, two had knives.

All five charged.

Jesus. He dodged a club, gripped the guy's wrist, and punched. As the elbow joint fractured, the man screamed. Gabe grabbed the club for his own, whirled—and caught a fist in the forehead. Ignoring the blast of pain, he ducked the swinging baseball bat and slammed the club into a knife-wielder's knee.

Bellowing, that bastard went down.

A long burn seared Gabe's upper back. The other knifeman had cut him.

With a dive and roll, Gabe broke free of the ring of men. Regaining his feet, he swiped away the blood impairing his vision.

Three left.

Gabe's head and shoulder hurt. The bleeding from the knife wound was more urgent. He needed to finish this up.

As baseball bat guy charged, the other two attacked from the flanks. Ah, hell, they were coordinating their movements.

Gabe kicked one in the gut, but the bat caught him a blow on the head. Skull exploding with pain, he fell to his knees.

At a glint of metal, he threw up an arm barely in time to block the descending knife. Viciously, he punched the man's vulnerable inner thigh.

With a shout of pain, the guy staggered back.

Growling, Baseball bat guy lunged forward—and suddenly yelled and spun to face the other way.

Gabe blinked. A knife stuck out of the man's upper back.

With a shout of pain, the guy ripped the knife out and whipped around. The man took a step back, the blade dropped to the ground, and he sprinted away.

All of the assholes were running, one helping the man with a fractured knee. A vehicle revved its engine farther down the alley. They had an escape car waiting.

Head still spinning, Gabe sucked in air. He'd move in a minute. Yeah, a minute.

Caz sauntered over.

Fuck, that'd been close. "Thanks, bro."

"*No hay problema.*" Caz gave him a gleaming white grin. "You'd have managed the last two. The *cabrón* with the knife didn't know which end was the pointy one."

After accepting a hand up, Gabe looked over his shoulder. Blood covered his back. "I'd say he found the pointy end, thanks."

Chuckling, Caz scooped up his knife. "Come, *viejo*. I

happen to run a clinic with all sorts of nice bandaging materials."

"There's a plan." After picking his Glock out of the gravel, Gabe scowled. "Dammit, I'm going to be late for supper."

Audrey sang along with Green Day's "21 Guns" as she measured out brown rice. The asparagus was cut and ready to steam. A salad was in the fridge. The salmon was prepared to go in the toaster oven to be broiled.

Everything waited for Gabe's arrival.

Lillian had talked about being with a cop because the Brit had once dated a sheriff. Audrey grinned. Of course, she had. The woman embraced and sampled life with an enviable vigor. In an ice cream shop, Lillian was the type to ask for a taste of every flavor.

But from painful experience, Lillian had advised Audrey a law enforcement officer's life wasn't his own. He wouldn't always be home on time or even be able to call and say he'd be late.

Audrey shook her head. Not a problem. She could make flexible-timed meals. And she was old enough to eat if she got hungry before he returned.

Twenty minutes later, she heard the garage door rise. His footsteps sounded in the hallway.

She stiffened. Gabe was normally so silent that he

could be behind her before she sensed him, and he'd learned to speak to warn her before his touch warmed her skin.

The heavy thud of footsteps was out of character.

Worried, she hurried into the living room. "Gabe?"

He stepped out of the hallway.

His eyes held a cold darkness like a stark winter's night. A gauze pad was taped on his forehead. Purple bruising showed around it. The lines in his face had deepened, roughening his face. He moved stiffly, without his usual smooth, prowling grace.

That wasn't the khaki shirt he'd worn this morning.

She ran across the room and skidded to a stop in front of him. "Where are you hurt? How bad is it? You should go to a hospital. I'll take you. Just let me get my purse. Show me where—"

"Sweetheart." His eyes lightened. "I caught some damage, but nothing major." As if to prove it, he drew her into his arms.

Yes, that was what she'd needed, although even as she breathed him in, her hands ran over his torso. The front seemed all right.

There was a big pad on his upper back under the shirt. *Oh, God.* "Tell me the damage. Now."

"You saw my face. Got a few bruises. A slice on my back. And I got hit on the head—just a lump—but I do have a headache. Don't worry. Caz stitched me up and gave me a once-over."

He'd be all right. He would. She rubbed her cheek against his solid chest.

He chuckled, curved his fingers under her ass, and squeezed lightly. "After a fight like that, I'd've liked to screw the Goldilocks who's sleeping in my bed, but...*headache*."

A sputter of amusement hit her at his disgruntled tone. Yes, he was all right. "You sit down, and I'll get some aspirin. No, I'll get Tylenol. That'll be safer if you're bleeding."

Smiling, he lifted her chin and bent to kiss her. "You are a miracle, sweetheart. Thank you."

She got him on the sectional and medicated, then lost the argument about no beer after injuries.

As she passed him the bottle, she felt a cold chill in her bones. Even though he wasn't badly hurt, he was awfully banged-up. *Too* banged-up.

Bull and Caz had often told stories about their brawling. Bull won by sheer size alone, Caz was never without a knife, Hawk was a berserker. In spite of their talents, they said Gabe won most of the fights because he was just that good of a fighter. She'd seen the efficient way he'd taken Knox down—and how unworried Bull had been.

She frowned. "Were you attacked by more than one?"

After a sip of beer, he eyed her. "Why do you ask?"

"I'm not stupid. I bet you wouldn't be this hurt if you'd fought only one man. How many were there?"

When he didn't answer, she tilted her chin up. He wouldn't win *this* argument.

"Five."

No way. She stared at him in mingled awe and horror. *Five.*

He laughed ruefully. "I'm not Chuck Norris, Goldilocks. I did all right with three, might have managed the fourth. It's good Caz was still in the clinic and heard the noise."

Heard the noise. This hadn't been a bar fight. "Where did this happen?"

"Behind the station. They'd been flattened up against the back of the building so they could ambush me." His mouth thinned. "I'll be more careful. And I'll put up a mirror so I can see what's out there."

"Caz joined the fight?"

"In a way. He stood in the doorway and took one out with a knife. He insists the reason he throws knives is because medics shouldn't risk damaging their hands. Sure it is."

Audrey tilted her head. "The reason sounds logical to me."

"Except that he started pitching knives when he was around ten."

Throwing sharp knives at that age? What had Mako been thinking? But, he'd taught his boys how to fight, and thank God for that.

She ran her tongue over her dry lips. Her heart seemed to have crammed into her throat, and she forced her voice to stay light. "The traditional saying is 'you should see the other guy,' How bad are the five other guys?"

Gabe set his beer down, pulled her against his side, and leaned his head against the couch back. "One got Caz's blade in his back. One has a knee that'll need surgery, same with another bastard's elbow. The other two just have bruises."

She put a hint of amusement into her words. "Oh, well, that's not so bad."

And then she swallowed against the bile trying to rise. *Don't throw up, don't throw up.*

Hours later, Gabe woke in bed. He was lying on his back, Audrey snuggled against his side. The cool night air from the lake ruffled the bedroom curtains and revealed the twilight glow. It must be sometime between midnight and 4 a.m.

Once his headache had eased up, Gabe had shared an amazing meal with Audrey. There'd been no recriminations or glares about being late. No telling him that the food was ruined. When he'd apologized, she'd laughed and said none of the meal was ruined from the delay.

Fuck, she'd been sweet. Had he ever had anyone care for him with such a loving mixture of practicality and worry?

After they'd eaten, she'd snuggled against him and picked a movie about a woman who wanted to be a spy. Light and funny. By the time it ended, the knots in his gut had disappeared.

Battles added up. Didn't matter how much experience a man had, his body would react to pain and danger. It always took a while to descend from that adrenaline peak.

A shame he hadn't gotten to enjoy sex, though. He liked the zing that adrenaline added. However, sex would've increased his blood pressure and probably exploded his aching head.

Turning his head one way, then the other, he smiled.

Headache was gone.

Mentally, he opened up the rules of engagement manual for male/female relationships. In the military, ROE defined the circumstances and manner in which the use of force might be applied. But for this...

He stroked over the sweetly curved body beside him in hopes that she'd wake and be in the mood. If she kept sleeping, he'd stop. Only a classless idiot pushed a woman into sex if she wasn't interested. However, *luring* her into the mood? That fell in the sneaky-but-permissible category for the rules of engagement.

Hearing her breathing speed up slightly, he grinned and rolled far enough he could capture a breast. Fondle it. Was there anything nicer than the feeling of a breast cupped in his hand?

Blinking, she tipped her head back. "Gabe?" Her voice was husky with sleep. Damn sexy. As was the way her nipple suddenly puckered.

"Mmm."

"Why do I get the impression you woke up wanting to play?"

My little librarian. "Is *wanting to play* a...what do you call it for sex?"

"Euphemism—and yes."

"Then, yes. Let's play." He tugged on the spiked nipple and felt her hips give a tiny wiggle. Ah, the lure was working.

With a tiny giggle, she tipped her head up so he could kiss her.

Yes. He started to roll over on his soft, willing woman— and pain stabbed through him. A club to the shoulder, a knife to the back, and every muscle and joint ached. "Hell."

"Oh, God, I forgot you were injured." Eyes wide, she sat up.

His hand regretted the loss of the sweet breast. And he had to grit his teeth to keep from growling...because his erect dick throbbed almost as bad as his back.

"Oh, such a face..."

His eyes narrowed. "Did you just giggle?"

Her lips clamped shut, which meant she gave a set of laughing snorts.

She sounded so funny he had to grin. "Dammit, I really wanted to fuck."

"Ah, poor Chief." She shook her head and stroked his bare chest in sympathy. "It'd put too much strain on that slash. I'm sorry."

"When I find those bastards, I'm going to..." He blinked as she pressed a kiss to his chest. Rubbed her satiny cheek against him. Licked around one nipple, then the other. Kissed her way lower.

"Sweetheart?" His voice came out gruff.

"It's so totally my turn." Her mist-gray eyes held a smile, and her tongue ran over her teeth.

Damned if she didn't sound both smug and enthusiastic.

Then, to his pleasure, she settled between his legs and took him in her mouth.

She was getting good at sex. Practice made perfect, right? And blowjobs were fun. At least they were with Gabe.

Audrey licked over the mushroom-like head, enjoying the diverse textures. The head like spongy velvet, the shaft silk over iron. Elastic-like veins just begged to be traced with her tongue.

She'd learned curling her fingers around the base kept her from gagging herself, but she was improving. As she took him even deeper, he rumbled low in his throat.

She grinned. "Is there anything in a blowjob you don't like?"

"Hell, no."

He was getting even harder. As his heavy testicles drew closer to his body, she molded them in her palm. She hadn't tried playing with them before. So...

His hand closed in her hair. "C'mere, woman."

His jaw was tight, his body tense. She glanced at his erection—very thick and big. "But..."

Without looking, he took a condom from the night-stand and unwrapped. "Put this on me, please."

Admittedly, she'd watched him do it lots of times... because, face it, watching him handle himself was really erotic.

Putting the top over his shaft, she rolled the condom down. "Gabe, your wound didn't heal up in the last few minutes. You still can't—"

"Be on top. I know." He smiled slowly. "But you can."

Sit on him? Hmm. Although they'd made love in a lot of different positions with far more variety than Craig had ever shown her, she'd never been on top. She almost laughed because no matter how inventive Gabe was, he always took the uppermost positions. Her alpha. "Sounds like fun."

Carefully, she straddled him, one knee on each side of his hips.

His lips curled into an easy smile. "Now grab my dick and lower yourself on it."

That sounded excellently wicked. Carnal.

"Look at you grin," he muttered.

Her face turned hot, but she gripped him firmly and put the first inch inside. *Mmmm, lovely*. Her hips wiggled, but she stayed in place, poised over him, only an inch inside.

And watched his face tighten at the delay.

He broke first. With a rough growl, he gripped her hips and yanked her down on him.

"Oh my God!" The sensation of fullness, the stretch, the heat bloomed in her core. He felt bigger in this position, went farther.

When she rocked forward, his pelvis rubbed her clit. Oh, that was nice.

Crinkles appeared at the corners of his eyes. "At this point, you have to do the moving, sweetheart."

"I can do that." Leaning forward, she braced herself with her hands beside his shoulders. Her butt went up, his shaft slid out. Then she settled into a rhythm, rocking forward and back, feeling his erection going in and out.

"Oh, nice." She was going to make this last forever. Torture him slowly. Drive him mad the way he had her so many times. She rose and lowered ever so slowly.

She was in charge and probably didn't manage to conceal the smirk.

Even though she hadn't spoken, his lips quirked. "I don't think so." Without moving his sore shoulder, he kneaded her breast.

When his knowledgeable fingers slid over her clit, shockingly exquisite pleasure shot through her. His touch and the thickness inside her were overwhelming.

The urge to speed up was uncontrollable, and her slow rhythm fell to pieces. She rocked faster and faster, adding wiggles to make his finger slide crosswise over her.

Tremors started low inside, the pressure growing. She tightened around him until she could feel each inch moving in and out.

"Oh, oh, oh, I need…"

With a low chuckle, he gripped her hips and slammed her down on his cock, lifting his hips at the same time, penetrating hard and deep.

Her insides clenched and spasmed in wave after wave of pleasure. When he came at the same time, the sense of sharing pleasure was incredible.

As the energy drained from her muscles, she sank on top of him, her cheek to his chest. His heart made a lovely thumping sound under her ear.

His arms closed around her, holding her, stroking her hair. "Thank you."

Lifting her head, she kissed the side of his strong jaw. "You're welcome, Mister Bossy Chief who hates to give up control."

She felt his smile even as he asked, ever so innocently, "Didn't you want me to use my fingers? I thought you liked that."

Sitting up carefully, she put her hands on each side of his face and gave him a stern frown. "You knew exactly what you were doing."

Laughter appeared in his eyes, and oh, she liked that look on him. "Sometimes, I'm not all that sure what I'm doing, no, but I do know this." His gaze went serious, and he tangled his fingers in her hair. "I care for you, Audrey. No, that's bullshit—I *love* you, woman."

What? *What?* Fireworks of delight sparkled around her, even as a thickness filled her throat. She shook her head. "No, no, you're wrong. You can't love me."

"No?" He tilted his head as if thinking. "Seems like I do. Yeah, I love you."

"It's not funny." He was injured. She couldn't hit him.

His gaze met hers. Straight. Clear. Honest.

He loved her? He really did?

Oh my God. What should she do? "I...I'm not ready. No, not ready for this."

Fear constricted her lungs. Craig had loved her, and then he hadn't. If she stayed and Gabe changed his mind, then... "I can't, I don't belong here. You shouldn't love me. This isn't right. I'm not ready. No. I have to go back to Chicago. I have a life there and—"

Babbling. She was babbling. Clamping her mouth shut, she stared at him. Shivers ran over her skin.

"Audrey, it's all right." He ran his hand over her cheek and smiled. "You tuck that in your head—that I love you—and stew on it for a while."

His order sounded almost insulting, yet he knew her well. She needed to stew.

After a quick kiss, he made a trip to the bathroom and returned. Rolling onto his back, he tucked her beside him, her leg over his, her arm over his waist.

"Go on to sleep, sweetheart." His voice dropped. "Gotta

say, having you here in my arms is about my favorite thing in the world."

With a sigh, she laid her cheek on his broad, warm shoulder. With a rumble of pleasure, he kissed the top of her head. As she breathed in his masculine scent, she knew she'd never felt so completely content.

CHAPTER TWENTY-SIX

In the station, Gabe watched the video play out the previous night's ambush in the parking lot. "Seems like moving the security cameras worked."

Sitting in the corner, Bull grunted his agreement.

Although Gabe's trap had worked, the results made him want to puke.

Onscreen, the men surrounded him. He hit pause and reset the video to the spot he wanted. No need to watch it again. He had enough bruises to remember every blow.

The door to the station opened and closed.

Bull muttered, "The bastard's here."

"Yeah. Guess we finish this game now."

Footsteps sounded in the office. Baumer had shown up for his Friday shift, right on time. "You in the office, MacNair?"

"Yeah. Come in."

"Nice day out, isn't it? Hey, Bull." Baumer leaned on the doorframe. "Did you want a meeting today? Anything going on I need to know about?"

"I'm afraid so." Gabe's anger was a low flame in his gut. "I got attacked by a bunch of cowardly wimps last night in the parking lot." Unable to resist, Gabe glanced at Bull. "Five men to just me. Am I really that scary?"

Even as Bull barked a laugh, Baumer's face went red. Satisfying as hell.

Gabe leaned back...and laid his hand on the pistol lying in his lap. Because he wasn't an idiot. "I have to wonder, are you off your meds, Officer Baumer?"

Baumer froze before giving a light laugh. "Very funny. I take it you want me to look for your attackers?"

"No, I'm looking at the leader. Nice brass knuckles you own, Baumer." Not that he'd used them much. No, the officer had stayed back and let his comrades do most of the work.

"There's no way—" Recognizing his mistake, Baumer smoothed his expression. "Why in the world would I attack you? Tell me more about what happened, and we'll look for the perpetrators."

"You're fired. Hand over your badge and keys."

"You can't do that. I... You don't have any reason to fire me. No proof."

Oh, proof they had, but why waste it on this asshole. Gabe smiled grimly. "You're on a ninety-day probation, which means I don't need a reason."

Baumer's gaze turned from Gabe to Bull and back as he tried to figure a way out of the hole. Then he pulled his badge off, dug out the station keys, and tossed everything onto the desk. "I didn't like working for a pussy like you anyway."

Ignoring the insult, Gabe said, "Tell Parrish the next time his Zealots—including you—overstep, I'll show up at the compound with a warrant and search the place from top to bottom."

Most certainly, the asshole reverend had munitions out there that weren't legal. "Tell him to keep his people in line."

Baumer froze. "I'm not one of them."

"Save it," Bull rumbled. "We know you live on the grounds."

Gabe didn't bother to add that Audrey'd found pictures of Baumer and his wife socializing with Parrish and other known Zealots. The dumbass's wife had posted the pictures on Facebook. "Isn't it a shame I didn't leave anything interesting in my office for you to pass to him?"

A flush reddened Baumer's face.

Yep, the asshole was the one who'd gone through the papers on Gabe's desk.

When Baumer didn't move, Gabe motioned to the door. "Dismissed. Regina has a box with your personal effects."

"Fine." Baumer's face turned purple with anger. "At least I'm not a bleeding-heart liberal kissing up to the bunny-huggers. This town will never amount to anything, and that's what we like. No one wants a trumped-up city cop here."

Baumer stomped out. The door to the station slammed a minute later.

Bull shook his head. "Bad loser."

Uneasiness roiled inside Gabe. Baumer had told the truth as he saw it. No one liked law enforcement, especially the rugged subsistence-living types and those living off the grid. All they knew of Gabe was that he'd worked in Anchorage and LA. *City cop.* "You think he has a point? Mako might've been wrong to think we could revive this place."

Bull ran his hand over his goatee. "We won't know unless we try. If we give up, tourists will avoid this place, even with the resort open. The Zealots would see to that."

"And Dante, Sarah, and the businesses will go under."

"Yeah. We need to win this, bro. Not for Mako—he's dead. Not for us—we'll do all right no matter what. We need to win for them."

Bull had a big heart, and he was right.

Gabe sighed. There were good people here, ones who deserved help.

It seemed he wouldn't be retreating to Mako's wilderness cabin. That wasn't who he was. He'd been fighting for others since he was born. Thinking he could stop was just bullshitting himself.

He glanced at Bull. "Yeah."

The one word was all Bull needed. "Good. We couldn't do this without you."

Gabe holstered his weapon. "I'll give a copy of the security video to Sarah. She can use it when she needs it, and it'll shut Parrish up for a while."

"Now, that'd be a sight worth seeing." Bull rose. "How much trouble will Baumer give you now?"

"Some. Maybe. He's lazy. Trouble is, he's also a weasel. He won't attack from the front. But he also knows you'll gut him and leave him for the wolves if I get hurt."

Bull grinned. "I figured that's why you wanted me in here instead of Caz. For intimidation purposes."

"Exactly." In all reality, Caz was more deadly than Bull. Mr. Intimidation simply liked to fight, nothing more deadly. Although Caz avoided killing, when he did dispatch someone, he was so silent that his targets never heard him before they were falling.

Bull shook his head. "If Baumer had any idea of your body count, he'd shit himself."

"Ewww." Audrey stood in the door. "Who'd soil himself and why?" She wrinkled her nose.

Gabe exhaled in relief. She'd only heard the last part of the sentence.

He walked over, gripped her upper arms, and pulled her to her tiptoes for a quick kiss.

He probably shouldn't have told her he loved her, yet, this morning, she was still beside him in bed. Hell, she was with him anytime they could be together. Maybe she hadn't said the words, but...he knew. Mako had taught him the art of patient waiting.

She was worth all the patience he had.

"So what happened?" she asked.

"He's now unemployed."

"Good riddance." She smiled up. "Let me know when you start interviewing for his replacement. I'll do some snooping in case there's stuff that's not on their official resumes."

"You have a sneaky side, don't you?" Gabe looked down into the wide gray eyes that held a wicked sparkle. "I like it."

CHAPTER TWENTY-SEVEN

Tuesday afternoon, Audrey crossed from Gabe's back deck to the tall shed—the coop—that housed the chickens. A wire enclosure was their yard. She thought country chickens would get the run of the fenced compound, but Gabe had set her straight. Apparently, big birds scratching in the garden for bugs would uproot seedlings and destroy plants. Bull had added that hawks and eagles found fowl to be excellent dining.

She never wanted to see that. Ever.

So the chickens stayed in their yard. Like chicken-shaped zebras, the Barred Rocks had black and white feathers with decorative red combs and wattles.

Bull called them sweet. And, although the sharp, yellow beaks had worried her, she'd come to like the pretty hens. Whenever she collected eggs, they'd come to the fence, clucking happily and expecting treats.

Gabe laughed at her because she felt guilty if she didn't have some.

On the side of the shed, she unlatched the hinged door to the nest boxes and gathered the eggs. A full dozen.

Excellent. She was going to make Gabe a cake. Not for any reason other than...well, because feeding him was a way to show she cared.

And she enjoyed cooking for him. He still seemed surprised when she did, as if no one had ever made him sweets.

She frowned. His mother had died when he was three, and his grandfather, who kept him for a few years, had worked a lot. Then there was foster care, which probably didn't dispense a lot of love with food. After that, he went to Mako who had a *no work, no eat* philosophy. Their sergeant hadn't been a very gentle person.

The thought of Gabe as a small boy, lacking for love, made her heart hurt. Their childhoods had been more alike than she realized.

As she carried the basket of eggs into the house, she made a vow that she'd see her man was well fed and well loved...while she was here.

But it was already July, and the end of the summer approached.

Propping up her phone so she could see the recipe, she beat the sugar, eggs, and butter into a smooth mixture.

At the end of August, she'd leave Rescue. Leave Gabe.

Her chest hurt.

In Chicago, even in the university library, she'd never felt as much a part of everything as she did here. Friendships didn't last long in a city. People changed jobs and moved away.

Some of her friendless state was her fault. She never attended university activities.

Face it, she was a hermit.

Yet, being broke in Rescue had sure ended her isolation. Her jobs here required more than a polite, efficient librarian —Dante and Bull expected her to be *friendly*.

She couldn't even hole up to do research—not with an internetless cabin...and people talked to her in the coffee shop.

Then, after talking the town into reopening the library, well, she had to prove how essential the place was. And it was working. More and more people came into the library. Had her order their favorite movies. Talked about books. Asked her help in selecting children's stories.

Then there was Knox. Satisfaction bloomed in her heart. He'd already mastered the alphabet. He was so much smarter than he believed, and she was proud of him. And he was changing as he viewed himself in a different light.

In the same way, her self-image had improved. After years of believing a nerd could never be accepted, she'd become a part of this town. They *liked* her.

How could she go back to being lonely?

And...she stared down at the cake batter. Her way of telling Gabe she loved him.

How could she leave *him*?

I don't want to.

Could she stay? Would he want her to?

He'd said he loved her, and oh, God help her, she loved him so very much.

She swiped up some cake batter and licked it off her finger. Could a helping of sugar make a girl braver? Somehow, she needed to summon up her courage and actually tell the man.

"I love you." She cringed at hearing herself say the words. Last time, when she'd blurted it out, her boyfriend had laughed at her. Because he'd been planning to leave and had already found a perfect status-enhancing girlfriend. "*I need someone at my side who likes people.*" With two sentences, he'd shattered her ego.

Gabe wouldn't do that. He *wouldn't.*

Would he?

No, she knew him better. Mr. Terse and Honest sure wouldn't say he loved her if he didn't.

He wants me to stay. Me, the nerd. He could have the gorgeous Brooke, but he'd chosen Audrey.

He'd change his mind; surely he would, and break her heart.

But what if he didn't? Could she risk it?

She had to. She'd tell him. She *would.*

And then the front door opened. Gabe walked in, scattering her willpower to the winds.

"Um. Hi."

He stopped, his eyes narrowing. "Sweetheart, you're flushed."

"It's the heat of the oven. I'm making you a cake."

Imitating her action, he swiped a fingerful of batter, ate it with a hum of pleasure, and turned his body to trap her against the counter.

"Gabe."

His kiss was sugar-sweet before he pulled back and murmured, "The oven isn't on, Audrey. Now answer me honestly, why do you look shaken up?"

He had his cop face on, and his fingers under her chin kept her from hiding her face against his chest.

Where had all her courage gone? "I...I did some thinking about stuff."

His lips twitched. "Stuff, huh?"

When she pulled in a shuddering breath, any trace of laughter died in his face. Putting that compelling sexuality of his away, he slid his hands down to grip her waist. "Did you come to any conclusions?"

"Oh, you jerk. Is it any wonder I love you?" she muttered.

Light filled his eyes, and he pulled her back into his arms. "You do, huh?"

When he brushed his cheek over hers, the slight rasp of stubble was as heady as champagne. "Can I have it in the proper form, a real sentence and all that?"

"You're such a rule-bound, law enforcement person. Will

I get a ticket if I don't say it properly?" She couldn't keep her lips from turning up.

"No." His nip on the edge of her jaw sent tingles quaking through her. "If needed, I'll interrogate you."

His teeth nibbled on her ear lobe. "As long as needed. Maybe all night long."

Oh...my.

"Tell me, Audrey." His whisper in her ear was husky and deep.

Courage. "I love you, Gabe MacNair." Her knees started to buckle.

His arms tightened, and he held her firmly against his solid body. "That's a good start."

His long exhalation said he'd been worried.

Worried if she loved him? Arms around him, she burrowed closer.

"What about Chicago, sweetheart?"

"If...if it's all right, I'd like to stay." She had just enough courage to lift her head and watch his face. If he looked unhappy or displeased, she'd...she'd just die.

Instead, he grinned.

Grinned.

"Fucking-A and yes, it's all right." He squeezed her so hard her ribs complained. His mouth came down on hers.

As he lifted her to carry her up the stairs, her head spun. "What are you *doing*?"

"I think it's an old tradition—celebrating."

"People eat when they celebrate."

"I can do that. In fact, I will do that. Yeah, before I'm through, the only word you'll be able to say will be *please*."

His merciless grip and his dark, sexy promise sent heat combusting through every cell in her body.

CHAPTER TWENTY-EIGHT

In the screened gazebo, Audrey wiggled, trying to get comfortable in the Adirondack loveseat. Really, the slatted wood chair was nice. She just couldn't settle. Because of what was to come.

A door shutting caught her attention. Caz was coming out of his cabin. All five log houses had the same architecture with decks and tall windows facing the lake and compound. But each cabin held unique touches. Gabe's shutters and trim were a gray-blue. In contrast, Mako's were a solid black. That sure fit what she'd heard of the sergeant.

Bull left his house, crossing his deck filled with flowering plants. She hoped to do the same for Gabe's place.

If she was here. She bit her lip as Gabe walked out, carrying a couple of beers.

It'd been a nice Sunday. She and the men spent the morning together doing outside chores before enjoying a mid-afternoon barbecue. After cleaning up, Gabe decided he needed a beer before facing the town meeting tonight. His brothers had laughed and agreed to hang out in the gazebo.

Audrey wished for a few shots of tequila rather than beer.

She and Gabe had kept quiet about her decision to stay until they could all be together. She'd thought it would happen on the Fourth of July last Wednesday, but that hadn't worked. The roadhouse had been open. Caz'd been called to the health clinic to deal with some scorched fingers for two young men who'd mixed alcohol and fireworks.

Not that there had been many fireworks. When the sun pretty much didn't set this time of year, what would be the point?

Today, everyone was home. She rubbed her damp palms on her thighs.

As Gabe settled next to her and handed her a beer, Bull dropped into a chair across from them.

Caz sat down, and his smile disappeared. "What's the matter, *chiquita*?"

"Um..." She glanced at Gabe.

His concerned look disappeared, and understanding filled his gaze. Wrapping his hand around her nape, he pressed his forehead against hers. "You, Goldilocks, worry too much," he whispered.

No, no, she didn't. His brothers might like her, but

there was a big difference between being an occasional overnight visitor and a real, live-in lover. At least, that was the impression she'd gotten from listening to her colleagues chatting.

"Okay, sweetheart, let's get this out of the way." Gabe put his arm around her. "My bros, she's terrified you'll be unhappy that I fell in love with her and plan to keep her."

The silence lasted and lasted...

Caz jumped up and pulled her from the chair, and she realized it had only been a second. "*Eso es excelente!*" He hugged her and kissed her cheek. "The *viejo* is a lucky guy."

Bull took her and squeezed the air right out of her lungs. "I can't think of anyone more perfect for him."

Smiling, Gabe drew her back down and put his arm over her shoulders. "See, Goldie?"

Oh God, she was going to cry. She buried her face against his neck until she got control.

As she took a shuddering breath, he just chuckled. "Better?"

Surreptitiously trying to wipe tears from her eyes, she sat up. Seeing his brothers' pleased grins almost had her crying again.

"She's moving in, right?" Bull asked Gabe.

"Damn straight." Gabe gave her hair a teasing tug. "She wouldn't tell Dante he could have the cabin back until you guys knew. In case you disapproved."

Bull's serious gaze met hers. "Even if we hadn't approved, Gabe wouldn't have let you go, Audrey."

"He'd have pounded on us until we saw it his way," Caz said.

Joy filled her, streaming light through every cell.

Gabe tilted his beer toward his brothers. "It's as if you could read my mind."

"Bet Lillian was thrilled to hear she can keep her chick here," Bull said.

"What makes you think Lillian already knows?" Gabe asked.

"Bro, seriously?" Bull shook his head. "A female will ferret out every detail before a guy even knows there's a secret."

At Gabe's disbelieving look, Audrey said between giggles, "She did. And she's pleased." In fact, there'd been tears in Lillian's eyes as she squeezed Audrey's hands.

"Yep. Told you," Bull said smugly.

Caz lifted his beer. "To the new member of the family."

As the guys gave a rousing shout and *clinked* their bottles together, Audrey pressed her face against Gabe's shoulder again.

She had friends.

She had a family.

And she had Gabe.

How much happiness could a heart hold?

Gabe's hand covered hers, and she looked up. He was watching her...the way he did so often.

She gave him a smile and rubbed her cheek against his ever-so-hard biceps. Was it possible for love to keep growing? Sometimes it felt as if her heart would burst from her chest.

A ringing sound came from Gabe's house.

"Oops, that's my cell." Audrey dashed across the grass, across the deck, and into the house.

Dennison's name showed on the caller ID. Although she'd given him her number after Spyros was caught, this was the first time he'd used it.

"Hello."

"This is Special Agent Dennison."

"How are you doing?" She headed back outside. "Don't you get weekends off?"

"Not this weekend. There's trouble." His voice was grim. "Several hours ago when Spyros was being transferred to a longer-term facility, a semi ran the prison transport vehicle off the road. A second team in an SUV shot up the guards and got Spyros free. He's escaped, Audrey."

"B-but..." Free? Spyros was free? Fear hit like a sledgehammer, and she stopped dead in the center of the lawn. Pushing back panic, she whispered, "The guards. Are they all right?"

There was a pause. "I'm afraid not. It was ugly...and it's on every news-station. The semi deliberately plowed down pedestrians. Spyros's men shot people—children—to force the guards to release Spyros from the prison van. It was a bloodbath, Audrey."

Her knees started to buckle. Those people, those poor

CHERISE SINCLAIR

people. Her heart sent up a prayer for them. "And he got away."

"Every agency is working to recapture him, but this was well-planned. They had resources in place for them all to disappear."

Spyros would be coming after her.

Paralyzing fear filled her, freezing her in place, freezing her thoughts.

"Audrey?" Gabe wrapped an arm around her. "What's wrong?"

She stared into Gabe's blue eyes and couldn't speak.

Brow furrowed, he plucked the phone from her grip. "This is MacNair, Chief of Police. Who is this?"

The buzz from her cell was Dennison's voice.

Gabe's face darkened. "What the *fuck*?"

"That doesn't sound good." Bull pulled her from Gabe and tucked her against his massive chest.

Her breathing hitched, and she burrowed against him.

When Caz took a position at her left, she was surrounded by Mako's sons, the toughest men she'd ever known. Something in her chest loosened, letting her manage to inhale.

"*Chiquita*, can you tell us what's wrong?" Caz's voice was gentle.

"Spyros, the murderer who was after me... He's escaped. That's an FBI agent on the line."

Still talking, Gabe surveyed the enclosed area, the lake,

384

and the houses as if already at war. "You've got my number. Keep me informed. We'll keep her safe."

After swiping the END CALL, he handed her the phone and pulled her back into his arms. Looking over her head at his brothers, he asked, "She told you?"

Bull nodded. "The assassin is loose. What are the chances he'll come after Audrey?"

"Too good, although Dennison thinks he'll hole up until the hunt dies down some. Spyros is apparently patient that way. But he wants revenge. Badly." Gabe gave her a tiny squeeze. "Because of her, he only has one eye. His shooting ability is affected, and his reputation has been shredded. He was crippled by a damn librarian."

Bull snorted.

"Does he know where to find Audrey?" Caz asked.

"Yeah. He was originally caught trying to board a plane to Alaska. He had informants in the Chicago PD who told him about Baumer's query." Scowling, Gabe led the way back to the gazebo.

"What's the plan, *viejo?*" Caz followed.

"I should leave," Audrey said. "I should—"

"Don't decide now, sweetheart." Gabe pressed a kiss to the top of her head before pulling her down on his lap. "We can batten the hatches, hunker down, and prepare for war."

Bull nodded. "And if an Outsider shows up looking for trouble, we'll give him all he can eat."

But she'd put them in danger. Only, she hadn't put those people in Chicago in danger—they'd died anyway. What would Spyros do if she wasn't here? Would he torture people to find out her location?

She closed her eyes, feeling hopeless. No matter what she did, someone would be in danger. Maybe it was time to stop running.

Maybe, with all of them, they could come up with a plan and stop him for good.

On Sunday night, Gabe waited as Audrey chatted with Regina in the municipal building lobby.

It'd been a difficult day.

First, he, his brothers, and Audrey had hammered out plans...because she'd agreed to stay. *Thank fuck.*

Spyros wouldn't forget about her, and she couldn't stay hidden forever, not in this interconnected world. Not even in Alaska. No matter where she went, sooner or later, the bastard would find her. No one could stay on guard forever.

It would be best if Spyros came when they were alert and prepared. Audrey had agreed, but had taken the "prepared" idea a step further.

She'd asked him for a knife and a pistol. *Jesus.*

Maybe he was infected with Mako's pessimism because he'd figured she needed to be able to defend herself if the shit hit the fan. He gave her his ankle-holster backup weapon and worked with her all afternoon until she'd proven she could mostly hit what she aimed at.

Caz must have felt the same. He gave her a knife and dug out one of his old arm sheaths from when he was a skinny teenager.

Watching her buckle on weapons had given Gabe an icy chill in his gut.

He hated how much danger she was in. She was...everything, and he'd go through anyone or anything that would hurt her. He felt the same about his brothers, but this was even more. She wasn't a hotshot ex-military combat vet; she was a sweet, far-too-fucking-innocent, librarian.

And he loved her more than he loved living.

It would've been good to know exactly who they would face. Dennison said Spyros might or might not come with a team.

Gabe frowned. Once upon a time, he'd been on a SEAL team. They'd been as tight as men sharing blood and battle could be, but over the years, they'd scattered. It would've been good to have them at his back.

Then again, he now had his very first team—his brothers. His mood lifted. Considering the end of the parking lot fight, he knew Caz's skills hadn't declined.

If the town wouldn't help, Gabe and his brothers would manage.

As Gabe walked over to the reception desk, Regina scowled and asked him, "What's the world coming to when a murderer gets free like that?"

Ah, Audrey had told Regina about Spyros.

"I agree." As a thought occurred to him, Gabe's jaw

tightened. Silently, he tucked an arm around Audrey and motioned for Regina to walk with them to the town meeting room.

Audrey glanced up. "You look even unhappier than earlier."

"Eh, I was thinking Spyros and I have more in common than is comfortable." Spyros worked on a team, much as Gabe had, and probably took pride in doing a good job. "He took money to kill people, and when I worked for the mercs, so did I."

She gave him an incredulous look. "You took money to kill innocent women?"

"No."

"Would you have?"

"No." Not for all the money in the world.

"Spyros lacks any moral code. You have a very strong one. Being a mercenary wasn't a good fit for you." She went up on tiptoes to kiss his cheek.

Well. His mood lightened. Goldilocks was right. There were lines he wouldn't cross.

Smiling, he kissed the top of Audrey's head. She certainly had a talent for putting things into perspective.

As they walked into the meeting—late—he saw the place was packed, again. At the front, Dante was announcing that Baumer had been dismissed.

"That seems very high-handed of Chief MacNair." His deep-set eyes flashing with anger, Parrish leaned forward, looking at the townspeople. "We've perhaps given an

Outsider too much control over our town. What does a police officer from the Lower 48 know about Alaska and how we operate here?

"Oh, he knows." Guzman snorted. "He can also track better than anyone I've ever met."

Chevy rose, moving stiffly. "He saved my son. I'd say he knows a damn lot."

"Knows how to deal with moose," another yelled.

Dante's wheezing laugh stilled the comments. "Gabe an Outsider? Bullpucky. He grew up in a dry cabin down by Seward. His father was a Green Beret buddy of mine. Our chief here was a Navy SEAL—yeah, served our country—and an Anchorage cop."

A SEAL...Anchorage...dry cabin? Whispers ran around the room.

Jesus. Who knew the whiskered old man was so chatty. Gabe frowned at Dante.

Parrish scowled. "He worked in Los Angeles."

Unfazed, Dante grinned. "For a bit. He fell for an Outsider woman who dragged him to the States to work. But now we got him back home, and we're not going to let him go again."

The cheers and hoots of agreement made Gabe freeze. Cheers?

Abandoning the Outsider argument, Parrish pointed to Gabe and shouted, "You fired Officer Baumer for no reason."

It was time to lay some cards on the table. "You mean I

fired your boy, Mr. Parrish?" Not *reverend* because he was sure no man of God.

Parrish stiffened. "Officer Baumer isn't one of mine."

"He lives in your compound. He's yours."

The man's mouth compressed.

"Let me show you the reason he was fired." Gabe nodded to Uriah who'd set up equipment to project the video on the white wall behind the council members. "For crime prevention, security cameras were installed in high-risk areas. Since medical clinics are high risk, there's a camera in the parking lot here, behind our municipal building."

Parrish frowned and the color drained from his face.

"Earl Baumer was fired because of this..." Gabe waved at Uriah to start the video.

The room went silent as the video showed Baumer and four other men crossing the parking lot. Their faces were easily identifiable...as were the weapons they carried. They all put on their ski masks. When Baumer pulled brass knuckles from his pocket, gasps ran through the room.

As the five men flattened themselves against the wall, Uriah said loudly. "The fools were there a long time. Seems they didn't realize how many hours a day our chief puts in." He fast-forwarded.

The time of day showed on the screen as Gabe stepped out of the building. The man with the club swung. Gabe dove forward—and the brawl began.

The video stopped. Voices protested.

"It gets violent," Uriah said, "and we have minors in the room. After the meeting, I'll play it for any adult who wants to see the rest."

The objections died.

A man yelled, "Besides Baumer, at least two of those bastards are in the PZs. Parrish, did you sic them on our chief?"

Our chief. Seems he had been claimed by the town. The warmth around Gabe's heart expanded.

Parrish was busy denying everything, doing damage control, spinning for all he was worth. *Asshole.* This'd shut him up for now, but the fight wasn't over. Parrish had too much invested in the area to leave.

The noise increased. People were getting too riled up.

Gabe moved to the center of the room. Dammit, he wished Parrish and his PZ people weren't present—but they were, and this was the only chance Gabe had to reach almost everyone in town. "I have a request that's a bit unusual."

He waited as the noise died down, then Tucker shouted from the back, "Let's hear it, MacNair."

Mentally, Gabe crossed his fingers for luck. He pointed to Audrey who sat in the back beside Regina. "Most of you know our librarian. When she arrived, she told us her name was Julie because she was hiding from a Chicago murderer by the name of Spyros."

Hearing her name, she jerked straight.

"You've seen her trying to make a living, working in

Dante's grocery, at Bull's Moose, and now running our library."

The buzz of approval made him smile.

"When they caught Spyros, she told a lot of us the story, and that her real name is Audrey. However, last night, Spyros escaped. You might have seen it on the news?"

Those that had caught the story began sharing it.

Gabe waited for the racket to die down. "Audrey was the one who, when fighting for her life, deprived him of that eye."

Gasps.

The man closest to him muttered, "She's tougher'n she looks."

Gabe grinned at the variations on "Way to go, girl!" Some of those old sourdoughs—male and female—were damned bloodthirsty.

"The FBI figures Spyros and his team will come after Audrey." Gabe hated the way Audrey's face paled. "I'd like you all to watch for them. I don't want heroics. These are skilled hitmen, and they'll kill anyone in their way. What I'm asking is that you keep your eyes open.

"How will we know?" Felix called. "The town is full of fishermen."

It was salmon season, dammit. "True. But these men are predators. And one man is missing an eye. If you get an off feeling, call the line to the station direct, no matter what time. It'll get relayed to me."

Uriah tapped a key on the laptop, and the number for the station came up on the projection.

Just about every person in the room pulled out a phone or pen and paper to record the number.

Gabe stared. Swallowed. Then had to clear his throat. "That's it. Thank you all."

After Mayor Lillian ended the meeting, Gabe grabbed Audrey as she was leaving.

Her eyes narrowed.

He kissed away her cute frowny-pout and pulled her close. "Sorry, sweetheart. I know you don't like being the center of attention."

Before she could speak, Guzman stepped in front of them. "But she's such a pretty center of attention." He gave Gabe a level look. "Tucker and I'll stay close to town for a while. Watching. You've got back-up if you need it."

Gabe shook his hand.

Several more people came forward to say essentially the same thing, including every member of the search team who'd looked for Chevy's kid.

By God, he liked this town.

Maybe, maybe together they could keep Audrey safe.

CHAPTER TWENTY-NINE

At Lillian's house, as Audrey climbed out of Gabe's car, she still couldn't get her mind around the towns-people's response.

Last night, Rescue had volunteered to keep Audrey safe, and people kept repeating the intention today.

Earlier, in the coffee shop, a man patted his holstered pistol and said he was carrying today in case those bastards came after her. He assured her he was ready to "perforate" them. Two men and a woman had laughed in agreement and stood to show her *their* weapons.

She'd come very close to bursting into tears.

In Chicago, fleeing for her life, she'd had no one to turn to.

In Rescue, all day, people had offered her sanctuary with variations of: *Those bastards will never find you at my place; it's off the road. Come and stay with me.*

God.

The feelings inside her were so big, so overwhelming, she had no way to express them.

Gabe felt the same way about the town's response. As they walked up the sidewalk to Lillian's, she took his hand. He squeezed her fingers with a smile.

How could she feel so frightened...and so blessed?

He'd held her hand when she called Dennison to say she wanted to be bait. After a long pause, the Special Agent had reluctantly agreed. Then he'd shared that the Chicago police hotline had received reports of Spyros and his men at a gas station. The hitman hadn't headed for Alaska yet.

The sense of relief was overwhelming.

Nonetheless, Gabe had still insisted on giving her guards. Just in case. Because he loved her.

How could she argue when he said stuff like that?

Gabe bent to give her a long, lingering kiss. He followed the sweetness with a stern look. "Call me when you're ready to leave."

She wouldn't do anything to add to the worry in his expression, so she smiled up at him. "Yes, Mister Bossy Chief. I'll be good."

Her reward was the slight relaxing of his jaw. "Thank you, sweetheart."

"I'll keep her safe, Gabriel." Lillian stood in the doorway.

Gabe's kisses were awfully potent. Audrey hadn't even heard the door open.

Gabe smiled slightly. "Thank you, Lillian."

As he headed back to his car, Audrey noticed two men leaning against a parked pickup.

Her muscular guards nodded at Gabe, then smiled at her and Lillian.

"Come, child." Lillian led her through the house to the back. "There's gardening to be done."

Good. She needed something to occupy her hands. "I know. It seems wrong to have fun while those men are stuck out there, just wasting their time."

"Protecting you is not a waste of time." Lillian positioned a folding chair next to the garden cart beside the row of carrots and sat down. "Let me teach you the fine art of thinning—also known as the slaughter of innocent seedlings."

Even as Audrey laughed, a tremor ran down her spine.

Kneeling in a garden row an hour later, Audrey sang along with Lillian as she harvested lettuce and beets. The song by Hobo Jim—and what a name—was a melancholy ballad about a fisherman who hadn't returned to his woman.

The woman was probably imaginary. Even so, the sad tune had Audrey choking up. Because she couldn't bear it if something happened to Gabe.

Romance books were all about the wonders of falling in love, the sex, even the fighting. Didn't they ever mention how a woman could fold at just the thought of losing the new center of her universe?

Gabe *was* her center.

As Lillian took up a haunting descant to the melody, and the song turned even more sorrowful, Audrey blinked back tears.

Catching her friend's worried look, she tried to smile. What had Lillian done when her husband died? How had she survived?

As the sun disappeared under encroaching clouds, the world grew darker. Colder. Audrey couldn't take it. "It's starting to sprinkle. Let's get everything inside, and go warm up."

"Good idea." A man's voice made Audrey scramble to her feet.

Earl Baumer stood in the open garden gate.

Audrey gasped. "What are you doing here?"

"Came for you." He lunged at her.

No time to draw her weapons. Dodging, she stuck out a foot and tripped him, then sprinted toward the side of the house. Her guards were in front.

She'd reached the corner when she heard, "Stop or I'll kill her."

His yell made Audrey look over her shoulder.

No.

She skidded to a halt and grabbed a tree to catch her balance.

Earl had Lillian pinned against him, her back to his

chest. One hand gripped her white hair as he held a knife to her fragile neck.

"Earl Baumer, you are a sodden-witted bull's pizzle." Lillian's face was tight with pain. She looked at Audrey. "Run, child, you—"

Her voice cut off as Earl dug in the point of the knife. A thin trickle of red ran down her white neck.

"You might get away, Audrey, but the old lady'll be dead." Earl's voice was ragged and strained. His reactions were...unpredictable, and Audrey's nerves tensed.

He stared at her. "Can you live with that, slut?"

Everything in her screamed *run*.

Lillian's mouth formed the word. *Go.*

Audrey hesitated, fear raising the hairs on her nape. Yet she couldn't survive if she ran and Lillian was hurt. "I'll go with you."

"Come here."

No choice. Hands in fists, Audrey crossed the yard back to the garden.

With a shout of victory, Earl grabbed her and shoved Lillian away.

The older woman staggered and tripped over her chair. Her head hit the wooden garden cart with a ghastly thump.

She fell, limp.

"No!" Audrey yanked Caz's knife from the arm sheath. She slashed at Earl's restraining hand, cutting his wrist.

With a shout of pain, he let go—and then punched her

arm so hard that her fingers went numb. The knife dropped.

Before she could jump away, he backhanded her. Pain exploded in her face, and she reeled back, stopped from falling when he grabbed her shirt. Blackness flickered at the edge of her vision

"Stupid slut." As she struggled, he yanked her arms behind her back and cuffed her. Gripping her shirtfront, he dragged her to the front of the house.

Tears streaming from her eyes, she looked frantically for the two men who'd volunteered to watch over her.

No one stood at the pickup. Audrey's breath froze in her lungs.

"Oooh, did the bitch lose her guards?" Earl's mocking voice made her freeze.

"What did you do to them?"

"Heh. Stupid bastards were watching for a guy with an eye patch, not me." He grinned. "I went over to talk—and then tasered them. They're tied up in the truck bed. It's good the old biddy lives on such a quiet street."

Her breathing restarted. The men were alive.

Oh, God, Lillian, are you all right?

Earl yanked her over to a big SUV.

You won't get away with this. She didn't say the words because he might. How could she escape? Her knife was gone. She couldn't reach the pistol strapped to her ankle.

Opening the sliding side door, he started to shove her in.

Edging sideways, she braced a shoulder against the doorframe and kicked him violently between the legs.

With a high whining scream, he dropped to his knees, holding his crotch.

Yes!

Someone inside the SUV grabbed her handcuffs and the back of her T-shirt.

Screaming and struggling frantically, she was dragged backward, scraping her shoulders and her head on the doorframe. She fell onto her back, landing painfully on her handcuffed arms.

A boot came down on her belly hard enough to knock the wind from her.

"Look at this. Spyros is gonna be in a better mood now."

Heart hammering, Audrey stared up at the man who sat above her.

Buzz-cut blond hair, busted nose, thick New York accent. He'd been with Spyros in her apartment.

The fired police officer hadn't grabbed her just to get revenge on Gabe. Earl was working with Spyros.

Oh, God.

"But Spyros is in Chicago. He was seen there." The words burst out in a stupidly futile protest. As if her wishing could make it true.

The New Yorker's ugly grin held open menace. "Not so, cunt. He boarded a private jet a half hour after we got him loose. The people who called the hotline about spotting us at a gas station? They got paid really well."

Spyros was here. *Here.*

A boulder of fear weighed down her chest as she fought to inhale.

"You can't kill her in my ride." After wrapping a cloth handkerchief around his slashed wrist, Earl jumped into the driver's seat. "I don't want any of her blood splashed around in here."

"Don't worry. The boss wants to take his time." The New Yorker dug the heel of his boot into Audrey's stomach, and a whine of pain broke from her. "He's gonna leave her body—what's left of it—someplace nice and public in Chicago."

Earl grunted. "He wants to make a statement that no one gets away from him?"

"Yeah." The guy grinned. "He'll leave one side of her face intact so she can be ID'd. The rest'll look like a horror show."

No. Oh, no. As tremors of fear shook her body, Audrey shut her eyes. *Don't cry. Don't cry.*

But tears seeped from beneath her eyelids.

Tucker, Guzman, and Bull crowded around Gabe's desk as Lillian spoke over the speakerphone.

Gabe's hands fisted as he listened.

Thank God, the elderly Brit had bought herself a medical alert system. When she'd regained consciousness in the garden, she'd pressed the button. Obeying her demand, the monitoring company had patched her call straight to the station.

"Audrey could have gotten away, Gabriel, but that abortive, rooting hog named Baumer held a knife to my throat. The girl came back. For me." The suppressed sobs in the old woman's voice echoed the ones in Gabe's heart. "Find her, Chief. Please, hurry."

She started to weep, and then silence indicated she'd disconnected the call.

"Tucker." Gabe looked at the sturdy old sourdough. "Can you and Guzman go check on her and the two guys who were on guard duty? Bring Lillian back to the station if she wants."

Tucker and Guzman left, pushing past the people outside the office door.

"Regina is alerting everyone she can." Caz came in, followed by Knox and Chevy.

"Baumer kidnapped her." Knox rubbed his face in disbelief. "I thought he was a good guy. I even believed his shit about tourists—ate it up like candy."

"We both did." Chevy's color was pale.

"That's water under the bridge. Move on." Gabe waved their remorse away. "Where would Baumer take Audrey? Probably not the PZ compound."

Parrish undoubtedly wanted Gabe's head, but a successful con man like him wouldn't act this openly. He sure wouldn't give Gabe a chance to search the compound, especially after last night when Baumer had been identified as a PZ.

In fact, going by Parrish's past reactions... "I bet Parrish kicked Baumer out of the group hug."

"He did," someone said from the back. "Earl hit me up for money this morning. Like we'd still be friends after I saw that tape and how he and the other assholes attacked you from the back? That's fucked up."

"Where's he staying now?" Caz asked.

The man shook his head. "He didn't say."

Baumer wanted revenge against Gabe...and Audrey would pay the price. Dammit, he'd never have thought the bastard would go this far. Would attack a woman or a civilian.

Gabe forced his fear back, needing to think, not react. *Audrey, where are you?*

First, they needed to ensure Baumer couldn't get her out of the area. He pressed a button on his desk. "Regina, can you have spotters on the Sterling Highway, east and west? Baumer's probably not more than fifteen minutes out. Text everyone a picture of him, his car, and license plate number. Let's make sure he's not leaving the area."

For the first time, he was pleased with the lack of roads in Alaska. The only way out of this area was the Sterling Highway.

"I've got plenty of volunteers. Consider it done." Regina clicked off.

As thunder rattled the window, Gabe glanced out. The rain had turned into a downpour.

Focusing only on each task that needed to be done, Gabe notified the state troopers.

A knot of pain filled his gut. Everything inside him wanted to go out and search for her himself, not sit here inside. Making calls.

However, this was where he was most useful.

If Baumer couldn't get out of the area, where would he go to ground? Who would know? Followed by Caz, Knox, and Chevy, Gabe walked into the bullpen.

It was crowded with people waiting to help. "Does anyone know where Baumer's staying? I'd like to speak with his wife. She might have some knowledge of his plans."

Erica, one of the two women who'd helped search for Niko, raised her hand as if she was in a classroom. "Last night, Earl, MaryEllen, and the children stayed with my mom here in town. I called Mom a few minutes ago. Earl left this morning, but his wife is still there."

In town. His hopes rose. "Can you take me there?"

"Sure, Chief."

Five minutes later, Gabe followed Erica and her mother through the small house off Dall Road. Caz—the pro at getting information from people—was beside him. The others waited outside.

"Chief MacNair and Caz." In the kitchen, Erica pointed

to a strained-looking, thin redhead who stood next to the table. "MaryEllen Baumer."

Erica's mother had a gentle voice. "MaryEllen, the Chief has some questions about Earl."

MaryEllen had a baby in her arms and a toddler clinging to her ankle-length black skirt. She looked Caz over, and her nose wrinkled slightly.

Turning to Gabe, she stared at his badge. Not meeting his gaze, she took a step back. "We've been kicked out. Lost our home."

He could hear the part she didn't say: because of you.

Earl was the type to blame others for his poor choices—and this pitiful woman wasn't one who'd stand up to her husband.

"Earl is not here, but I don't think he would want to see you," she finished.

"I don't particularly want to see him either. Unfortunately, he put a knife to Mayor Lillian's throat and kidnapped Audrey Hamilton." Gabe watched her closely.

All color left her face, and she sank onto a chair at the small table. "No. It wasn't supposed to be like that."

Gabe glanced at Caz, waiting for him to take over.

An infinitesimal shake of the head said no. Caz ran a finger down his brown skin and shrugged. True enough, a bigoted person probably wouldn't confide in a Hispanic.

Dammit.

MaryEllen's gaze stayed on the floor as she whispered. "I think you should leave."

Gabe rubbed his neck as he studied the woman. Long skirt, hair in a bun, blouse buttoned up all the way. She might be kicked out, but her heart was still in the PZs. Even as urgency stampeded over his nerves, pity grew inside him. She hadn't been allowed to think. Had been indoctrinated into the PZ's belief system.

That couldn't matter. Although Baumer undoubtedly made the decisions in the family, MaryEllen had heard enough to know what was going on and that laws were being broken. Now she'd have to make some decisions of her own—and would hear some truths she'd rather not know.

In his head, he cursed Baumer again. Not only for Audrey and Lillian, but also for not caring enough for his family to keep them out of harm's way.

Sitting down at the table to keep from looming, Gabe softened his voice. "MaryEllen, kidnapping is a federal crime, I'm afraid, and you will be considered an accomplice. If you help us stop this, I might be able to keep you out of prison." He dropped his gaze to her children.

"Dear sweet Jesus," she whispered, pulling her toddler closer.

"Tell me."

She shook her head. "No, no, no. A woman must obey her man. Mustn't—"

Caz said very quietly, "Does a loving mother abandon her children? Who will guard your babies?"

Her arm tightened around the infant she held, and her gaze turned to the toddler. "Oh, God, what should I do?"

She swallowed then started talking, her voice still never louder than a whisper. "Late last night, Earl got an email from someone who said he would pay ten thousand dollars if Earl arranged for Ms. Hamilton to be somewhere isolated today. There wasn't supposed to be...violence."

Gabe stared at her. An email? Ten thousand dollars? *Spyros.*

Gabe saw the dawning horror on his brother's face. Baumer hadn't done this for revenge—or not solely for revenge—but because Spyros had hired him.

Not understanding their silence, MaryEllen jumped into excuses. "After you showed that video last night, the Reverend threw us out. Earl is...is very angry with you."

"I see."

MaryEllen flushed. "It's wrong to live in sin without the bond of matrimony. Earl said the woman is your lover."

"She is." And the very air he needed to breathe. "Earl has Audrey in his car. Where is he taking her?"

"I don't know."

At their disbelieving looks, she raised her voice. "I *don't.* A man called this morning and told Earl to pick him up. He wanted to be in the car to facil...facil...the delivery."

"Facilitate the delivery?"

"Yes. Once she...when she was in the car, they'd meet someone and hike to a zone." She rubbed her cheek against her baby's head. "I didn't hear everything."

She'd probably been hearing only Earl's side of the conversation.

A zone?

"A landing zone," Caz said quietly.

Gabe nodded, even as cold ran through his veins. If Audrey got in a plane, the chances of finding her grew infinitesimal. He forced his mind to keep working. "Helicopter or float plane?"

"Earl said something about a chopper and started making suggestions, but Matthew Mark woke up, and I didn't hear more." Tears filled her eyes. "Earl left. He didn't say goodbye; he just left."

Because he was in a rush to get revenge on Gabe. To get his blood money. The asshole. And this woman had known and...

He shook his head and kept his voice gentle and firm. The woman was in a cult. Brainwashed. "Have you heard from him since?"

"No," she whispered. "Phones are for men, not women."

Jesus. Gabe bit down on his temper. He'd be looking more into the Patriot Zealots in the future, oh yes, he would. "I understand, MaryEllen."

After a few more questions, Gabe and Caz left her sitting in the kitchen.

Erica and her mother were in the living room, and Gabe paused to ask the two women to keep an eye on MaryEllen. That she wasn't to leave or use the phone.

"No service out here anyway." Erica sent an angry look toward the kitchen. "We'll keep her here for you, Chief."

"Thank you." He hesitated. "Erica, this mess isn't her fault."

Caz took over. "You know, the Patriot Zealots believe a man should do all the thinking. Foolish, yes, but it is what she believes, which means, without her husband to make her decisions, she'll be lost. I'll notify social services, but they can be slow to respond. If you could help MaryEllen get by..."

"You're right." Erica gave Caz a rueful smile. "She's going to have a rough time coping, isn't she?"

"She is." And how many more MaryEllens were there behind the compound's razor wire-topped fences?

Back at the station, Gabe and Caz hugged a frail-looking Lillian. The guards were there, shamefaced and furious at being tricked.

After Gabe updated everyone, Bull and Dante pulled up a map of the area on the computer, looking for potential landing areas outside of town. They eliminated clearings with obstacles, unstable or rough ground, or not enough room. Once a possible site was found, volunteers headed out to check for parked vehicles—especially Baumer's or rentals.

Chevy and Knox were using Gabe's computer.

"Yeah, a copter could land in any of those," Chevy said. "Hey, Chief."

"Find something?" Gabe joined them.

Knox tugged on his hefty mustache and pointed to the three-D map display. "Earl and I hunted up there a while back. There's a bunch of unmarked trails, a couple of cabins and stands. The trailhead is behind some undergrowth. A 4-wheel can get back there to park and can't be seen from the road."

Shifting uneasily, Knox flushed. "Means that the wildlife troopers aren't liable to catch someone who's hunting off-season."

Gabe only sighed. "Does that area have a place for a chopper to land?"

"Yeah, a few." Chevy pointed to the clearings on the display.

Dante and Bull had followed them in. Dante frowned. "Huh. I didn't know there were trails in that area. I didn't send anyone to check it."

Gabe studied the monitor. Hidden parking, unmarked trails. That'd weigh heavy for Spyros.

If there was a cabin where the kidnappers could wait out the rain until the chopper could land? Well, Baumer liked things easy.

"You know how to get there?" Bull asked Knox.

"Been awhile, but yeah."

Hang in there, Audrey. I think we might have a lead.

Gabe looked around the squad room. The last few people had headed out to scour the roads, randomly looking for Baumer's car. The only people who remained were his brothers, Knox, Chevy, Dante, Lillian, and Regina.

And Gabe. Damned if he'd stay behind at this point.

"Dante, can you, Lillian, and Regina hold down the fort here? Coordinate efforts as needed." He gave the old vet a smile. "I know you haven't forgotten how."

"Can do." Dante glanced at the weapons locker. "Arm your men, Chief."

Gabe already had the keys in his hand.

The cold rain beat down on Audrey and plastered her inadequate T-shirt to her chilled body. Her strength was fading as she stumbled behind Earl Baumer on the narrow forest trail.

Despair weighed down her heart even more heavily than the useless pistol dragged down her right ankle.

Walking behind her, Spyros jabbed his fingers into her spine. Cruelly. Painfully. "...and then I'll cut you here."

Since the first step on the trail, he'd been telling her how she'd die.

Earlier, at the trailhead, Earl and the New Yorker had dragged her out of the SUV and thrown her on the ground. Another car had pulled in. Four men climbed out.

And then she'd looked up...into the face of her nightmares.

Spyros. Oh God. Terror flooded her, drowned her. His right eye was gone, the lid scarred and sunken. White scarring stood out starkly against his swarthy skin.

"You got the maláka. *Good, good."* He gave her a malice-filled smile before asking the New Yorker, *"The backup team?"*

"On schedule."

Earl frowned. *"What backup?"*

"Just a few more men. A precaution. In case we run into trouble." Spyros yanked her to her feet. With the two vehicles concealed by the shrubbery growing next to the shoulder, the group headed up the trail. Along with Spyros, Earl, and the New Yorker, there were three more brutal-looking men.

Too many men. She was going to die.

She'd known it then—and knew it now.

He'd been telling her that, in Greek and English, with every step on the trail. As the thunder grew loud enough to drown out his voice, she was grateful for the small break. For being able to try to think past her fear.

What could she do? Was there *anything* she could do?

By now, Gabe must know she'd been taken. Her heart ached because he'd be pushing his fear for her down so he could stay in control. He'd do everything he could to find her. But, if she didn't survive... He wouldn't handle it well. He'd blame himself.

Oh, Gabe.

Like she was blaming herself. For his pain.

For Lillian. Over and over, her mind replayed the moment when Earl had shoved Lillian, her fall, hitting the cart.

I'm sorry, Lillian. Her heart ached.

Staying in Rescue had been the wrong choice. Lillian would have been all right if Audrey had just left.

Hopelessness seeped into her bones, weakening her muscles. She tripped over a moss-covered boulder. With her wrists cuffed behind her back, she couldn't catch herself and landed painfully on her front.

New scrapes burned. Her shoulders ached. She managed a gasping breath—

Spyros picked her up by her hair.

Her cry of pain made him laugh. "You won't slow us down with your antics, *poutana*." He slapped her left cheek, backhanded her right.

Hot tears mixed with the cold rain on her burning skin. She didn't speak. Any response would only be a reason for him to hit her again.

"There's no hurry," Earl called. "Your helicopter can't land till this shit clears up some."

"Good. I'll have some fun first," Spyros said, adding something in Greek.

"If you cut her up too badly, that chopper-head we hired might not let us board," the New Yorker warned. "He won't want blood all over his copter."

"Fine." Spyros slammed her between the shoulders, making her stagger forward. "Walk."

Gabe, find me. Please, please, please, find me. More tears trickled down her cheeks. *I don't want to die.*

Then her muscles tensed as she thought of the six

413

vicious men with her. All the weapons they carried. The "few more men" in their backup.

Knowing she was a captive, Gabe wouldn't back down. He'd charge in, no matter the danger to himself.

They'd kill him.

No, no, I take it back. Stay away, Gabe.

CHAPTER THIRTY

M urphy's Law of combat: there is no limit to how bad things can get.

They'd found a rental car and Baumer's SUV concealed at the trailhead.

Unable to get a cell signal in the isolated spot, Gabe had chosen Chevy to return to town, update Dante and the troopers, and fetch reinforcements. The man had tried to refuse, insisting he'd recovered from the bear attack. Quite likely, but he was also the only one of them with children.

Best he stay safe.

Gabe'd checked the tracks as they started out. From the footprints, Audrey had at least five or six captors. Not good.

Audrey's footprints were smaller. He'd spotted when she'd fallen. How she'd staggered to one side—probably from being shoved. But she was on her feet. Alive and moving.

He tried to take hope from that.

Gabe's group—Bull, Caz, and Knox—were all hardened Alaskans. Needing speed more than anything else, they'd weaponed up with handguns. And they moved fast—hopefully faster than the Outsiders ahead. Unfortunately, as trails branched, he'd had to stop and search for sign in the rain and dim light.

As he led the men upward, the trail sign got fresher.

The rain was a bitch, but damned if he didn't bless the weather. Thunderstorms weren't common in Alaska, and chopper pilots hated them. The lightning and heavy clouds would delay Spyros's helicopter for a time.

As they hiked ever upward, and the worst of the storm passed, icy mountain winds created a thick cloud layer. With the vertical mountainsides and tall forest, and the dense fog covering the landing site, a pilot wouldn't risk coming in.

Not yet.

Knox touched his arm.

Gabe held up his fist, bringing everyone to a stop.

"See how the trees open ahead? There's a cabin up past this curve," Knox said in a barely heard voice.

Gabe looked around at the others, all wearing the silent camo raingear they used for hunting.

This time they were hunting human game.

Despite the muffling effect of the drizzling rain, an alert

sentry might hear them. "We go slow and quiet." Gabe eyed the trail. "Knox, stay right behind me and tap my back if you need my attention."

A few minutes later, Gabe stopped in the shadows at the forest's edge. Glimpses through the fog showed a level, wide clearing—one adequate for a helicopter landing.

A rough log shanty with moss-covered wood shingles sat at the west edge. Probably an old trapper's cabin. Under the low overhang, a man stood guard outside the plank door. He had his pistol out and ready. Gabe growled low.

A stack of logs and split wood lay beside a rock-ringed fire pit in front of the cabin. To the right was a massive fallen spruce surrounded by dead branches.

Gabe frowned. How many were here, and how were they armed? The small cabin window beside the door was shuttered, providing no hint of what was inside. He kept his voice low. "Knox, is there another window?"

"Seems like it had a window in the back wall. Too small for anyone to wiggle out. No glass. Shuttered to keep the wildlife out."

The urgency to see if Audrey was all right was fucking with Gabe's brain. He made himself stand still. He didn't have enough information to formulate a plan of attack.

His brothers and Knox waited quietly.

Gabe looked at Bull. "I'm going to check the back. Maybe get an idea of what we're facing." Coordination without comms was going to suck. "However, if the chopper arrives, you do whatever you must to keep Audrey off of it. If they lift with her onboard, she's dead."

Expression rigid, Bull nodded. His pistol was in his hand.

Gabe motioned for Caz and Knox to follow. Staying in the forest shadows, he circled to the back of the cabin. Stationing the others to guard his flanks, Gabe crept up to the back wall. The window shutter was closed, but the aged wood had warped, leaving large cracks.

He looked inside.

Hanging from a wall hook, a kerosene lantern illumined the single room.

There was Audrey. Alive. Gabe pulled in a breath at the rush of relief.

She sat on the plank floor, her shoulder against the left log wall. Her wrists were handcuffed behind her back, but her legs were free. Her soaked, tangled hair was filled with twigs and dirt. Mud, scrapes, and bruises marked her face and bare arms. Her T-shirt was ripped.

Although she trembled visibly, her head was up.

Yeah, that was the woman he loved.

Focus, MacNair.

Five men in the room.

Face pale, Baumer sat on the floor, his only weapon a sheathed belt knife. Maybe Spyros didn't trust him? Fabric wrapped around his wrist was stained with blood.

A barrel-chested, buzz-cut blond leaned against the front wall. His shoulder holster held a handgun.

Two more thugs sat on a plank bench on the right wall. More pistols.

The last man...

From the photos Dennison had sent, Gabe recognized Spyros. Of course, the sunken right eyelid made his identity obvious. Short black hair. Several days unshaven.

With a pistol holstered at his hip, Spyros sat on a tree stump chair beside Audrey. He held a Bowie knife, flipping it repeatedly, watching Audrey like a weasel hunting a mouse.

Catching the knife, he said something to her—and drew the knife down her arm.

Gabe's jaw clenched.

Making no sound at all, she flinched. Gabe saw blood trickle down her upper arm...joining tiny streams from previous cuts.

Red, the color of her blood, filled Gabe's vision, hammered at his head, filled his world until every inhalation seemed hotter than fire.

He bit his lip until it bled, then backed up, silently.

If Spyros was toying with her, they had time.

"This is just a sample, a hint of what awaits you, *poutana*," Spyros grated. The knife sliced down Audrey's arm again.

Teeth clamped together, she forced herself to remain still...because if she moved, he cut deeper.

Her skin split under the finely honed blade. A second later came the searing flash of pain and hot oozing of blood. Turning her face away, she blinked away the flood of tears. Her whole upper arm was one throbbing mass of pain.

And she was so, so scared.

Earlier, she'd decided not to taunt him or force him to kill her. Not right now. Not until the helicopter arrived. Maybe, maybe Gabe would find her. But as the trail led higher and higher, her hopes had faded until they'd arrived at this tiny cabin in the middle of nowhere.

Did Gabe even know Spyros had her? What if Lillian had died...because of Audrey? Over and over, guilt battered at her heart. She sagged against the wall.

Why had she ever come to this place? Made friends? Put them at risk?

Loving people hurt far worse than anything else.

"Yes, you're beginning to see, to know how you'll die, screaming and screaming." Spyros's lips closed over the words as if savoring the taste.

Because he got off on scaring her.

Rage seared away the fear. "A man who'll fight another man, one on one, is impressive." Even as her response snapped out, she tried to hold the words back—and failed. "I'm not a man. No, I'm female, a hundred pounds lighter than you, and tied-up. But you still need five minions to hold your widdle hand. Aren't you *brave*." Her rant was cut short by Spyros's roar, and his fist smashing into her jaw.

A cry of pain escaped her.

Knocked sideways, she fell. As her shoulder struck the rough flooring, splinters dug into her arm and cheek. As the whole left side of her face throbbed with pain, tears trickled from her closed eyes.

A couple of the men laughed.

Okay, maybe that had been stupid.

Back with the others, Gabe paused in his instructions as a yell of anger and cry of pain came from the cabin.

Audrey. Blind rage swept over him. *Kill.* He started to charge forward.

Bull grabbed his shoulder. "No, bro."

Gabe growled. A war raged inside him. He had to get her out of there. *Now.*

But his stupidity would get her killed. Finish the plan.

Go on, MacNair. He sucked in air through his nose. Focused. "Spyros is seated beside Audrey and cutting her with his knife." He held up his hand to keep Knox quiet. "The cuts aren't life-threatening, but a knife that close to her means we can't risk breaking in."

Spyros would slit her throat before they could kill him.

Damn cabin.

Small shuttered windows. A heavy door that opened outward. Excellent deterrents to keep a bear from breaking in. Excellent deterrents to keep his team from breaking in quickly enough to keep Audrey alive.

"The *cabrón*." Caz had pulled one of his knives. "We wait until he brings her out of the cabin?"

"That's our best chance." Gabe glanced up. The storm clouds had blown through, and the fog was lifting. "The chopper should be on the way."

A muted hiss came from Knox who was watching the door sentry.

Everyone froze.

After taking a piss against a tree, the guard started on a circuit of the cabin.

In the distance, Gabe heard a chopper. His pulse picked up. Perfect. The noise would distract the guard.

Now, the plan. Bull and Caz could operate without detailed instructions—they'd worked as a team all their lives.

And Knox... Audrey was special to him. He'd shown that in the bar. He'd protect her well.

"Caz, you and Bull grab the sentry and bring him to the front. I need him capable of talking. They need to think he's still on guard."

Bull and Caz nodded.

"Knox, you and I will wait on each side of the door for them to come out. When I yell 'Go', you grab Audrey." Gabe narrowed his eyes at the man. "Your *only* job is to yank her out of the doorway—no matter what damage she might get in doing so. Then you keep her safe. The best cover will probably be prone behind the woodpile or around the cabin. Use your judgment, and stay out of the kill zone."

"Got it."

"Here. They have her cuffed." Gabe gave his spare handcuff key to Knox and turned to his brothers. "We have Spyros, Baumer, and four unknowns. These bastards aren't innocent bystanders; they know Spyros intends to kill Audrey. Take them down as hard as you need to."

They nodded.

"How about the pilot?" Knox asked.

"He's probably a hire from Anchorage. Unless he jumps in, don't shoot him."

Caz tossed off a salute.

Bull gave Gabe a smile. "We'll get her out."

Gabe tried to smile back and knew he'd failed. The odds...sucked.

Still lying on her side, Audrey heard a whirring, and her heart sank. *Oh, God.*

Earl Baumer tipped his head. "Is that the chopper?"

It was.

The cabin fell silent. The engine sounded funny. Loud, then soft.

The New Yorker frowned. "Almost sounds like there are two of them."

"Noise tends to echo off the cliffs." Earl slung his pack over his shoulder. "I can't wait to get out of here."

A thud on the door sounded, and the outside guard called, "Copter is coming in now."

"Let's go." Knife in one fist, Spyros grabbed Audrey's T-shirt with his other hand and yanked her to her feet.

She staggered, almost falling when he shoved her forward.

Get it together, Audrey.

Once outside in an open space, she might be able to break free. Head down, she tensed and relaxed her muscles to get the circulation going. She'd run—and if the way wasn't clear, she'd dive into the tail rotor and die fast.

Her heart quailed. *Die.* She didn't want to die.

She would. She must.

The door opened, and Earl walked out.

Behind Audrey, Spyros gripped her hair. "Wouldn't want you to run, now would we?" The yank on her head pulled her backward a step.

As her hopes died, despair emptied her mind.

Flattened against the wall beside the front door, Gabe waited.

Bound hand and foot, the terrified sentry had recited his *"Copter is coming in now"* nicely. Caz's knife pricking his eyelid had proved an adequate incentive for cooperation.

Bull had knocked the guy out, tossed the body around the side of the cabin, and took up position there.

Caz was stationed at the other corner.

Knox and Gabe stood on either side of the door.

Overhead, the helicopter started to descend. The tree branches whipped in the turbulence stirred up by the helicopter blades.

The door opened. Gabe tensed.

Baumer came out, hand over his eyes as he looked at the helicopter.

C'mon, Spyros. Be next. Keep the bastards inside.

Fate wasn't listening. The buzz-cut blond walked out and frowned.

As the two thugs followed, Buzzcut scowled. "Look for Jones. He must be taking a piss."

Laughing the two separated.

Gabe stiffened. They'd see him and Knox any—

Audrey stepped out. Spyros came right behind her, left fist in her hair, knife carelessly to one side.

Now. Gabe punched Spyros's forearm, paralyzing the nerves, deadening his grip on Audrey's hair. "Take her!"

Even as Knox yanked Audrey away, Spyros tried to stab her.

Gabe lunged and knocked him against the doorframe.

Braced by the wall, Spyros twisted, catching Gabe's coat with his left hand and stabbing with the knife in the right. Barely slowed by Gabe's raingear, the sharp blade punched into Gabe's side.

Fiery pain burst along his ribs as the blade scraped the bone. *Jesus.* With a furious downward block, Gabe knocked the knife into the dirt, then head-butted Spyros. The asshole's grip on his coat loosened.

Gabe ripped free.

Firing broke out across the clearing.

"*Gamóto!*" Spewing Greek curses, Spyros staggered forward and yanked out his pistol.

Hell. Powering from his legs, Gabe slammed a right hook into the man's jaw.

Spyros dropped, landing on his side.

Drawing his pistol, Gabe snap kicked him in the head, knocking him out. A flick of his foot sent Spyros's handgun under the cabin.

Good. A quick check showed one thug motionless on the ground and another dead with a knife in his chest.

Ignoring everything, Baumer was running toward the helicopter.

Near the fire pit, Buzzcut spotted Gabe and charged, snapping off shots.

A bullet whizzed past. Gabe dodged sideways, aimed—

"Noooo!" Directly between Gabe and the man, Audrey jumped up from behind the woodpile.

Fuck!

Pistol out, she fired at Buzzcut. Missed. Kept firing.

Staggering back, the bastard shot at her. Shot *her*. She dropped.

No. God, no!

Target now clear, Gabe shot the bastard between the eyes, turned.

With a roar of fury, Spyros tackled him from the side.

Barely hanging onto his pistol, Gabe landed on his hip. A fist slammed into his kidney, sending a blast of pain through him. Twisting, he rammed his elbow backward into Spyros's face. He rolled to his feet.

Spyros had his knife.

Gabe shot from the hip—double-tap.

The bastard fell.

Audrey. Gabe charged across the clearing.

Bull was already there, bending over her. He saw Gabe. "She's okay."

As she sat up, the relief made Gabe's head spin. *Thank God.*

He made a quick assessment. All the bad guys were down but one.

Baumer.

At the helicopter, the ex-officer yanked open the rear door and climbed in.

Gabe sprinted toward the chopper.

The sound of the engine changed. Rather than taking off, the chopper powered down. *What the hell?*

Pistol in one hand, keeping out of the line of fire, Gabe sidled up to the open door.

Fingers laced on top of his head, kneeling between the passenger seats, Baumer didn't move.

Gabe blinked and glanced at the pilot.

Pistol aimed straight at Baumer's head, Hawk smiled at

Gabe. "What the fuck, bro. You threw a party and didn't invite me?"

Fist pressed against her mouth, Audrey tried not to scream for Gabe to be careful. She tried to rise, but her leg gave out and dropped her back onto her butt.

"Hold on, champ." Bull wrapped his coat around her. "I think your ankle got messed up when Knox landed on you."

"Help Gabe. Leave me and help Gabe." Her heart pounded so intensely she had trouble speaking. Gabe wasn't moving, was staring in the helicopter door. Did someone have a gun on him?

Then Gabe grabbed his handcuffs from his belt and leaned into the helicopter. A minute later, he dragged a cuffed Baumer out and shoved him to his knees.

When the pilot came around the helicopter, Gabe slapped his shoulder.

Gabe knew the pilot?

Audrey's view was blocked when Caz dropped down on a knee beside her and pulled Bull's coat back. "Your arm needs tending, *chica*."

She pushed him back. "Knox needs help first. Something hit him in the head."

Caz's gaze swept over her, then he nodded and gave her a fleeting smile before turning to Knox. "Let's see."

Hand to his bloody head, Knox sat up. "Don't think I cracked anything."

Still standing guard over everyone at the woodpile, Bull raised his voice. "Yo, we got company, Gabe."

A wave of people emerged from the trail and spread out into the clearing.

Oh God, no. They must be Spyros's backup men. Heart sinking, Audrey straightened her shoulders. "I need some bullets. Who has bullets?" She braced for the shooting to begin.

"Don't shoot them, *chica*. They're ours." Caz opened his pack, pulled out a first aid kit, and tossed gauze to Bull. "Put pressure on her arm for me, *sí?*"

When Bull grunted agreement, Caz tilted Knox's head up. "Looks like wood from a bullet ricochet caught you. You'll be fine."

"The men are ours?" Audrey asked as Bull knelt beside her. He pressed the gauze to the cuts and wrapped his hand around her arm. Her teeth ground together at the blast of pain.

"Yeah," Bull said. "That's Chevy with reinforcements."

As the group came closer, she recognized Chevy in the lead. He gestured, and Tucker, Guzman, and others headed for Gabe. Uriah led some toward the cabin.

Oh, there was Zappa from the gas station. Didn't hippies hate guns?

God, her thoughts were getting weird.

"Hey, Chief, we caught some weasels for you." Chevy

motioned toward more men—and some had wrists tied behind their backs. And looked roughed up.

"They *got* them." Audrey turned to Bull. "Spyros had backup coming, he said."

"Good job." Gabe shook Chevy's hand. "Just think, there's no hunting season restriction on bad guys."

A wave of laughter swept the clearing.

"Chief, the blue shirts are on the way," Uriah called.

"There's a relief." Gabe yanked Earl to his feet and shoved him toward Guzman. "Take charge of this one until the state troopers get here, will you?"

"Be a pleasure." Guzman gripped Earl's arm. Face pitiless, Tucker took the other arm.

Earl's shoulders slumped.

Gabe's gaze met Audrey's—and held. The hardness in his face eased. He slapped the pilot on the shoulder and headed over at a jog.

Audrey could feel her muscles loosen. He was all right. Alive. Moving.

"Audrey."

She realized someone wanted her attention. With an effort, she pulled her gaze away.

"*Chica*, look at me."

She turned her head and looked into Caz's dark brown eyes.

"That is better." He held up a roll of gauze as Bull stepped back. "I'm going to put a pressure dressing on your arm so Bull doesn't have to hold it for you."

"Sure."

"Hey, Bull, you should say hi to the pilot." Gabe dropped to one knee beside her. "Caz, did you see she got shot? Did she tell you?" His hand wrapped around her nape, and he leaned his forehead against hers. "Jesus, I saw you go down, and hell, I didn't know I could be so damn scared. Are you all right?"

She was. Now that he was here, was touching her, the tightness in her chest was loosening. "My hero," she whispered and touched his face. "I'm not hurt. I dropped down because I ran out of bullets. I'm fine. Really."

Caz made a sound of disagreement that had Gabe looking at him.

"Report, bro." Gabe's hand was still around the back of her neck, so wonderfully warm.

"Her arm—mostly superficial, but far too many cuts. But why blood on this side?" Caz scowled as he pulled Bull's coat away farther and tugged at her soaked clothing. "Sí, there's blood here. Audrey, let me see your hip."

As Gabe leaned forward to unzip her jeans, her gaze fixed on his raingear. At the place where the camo spots all ran together...with red.

"Oh, no. No, no, no, you're hurt." A buzzing started in her ears. So much blood. "Fix Gabe. He's hurt. Fix him."

Her breathing was getting all funny and fast as she turned to Caz. "Fix him."

"Shhh, shhh." Caz ran his hand over her back. "Strip

down some, Gabe, while I check out her wound. And I'll deal with whichever of you is hurt worse."

"You will care for Aud—" Gabe broke off at the high growl she made. Chuckling, he doffed his coat and unbuttoned his shirt.

Seeing the bleeding, gaping wound along his ribs, she started to cry. "Noooo. He hurt you."

"Been hurt worse." Gabe's eyes darkened as Caz peeled down her jeans. "Jesus, that looks nasty."

She looked down. A bloody furrow ran across the outside of her hip. Well, *eff-it-all*, the New Yorker's bullet had hit her. She only had a second to see it before Caz had rinsed it off and put on a pad, followed by a thicker piece of gauze. He taped it down tightly enough to make her wince.

"You were lucky, *chiquita*. The bullet just made a gouge on the way past. Missed the bone, missed the joint, only got tissue." After pulling Bull's coat back around her, Caz rose and stepped to Gabe's side with his first aid kit.

"Your ribs turned the blade. You were lucky, 'mano," Caz muttered.

"Yeah, we all were."

After the knife puncture on Gabe's ribs was cleaned and covered, Audrey found she could breathe again. He'd be all right.

"Look who's here, Caz." Bull approached with the pilot beside him. The man had short caramel-colored hair, fair skin with a weathered tan. A long jagged scar ran across his forehead. Another one on his cheek disappeared into a short beard and pulled his upper lip into a slight sneer.

"*Hawk.*" Jumping to his feet, Caz hugged the man. "*Dios.* Where did you come from, bro?"

"Talked to Bull a couple of days ago. I heard the old man's girlfriend had trouble."

Why did this Hawk's intonation sound more like the "the girlfriend *is* trouble?" Perhaps because of the way he was studying her with cynical blue eyes.

Hawk turned away from her to Caz. "I was flying to see you, but when I called the Rescue PD on where to land, Dante said shit was going down. So I came here."

"Good timing." Caz eyed the helicopter. "Knox, Gabe, and Audrey need a ride to town, and I need to go with to patch them up."

"She sure can't walk out. She's not only half-frozen, but did you see her ankle, Caz?" Bull glanced at Hawk. "You can take the prisoners, too."

"No, I'll only haul Caz and the injured. Can't take anyone else," Hawk said. "I'm low on gas."

As Caz started examining her ankle, Audrey winced. Somehow, this pain was one pain too many. Her hands closed into fists. *Ow, ow, ow.*

Gabe knelt and wrapped a reassuring arm around her shoulder before asking Hawk, "Low on gas? Were you waiting out the storm in the air?"

"Nah, the clouds were thinning when I got here. Problem was the other chopper wanted to land." Hawk's lips twisted into a malevolent smile. "After I dive-bombed him a few times, he changed his mind."

Bull's laugh roared out across the clearing. "Only you think a knife fight means chopper blades."

"Caz might carry more blades, but mine are bigger." The pilot's smile didn't reach his eyes.

Audrey leaned her head against Gabe's chest. She hurt, oh God, how she hurt, and *none* of that mattered. Gabe was alive, his heartbeat slow and strong under her ear.

"Is Lillian all right?" she whispered, tilting her head back to look at him.

"Yeah, she is." He kissed the tip of her nose, then her lips. "You should have heard her cursing."

Audrey laughed. She'd been present when a blackberry vine had raked down Lillian's arm. The poor vine probably withered away from shame by the time the Englishwoman had finished describing its parentage.

Caz tugged at Audrey's shoe, and her laugh stopped abruptly as pain stabbed into her ankle.

"Sorry, *chica*. Let's forget getting your footwear off." Caz wrapped a stretch bandage around the outside of her boot. "Keep it on until we reach the clinic."

"I like that plan." Her words came out through clenched teeth, and Gabe's arm drew tighter around her.

"Crap." Chevy stood beside Caz, staring at Audrey. "You look like...like bad."

"Man, that isn't the way to charm a woman." Bull winked at Audrey.

Looking worried, Chevy shook his head. "Our sweetheart librarian doesn't worry me. It's the mayor. When I picked up the reinforcements, the Brit said she'd gut me with a dirty fish knife if I didn't bring her girl back safe and sound."

Tucker joined them. His assessing gaze took in Audrey's bloody jeans, her bruised face. Anger and worry narrowed his eyes before he looked at Gabe as if for reassurance.

"She'll be all right," Gabe said.

"The asshole who took her..." Tucker's voice was tight. "Before you take him back, I wanna chat with—"

"He's dead, Tuck." Gabe's words were cold and even. "He won't hurt anyone ever again."

Audrey realized most of the men were watching, listening, and their approval sounded clearly in the cold mountain air.

"Good." "Got what he deserved." "Drag him out of hell and kill him again." "Teach him to screw with our pretty librarian."

Tears burned her eyes as she realized no one blamed her. That they'd come, armed and ready to risk their lives...for her. *Our librarian.* Misty-eyed, she looked from man to man. Had she thought she didn't belong?

"Thank you." Her voice cracked but carried through the clearing. "Thank you all."

CHAPTER THIRTY-ONE

When a man bleeds to save your ass, you know you got no finer a friend. - First Sergeant Michael "Mako" Tyne

Gabe listened as a blue-grass trio played the classic "John Henry" song to an appreciative audience. The Lynx Lake Park bandstand was nothing fancy, just a two-foot high raised platform with a roof over it, but it served the purpose. Everywhere he looked were clusters of people, some at picnic tables, some on blankets on the grass. Bright coolers and picnic baskets added color. The early August Saturday evening was clear. At ten-thirty, the sun was starting to set. A breeze past the park's pedestal grills brought the fading aromas of burgers, hot dogs, and salmon.

It'd been an interesting three-or-so weeks since what the

townsfolk were calling "The Kidnapping." Personally, he'd titled it the "clusterfuck of a day." It'd be a long time before he got past the sight of Audrey getting shot. Falling.

He also remembered her sheer courage, the fury on her face, as she'd stood, firing bullet after bullet at Buzzcut. If she hadn't diverted the man's attention, Gabe would be dead.

Damn, she was something.

And his nightmares—and hers—would fade with time. The law enforcement, reporters, and everyone else in the known universe were finally gone. Aside from the trials awaiting the survivors on Spyros's team and Baumer, life in Rescue had returned to normal.

In fact, he'd started interviewing people for Baumer's old police officer post.

Strolling through the park, he greeted people, dodged children, and considered going back to the grill for another burger.

"Hey, Chief."

At Uriah's call, Gabe stopped. "Evening, you two."

On a dark blue saddle blanket, Sarah and Uriah were enjoying their drinks while their daughter Rachel finished off a hot dog. Sarah tilted her head back. "So, Gabe. Are you enjoying the mini-fest?"

"I am."

"I have a feeling the townsfolk will go for a bigger event next year," Sarah said. "The entire atmosphere is more welcoming to tourists these days."

Mayor Lillian had called this a "test day" to see if Rescue wanted to hold a true harvest festival next summer. This trial run was merely a town event—an evening in the park—although it'd drawn a fair number of tourists from the resort and fishing lodges. The council had provided burgers and hot dogs; local fishermen donated salmon. Volunteers manned the grills. Several picnic tables held a community potluck of side dishes and desserts.

"You know, I think you're right." Gabe grinned as a bevy of young children raced past with streamers, avoiding the older children playing soccer in a grassy space.

People were having fun.

Even better, there'd been no incidents. No stealing. No vandalism. Not even any brawling, which was probably a record.

Huh. That would be his goal for events—no fights.

A burst of clear, musical laughter caught his attention.

In a nearby group of women, Audrey was describing—and acting out—her battle with the salmon she'd caught yesterday. She finished by pointing to the grill to show who'd been victorious. A chorus of congratulations came from the women.

Wasn't it odd that the woman who worried she had no social skills had been instrumental in breaking down the barriers between people? Aside from the PZs, the various factions had united to save her...and discovered they had more in common than they'd thought.

The mini-fest tonight with food, activities, and a wealth

of children was also creating new connections. With the first of the playground equipment in and a grassy space for sports, the kids weren't concerned if someone's parents ran businesses or lived off the road or were fishing guides. They just wanted to play.

Soon enough, parents were setting their own differences aside, at least for one evening.

In a crackle of loudspeaker static, the trio's fiddle-player announced from the bandstand, "We're taking a break now, and Mayor Lillian says she's going to get Caz and Bull—and even our Chief of Police up here next."

Gabe frowned. Since when had he volunteered to play?

Glancing around, he spotted Caz and Bull carrying their instruments. Bull had Gabe's guitar. Damned if Hawk wasn't following along with his fiddle.

Guess he'd been drafted. Wouldn't be the first time. They would sing together in the military, on drunken nights of carousing, even while helping Bull with his first bar...

If Mako's sons were together, they eventually ended up playing music together.

As he headed toward the bandstand, he stopped at the group of women and tucked his arm around Audrey.

She smiled up at him. "I hear you're going to—"

He took her lips. *Oh yeah.* Pulling her closer, he enjoyed the hell out of kissing her. Somehow, he couldn't foresee a time he wouldn't. "Mmm."

Despite looking thoroughly well kissed, she attempted to glare at him. "Chief MacNair, there are *children* here."

He gave her an innocent look. "Hey, I kept my dick in my pants."

That set off all the women around her, including one who must've been about ninety.

As Audrey pressed her face against his chest, trying to smother giggles, he pulled her along with him.

"Where are we going?"

"We need a soprano"—he grinned at Caz who was on the stage—"right, bro?"

"Very true." Caz leaned down to take Audrey's hand and help her onto the stage. "Don't look so worried, *chiquita*. You know we sound better with you singing."

"That's right." Bull smiled at her and started the lead-in to "Rainy Day People."

When their voices rose, there was a sweet soprano with them.

Twenty minutes later, someone said loudly, "One of these things is not like the others."

Gabe looked up from his guitar.

In front of the stage, a large number of Patriot Zealots in jeans, work shirts, and patriotic-sloganed baseball caps stared at Caz.

Gabe'd never seen any of them before. For fuck's sake, how many men did Parrish have at his compound?

A red-bearded man held his throat and made gagging sounds.

A guy with tats running up his arms said, "I crossed two borders to get away from the stinking beaners. And here's one, front and center."

Son of a bitch, their target was Caz for being Hispanic.

As the rest of the PZs descended into sarcastic agreement, Gabe's fingers tightened on the fret, flattening the sound of the strings. He stared down at the bigoted idiots. "Move on. Now."

They ignored him.

"Of course, the wetback made it here to Alaska. You know, like oil, greasers slide everywhere." The man, all three hundred pounds worth, grinned as if he'd said something brilliant.

As Caz growled, Gabe winced. His brother endured this dumbass intolerance and even managed to ignore it most of the time. But there was a breaking point. And that sound meant he'd reached it.

Hell.

Gabe leaned forward. "Last chance. Get out of here before you regret it."

"Oooh, the pussy cop is defending his tacohead friend. I'm so scared." A squat guy with the face of a weasel pretended to cringe away, bumped into a young woman—and shoved her out of his way.

As she staggered, almost falling, a man dressed in black caught her.

"What a cunt," Weasel-face muttered.

"Yeah, shouldn't let women out of the kitch—"

"That's it." Caz stepped from behind his drum, launched from the stage, and hit the front-most man, knocking him to the ground.

In typical cowardly style, four of the bastards jumped on Caz.

That was definitely *it*. "You take the dogpile, Bull." Gabe set his guitar down and dove at three more men getting ready to jump on.

His targets went down like bowling pins.

Bull gave a happy roar as he leaped off the stage. When he reached the dogpile, bodies went flying. Off to one side, Hawk waited politely for his opponents to be tossed to him. It was nice to see his brother laughing.

Good times.

A couple of minutes later, Gabe'd finished with his three, leaving them sprawled and groaning on the ground. As he moved away, his jaw throbbed from a fist he hadn't dodged quickly enough, and his healing ribs ached from a stray kick.

Surprised that more PZs hadn't come to the assistance of his three opponents, he checked the brawl.

Damned if small fights weren't going on all over the grassy space.

Smiling cruelly, Hawk stood with his foot on the three-hundred-pounder's thick neck. The corpulent bastard's face was a dark red—not blue—so he was getting enough air.

Gabe grinned.

A familiar-looking man in black—the one who'd caught

the girl—landed a sweet right jab to a PZ belly and followed it up with a knockout punch.

Tucker, Guzman, Uriah—hell, a large number of men had taken on the PZs. There was Knox along with several more male and female residents he didn't recognize.

Now it was the PZs who were out-numbered.

Dogpile gone, Bull dragged two half-conscious men—by the feet—off the field of battle and toward the onlookers.

Near a picnic table, Audrey had a black cane in her hand and an unconscious Zealot in front of her. She nudged him with her foot. When he didn't move, she gave the cane to a scrawny, old man at the picnic table.

Gabe eyed the cane, then the tattooed bastard on the ground. *Uh-huh.* Yeah, he was going to keep this woman.

Two brothers and one woman were accounted for. Where was Caz?

Ah, fuck.

Straddling the red-bearded man, Caz had a knife to the asshole's neck.

Moving closer, Gabe cleared his throat. "Jesus, Caz, I'm gonna be pissed off if you kill him. Do you know how much paperwork I'll get stuck with?"

The blade didn't move. "*No hay problema*—I'll just cut him up a bit."

"Now, let's think this through. Who, exactly, will be stuck stitching up the bastard?"

Caz gave Gabe a narrow-eyed stare before staring down at his victim. The knife moved an inch. A whisper whitened the asshole's face to the color of fresh fallen snow.

Good. Threats were good. Gabe let out the breath he'd been holding.

After flipping the knife and shoving it into his boot-sheath, Caz rose. He gave Gabe an aggrieved stare and walked away. "I need a drink."

"Hey, old man." Bull handed Gabe a beer and looked toward Caz. "He really hates when you won't let him draw blood."

"Yeah, well, you'd think a health professional would be more careful about hazardous waste. It's a park, after all."

"You'd think." Laughing, Bull headed after Caz.

Drinking his beer, Gabe looked around to assess the aftermath of the fight.

Townsfolk were dragging the PZs to their feet and shoving them toward the parking lot.

The rest of the people hadn't moved. Were shaking their heads.

Probably at the crappy behavior of their Chief of Police. *Fine example you just set, MacNair.* Gabe raised his voice. "Sorry for the brawl, people."

"Hell, Chief, it was a great fight," someone called.

After a second, Gabe realized the buzz of conversation was enthusiastic. Appreciative.

"...fine teamwork. I liked the way Bull tossed the idiots to the chopper pilot for disposal. Nice."

A young man bounced on his toes. "Did you see the chief's uppercut? Sweet."

"Told you MacNair was a sourdough to his toenails." Grinning at an older woman, Tucker rocked back and forth on his boots.

Off to one side, two teens were re-enacting their favorite parts of the fight.

Crazy Alaskans.

Rubbing his aching ribs, Gabe sat down on a newly constructed picnic table.

"Do you need medical attention?" The deep smooth voice came from one side.

He knew that voice. Gabe turned.

It was Zachary Grayson, dressed in his usual all black. No wonder the guy in black had looked familiar.

"What are you doing this far from Florida? Especially with a new baby. Congratulations, by the way." Gabe held out his hand.

"Thank you." After shaking hands, Grayson joined him on the picnic table. "I'm here because I promised Mako I'd keep an eye on his boys."

His *boys*. The grief had eased to a dull ache, and the memory was sweet. Even after they'd reached adulthood, the sarge had always referred to them as his boys.

Gabe motioned to the battlefield. "As you can see— we're not doing so well."

"Actually, I'd disagree." Grayson's mouth twitched. "Aside from Caz, you all appeared to be having fun."

Gabe took a sip of his beer. He had no good response because the observation was dead accurate.

"I see I'm not the only one pleased that you're no longer isolating yourself in a cabin."

"What do you mean?"

Grayson smiled slightly. "Your town was content to watch the fight until you got punched. Then every man in the area charged in to save their chief."

"They what?"

Grayson's level gray eyes met his. The man wasn't bull-shitting.

"Well. I'll be damned." Looked like the town he guarded felt the same way about him.

"You've done well, Gabriel."

Gabe smiled. Grayson's approval was almost as tough to earn as the sarge's had been. "Do my brothers know you're here?"

"Not yet. Ah, I see Cazador still hasn't found the right woman."

Gabe followed Grayson's gaze.

Caz was flirting, and the pretty woman had just plopped down in his lap. No surprise. His brother had a lethal charm. "Caz is upfront that he has no intention of finding the right woman. His women know that a few hours or days is the extent of his desire."

Grayson shook his head. "Eventually, that practice will come back to haunt him."

"It's served him well so far." On the other hand, now

that Gabe had Audrey, he knew how much...joy...his brothers' lives lacked.

"So far is not forever." Grayson turned to watch three PZs climbing into a pickup. "Interesting. Religious militia?"

"Oh, yeah." Gabe watched the pickup drive away. "There's nothing I can do about them...yet."

"Indeed." Grayson's eyes narrowed, and his smooth voice took on an edge. "Let me know if you need help when the time comes."

With the offer, Gabe remembered Zachary Grayson held a doctorate in psychology. "I will. Thanks, Doc."

Grayson squeezed Gabe's shoulder before rising. He motioned toward Caz. "I think it's time for a chat with your brother."

Gabe studied him. Over the years, Grayson had come to check on the boys at Mako's old cabin at least once a year. He'd spent time talking with them, listening, counseling. *Helping.*

"About those *chats* of yours." Gabe held out his hand. "I don't think I ever said it as a kid, but...thanks."

Grayson took his hand. "You're very welcome." Without another word, he strolled away.

Look out, Caz. Gabe grinned and drank more of his beer.

Over at the stage, Hawk picked up his fiddle, looked around, and headed toward Gabe. The sun highlighted the sleeves of tattoos running up his arms. Seemed like he'd added some new ones.

When a bevy of young women skittered out of Hawk's

path like startled grouse, Gabe frowned. Admittedly, his scarred-up brother had a daunting appearance, but he was a good man. Why didn't women ever see that?

It'd been good to have him home. To hear the fiddle again. To fight together. Filled a hole, dammit.

"Which beer are you drinking?" Hawk settled on top of the picnic table, his feet on the bench.

"Beartooth." Gabe held the bottle up for him to sample.

Hawk took a swallow. "Eh. Nope."

They'd never liked the same beers—Gabe enjoyed malt, Hawk was more into hops. Hell, they didn't agree on much, really.

Gabe nodded at the fiddle. "You're not going to play more tonight?"

"Heading out." Hawk stared at the water where two kayakers silently skimmed along beside the shore.

Gabe turned to face him. "Back to the merc outfit?"

"No. Quit." That was Hawk. Never use three words where two would serve.

"Then..."

"Not sure."

"You have a house here. Things to do. Mako left the trust to all of us, you know."

"I know."

"Be nice if you stayed."

Hawk's lips edged up slightly. "Good to hear. I wasn't sure..."

"Are you ever going to tell me why you quit the squad?" Gabe asked.

"Maybe. Someday."

"All right." Typical.

The last of Gabe's anger at his brother's leaving the squad without explanation had disappeared when Hawk showed up to help find Audrey. "Thanks for the help. On the mountain."

"Sure." After a pause, Hawk added, "I like her for you."

From his brother, that was a glowing accolade, especially since Hawk had watched her with open suspicion at first. "She likes you, too.

Hawk shrugged.

Yeah, act as if you don't care. You do. Gabe shook his head. "You know, even though you're a bull-headed dumbass, you're still my brother. And I love you."

When tears appeared in Hawk's eyes, Gabe hastily looked away. Clearing his throat, he pointed at a young boy playing tug-of-war with a fluffy pup. "That's the kid I told you about. Niko. The one who escaped a pissed-off sow."

Hawk's jaw was tight, his gaze on the child and dog.

"You all right, bro?" Gabe asked softly.

"Good enough, yeah." Hawk watched as the kid lost his hold, landed on his ass, and burst into infectious giggles.

"Fuck, I'd forgotten that sound." As if that'd used up his quota of words, Hawk jumped off the table and punched Gabe's arm. "See you later, old man."

"Soar high, bro."

. . .

Audrey watched Gabe's blond brother move toward the parking lot. Walk wasn't the right word for the menacing way he moved. *Stalk* was closer.

Caz moved so silently that he'd scared her more than once. Bull didn't have the same grace, but no one ever got in his way.

Now, her Gabe had a prowling gait that was as sexy as anything.

She looked around for him and realized he was watching his brother leave with a tight expression of unhappiness.

Her heart ached for him. He'd often talked about Hawk and how his taciturn brother had disappeared without a word.

Turning, Gabe noticed Audrey's gaze. His face softened, and he gave her that look, the one she'd only seen him wear for her. Because he loved her.

She swallowed hard. He *loved* her.

Gabe was up and moving across the grass to her.

"You okay, Goldilocks?" He tipped up her chin as his baritone deepened. "Did the fighting scare you?"

Beside her, Cecil gave a loud snort. "Scare her? She saw that putz heading for you, grabbed my cane, and gave the asshole—'scuse me, miss—the *cretin* a smack up alongside the head that laid him out, sweet as ya please."

Her face heated with a flush as pride—*I'm a badass!*—and embarrassment—*I hit a man!*—danced through her. "Um..."

"I saw." Gabe grinned down at her. His warm hand cupped her face. "Good to know you have my back."

"I'll always have your back." She rubbed her cheek against his palm. "You're my hero, you know. I should buy you a red cape."

Gabe stared at her, then closed his arms around her so tightly she had trouble drawing a breath.

"Yeah, the chief is livin' up to the finest tradition of Rescue residents." Cecil stroked his short white beard.

Gabe looked at him curiously. "How's that?"

"You never heard the origins of our town?" With a contented smile, Cecil leaned against the picnic tabletop, settling in for a good story. "See, this section of the trail was just known as Pearl's Roadhouse, way back in the ugly winter of 1896. The thaw came late. With everything still under snow, the bears out of hibernation had nothin' to eat."

As he went on to describe the horrendous conditions, Audrey smothered a smile because he sounded as if he'd been there.

"An' Pearl—she owned the roadhouse then. The building burned down after World War II, but it's where Bull's place is now. Anyways, she was takin' the garbage out, and a hungry griz decided it wanted the leftovers—and Pearl, too."

Audrey stiffened. She had enough nightmares without adding a bear horror story. "Was she all right?"

"Well, she screamed bloody murder, and wouldn't you

know, there was Rusty, pretty near passed out inside. The old musher'd busted his leg the hell up—*sorry, miss*—and was stuck at the roadhouse, trying to earn enough money for boat fare back to Seattle. Only he kept drinkin' it all. So, the ol' drunk grabs his cane and charges out. He wallops that bear, fast and furious, and although he catches a swipe that rips up his arm, the bear runs off. Bleeding like a stuck hog, Rusty drags Pearl into the roadhouse. And she plants a big ol' kiss on him. Called him her hero."

Gabe chuckled. "So, that's how the name changed from Pearl's Roadhouse to Rescue?"

The old man moved his shoulders with a funny smile. "In a way. See, Rusty saved Pearl, yeah, but the real rescue was him giving up the bottle...and marrying Pearl. Said she rescued him. Turned his life around. Love will do that, you know."

Gabe's arm around Audrey tightened, and her heart melted at the look in his eyes.

He ran his finger down her cheek, and his voice was soft and deep. "Yeah, I know."

Want to be notified of the next release?

Ready for the next book in the
Sons of the Survivalist series?
Lethal Balance

*"Cherise Sinclair swept me away on a tidal wave of heat,
feels, intensity and a stunning environment that left me once
again, breathless!"* ~Marie's Tempting Reads

His name means hunter.

Once the best assassin in black ops, Cazador is now the best at saving lives. His path has changed from seeking bloody vengeance to running a health clinic in Rescue, Alaska.

He will never again risk loving someone he can't protect.

His mother and sister were murdered in front of him, his fiancée slaughtered in a war zone. Despite his popularity with women, he's determined to remain unattached. His heart can bear no more loss.

Unfortunately, the universe isn't listening.

First, his brother hires JJ, a fiery-haired, tough cop who lives on the edge of danger and has the biggest heart of anyone he knows. And then, his disreputable past returns in the shape of an adorable, foul-mouthed nine-year-old daughter. Now he has two loved ones to protect. An impossible task, because...

Life is dangerous. Especially in Alaska.

EXCERPT FOR LETHAL BALANCE

Embarrassment stung as JJ looked at the man. First, she'd butted in on his secluded sitting area then slugged down a potent drink. Damn, she already felt the alcohol humming in her veins. The guy must think she was a real idiot.

Even worse, he was intimidatingly good-looking.

Not a fancy meat-market gorgeous though. His clothing was an understated casual—black jeans, black boots, long-sleeved, button-up shirt. He looked Latino. Fairly tall, closing in on six feet. And his build wasn't bulky like a power-lifter, but sheer streamlined muscles. The rolled-up sleeves on his hunter green shirt revealed corded forearms.

His black hair was short, with a few strands falling over his forehead, and his eyes, so dark a brown as to match his hair. His skin was a beautiful light brown, the tone she often longed for since her skin was all freckles. A dark beard shadow gave him a dangerous edgy look.

But handsome men reminded her of Nash. Sad as it was to admit, males, ugly or not, no longer interested her. Not after all the harassment of the last year.

Unconcerned at her perusal, he sipped his beer and looked her over in turn. "Do you have a name you would share, Nevada?"

She smiled at the polite phrasing. "Jayden. JJ."

"Jayden. A beautiful name."

"It sounds even better the way you say it." His Spanish accent softened the J, giving it an even more musical sound. Truly, he had an amazing voice. She didn't want a man, any man, but she'd be happy to listen to this guy read the phone book.

And then she blinked and glanced at the bar, remembering Kiki's comment about a man with an accent. *"Keem-bear-ly, I told you, did I not, that we would enjoy one night together and one night only.""*

This was the notorious Cazador.

Following her gaze, he looked around the back of his chair and spotted the three women at the bar. His eyebrows lifted. "My name is Cazador—but, perhaps, you already know it?"

She had a feeling her cheeks had turned the dark red of the loveseat. "I...yes. I heard them talking about you."

He didn't appear offended. Or gratified. Simply slightly amused and somewhat indifferent. As if he didn't particularly care what others' opinions were.

Envy stabbed her. "They sounded as if they come here

often?" He'd obviously been around this place before. Maybe she could learn something about the area so as not to sound like a total idiot at the interview tomorrow. She might even learn if she'd want to live here.

"McNally is close enough to Anchorage that women come to enjoy the mountains and be pampered. The spa is gaining a good reputation." He gestured toward the group of men at a table. "Not every fisherman wants to spend the night in a sleeping bag. Some prefer to be picked up in the lobby and driven to the boat. After a day of fishing they're brought back while their salmon is cleaned, iced, and packed to take home."

She studied the men. "I pretty much thought of fishing as a grungy tent or RV sort of activity, but the resort's method would be nice." Cazador was probably from Anchorage, too. A city guy, if Anchorage could be called a city. She settled into her chair, feeling more comfortable. Her hunger was assuaged, and her brain had a pleasant fizzing sensation going on, thanks to the drink.

Even better, she had someone to talk with. A man who wasn't putting moves on her but was interested in conversation.

He picked up his beer and took a sip. "What do you like about living in Nevada, JJ? I've never been there."

"Nevada's the only state with Area 51 and UFOs."

When he laughed, she grinned and continued. "Really, it's a state of contrasts." She told him about the quirks of Nevada—the gambling city of Las Vegas surrounded by gorgeous, wide-open land and wild horses. Desert, yet with snow-capped mountains and forested valleys. The Burning Man festival and Nevada Day. And, as she talked, homesickness swept over her. She loved her damn state. How could she move?

Turning her gaze away, she pulled in a hard breath.

"Ah, chica, you go home tomorrow." His voice was soft. Sympathetic. As if he could tell her throat had clogged with homesickness, he took over the conversation, offering intriguing Alaska tidbits, as well as comparisons to South America, the Mideast, and Europe.

Although the man had been everywhere, he wasn't all about his adventures but asked her questions. Listened. Was obviously interested in her opinions. When she asked him about dangerous Alaska wildlife, he took out his phone and moved to sit beside her on the loveseat. He had amazing pictures: a moose with a baby, a moose walking through a downtown area, a moose attacking a car—that one widened her eyes.

"What about other predators?" She flushed. "I mean, I know moose aren't technically predators, but—"

"But they're more liable to charge a person than our lazy brown bears."

She was holding his phone, and rather than taking it back, he closed his hand around hers to pull up a different set of photos.

"Oh, it's Hagrid." A second later, she realized he hadn't released her hand. Their knees bumped.

She tipped her head to look up at him, and they were too close, their faces only a few inches apart. Her gaze dropped to his mouth. His lips were sculptured, not puffy like a girl, but not thin. Just...perfect.

He leaned forward and brushed his lips against hers.

She jerked back. "No."

"No?" Heat simmered in his so-very-dark eyes.

Suddenly, she was far too conscious of how close he sat, how his shoulder brushed hers, the heat of his body. She pulled back. Dear God, she'd been staring at his mouth—of course, he'd thought she was flirting. "No."

"Ah, I misunderstood. Please forgive me." All the heat and sexuality disappeared, and he politely moved a few inches from her. His expression showed honest regret—without anger. He wasn't blaming her for giving mixed signals or himself for misreading her.

Instead, he motioned to the phone she was still holding. To the shaggy bear on the display. "You said the bear reminded you of Hagrid. Is he a relative?"

"Uh, no." She shook her head in mock horror. "You don't read Harry Potter?"

"I fear he's escaped my notice. Are those the books with a young wizard?"

"Movies, too, yes." She frowned. "You're not a flat-earther, right? Tell me you've seen *Star Wars*."

"And *Star Trek*, as well." When he grinned, she could see why numerous women had fallen for the man-ho. "So, who would you pick for your captain—Kirk, Picard, or Janeway?"

Now that was a question she could hash over forever. She drained her drink and set it down. "There's absolutely no question; the best one is Picard."

Their battles raged over starship captains, to white orcs that should have died the first time, to whether the Hulk could beat up Superman. She and her training officer, Gene, had enjoyed science fiction and fantasy discussions, but Cazador was even more fun. She pointed at him with a severe expression. "If Superman could—"

"Last call."

The voice made her jump. She looked up. "What?"

The bartender stood by the fireplace. "It's last call, people. Bar's closing shortly."

"Oh." Time to leave.

"Thank you for letting us know." Cazador turned to JJ, and his grin flashed. "Did you want another *sweet iced tea?*"

"Now that's just mean." She smiled at the bartender. "I'm through. Thank you."

"It was a pleasure, ma'am." The bartender hesitated, looked from her to Cazador, then left.

JJ frowned. "Did she seem...?" She shook her head, thinking how easy he was to talk with. As if they were friends rather than two people passing time in a bar.

"She wanted to warn you that I enjoy women. Which is true." He rose. "I need to be going. I hadn't realized we'd talked so long."

It really was late—and she'd had fun. "I need to head back to my room, too."

"Then, might I escort you to the elevator?" He held his hand out to help her to her feet.

"Sure." She let him pull her to her feet, and they walked out of the bar and across the hotel lobby. Only two front desk clerks remained. One smiled at her and nodded. The other one, a curvy blonde with big hair, frowned and turned her back.

As she got in the elevator, she smiled at Cazador. "Thanks for the escort—and the conversation."

"It was my pleasure. Good night, Nevada." With a smile and a nod, he walked toward the rear of the hotel.

She shook her head. That was one amazing man... although she still felt a bit embarrassed about the aborted kiss. Just as well she'd never see him again.

~ Buy now! ~

ALSO BY CHERISE SINCLAIR

Masters of the Shadowlands Series

Mountain Masters & Dark Haven Series

Master of the Mountain

Simon Says: Mine

Master of the Abyss

Master of the Dark Side

My Liege of Dark Haven

Edge of the Enforcer

Master of Freedom

Master of Solitude

I Will Not Beg

The Wild Hunt Legacy

Hour of the Lion

Winter of the Wolf

Eventide of the Bear

Leap of the Lion

Healing of the Wolf

Sons of the Survivalist Series

Not a Hero

Lethal Balance

What You See

Soar High

Standalone Books

The Dom's Dungeon

The Starlight Rite

ABOUT THE AUTHOR

Cherise Sinclair is a *New York Times* and *USA Today* best-selling author of emotional, suspenseful romance. She loves to match up devastatingly powerful males with heroines who can hold their own against the subtle—and not-so-subtle—alpha male pressure.

Fledglings having flown the nest, Cherise, her beloved husband, an eighty-pound lap-puppy, and one fussy feline live in the Pacific Northwest where nothing is cozier than a rainy day spent writing.